She worked all day long on a street named despair
In a town with no pity, she was going nowhere
Well funny how her heart, well it grew colder and colder
With the weight of the world crashing down on her shoulder
But when the going gets tough
And the tough are long gone
Walk On, Walk on, Walk on, Walk on...[1]

[1] "Walk On", By Jeff Borders and Gayla Borders, 1994, Grayson Castle Songs, Tree Publishing, Along The Road, Susan Ashton, Margaret Becker, Christine Dente,

Also by Susan McGeown:

A Well Behaved Woman's Life

A Garden Walled Around Trilogy:
Call Me Bear
Call Me Elle
Call Me Survivor

Recipe for Disaster
Rules for Survival

The Butler Did It

Rules

for

Survival

By Susan McGeown

Faith Inspired Books

Magnificent Cover Art courtesy of Laury Vaden
magentaswan@patmedia.net

Published by Faith Inspired Books
3 Kathleen Place, Bridgewater, New Jersey 08807
www.FaithInspiredBooks.com

Footnote credits appear throughout this work.

ISBN: 978-0-6151-4407-8
First Printing: March, 2007

To North Branch Reformed Church
of Bridgewater, New Jersey,
which is a church just like Riverside Church
(but the "main minister" is a lot neater!)

Table of Contents

★

★ ★ · ★

★ ★

My shadow's my only, only companion and at night he leaves too ...[2]

One: Men Always Have Hidden Agendas

Glancing down at her watch, she cursed under her breath. She was going to be late. *Again.* Nothing could ever be simple, could it? Certainly not for Claire Jenkins. *Never* for Claire Jenkins. Something always seemed to come up and complicate her life. She cursed again. Glancing in her rearview mirror she determined to risk a speeding ticket and gain a few precious moments. Pressing down on the gas pedal she had a moment's confusion, and then an enormous wave of dismay. Rather then speeding *up* the car was slowing *down*. Claire floored the gas pedal and heard the distinctive shudder and cough of the engine as it quit all together. Cursing loudly and passionately, she coasted the car toward the side of the road, coming to a slow halt. Putting her head down on the steering wheel, she let out a blood-curdling scream that rattled the car windows. *Not now. Not again. Not today.* Would she, could she, *ever* catch a break?

This was the third time in as many weeks that the car had failed her. She shifted into park, turned off the key, took a deep breath and sent

[2] "Valleys Fill First", words and music by Aaron Tate and Ed Cash, Caedmon's Call, Long Line of Leavers, 2000, Cumbee Road Music

up a plea to the great car fairy in the sky. Turning the key, Claire tried to start the engine. Nothing. *Nada.* With her throat still sore from her screams, she put her head down on the steering wheel again and burst into tears.

"Got a problem?" Claire heard over her sobs through the closed window. Tap. Tap. Tap. "Hey, lady! I said, *'Got a problem?'*"

Hastily she wiped her sopping wet face and sniffed loudly. An enormous man with a days' growth of salt and pepper beard, a hard hat, and sunglasses was bending down and peering into her none too clean window. "It just died," she said through the closed window. "I don't know what's wrong."

He nodded. "Pop the hood," he said as he straightened and walked to the front of the car. They stared at each other for a few moments through the window, he expectantly, her suspiciously. Claire had a flash of regret that she'd taken this meandering back country road in an effort to gain a few more precious moments. There was little traffic. She was alone. Weren't there always stories about women who were attacked and killed in circumstances like this? With her luck …

"Look," she heard him say to her as he put his hands on his hips above his tool belt, "if you'd prefer, I'll just go. Do you have a cell phone? Can you call a road service? I don't want to cause you any further *distress* …"

Did he look like a killer-man-rapist? She knew for a fact that they didn't skulk around with "I'm a rapist and proud of it" on their tee shirts. But she also knew that no man, *ever* could be trusted. Rules Number One through Three of the Claire Jenkins Rules of Survival Book: *Men always have hidden agendas. Men will do anything to achieve said hidden agendas. Stay away from all men.* She looked at her watch again. Tyler would be waiting for her, and she really had no choice. She popped the hood.

"Try turning it over," she heard him shout.

Again, nothing happened.

He slammed the lid down and came around and squatted down by her car door. Even squatting he looked enormous. "I'm not a expert on cars," he spoke in a voice louder than normal to be heard through the closed window, "but it's pretty obvious that you're out of gas." Claire gaped at him in astonishment. It couldn't be. She could not have been *that* stupid. And then she looked at the fuel gage. He was absolutely right. She put her head down on the steering wheel and fought the wave of anguish that threatened to well up inside again. She was such a complete screw up.

"Do you have a cell phone?"

She shook her head. *She couldn't afford one.*

"I can let you borrow mine …"

She shook her head. *There was no one she could call.*

"Is there someone you can call?"

She shook her head. The tears started then as she stared out the front windshield, totally oblivious to anything but the disaster of her life. Nothing, *nothing* had ever gone right in her life. Except Tyler. And she was doing her level best to destroy that as well.

"Look, lady, I can't just leave you here. What do you want to do? Come on, pull yourself together and think."

Think, he said. Claire worked to repress the cloak of self-pity and loathing that she was working so hard to weave around her and did as the guy said. *I should call the school*, she thought in a flash. At least she could let them know of her situation and they would keep Tyler safe until she got there. She turned to look at the man still peering at her through the dirty car window. He looked kind enough … He'd appeared concerned and willing to help. Claire knew for a fact that those were the ones you should trust the least.

She wiped her face with the back of her sleeve, released the lock and opened up the door. He stood and stepped back, as if sensing she needed a wide berth. God, he was massive. She peered up at him and saw her reflection in his sunglasses. "If I could borrow your phone, I could call my son's school and tell them I'm going to be late (*again*, her head said) to pick him up. That way he won't worry."

He nodded, seemingly pleased that she wasn't still spiraling down into the pit of despair. "Hang on, I'll go get it."

She stood by her useless car and watched him hoist himself up into his truck. It was a power company truck, one of the huge ones with a cherry picker on top and lights and all manner of tools and contraptions attached to every available space. Claire watched him walk back to her in an easy loping gait, tools clanking musically at his side, his hand extended with the phone. "Thanks," she said and was embarrassed that she had to sniff loudly to keep her nose from running.

The secretary at the school, Ms. Briggs, was snotty. But to the best of Claire's knowledge, Ms. Briggs was always snotty. Perhaps that was part of her job description? *Intimidate all parents who have the potential to cause complications over the course of a typical school day.* When Claire finished explaining her situation, Ms. Briggs said condescendingly, "Ms. Jenkins, I believe that Principal Thompson has talked with you about your *numerous* late pick-ups of Tyler."

"Look Ms. Briggs," Claire ground out, conscious of the mountain of a man standing within earshot, "I'm doing the best I can. My car is old and unreliable. Please tell Tyler to wait in the office and I'll be there as soon as I can get a tow truck."

Remain firm and unbending despite any and all extenuating circumstances. In the face of confrontation forge on fearlessly with whatever difficult information that must be delivered. "I believe that Principal Thompson wished to speak with you about an incident with Tyler on the playground today at recess," Ms. Briggs said rather smugly.

Oh God, not again …

"Yes, well, I'll be happy to speak with her once I get there, okay?" She hung up before Ms. Briggs could say anything else.

She looked up at the silent man leaning casually with arms crossed against her useless car. She hated having to ask anything of anyone. Why did her life always seem to be pushing her into situations just like this one? "Is it okay if I call a tow truck?"

He studied her for one brief flash and then said, "Got money to do that?"

She felt of wave of anger wash through her. "What business of it is yours?" she shot out. How dare he!

He shrugged. "I could offer you a ride."

Claire gave him an impatient look, struggling to keep herself from diving off the edge of control she was tottering on. "Oh yeah," she heard herself say in a tone dripping with venom and sarcasm, "you really want to drive all the way to Hillside Elementary School, wait for me while I get reamed out by the principal for something my kid did, and then drive us home? I had no idea that the power company gave you guys so much free time. That must be why my utility bill is so high."

He grinned at her then. A smile whose size was in compliment with the rest of him – huge. "You're pretty feisty considering I'm only trying to play the Good Samaritan. For your information, I've just finished a double shift, eleven to seven and seven to three so I'm done for the day. All I've got to do is return my truck and go home and catch some much-needed zzz's. But if you're not interested in my offer then go ahead and call your tow truck. From the look of this car, I'd guess you've got the number memorized." He leaned back against her car again, slumped his head forward onto his chest, and appeared to go to sleep.

She didn't have the money. Not in cash, check, or credit card. Why was she being so ornery? Because this kind of thing *always* happened to her and she was just *sick* of it, that's why. Because nobody did *anything* for *nothing* and consequently she never accepted charity, that's why.

The clock was ticking. Reality loomed its ugly head: Tyler was waiting and Claire had no choice. She would have to make nice and accept his offer. Her skin literally crawled. She cleared her throat and sniffed again. *What she wouldn't give for a lousy tissue.* "Look, it's been a bad day and it seems to have the makings of getting worse. *I'm sorry*, okay? I appreciate your stopping, and I would like to take you up on your offer." There. That should do it. She extended her hand, trying to be mature, "My name is Claire. Claire Jenkins."

He picked his head up and studied her for a moment. He looked down at her extended hand, but didn't accept it. "Name's Paul. Paul Williamson. Get your stuff and then I'll help you into the truck. Make sure you lock up that wreck. You wouldn't want anyone to steal it." He chuckled at his own joke.

Mr. Paul Williamson was waiting for her on the passenger side of the truck with the door open. He pointed, "See the step there? See the handle? Grip that, step there and then hoist yourself into the cab." He grinned at her. "If you start to fall, don't worry, I'll catch you." The thought of him touching her sent Claire into such a panic it must have shown clearly on her face. As she looked into his sunglass shaded eyes, he said, "*I'm kidding*," and shook his head in exasperation.

She made it up and in and was quite pleased with herself that she did it on the first try *without his help*. Claire was amazed at the different perspective from so high up and was looking out the front windshield when he climbed in and settled himself behind the steering wheel. He smiled at her as he started up the truck and pulled out onto the road. "Whole different world up here, huh?"

"Tyler's going to go nuts," was all she could say.

Turned out he knew exactly where Hillside Elementary School was. "Done work there a while back," Paul said by way of explanation. She noted that the inside of the truck was surprisingly neat. No discarded coffee cups or empty food bags. He seemed content to drive in silence.

"Do you make it a habit to rescue stranded roadside travelers?" she asked, growing uncomfortable with the quiet.

He never looked at her. "Only the pretty ones," he said with an absolutely straight face. That shut her up for the rest of the ride.

He parked the truck in the school parking lot and she walked in, mentally preparing herself for Tyler's impatience, Ms. Biggs condescension, and the principal's impending lecture. Why did she always feel like *she* had done something wrong and that *she* was being sent to the principal's office?

"Mom!" Tyler said when she walked into the office. His left shoe was untied (as usual) and there was a new rip in the knee of his trousers. *Great.* She could see in his face the effort it was taking for him to sit in his chair and act cooperative. *Uh oh. This must be really bad ...*

"I'm sorry I'm late, big guy," she said as she ruffled his sandy blonde hair. "The car broke down again." She leaned over and whispered, "This time it's all my fault though. I ran out of gas. Can you believe it?"

"Oh, Mom," he rolled his green eyes like he was twenty-three instead of seven.

Claire looked at the stern countenance of the school secretary.

"Ms. Briggs, does the principal still want to see me?"

The computer keyboard continued to click. *Always keep nervous parents on the edge and uncertain. Never let them acquire the upper hand.* Finally, Ms. Briggs stopped typing and looked up at her. "One moment and I'll see," she said. She acted like she was the secretary for Donald Trump, not some tiny elementary school in central New Jersey. "Principal Thompson? Ms. Jenkins is here, do you still wish to talk with her about lunchtime's *incident?*" She listened for a moment. "Fine, I'll send her in." She looked at Claire. "You may go in," she intoned and went back to typing on her computer.

"Tyler, you wait here," Claire said in a firm voice. "Start your homework."

"I don't have any."

They exchanged glances. Two pairs of green eyes looked at each other; one pair tired and impatient, the other pair manipulative and shifty. Claire glared at him. This was the afternoon dance they did every day. The teachers assured her that he had homework each and every night, Monday through Thursday. And each and every night Tyler came home insisting he had none. *Honest, Mom.* Sometimes, if she was lucky, Claire managed to find a mangled math worksheet down in the deep, dark, dank recesses of his backpack. But rarely. "I *know* you have reading to do, I *know* that you have to have spelling words to study, I *know* you've got to have at least some kind of math homework ..."

Tyler looked at her with the innocence of a saint. "Honest, Mom, I don't have any. I got it all done in school."

Claire was too old for this and she was only twenty-five.

Parents need to be continually reminded of the valuable service that the school system provides for them. "Principal Thompson is waiting, Ms. Jenkins. She has a very busy schedule you know," Ms. Briggs spoke without looking away from her computer screen.

Claire glared at Tyler and then at Ms. Briggs. *I'll fight this battle later without an audience*, she thought as she walked into the principal's office.

"Hi, Principal Thompson. You wanted to speak with me?" Claire fought down the urge to grovel. To stand up straight. To try to look innocent in the face of impending doom. She hoped her eyes didn't look manipulative and shifty …

Claire was greeted with a practiced smile. "Hello, Ms. Jenkins. Won't you come in and sit down? Let me shut the door." Principal Thompson always looked impeccable. Whether it was 8 a.m. during morning arrival or 8 p.m. at an evening function. There was never a hair out of place, never a drop of sweat on her face, her nails were always professionally manicured and even her lipstick always appeared fresh. Claire looked down at her waitress uniform and stained white sneakers.

It was so obvious that they lived on different planets.

Trying to sound adult and professional, Claire said, "I understand from Ms. Briggs that there was a problem with Tyler at lunchtime today?"

Principal Thompson seemed to collect herself, took a deep breath, and then looked directly at Claire. "Yes, and this incident transcends all the other incidents for it directly impacts another student's emotional and physical well being. It is a very, *very* serious situation."

"What's he done?" Claire breathed with real trepidation, all efforts to maintain her composure evaporating. Dread and despair filled her.

"While on the playground at lunch recess, Tyler accosted another boy and pulled his pants down in front of everyone. The boy was so traumatized that he was sent home to recover. As you can imagine, this is not a situation that we can simply address with words and admonitions. I've spoken with another principal in the district, as well as the Superintendent of Schools, and even though Tyler is only in second grade and seven years old, it has been determined that he will be suspended from school for three full days. That means he will not be permitted on school grounds until Monday."

Claire just sat there for long moments, unable to think of what to say or how to react. Finally she choked out, "Did you speak with Tyler about this?"

"Yes, we did. Both myself and the school nurse, Mrs. Lane, did."

"And? What did he say?"

"Very little, to be quite honest with you. He said nothing other than to admit that the account that the lunch aid had given us was correct and he had indeed done what he had been accused of. He offered no defense or explanation of his actions whatsoever. And the child he accosted insisted that the attack was completely unprovoked. There were a number of children who were in the immediate vicinity of the incident. When we talked with them none could provide us with any additional details."

Principal Thompson looked pointedly at Claire. "Perhaps over the course of his suspension, he will provide you with some more insight. Should he do this, I'd appreciate your letting me know."

"I'll talk with him tonight after I finish work …"

"Yes, I suggest you do."

Claire struggled with what she had just heard about her son. Tyler had always been kind, loving and sensitive. He was a regular kid though: mischief happened when he got bored, retaliation happened when he was attacked. His sense of humor was not so well developed simply because there was very little to laugh about in their lives. Jeeze, what was going on in his head that he'd do such a thing? Claire looked at Principal Thompson, "He's never done anything like this before. Harm another child, I mean, has he?"

Principal Thompson shook her head. "No, all the other prior incidents have involved simple mischief and testing of the rules. I really do not believe that Tyler is a malicious child, Ms. Jenkins, but this situation cannot be brushed under the table and forgotten. An entire lunch period of children witnessed your son's brutality and another child's humiliation."

Principal Thompson hesitated and then continued. "There is one other thing, Ms. Jenkins. I'd like the school psychologist to talk with Tyler. His disruptive behavior seems to be escalating. I believe it would be wise that we make use of the avenues available to us within the school system to see if we can shed some light on what's going on in Tyler's head."

"You think he needs a shrink?"

Principal Thompson leaned forward toward Claire. She was wearing a huge diamond ring and had, what looked like, a very expensive gold watch and gold bracelet on her wrist. "Can I be frank with you, Ms. Jenkins?"

Is there any way I could possibly stop you? Claire nodded.

"What your son did borders on criminal harassment. There is now zero tolerance for abusive, threatening behavior on school grounds. The parents of the young boy whom Tyler accosted could, conceivably, press criminal charges against your son. It is in your own as well as Tyler's best interest for you to appear cooperative, concerned, and contrite regarding this incident. Am I making myself clear?"

Claire nodded again.

Principal Thompson seemed to soften just a bit. "Besides Ms. Jenkins, don't you want to know what's causing all of this? Wouldn't you like the opportunity to get a handle on things before the situation gets so uncontrollable it becomes hopeless?"

Who the hell did this woman think she was, sitting there with her polished nails and diamond jewelry? Claire felt the tears coming like the inevitability of a tidal wave, when the sea water is drawn far away from the shoreline and you *know* something horrible is going to happen. *Don't cry now, Claire. Save it for later. You know you can do it.* She nodded again but could not find any words. She didn't dare. Who knew what would come out of her mouth if she opened it? She could curl Principal Thompson's hair with the curses she desperately wanted to spit out. Blindly she reached for her purse and hurried out of the office.

"Ms. Jenkins!" she heard the principal calling after her. "Wait! We haven't finished discussing-," Claire didn't even slow down.

She rushed past the evil Ms. Briggs, grabbed Tyler's arm with one hand and his backpack with the other, and rushed out of the office out into the bright sunshine.

"Mom ..."

"Don't say a word to me," she gasped unable to fight the tears that were streaming down her face. *Wouldn't you like the opportunity to get a handle on things before the situation gets so uncontrollable it becomes hopeless?* Principal Thompson had no idea. *The situation had been uncontrollably hopeless for years.* Probably her whole life.

Welcome to my world.

Tyler, unable to be quiet for longer than thirty seconds, was not particularly fazed by her words or her tears. "I know I'm not supposed to say a word to you, Mom, but how are we getting home? I don't see the car."

Oh God, *oh God*. Not only did she have to face her potentially criminal minded son, she had to deal with this stranger acting like a - what did he call himself? – a *Good Samaritan*. She looked up frantically and was horrified to see him walking slowly toward them. He'd taken off his hard hat and tool belt but still wore his sunglasses. She was so done in. She just stood there still clutching Tyler's arm and watched him approach.

"You okay?" he asked when he got within earshot.

"Who's this guy?" Tyler asked her with a tinge of hostility.

Claire couldn't speak. She was completely and totally done in. She just stood there, still crying. *I'm done, I'm done ... I'm done.*

"Hi, Tyler, my name is Paul Williamson. I came by your mom when she was stranded on the side of the road and offered her a ride."

"We're gonna ride in that truck?" Tyler's excitement was evident, always willing to seize the moment, capitalize on a good opportunity.

Claire numbly registered Paul's smile at her son. "Yeah, you think you can handle that?"

"Can you put me up in the cherry picker?"

"No, sorry, I can't." Paul looked at her. "Claire? Come on, I'll take you two home, okay?"

She just looked at him. She could hear him saying to her - not an hour ago - *Come on, pull yourself together a bit and think.* She walked down the steps still clutching Tyler's backpack and dragging him along with her.

Once they were all settled in the truck, Paul asked, "Which way's home for you guys?"

"Oh, we don't go home *yet*," Tyler volunteered, a font of information. "Mom's got to go back and finish her shift at the diner. It's the *All American Diner* on Route 28. Do you know it? It has really, *really* good chocolate chip cookies, but disgusting green beans."

Paul hesitated, and then asked Tyler, "What do you do while your mom works?"

"Well, if I've got any homework – which I hardly ever do – I work on that at one of the empty tables. If I don't have homework, I play my Gameboy, or if the weather's nice there's a basketball hoop in the back for the busboys when they're on break."

"What time is Mom's shift over?"

"Nine."

"*Nine p.m.?*"

"Yeah, it's not so bad. I get a free dinner every night and any dessert I want as long as I eat my *greens*," Tyler said with an obvious shiver of revulsion.

The tears had stopped. Claire had continued to stare out the front of the truck since she had climbed in, but felt Tyler glance at her. His voice dropped down into a conspiratorial whisper as he continued to speak to Paul. "Mom's usually pretty busy around dinner time so I can usually scam it pretty good." She heard Paul chuckle in spite of himself.

"Claire?" Paul addressed her. "Is Tyler right? Am I taking you two back to work?"

She had to pull herself together. *C'mon girl, you've done it a million times*. She took a deep breath and looked at him. "Yeah, you're taking us back to my job."

Paul knew where the diner was, so she was spared having to make any more conversation. While they drove she struggled for composure; crabby/hysterical waitresses made really lousy tips. Outside the diner, Paul came around to help her and Tyler down.

She had pulled herself together enough to make eye contact with Paul and say, "Thanks for your help. You get the Good Samaritan Badge of Honor."

He studied her for a moment and she felt uncomfortable under his scrutiny. "You're welcome. I'm glad I was able to stop. I don't believe in coincidences, so it was a pleasure to be of service."

She was too wiped out to ask him to explain what he meant. As she walked up the steps of the diner Paul called out to her, "Hey! How will you guys get home?"

Claire hadn't thought of that. Finally, she shrugged. "I'll ask one of the girls to give us a lift. They've done it before. They'll probably have to do it again." The noise of the diner drowned out the sound of the truck engine pulling out of the parking lot.

Tyler was on his best behavior at the diner that night, suspecting the confrontation awaiting him once they got home. Each time she looked over at him he seemed to be obediently doing what was expected of him: reading, working on a school paper, eating green beans (with the requisite shiver), and then playing his Gameboy.

When it got close to the end of her shift she approached Sally, the cashier. "Who's off at nine, tonight? I need to catch a ride home."

"How come?"

Sally was Chief Gossip in the diner. She was Dan's youngest daughter and the hostess/cashier. Dan owned the diner. Sally's most distinctive feature was the big wad of gum she was continually chewing and popping. If you needed info you sought her out; if you had a secret you avoided her. "My car. It died this afternoon on my way to get Tyler. It's a problem I'll have to deal with tomorrow. It's sitting on the side of some country road on the way to Tyler's school."

"That's funny," Sally said with a frown glancing out the window, "Dan said to tell you that the next time you park your car in customer spaces he's going to dock you."

Claire turned to follow Sally's glance, looking out into the parking lot. Sure enough there was her car parked underneath the flickering fluorescent lights. She looked at Sally who gazed back at her, popped her gum, and shrugged.

Even though she still had two tables, she walked out into the cool spring evening and over to her car. There was a white envelope under the windshield wiper. She opened it and read:

Claire,

You left your keys in my truck. I took it as another opportunity to be of service.

Paul

Enclosed in the envelope were her keys. She got in behind the wheel, put the key in the ignition, and turned it over. The car started right up and she took note that there was a full tank of gas. No one ever did kind, helpful things for her. She didn't allow it. Claire was an independent, self-supporting woman. She and Tyler might live close to the poverty line but it was her own sheer determination and willpower that kept them from the brink. She didn't need anybody. Never had. Never would.

But the guy had been nice. He'd helped her out of a difficult spot and briefly had made her life slightly less complicated. "Thanks, Paul," she said into the darkness, "Thanks a lot."

And she meant it.

I built another temple to a stranger, I gave away my heart to the rushing wind,
I set my course to run right into danger, sought the company of fools instead of friends.[3]

★
★ ★ · ★
★ · ★

Two: Believe What You See, Not What You Hear

D riving home from the All American Diner that Tuesday night, Paul Williamson pondered the question: Were you supposed to love your brothers and sisters? He knew that you were supposed to honor your father and mother and love your neighbor as yourself but *technically*, neither his two self righteous sisters nor his two all knowing brothers fit in either category. Was there a Bible command that said he had to love them? Or worse yet, pay attention and always listen to them? He could break out in a cold sweat over that one! Even though he was twenty-seven years old, had a solid, reliable job, and lived in his own home, a week rarely went by that they didn't make him feel like a five year old pain in the ... butt.

Actually the reality of whom and what he had become was much worse than that. He was a full-grown example of a complete disappointment. Even more disturbing was the fact that the opinion his family and friends had of him was based only on the *partial* picture of what he truly was. No one knew the entire, disgusting, depressing story. Were

---

[3] "Jealous Kind", Jars of Clay, Who We Are Instead, 2003

he to admit it to himself in the deepest, darkest parts of his soul, his greatest fear was that what his siblings had been thinking about him all this time was absolutely right.

He had grown up in a strong Christian home with loving parents as the youngest of five children. It was in his adulthood that he realized the magnitude of what his parents had given him: a spiritual foundation as well as an example of a solid, loving family. It was quite a shock to realize that the upbringing he had taken for granted was very unique. Paul had friends who had grown up in intact families, or who had felt loved and treasured, or who had been taught right from wrong, respect from insolence, or who had been given the important knowledge of salvation. But he'd never met anyone, like himself, who had had all of those things in one complete package. That realization, when he had been in his early twenties, had brought him up short.

For a bit.

Paul felt he was in a continual, never ending battle with himself - it was a war between the person he desperately wanted to be and the person he had so easily let himself become. And no matter what admirable decisions he made *now,* he could not escape the glaring scars of the past. It seemed as if, in the blink of an eye, he had become the epitome of the worst kind of man imaginable: egotistical, thoughtless, and foul. The discovery of what he truly was, without the parental imposed veneer of a nice Christian boy, still shocked and depressed him.

He sighed and shook his head in disgust. How much of his personal time did he loose in thoughts like this? Regrets. God, he had so many of them it felt like he was dressed in a suit of lead. Maybe he should have bought a home in a different state. Perhaps he would have been able to forget (never forgive) more about himself had he removed himself from everything familiar. But in reality, distancing himself from family and old friends hadn't worked. Drawing rigid boundaries around himself in an effort to control his behavior and thoughts hadn't worked. The guilt he carried around was as much a part of him as his internal organs. There was nowhere he could go to escape *himself.* The person he *was* and the things he'd *done* would always be a part of the person he was *trying* to become.

How could you move along in life with such a past and expect to put it out of your mind? *Forget about it.*

Thoughts about regrets and the massive failures in his life always led to thoughts about Karly. Paul sighed. Even after all these years … The monumental responsibility he felt for the hurt, humiliation, and disaster that he had caused in her life was something he could not reconcile himself to. Ever.

The Guilt he still felt regarding *everything* about their relationship was powerful enough to make his heart pound, even after all this time. Five years ago. *Five years.* He and Karly dated for almost four years, through most of college. Years of patience and persistence on his part had finally paid off though; he'd managed to completely destroy the prettiest and sweetest girl he'd ever known.

Truth be told, the enjoyment of women had been with him forever so he supposed it was destined to be his greatest downfall. One of the best things about youth group and church socials had always been the girls. Paul had been gregarious and popular with everyone at church, but most especially the girls. Things just shifted into overdrive once he hit college and threw caution and Christianity to the wind. He supposed, if it were possible to map out his decline and fall from grace, it was women from start to finish that had brought him to the cliff of no return.

Karly had blonde hair, blue eyes, and a figure that had no business sashaying down a church aisle. They'd met at a fraternity party during the first few weeks of college in their freshman year. She had tagged along with a girlfriend of hers. Over the years that they dated, everyone who knew the two of them at college had assumed they'd eventually get married. And what Paul knew better than anyone was that despite the level ten sex kitten exterior, Karly was a grade A Christian young woman inside. Passionate and committed to Christ, all she had wanted to do was become a missionary. At the time they'd started dating she'd already been to Kentucky and Georgia to build homes with Habitat for Humanity and was actively planning on traveling to Mexico to help build a start up church near Tijuana. While Paul had gone reluctantly to the local state college for an accounting degree, Karly had attended the nearby Christian college excelling in all of her biblical studies and avidly researching where the Lord wished her to go for missionary service.

Meanwhile, Paul had slipped one step at a time over to the dark side. That pull, *to the dark side*, had been powerful and persistent: to make his own choices, his own decisions, ... and his own mistakes. Choices and decisions that had not been imposed on him by his family or his church. What was wrong with wanting to learn first hand what was out there in the big, bad world? In the end, Paul hadn't tried very hard to resist any of it.

During their senior year at college, Paul had reached a stage with his Christianity where it downright embarrassed him, making Karly's commitment to her life's purpose a glaring spotlight to Paul's own personal compromises. He actually began resenting her intrinsic goodness, challenging her unswerving beliefs, and battering continually at her desire to maintain a celibate relationship. His doubts and his new behaviors became a red-hot wedge that slowly and methodically drove them apart.

Except for one very important thing. Karly had (shockingly as it still was to Paul) really, truly loved him. She was willing to do anything in her power to fight for him and their relationship. The key word being *anything*.

They'd lost their virginity together in the end. Mere moments afterwards, he'd felt guilty as hell and she'd cried pitifully. The specters of eternal damnation and carnal lust had loomed largely while he had lain next to her trying to find the right words for comfort and redemption. Somehow, "Will you marry me?" seemed the best ones for that particular job.

Four months later found Paul with a degree in accounting, destined to be married in two weeks. And more miserable than he'd ever thought possible. Suddenly issues that had been vague and uncertain were now crystal clear and it was too damned late. He didn't *want* to be a church-going Christian man. He wanted to spread his wings and taste all the different flavors life had to offer. He didn't *want* to dedicate his life to the Lord. He wanted to throw caution to the wind and run wild. He didn't *want* to be a missionary. Hell, he didn't even want to be an accountant! He wanted a job that wasn't going to suck the life right out of him; just pay him and send him on his way. And most important of all, Paul didn't want to marry Karly. He wanted an opportunity to play with all the forbidden fruits he could get his hands on.

But he kept his mouth shut … Who would understand? How could he justify the sacrifice of Karly's noble calling to his selfish whims? How could he rationalize all she had given him by abandoning her? Watching the faces of his family and friends wreathed in smiles and giddy with excitement, Paul felt as though a noose had been tied around his neck.

He'd remained silent through the engagement party, the bridal shower, the bachelor party in the church basement and the bachelorette party at his mother's house. He helped stuff, stamp and address two hundred and fifty invitations that were mailed out to people who had known him and Karly since before they were born. Tuxedoes had been ordered, gowns had been made, rings had been sized, honeymoon plans had been finalized, menus had been selected, flowers had been chosen, and a DJ had been hired. He'd been positioned over the trap door, and the executioner's hand was on the release lever. His life would be over before it had even begun …

The morning of the wedding dawned clear and beautiful and found Paul standing on the front lawn of Karly's home bleary eyed from a night of no sleep. He'd been standing there for hours, waiting. He knew she walked her dog each morning. Said it was a peaceful time for her to pray and set her day on track right from the start. Just because it was her wedding day Paul knew she would never consider deviating from a routine that worked. At 6:00 a.m. exactly she breezed out the front door with Max straining at the lease, laughing and saying, "Hold on you dumb dog! Let me tie my sneaker or I'll break my neck. What are you so excited about?" When she saw him standing there on the front lawn she'd worked hard to give him her megawatt smile and said, "Oh, hi Paul …"

Afterwards, he'd played the scene over in his head a million times. He had come to the conclusion that the moment she'd seen him standing there she'd known what was coming. She had walked down the front path, hesitantly, with a puzzled smile on her face. "What are you doing here, honey? Don't you know you're not supposed to see the bride before the ceremony?"

Still, she had placed her hand on his shoulder and stood up on tiptoe to kiss him. He'd stood there like a statue and blurted out, "I can't do it, Karly."

Paul was certain that she knew what he had meant, but still she asked, "Can't do what?"

So he'd choked out, "I can't marry you."

Karly had laughed a tinkling little laugh that went with her blonde hair and sky blue eyes. "What are you saying, Paul? Are you saying *now*, *today*, on the *day of our wedding*, after almost four years of dating and the *level of commitment* that we've shared, that you're changing your mind *now?*" She had laughed again like it was some huge, funny joke.

Pushing the words out of his mouth had been the hardest thing he'd ever done. "Yeah. That's what I'm saying." Karly had turned to begin her walk, making every effort to completely ignore what he'd been killing himself to tell her. Roughly, he'd caught her arm to keep from having to run after to her. "I mean it, Karly. Do you want me to come inside so we can talk to your parents together?"

That's when she'd blown. Karly had rounded on him, all sign of laughter gone, fury etched in the lines around her eyes and mouth, and her newly manicured fingernails dug into his forearm. "*You can't do this*, Paul. Things are set. Done. Finished. Planned. I've given you *everything* I've had to give. You know who I am and what I am and what my hopes and dreams and plans are. We are in this together. *Two have been made one*, Paul. The vows maybe need to be spoken today, but this deal is already signed and sealed."

But he'd stood there, watching her completely fall apart right before his eyes, shaking his head, "I can't marry you, Karly. I don't love you."

"*You don't love me?*" Karly's voice rose in volume causing Max the dog to jump up at her and whine. "We're sleeping together!" she'd screamed loud enough for the entire neighborhood to hear. "We're considering a missionary call to Appalachia! We've got two hundred and fifty people getting dressed right now to come and see us be made officially man and wife in less than five hours! *AND YOU HAVE THE GALL TO STAND HERE AND TELL ME YOU DON'T LOVE ME?"*

From there, it had only gotten worse. Karly's mother and father had come out on the front porch to hear the last exchange. Rushing toward their daughter, they had tried to touch her in comfort, but Karly had slapped their hands away shouting at them, *"DO YOU HEAR WHAT HE'S TELLING ME? DO YOU HEAR?"*

"Come inside, dear, and we'll talk," Karly's mother had said firmly, grabbing her by the arm and forcibly dragging her daughter into the house.

"You'd better come inside, too, son," Karly's father said to Paul in a tone that offered no argument.

Inside the house, things did not improve. "Why's Karly screaming on the front lawn?" her wise ass ten year old brother Michael had asked as soon as they walked through the front door. "And what does 'gall' mean? Isn't that a body part?"

"Go back to sleep, Michael," Mr. Martin had said impatiently brushing past his son.

"But Dad …"

"NOW."

They'd all (minus Michael) ended up standing awkwardly and silently in the living room unable to sit, afraid to speak.

"I'm sorry," Paul had finally managed, unwilling to repeat what had been said but knowing more had to be offered. "I never wanted to hurt you, Karly. You don't see it now, but I'd only make you more miserable if you married me. I'm sorry it took me so long to realize that."

"Get out," Karly had ground out through gritted teeth, her fists clenched at her sides, her face contorted with grief and awash in tears. "I don't want to see your face or hear your voice. You are weak and cowardly, afraid to make a choice and take a stand! You're right, Paul, you would have made me miserable! You would have dragged me down into the depths where you seem so desperate to be! Get out! *GET OUT!"*

Paul had left under the condemning eyes of Karly's mother and the disappointed eyes of her father. But it wasn't facing Karly that had turned out to be the most difficult part of the day. It was facing his family.

Listening to his sisters rail at him and trying to ignore his brothers' constant requests for explanations had been hard enough. His mother's silent tears and his father's visible disappointment had made Paul want to leave the house he had grown up in and never come home. *Ever.*

After that day, it was a lot easier to dance along the dark side. At least there was no one to let down. He had blown off accounting and got a job working for the power company. The pay was great, especially with overtime bonuses thrown in. He got an apartment with a bunch of college fraternity brothers and began setting out to try all the forbidden things he'd dreamed of. His family continued to make overtures; the church continued to reach out. His youth pastor visited him twice at the apartment to invite him to come back to church. The last remaining threads that kept him from going over the edge grew taut with stress and strain.

Eight months after he'd broken off with Karly he received legal papers from Agape Christian Services asking him for his signature, signing away all parental rights to the son Karly Martin had given birth to on January 8th. He'd sat there in his filthy bachelor apartment hearing the last threads to goodness and light twanging around him as they snapped for good. *She'd had a baby.* His baby. And she'd given it up for adoption. She'd not become a missionary. She'd born the shame and heartache all alone. He'd done this to her because of his selfish vision of life and spoiled desire for everything he'd wanted to the exclusion of all else. There was not one ounce of redeeming goodness in him. *Just move on.* After he'd signed the adoption papers there had been no turning back. What was there but wreckage and ashes? The dark side became his very best friend; it was the only place he deserved to be. The "nice Christian boy" became tarnished beyond recognition. He developed new interests, established new friendships, and cultivated new passions. He became the life of any party and a connoisseur of women. Life became an opportunity to play games and acquire victories – especially with females.

And Paul would have stayed in that dark place forever … except for one person.

He felt the condemnation and disappointment of his parents, his siblings, his church friends, his minister, and his youth pastor. Did they know about the baby? Paul didn't know and he sure as hell wasn't going to ask. They seemed to look at him with eyes that said, *You weren't strong enough. We were always afraid of this. What a waste.* Interactions with any or all of them invariably ended up with sorrowful words of condemnation challenged with furious bursts of his newly discovered explosive temper. Consequently he'd avoided all old connections and most of them gradually gave up and slipped away.

Except for his grandfather. Paul had always had a special relationship with him. It was a relationship rooted in childhood love and adoration, fostered in a unique one-on-one bond of patience and sharing. Paul may have never felt he measured up to his older brothers and sisters, Paul may have often felt he disappointed his mother and father, but with Grandpa, Paul always felt that he was *just right.*

Grandpa steadfastly refused to behave any differently towards Paul when they got together. He remained silent at the rare family get - togethers Paul attended that were always *loaded* with innuendoes and condescension. Grandpa regularly called Paul on the phone, and talked about work and baseball, the weather and his hemorrhoids.

His grandfather commented only once on his absence from church saying, "I miss you sitting next to me, Paul." And the only thing his grandfather ever said directly about Paul's 'rebellion' (as the family chose to call it) was, "You can't live another person's faith, Paul. It has to be your own. I hope you take the time to examine your head and your heart and make sure you are on the right path."

But the reality was that he was having too wild a time to spend any time soul searching or in self-examination. About the only thing he thought about was enjoying himself. He lost *years*, leaving a trail of debauchery and destruction in his wake. Then his grandpa died and life brought Paul up short. *Then* Paul examined his head and his heart and his soul and he found what he saw too revolting to believe possible.

More years followed in which Paul slowly and carefully recommitted his life to Christ. He stood up out of the muck and the mire and did his best to clean himself off. The process of redefining himself was long and tortuous. He began attending church again – not his old one –

unable to face the familiar faces and deal with the old questions. He wasn't *that* strong. He found a new church near his house that was solid and welcoming. Determined that whatever he accomplished would be purely on his own steam, he strove to be fresh and forward thinking. He sought to surround himself with positive influences such as the church softball team, and he offered to coach the church sponsored little league baseball team. He learned to evaluate every one of his automatic reactions; gradually he became quiet instead of boisterous, thoughtful instead of reactionary. Old habits died hard though, especially when he was out and about with his friends.

He'd been able to get the drinking under control. *Thank God.* He wasn't an alcoholic, he was more a typical good 'ole boy who liked to have one, two, *eleven* beers to help himself loosen up and have a good, raucous time. It had been the easiest way to escape the God-fearing respect that had been dosed into him since his infancy and the inevitable guilt that was never far behind.

The language problem was tougher to overcome, because he couldn't get away from his mouth. He could avoid the bars, but his big mouth was always with him. He constantly battled with language that wanted desperately to shoot out of his mouth and prowled around constantly in his head waiting for release. Especially around his family. It could almost be funny. Around his family it was the worst! As he walked into his parents home or any one of his sibling's houses, he had an almost constant litany of smart ... aleck ... responses in his head, full of vivid curses and cutting remarks. His sisters and brothers were critical enough of him as it was. *If they could only hear his thoughts!*

But it was the woman thing that was the hardest by far. Paul had always been a natural charmer (ask his sisters) and for some reason he couldn't quite fathom, his rough, imposing looks seemed to appeal to women. Maybe because he was so big they just couldn't overlook him. At 6'5" and 245 pounds he certainly wasn't someone who faded into the background. Add in the thrill of the hunt and the rush of the catch and women were just about the most fun he could imagine. *Even now were he to be honest with himself* ... The past two years, the easiest solution had been to avoid women and dating completely.   His commitment to God was important to him, and he needed as little temptation as possible.

His mind wandered to Miss Claire Jenkins and those big green eyes of hers, despite his best intentions ...

Stop.

Claire Jenkins.   Paul didn't think he'd ever encountered anyone so down on her luck.   Finishing up his double shift with the power company, the only thing he wanted was a hot shower, a steak, and bed.   In that order. Had Claire's car not been the exact make, model and color of a car he used to remember his grandfather driving, Paul probably wouldn't even have noticed it on the side of the road.   He often drove that winding back-country road for the peace and quiet, taking the time to go over his day and night and apologize to God for all the times he'd failed once again.   When Paul had noticed her, he knew that if he didn't stop, she would have been in for a long wait until the next passing motorist happened by.

He wasn't sure, but Paul didn't think he'd ever had any female look at him as Claire had while he'd waited for her to pop the hood: that 'deer in the head lights' look with him feeling distinctively like the eighteen-wheeler tractor trailer.   Standing there waiting for her to decide if she was going to let him help her, he had an overwhelming desire to calm her fears and make her smile.   His immediate response was to tamp down any and all interest in the opposite sex *because he still couldn't trust himself* in that area.   That caused him to get impatient with her.   *Could we hurry this up a bit, sweetie, so I can get the ... heck ... out of here?*   He could hear his voice, sounding more fed up than he had any right to be, saying "Look if you'd prefer, I'll just go.   Do you have a cell phone?   Can you call a road service?   I don't want to cause you any further *distress* ..."

The kid, Tyler, was cute.   Paul had liked him immediately when he'd said, "Who's this guy?" with all the hostility a seven year old who barely reached to his belt buckle could muster.   His feistiness had reminded Paul of himself.   He still vividly remembered trying to stand up to his brothers, Elliot and Brian, as they tortured and teased him and then, later, when they were going to beat him up once he had tattled to his parents about them.   Sometimes he felt as if his life was a study of bad memories ...

Paul had liked helping Claire and her kid out.   Surprisingly, watching them walk into the diner, he'd felt almost *bereft* for a moment. How stupid was that? He had spent no more than an hour with this down-on-her-luck woman and her smart mouthed kid and yet he had felt lonely as they had walked away from him. It made no sense. It was then as he climbed back into the truck that he'd noticed Claire's keys. So he'd done one more good deed. One positive mark against the million marks he regularly chalked up on the negative side.

Paul's life was that of a typical bachelor, said with a touch of envy by his married buddies and inevitable sarcasm by his sisters, Rachel and Connie.   His   small   ranch   style   house   was   furnished   in   the minimalist/functional/hardy bachelor style with accents of sports enthusiasm in every available space. Purchased with money left to him by his grandfather, Paul knew how fortunate he was to be twenty-seven and owning his own home. Just another wonderful legacy from his grandfather.

He enjoyed all sports, but was not exceptionally good at any one in particular. That was more than okay with him, because the reality was that he simply liked to *play*. It didn't matter how, what, or with whom. He could stay erect and smash most opponents silly in the ice hockey rink, he could throw a fifty-yard pass without much trouble and strike sufficient fear to make most guys he was chasing run out of bounds rather than be tackled, and should he connect with a softball, which didn't happen as regularly as he'd like, he could send it out of the park. He also had golf clubs in the garage, a basketball hoop in the driveway, a mountain bike on the back porch, and a pool table in the basement.

As would be expected, his nieces and nephews loved him, and his friends considered his home the *place to go to hang*. When he could convince his brothers and sisters that he wasn't going to corrupt their children completely, he enjoyed having the kids sleep over. Most of his friends had keys to the house, and it was not unusual to find someone sprawled across his living room couch any given morning. In fact, he was happy and pleased with that.

Prior to his grandfather's death, during his lost years as he'd come to call them, Paul had worked hard to enjoy the freedom of answering to no one and the companionship of a multitude of friends. He'd discovered that if he concentrated on living for the moment – not dwelling on the past or agonizing about the future, he could get through the day just fine. Haphazardness ruled his existence. Any hollow emptiness he felt was determinedly attributed to the desire for bigger thrills or wilder experiences. It made him move faster, talk louder, and definitely think even less.

But after his grandfather's death, the emptiness was properly labeled and the haphazardness was duly faced. He could no longer avoid it. The reality was that Paul was rudderless with no place to go. He was a Christian man who was running away from his purpose and his destiny, unable to face his failures nor take responsibility for his actions. Try as he might, he was unable to escape The Guilt of Karly and The Secret that went with her because he carried it inside him every single … darn … moment. For a while he was tremendously angry with his mother and father. His parents had effectively ruined any attempt for him to live a life of complete and utter debauchery. What was that verse? *Train up a child in the way he should go and when he is old he will not depart from it*[4]. More like, "when he is old he won't be able to escape it"!

Once Paul began to face the hard things that were wrong with his life he realized that he desperately wanted back what he had spent his whole life running away from: stability, purpose, direction, protection, guidance, love … It was all true after all. Every word. *You don't appreciate anything half as much until it's gone.* He couldn't bring his grandfather back but he could for … darn sure … reestablish his relationship with Christ. He'd been working on it ever since. And he failed *all the time.* Granted, he was his own worst critic. But Paul sincerely doubted if he'd ever be worthy of being able to call himself a Christian out loud.

He hung around regularly with a group of five friends. It was a friendship rooted in work - they all worked for the same power company - but that had grown to include playing together as well. Separately, they were nice, good hearted and easy going men. Together, factoring in a few drinks and the inevitable raging testosterone, they were a wild partying force to be reckoned with.

---

[4] Proverbs 22:6

The guys saw a difference for sure. They teased him now calling him "Saint Paul", or just "Saint" for short. All of them had known him since long before he'd decided to rededicate his life to Christ. The guys had gotten to know him during his 'insane' years, so his transformation had been particularly stunning to them. None of them really understood his reasoning or the importance of it all, but a few of them regularly asked him pointed questions about his beliefs and opinions. He wasn't a Bible - banger. In fact, he'd be the first one to run in the opposite direction should he be faced with one. But he could no longer deny what he was and what he strove to be. He was a Christian who strove to be a man after God's own heart.

When Paul had decided to recommit his life to Christ, he'd struggled with the wisdom of continuing friendships that were based primarily on partying and playing. But the reality was *he really liked the guys*. A good part of the friendships were strongly positive. In Paul's opinion, the strength lay in their diverse individuality and easygoing acceptance of each other. Vince, probably the one he was the closest to, was loud and irreverent, never cowed into submission by voices of authority or rules of propriety. James was a lover, not a fighter, and although he did his best to hide it, treasured his relationship and new marriage with his wife, Maggie, above all else. Mike, was loud and obnoxious, a smoke screen he used to cover his profound lack of self-confidence. Simon was the voice of reason in the group, which was why the first goal of any evening was to get two beers into him. Joshua reminded Paul most of himself, for he seemed, most of the time, to not quite know who he was or what he wanted to be. The idea of severing his relationship with any of them caused Paul more anxiety than his separation from his family. In the end, after he'd prayed long and hard about it, Paul had decided that he owed it to the guys to be honest with them. He'd let them *leave him* if they felt they had to.

The guys quickly discovered that he was attending church on Sunday mornings and that he'd agreed to help out coaching the church-sponsored little league team. They also knew that beside their regular Thursday night softball game, he played on the church softball team as well. Paul had even managed to get two of them to join because the church team was so ... darn ... pathetic.

It had been his profound pleasure that as soon as he'd made the choice to change direction, the Lord had opened up doors. And they were all to places Paul gladly wanted to be. All of the things that he enjoyed – sports, the outdoors, and fellowship – surprisingly fit right into his new life. He stopped counting the surprising *coincidences* he found at the church he began to attend: they had a softball team and needed players, they had a little league team that needed another coach, they had a campground up north where they regularly went on retreats ... Seemed like God was a sports fan and a nature enthusiast just as he was. *Cool.*

The guys had first noticed things were different when he'd begun to order sodas at the bar. Paul's decision to stop drinking was based solely on the fact that he had enough trouble controlling himself sober. He didn't want to court disaster once he had a few cold ones in him. At first, nervous about revealing too much about himself and fearful of their reactions, he'd made vague excuses about 'stomach problems' and 'cutting down for a while to dry out'. Finally, after persistent inquiries, he'd just blurted out that he'd decided to quit. He hadn't had the courage to elaborate any further. For a couple of months he let them think that he was a recovering alcoholic until The Voice in his head that sounded distinctly like his grandfather's had quietly pointed out how pathetic it was that he'd rather his friends think of him as a drunk rather than a Christian. *How pitiful was that?* So, one night at his house - they almost always ended up there after Thursday's softball game - he'd told them the real reason why he'd stopped drinking.

The guys had greeted the whole confession with lengthy moments of stunned silence.

"You yanking us around, Paul?" Josh had asked.

"Nope."

"You mean, you really plan on giving up drinking, and cursing, and ... *women?*" Vince had choked out in an incredulous tone. Vince made it sound like Paul had decided to give up breathing.

"Yeah, Vince. Believe it or not, I think I can do it."

"Fifty bucks says you won't make a month." Mike saw everything as a gambling opportunity. "You don't have an ounce of self control where any of those three are concerned. Why, I remember that night we went into the city-"

"I'm going to do my best, Mike," Paul had interrupted, also remembering that infamous night in the city, "and I think the hardest thing for me is going to be stopping the cursing because right now I'd like to punch your ... darn ... face in." Mike had laughed out loud.

Simon, always the quietest and the most serious of the bunch, finally spoke. "I give you credit, Paul."

"Does this mean we can't drink beer here and you're going to start praying before games and bugging us to attend church?" Josh asked. He looked moderately terrified.

Paul couldn't tell if he was serious or joking. He decided to treat the question as if he meant it. "I hope you'll respect my opinions about things, that's all."

"Hell, that's a relief," Mike blurted out. "I don't know about the rest of you, but all this God talk is making me thirsty. Who needs another cold one?"

"I look at it this way," said James, the only one out of the group who was married. (Vince was divorced.) "Maggie will be thrilled to know that you're trying to get respectable, Paul, and that should work in my favor. Maybe she won't give me such a hard time when I want to come out and play."

"And we'll always have a designated driver," noted Simon practically.

It had turned out to be no big deal, really. Paul and the guys had settled into a surprisingly easy existence. They still hung out at his house, but now brought their own beer. He always drove when things got out of hand. Vince continued to be the only one to tease, even going so far as to pay for a year's subscription of *Playboy* to be delivered to Paul's house. "Heck, big guy, you're going to have to do *something* ...!" And Simon and Joshua in the end had been persuaded to join the church softball team.

Despite the changes Paul introduced, the friendships had remained.

Once again, it had been Paul's family that had been the most difficult. For some reason he couldn't explain even to himself why he chose to keep this major spiritual decision to himself. The desire to prove himself, and then finally tell his family, was strong but not strong enough. Perhaps he was afraid that Connie or Rachel would say something negative, perhaps he was concerned that Elliot and Brian would still question his integrity, or perhaps he was unwilling to disappoint his parents yet again should he fail. Or perhaps it was because he was still living Karly's description of him – *weak and cowardly, afraid to make a choice and take a stand* ... Deep down Paul knew that it was all of the above, *and probably more.*

So he kept quiet. The family all thought he still lived a life of abject debauchery. Since he still hung out with the same guys, maintained the same interests, and continued to decline most family and church initiated invitations, no one saw any reason to assume anything but the worst. After all, he'd done his level best to prove them all correct so far ... The family's opinion of him was low enough, *and they didn't even know the whole story.*

However, lately this deception with his family had begun to wear thin. As with his friends, the desire to 'come clean' grew with each family visit. He was tired of his brothers' and sisters' innuendos, depressed by his parents' disappointed expressions, and frustrated from holding his ... darn ... tongue. Driving home after having delivered Claire's car to the diner - Josh had been willing to help with all the car shuffling that was involved - Paul tried to examine why he was still so hesitant to tell his family such positive news *after more than two years.*

It's a question of faith, his grandfather's voice said to him suddenly, *faith in yourself and your commitment.*

Paul sighed.

The Voice was right.

His phone was ringing as Paul walked into the house. Claire's car was waiting for her in the diner parking lot with a tank full of gas. One more good deed added to his meager list. "Paul? It's Connie. I hope I'm not calling too late."

"Hey, Connie, how're Mark and the kids?"

"Oh, they're fine. Evan would really like to do a sleepover again, but I'm concerned with some of the things you exposed him to the last time he stayed."

Paul sighed. "Like what, Connie?"

"He told me that you had a number of your friends over when he was there last time."

"Yeah, I did. Some of the guys came over, and we had a barbeque. I thought Evan had a great time. Did I miss something?"

"Oh, he had a great time all right. But tell me, Paul. Was there alcohol at the party?"

Paul hesitated. *Here we go.* "Yeah, Connie. Some of the guys bring beer."

"Do you think that that's an appropriate atmosphere for an impressionable ten year old?"

See what your deception perpetuates? His grandfather's voice said quietly to him.

Actually, he did. None of the guys had drunk to excess and Uncle Paul had abstained. He and Evan had had a wonderful time; they had talked a lot about what was important in life and what was not. But the reality was that whatever Paul said to Connie would not please her. So he stayed silent.

"Paul? Are you there? Are you going to answer me?"

Here's where feeling like a six year old kicked in. *Again.* "Is this why you called, Connie?"

He caught her up short. "Well, actually, no."

"Then what's up, Sis?"

"Rachel and I were talking and Elliot and Brian agreed that we should plan something for Mom for her 70th birthday. We've been working on it for a few weeks now and we were wondering if you'd be willing to help out."

He couldn't help it. "So, the four of you have decided to do something. Why call me?"

"Now, don't start your same old song, Paul. Just because you choose to live a life that is distant and separate from your family! *Your choices* shouldn't mean that you are resentful that we are closer and therefore communicate with each other on a more regular basis."

Patience, his grandfather's voice reminded him, *technically she's right, you know.* Paul took a deep breath. "What do you need from me, Con? I'll do whatever I can to help."

His sister's shocked surprise at his willingness radiated over the phone lines. "Oh! Well! Thanks! I appreciate that. First, we want you to reserve the second Saturday of June on your calendar. That's a week before her birthday, and we thought that would be the best choice for a surprise. Second, we were wondering, since you've got the truck, if you'd be willing to pick up all the food the day of the party and get it to the park."

"Sure Con, that's easy. I'd be happy to. Just tell me what to do and when to be there." They went over more details, discussing the foods that had been chosen. Three times she mentioned how important it would be for him to be *on time* the day of the party. Like he had been perpetually late his entire life, just because he wasn't as anal as she was over schedules!

After his shower and steak, he laid on the couch flipping through the television channels, dozing. His last conscious thought was of big, sad, green eyes and a mouth that never smiled.

*Never doubt that a small group of thoughtful, committed citizens can change the world.
Indeed, it is the only thing that ever has.[5]*

Three: If You Dream About It, It's Never Gonna Happen

The battle began first thing Wednesday morning. Cleverly orchestrated, the enemy was fully aware of his opponent's weaknesses, and his plan of attack was relentless. "Please, Mom, *please, pleeeeees,* let me stay home today. I don't want to go to the diner. I promise I'll be good." Tyler gave Claire that wide eyed expression that he had somehow come to understand got him what he wanted.

"I can't leave you home alone, Tyler. You can't be home all day by yourself! We're talking hours and hours and I don't know when or even if I'd be able to come and check on you."

He executed a perfect pout and crossed his arms. "I'll be miserable all day at the diner, Mom. *You know I will.* I don't care how much I read or write or study. *I can't do it for all those hours.*"

Claire put her hands on her hips. "Well, I guess you should have thought of that before you got yourself suspended from school, huh?" She had been completely unsuccessful getting him to explain what had happened yesterday on the playground. Tyler had remained stubbornly

[5] Margaret Mead

silent through all of her questioning last night. *This enemy was tough.* Claire glared at her son. "Maybe this will make you think twice before you do something like you did yesterday." Claire tried her best, stern expression. "Besides, Tyler, you're not *supposed to be* happy. You're suspended from school remember? You're not supposed to sit home all day watching TV."

Tyler's expression was mutinous. "I don't want to spend all day at the diner, Mom. And you know what? I bet you Dan doesn't want me spending all day at the diner, either. I bet you he's gonna be really sad when I show up with you. Please, *please* don't make me. What's the big deal? I'll stay home and be good, *I promise.*"

Tyler was getting too clever for her. He'd finally hit on the only thing that she was really worried about: Dan's reaction to having her kid sitting in the diner for three solid days. *Forty hours.* Claire was so certain about the impending poor reception, that she'd decided to just spring the whole thing on her boss rather than risk a refusal over the phone. She sighed, closed her eyes, and pinched the spot high on her nose between her eyes. Nothing was ever simple for her. Nothing. The pressure of having to keep all of her tables plus one very bored seven year old happy all day for thirteen plus hours was enough to make her want to jump off a cliff.

And there were going to be three full days of this.

She sighed another deep, world weary sigh, and this time Tyler looked triumphant, the prospect of victory visible on the horizon. His battle strategy had been brilliantly executed. "Okay, we'll try it today, but on *my terms*, Tyler. MY TERMS. If you don't follow them, *exactly*, then you'll spend the rest of your suspension sitting at a table in the diner reading and writing essays all day. Got it?"

Claire felt a wave of uncertainty and the prospect of disaster growing larger with each second, for Tyler could barely contain his excitement at the idea of being on his own all day. He nodded eagerly. "Sure Mom, anything you say. What're the rules?"

"Number 1: No going outside. Number 2: No cooking. Number 3: Only two hours of TV and Gameboy. Number 4: I want that book you were reading finished and a *two page written report about it* done by the time I get home."

Tyler tilted his head to the right, a frown of concentration on his forehead. "Only two hours of TV, Mom? How about four? Or could I at least have two hours of TV and then two hours of Gameboy?" *To the victor goes the spoils* …

She stood and stared at him not saying a word, refusing to elaborate on the specifics of the rules. Actually, she didn't really care, she was so tired and her day had barely begun.

"Okay, Mom …"

"I'll call every hour to see how you are doing. I'll put the number of the diner by the phone if you need to call me, okay?" She gave him a hug, he allowed her to kiss him, and then she left. As she turned to wave goodbye just before she walked down the steps, she could see he was scrubbing the side of his cheek with the back of his hand where she'd kissed him.

Claire had been working at the All American Diner now for almost seven years. She could probably work somewhere that got her better tips, but they let her bring Tyler after school, saving her money on baby sitters, which seemed to even things out. The customers were usually polite, Dan wasn't exactly a tyrant, and the other waitresses were okay. Claire didn't have any close friends at the diner, but she could honestly say that there was no one she worked with that she disliked.

Things went well until the middle of the lunch rush. Claire had called Tyler three times, and each time he had answered the phone promptly and had a plausible explanation about what he was doing. He seemed content and happy, rattling off what he had done, what he hadn't done, asking if he could have another snack or should he just have an early lunch … At 1:25 p.m. Sally caught her attention and held up the phone. "Claire! Your kid's on the phone!"

"Mom?"

"Yeah, hi honey. What's up? I've got seven tables full of customers and all of them are hungry and I'm in a hurry to get back to work. Talk quick."

"It was okay that I answered the phone, right?"

A small spark of concern ignited in Claire's gut just as one of her customers waved at her and held up his empty iced tea glass. "Yeah ..."

"Well," it all started to come out in a rush, "Principal Thompson called early this morning ... and ... well, I said you were at work ... and she wanted to know if she could talk to the babysitter and I said there wasn't a babysitter and ... then she wanted to know who I was staying with and ... well, I told her I was by myself but there were lots of rules that I was following and she ... well, she didn't sound real happy at all ... and well, now ..." Tyler paused and Claire felt wave of impending doom wash over her because this already sounded very bad, and obviously Tyler was worried about telling her something ... *worse.* "Mom, there is some person at the door and he keeps saying his name is "Dryfuss" or something ... and I don't know what to do."

Claire thought frantically while trying not make eye contact with her tables. Her head was suddenly too heavy for her neck. "He says his name is Dryfuss, Tyler? Are you sure?" she said in a puzzled voice trying to think who she knew by that name. "Did he say he was from the school?" Could he be the school psychologist already? Man, that was fast!

"Nah, he's definitely not from the school," he said with absolute certainty.

"How are you so sure?"

"Cause he already told me he was from the government."

"*The government!*" she exploded.

"Yeah, some agency or something ..."

All of a sudden she had a terrible headache. "The man is still there?"

"Yeah, he's outside the door sitting in the hallway with his computer. I can see him through the peephole."

"Claire," Dan came up behind her his voice tight with anger, "you've got at least five tables that need you. *Get off the phone.*"

She covered the receiver and said desperately, "Dan, something's going on with Tyler! He's home alone! I can't hang up ... yet, *please ...*" He glared at her for a moment and then stalked away toward her tables. She saw him pick up the coffee urn and make conversation while he refilled the coffee cups she should be refilling. She went back to Tyler. "Tyler, go to the door and ask the man to tell you again who he is. Tell him to speak nice and slow so you can tell your mother over the phone."

"Okay." Claire heard him going over to the door. "Hey, Mister! You still out there?" She could hear a muffled reply. "Well, my mom's on the phone and she says to tell me nice and slow who you are again so I can tell her who you are." She heard more muffled talking. "Okay, Mom, ready?"

She cradled her forehead in her left hand while her right hand gripped the phone so hard she thought she might break it. *Sure, go ahead, fire both barrels.* "I'm ready."

"He says his name is ... Daniel ... Alvarez ... from the Division ... of ... Youth ... and ... Family ... Services ... the ... State ...Agency ... concerned ... with ... child ... welfare. Hey, Mister," she heard Tyler shout through the door, "I thought you said your name was *Dryfuss*!!" Claire heard a lengthy muffled explanation. "Ooooohhh," she heard Tyler say, obviously mollified by what the man had said. Tyler's voice came over the phone to her, "What do I tell him, Mom?"

Just when she was certain every disaster had already hit. "Ask him if he'll wait until I get home," she said in a world weary voice. She heard the one-sided conversation between Tyler and Daniel Alvarez.

"He says he'll wait, Mom."

"I'll be there in a half hour."

Claire sought Dan out in a near panic. "Dan, I've got to go! I'm sorry, but I've got to get home!"

"*You're leaving me in the middle of the lunch rush?!*" Dan exploded. He looked at Claire like she had suddenly decided to serve botulism to all of his customers.

She was near hysteria and could feel the tears gathering like a darkening summer thunderstorm. Customers were looking at her. Sally, The Gossip, was listening intently, popping her gum at an alarming rate. Claire spoke breathlessly in low tones, mentally pleading with Dan to have some level of compassion and understanding. "Tyler says there's a man from the Division of Youth and Family Services outside our apartment door wanting to speak with me. *I've got to go, Dan.*"

Sally stopped chewing and popping her gum. Dan looked incredulous. "DYFS?! You've got *DYFS* calling on you, Claire? Christ, *do you know who they are?* That's the agency that takes kids away from their parents when they're not cared for right ... Jeeze, Claire, *what have you done now?!*" With a sob, Claire ran blindly out of the diner.

The agency that takes kids away from their parents. That was terrifying. But it was Dan's tone of voice when he said, *Jeeze, Claire, what have you done now?* that really did her in. She choked back another sob and tried to drive home without having an accident. Even her boss knew what a screw up she was. *Everyone knew.*

On the drive home, Claire had a long conversation with herself in the car. "Why is this always happening to me? Have I done something I need to be punished for? Was I born under an evil star? Am I just someone who will always have bad luck? What's wrong with me? Why can't I seem to do anything right? Why does everything seem to lead to a disaster? WHY CAN'T SOMEONE JUST CUT ME ONE FRIGGIN' BREAK!!!" she finally screamed at the top of her lungs.

Her throat was still sore from yesterday's screams.

Their apartment was in a rough part of town in an old run down building on the busy main street. One of six apartments on top of a greeting card store, it was built during a time when things were solid and roomy. She had two bedrooms, a tiny kitchen, a dining room, a living room, and a bath. All for the absolutely unaffordable price of $900 a month. It was a bargain by normal standards, an impossibility by hers. The rent ate just about her entire salary from the diner. And that was before utilities, phone, food, clothes ... Not to mention medical bills. Each month at bill paying time she fought an overwhelming sense of terror. Would there be enough money to make ends meet? A reoccurring nightmare haunted her that she and Tyler ended up homeless, living in their car. It was so close to reality that thinking about the nightmare caused her stomach to clench and she felt as if she were going to be ill. *Not now, Claire.*

As she pulled into the parking lot she looked up at her building. Had she been forced to admit it, she was quite proud of the place. It was clean, and it was home. Maybe not as bright as she would have liked it to be, but at least it had character.

There were two entrances, and Claire knew that Daniel Alvarez would be at the front door because no one but tenants used the back entrance. She parked her car in her assigned parking space and raced up the first long flight of outside stairs. These stairs brought you up from the parking lot to the flat roof of the card shop. A few worn benches made up the "back porch" the tenants were free to use. Her apartment was on the second of three apartment floors. She made her way to the next bank of stairs leading to her floor. Each apartment had a metal back porch area that was large enough to chain a bicycle (if you had one, which she didn't). This back entrance also qualified as the fire escape.

"Halo, Claire!" came a breathless voice from behind her.

"Oh, hi, Mrs. Santiago." This was not good. Not good at all. Mrs. Santiago liked to talk and talk and talk. She was an elderly, lonely old woman who lived in the apartment adjacent to Claire's. She was overweight, with bad knees, bad hips, high blood pressure ... you name it she had it. She was struggling with two big bags of groceries. "Here," Claire said, "let me help you with those." Claire walked halfway back down to take the bags from Mrs. Santiago, and then turned to haul them the rest of the way back up the stairs. Claire slowed her steps to keep pace with Mrs. Santiago, who huffed and puffed like she'd just run a marathon.

"These old bones," Mrs. Santiago gasped. "They just aren't what they used to be ..." The two of them began the long ascent up the second flight of outside stairs that led to both of their apartments.

"Oh, bless you, child. I've got four more bags downstairs in my trunk," Mrs. Santiago panted. There was a distinct air of hopefulness in the comment.

"Look, Mrs. Santiago, I'm in a rush right now, but if you can wait, I'll be more than happy to bring the rest up for you in a little while. Do you have anything perishable that can't wait?" *Please say no.*

"No, this is my frozen stuff. You sure you don't mind, child? I'd so appreciate it if you'd spare these old bones the climb up and down the stairs ..."

"No, I don't mind. But like I said, I can't do it right now. I won't forget, honest." Claire dumped the shopping bags at Mrs. Santiago's back door and rushed to unlock her back door.

Tyler was waiting for her in the kitchen. "He's still there, Mom," was the first thing he said when she walked into the apartment. Tyler's empty cereal bowl and orange juice glass sat on the table and she quickly scooped them up and put them in the sink. She tried to look at the apartment with a stranger's eyes and couldn't really find any fault. It was sparse but clean and neat. It was easy to be organized when you had so few things to work with. But what did her opinion matter? She *was* the screw-up after all.

"Tyler," she said looking at him intensely, "*best behavior*, okay?"

"Yeah, sure Mom ... are you okay?" *He had no idea.*

She took a deep breath to compose herself before she opened the front door a crack. "Mr. Alvarez?" she said in as calm a voice as she could manage. She did not take the chain off the door.

A young man about her age with dark hair and glasses perched on the end of his nose was sitting on the steps. Papers were neatly piled about him while he typed furiously on his laptop. He looked up from his impromptu office. "Ms. Jenkins?"

She nodded, but could only manage a wan smile through the crack in the door. She watched him meticulously gather up his papers and his computer. Standing, he came over to the door and handed her his business card. It said, *Daniel Alvarez, New Jersey Division of Youth and Family Services, Field Agent,* along with his field office address and phone numbers. She took note of the official badge hanging around his neck as well. It was a photo ID. He looked real enough, she thought. What choice did she have? Claire undid the door chain and opened her apartment door to let this stranger in.

It was a monumental occasion, but only Claire knew its level of significance. Daniel Alvarez was the first man to ever set foot in her apartment in all the years she had lived here. Even her landlord had only been in the apartment once when she was first shown the place. It was her haven, her sanctuary. No one else was needed or welcome. Except Tyler, of course.

He shook hands with her then turned to Tyler and squatted down so that they were eye level. "Hi, Tyler. I'm Mr. Alvarez. You did a good job handling this situation. I'm impressed how you followed all the instructions that your mom gave you." Daniel Alvarez glanced at Claire and then back to Tyler. "Not every young boy would keep a level head and handle things so smoothly. Good job." Tyler gave him a tentative smile. "Would you mind, Tyler, if your Mom and I spoke privately for a bit? Then just you and I will talk, okay?"

Tyler glanced at Claire, and she tried valiantly to give him a reassuring smile along with a shaky nod. "It's okay, Ty, you can do what Mr. Alvarez asks. Why don't you go in your room and play your Gameboy?"

"Okay," he mumbled hesitantly, "does this count towards my two hours? I was saving it for as long as I could …"

"*Tyler* … " she said in a rather desperate tone.

"*Okay,*" he said, and walked down the hallway. He glanced back at her twice and each time she did her best to smile. It was a hard thing to do.

Daniel Alvarez settled himself on her worn couch, opened up his laptop and then looked at her very intently. "I'll get right to the point, Ms. Jenkins. A complaint has been filed against you on behalf of your son, Tyler, for concern regarding criminal neglect and child endangerment."

Claire was confused. "Tyler filed a complaint about me?" she said incredulously.

Daniel smiled. "No, an anonymous complaint has been filed on behalf of your son."

"I can't know who filed it?"

He shook his head. "No you can't. That's the way the system works, you see. We have a much better chance of receiving information if people can be assured of anonymity. People are much more willing to lodge complaints and provide information when they are assured that whomever they report can't turn around and somehow retaliate.

"It's a serious charge, Ms. Jenkins. Are you aware that you cannot leave a young child unattended for any length of time? Are you aware that what you have done today constitutes child neglect? Maybe first I should explain to you what the term "neglect" means, legally speaking. The formal definition states that neglect is 'an act or failure to act which presents an imminent risk of serious harm to the child.'[6]" Mr. Alvarez looked at Claire intently. "Ms. Jenkins, in leaving Tyler, who is a minor, unsupervised and on his own here at your apartment for an entire day you have placed him in imminent risk of serious harm. Such a charge, should you be formally prosecuted for it, could result in the loss of your maternal rights regarding your son."

Claire felt as if a massive hand were pressing down on her chest making it impossible to breath. Her heart pounded. Her palms were damp with sweat. Just when she thought that she had lived all the worse nightmares a person could live … She could only manage at first to shake her head 'no' while Daniel Alvarez studied her unblinkingly. Finally, she gasped out, "I wouldn't have done it if I'd known …"

She felt a wave of hysteria overwhelming her which forced a rush of words out of her mouth. There was no time to think or plan or analyze. *He can't have Tyler. He'll have to kill me first before he takes him.* "Look, I'm living on the edge here, Mr. Alvarez. Just missing the lunch rush today at the diner to meet with you will probably set me back enough that I won't be able to make my rent this month. I'm telling you that so that you can understand how desperate things are for us. I have no room to move or blink or even take a breath.

"Tyler - he got suspended from school yesterday! For *three days!* What was I supposed to do? I can't work *and* stay here and watch him. I have no family or friends. I can't afford babysitters. He didn't want to go to work with me and quite frankly, I was afraid I'd loose my job if I brought him for the whole day. I thought I did a good job! I called him every hour! I made rules!"

Her voice began to rise as she continued to speak. She felt herself losing it. Big time. But couldn't help herself. "He promised he'd be good! He's not a perfect kid, but I know that I can count on him to listen when I need him to."

She shook her head and looked down at her clenched, sweaty

---

[6] Child Welfare Information Gateway

hands. "You don't get it. No one gets it. I'm sitting here trying to explain my life to you in ten minutes and I can't even explain why things are the way they are *to myself* and *I've lived this life*. I'm terrified you're going to take my son away from me, while at the same time I'm sick with dread that my boss is going to fire me because I left him with five tables in the middle of the lunch rush!" She looked at Daniel Alvarez and felt the tears begin to pour down her face despite her best intentions to the contrary. She swallowed and tried to get hold of herself. Finally she whispered, her voice low and choked with tears, "I didn't know, Mr. Alvarez. *I swear I didn't know*. I won't do it again, I promise. Please don't take Tyler away from me, Mr. Alvarez. He's the *only good thing that I have in my life*. He's the *only good thing I've ever done*. If you take him away from me, I'll die."

Daniel Alvarez reached out and placed a reassuring hand on her forearm. She was too distraught to even notice. He spoke in a quiet, reassuring tone. "I'm not going to take your son away from you, Ms. Jenkins. Despite the reputation that DYFS has and believe me it's hardly all good - we don't go ripping children out of homes at the drop of a hat." He sighed. "I'm not going to lie to you and tell you that these circumstances are not serious or that the removal of a child from the home never happens - it does - but we also provide help and assistance to try and prevent that."

She studied him for a few moments and finally came to the conclusion that he was telling her the truth. He wasn't trying to trick her into implicating herself. Claire got up, walked down the hall to the bathroom and came back with a wad of toilet paper to blow her nose. She felt as though she had been crying constantly for the past two days. She blew her nose loudly and then looked at this man sitting in her living room. Twice in two days she'd had conversations with strange men who were privy to the most private and painful aspects of her life. "I feel like my life is completely out of control," she said more to herself then to Daniel Alvarez. "The more I try to make things work, the more things seem to fall apart. I'm only twenty-five, but I feel like a hundred."

"Okay," Daniel Alvarez said in a business like tone. "So let's get started and see what we can do for you, okay?"

She nodded reluctantly and began to answer the questions he asked as he typed information into his computer. He gave her a list of services with a pile of pamphlets describing what opportunities were available to her given her situation and income. She read through some of it while he sat with Tyler at the dining room table and had a private conversation with him. She could hear the murmur of their voices but not what they were talking about. God, she was so terribly tired.

"Ms. Jenkins?" She jumped up, startled that he'd caught her apparently sleeping. He smiled kindly. "Can I make one more suggestion, off the record?"

"Sure." *Now what?*

"My church has recently acquired the piece of property adjacent to it. They have refurbished it and decided to open it to single women and their children who need an opportunity to get on their feet and have a fresh start. The rent is prorated to what your income is, and many of the services I've just told you about come automatically with the residence. I don't believe in coincidences, Ms. Jenkins, and I think this opportunity might relieve some of the stress you've been under."

"I'm not good at taking charity, Mr. Alvarez. I'm pretty much a product of the system and look where it's gotten me. I've been trying to escape its curse for years."

He seemed to take a moment to gather his words. "This may seem like charity to you, but in reality, the goal of this mission is to help women become independent, vital members of the community, and at the same time provide their children with a level of stability that may not be possible otherwise. There is a time limit on the length of stay. Women and their children are given two full years, with an option to extend that by an additional six months if the situation warrants. Women are required to hold a full time job or a part time job and provide proof that they are attending some type of classes for educational or career skill improvement. Children must be enrolled in school full time, and if they are too little for public school they are given a prorated fee for the church's preschool and daycare center. You can't just sit home, watch soap operas, and eat bon-bons."

She turned stunned eyes at him and he laughed. "When was the last time you laughed, Ms. Jenkins?"

Claire didn't answer him because she had no idea. "You know, you're the second person in two days who've said you don't believe in coincidences. What do you mean by that?"

"Are we still off the record?"

"Why are we supposed to be off the record?"

"Because I'm not supposed to talk 'God-talk' at the same time I'm doing 'shop-talk' and I'm going to have to do that to answer your question."

"Oh." Her lack of enthusiasm was evident. "Yeah, we're still off the record."

"Then I'll tell you my personal opinion about the meaning of life." He smiled again at her as he started to gather up his papers and shut down his computer. He was a few inches taller than she was, with dark brown hair and eyes. Dressed in his suit and tie he looked professional and serious but when he talked he portrayed an air of easy going affability. Claire decided, should she describe him in just a few words, she'd have said he was calm and collected. "I don't believe in chances, luck, superstitions, or coincidences. I believe that God has a precise life plan for every single one of us - me, you, Tyler - and that *if we choose to embrace and follow it,* we will achieve a peace and satisfaction unlike anything we've ever experienced or dreamed of."

Claire couldn't help herself. She snorted in disbelief. "So you're telling me you've achieved this?"

Daniel seemed unperturbed by her skepticism, as if he'd dealt with this before. "Well, it's an ongoing process. I have significant moments in each of my days in which I experience it, yes." Daniel looked at her pointedly. "Please understand that I'm not saying that I've ended up with a life that's a bed of roses. I'm not implying that at all. Life continues to be difficult, stressful, and unhappy at times but with the assurance that God's in charge and guiding me through everything. I don't know if I'm explaining this right, but it just seems easier to deal with the rough times."

He pulled out another business card from his wallet, wrote something on the back, and then handed it to her. "This is my business card. You can call me if you're confused about all the services I've told you about. On the back is the number of the church mission I told you about. The woman who runs it - I put her name underneath the phone number - is Janice Strocco.

"Life is all about choices, Ms. Jenkins. God lets us make them - good or bad. We *are not* His puppets. As a result of these choices, we deal with consequences. That's life. At any point along the way we can ask for His help and His guidance and He will respond. *Faith* is listening when you get the answer, although it's not always as easy as that sounds." He grinned and scratched his chin. "Because sometimes the answers you get seem to make no sense."

Daniel extended his hand, and while she hesitated at first, eventually she shook it. "Thank you," she said.

"You're welcome. You'll get a copy of my report and you can expect some follow up contact." He leaned forward, making sure she was really listening. "It doesn't mean anything except we are doing our job, okay?"

She nodded and walked him to the door. "Can I ask you a rather bizarre question?"

"Shoot," he said, standing in the doorway.

"Do you know who the Good Samaritan is?"

He stared at her for a brief moment and she got the uncomfortable feeling that he was trying hard to read her mind. "He was a character in a parable Jesus told in the New Testament of the Bible. He rescued, cared for, and paid for the healing of a man who had been attacked and left for dead at the side of the road. Other people passed by, ignoring the dying man, but the man from Samaria stopped."

"Oh ..."

"Got a Bible?"

"No." She had never even touched one to the best of her knowledge, but she didn't tell him that.

"You should get one. You can get inexpensive paperback copies at most book stores. There's *lots* of stories of women, just like you, who were struggling with everyday life situations and just trying to survive. You'd be surprised." He stepped into the hall and smiled back at her. "I'll pray for you, Ms. Jenkins."

"Is that still off the record?"

He rolled his eyes. "Oh man, is it *ever.*"

She laughed briefly for the first time in a long time. It felt good.

Tyler was looking at her with a serious expression when she shut and locked the front door. "Are we in trouble, Mom?" he asked.

"Yes and no," she finally answered. "I can't leave you alone anymore, Tyler. It's against the law. I didn't know that, but Mr. Alvarez explained everything to me so now I do."

"But I did *everything* you told me!"

Claire walked over to him and pulled him into her arms. "Look, you're too young to be left on your own. Any number of things could happen that could put you in danger, and I should have trusted my gut feeling and made you come with me to the diner." She knelt down in front of him and took his face in her hands. "Tyler, you're the only good thing in my life. *I can't risk loosing you.* Okay?" She felt the tears again.

"Aww, don't cry Mom. It makes me feel like crap."

"Don't say 'crap'." There was a knock at the back door. "That's probably Mrs. Santiago. I promised I'd help carry up her groceries." Tyler immediately made a beeline for the front of the apartment, *away* from the back door. "What are you doing?" she asked him.

"I can't stand Old Lady Santiago. She's always telling me to keep my voice down and talking about her sore knees. Sometimes she even tries to give me a hug."

"Come on, I need your help. Please? If you help, then I only have to make one trip down to her car. She said she had four more bags."

"Okay," he said reluctantly.

It *was* Mrs. Santiago at their back door with her car keys so they could get the groceries when they had the time. "I'll do it in just a minute," Claire told her, "I just have to call work."

When Dan got on the phone, Claire offered to come back and do the dinner rush. She could hear in his tone of voice that he was still annoyed with her. "Look, Claire, take the day and get your life together, okay? I called Maddy and she came in, even though it was her day off. She's covering for you. So I don't need you for the rest of the day. *Make good use of your time, okay?*" The line went dead. She needed the money. She couldn't afford to take a day off to try to get her life together. In fact, taking a day off would probably make her financial life completely fall apart!

"Come on," she said to Tyler, "let's go get the groceries."

She ended up putting the food away, too, while Mrs. Santiago and Tyler sat at her kitchen table eating cookies and drinking milk. Mrs. Santiago's apartment was the same as hers in reverse. While Mrs. Santiago definitely did not have any more money to spend on fancy furnishings than Claire did, she obviously took great stock in her religion. There were religious pictures and plaques and crosses and statues everywhere you looked. Jesus on the cross. Virgin Mary bowed in prayer. Big angels, small angels, woven branches shaped like crosses, big candles with very religious-like people gazing out at you. And that was just in the kitchen!

Claire was quietly listening to the conversation as she unloaded and put away the groceries. Periodically, she tapped Mrs. Santiago on the shoulder and held something up with a *where's this go?* expression. As the talking progressed, Claire tried to be quieter and quieter because she was hearing things out of Tyler's mouth that she'd never heard before. He'd told Mrs. Santiago why he wasn't in school, what he'd done to get suspended and what had been the reactions from the school kids and officials. Jeez, Mrs. Santiago should be an investigative reporter, Claire thought.

"Tyler, Tyler, why would a nice boy like you do such a thing to another child? I just don't understand. You are always so nice and polite to me each time I see you. You are always quick to listen when I ask you to quiet down. You even ask me how my knees are feeling sometimes. *Why?*"

Tyler looked uncomfortable and then finally said very quietly, "I just was so mad at that stupid kid."

"Had he hurt you or made fun of you, child?"

Tyler shook his head no.

"Did he bother one of your friends?"

Tyler shook his head again.

"Then what did this boy do that deserved this horrible thing that you did to him? *What?*"

Tyler sighed a world weary sigh. "Every single day that stupid kid talks about his father. His father's a millionaire, his father plays football with him, his father took him on a long trip camping and fishing last summer, his father buys his mother all kinds of fancy jewelry." Tyler looked at Mrs. Santiago and said with complete disgust, "He even says his father is good at Gameboy."

Tyler had his back to Claire, who was now standing frozen in the middle of Mrs. Santiago's kitchen slowly dying inside. Tyler had no father. Tyler would never have a father. He knew that and she knew that. They had talked about it more times than Claire could count. She knew it bothered him, but she had done her best to explain in child's terms why there was nothing that could be done about it. As Tyler finished speaking and looked down at his napkin covered in cookie crumbs, Mrs. Santiago glanced briefly at Claire's utterly defeated expression. Carefully, Mrs. Santiago reached over and took his small hand in her old, gnarled one. "Do you think that all the things this boy says about his father are true?"

Tyler shrugged, still avoiding eye contact. "Who knows? All I know - and so does everyone else - is that I don't have a father, so all I can do is just listen to all that cr--, er, stuff."

"Does he always make sure to talk about his father when you are around?"

Tyler looked up at Mrs. Santiago. "He waits special until I show up to play kickball each day before he starts talking about his dad. He gets the other kids to tell 'Dad stories', too. Sometimes he asks me if I have anything to tell, and then he laughs and everyone else does, too."

"There are many other children who don't have fathers, too, you know, Tyler."

Tyler looked up at her. "I know that. My best friend Antwon doesn't have a dad, either. But even if kids don't have a dad who lives with them, they almost always have one that they see on weekends or can call on the phone or they at least have pictures or get a Christmas card now and then. I don't even have that." Claire was dying slowly and painfully standing in Mrs. Santiago's religiously decorated kitchen. Nothing was harder to bear than your child's hurts, hurts that you caused and could do nothing to fix.

"I grew up without my Poppa, you know," Mrs. Santiago said with a deep sigh.

"You did?"

Mrs. Santiago nodded. "Yes, he died when I was only two years old so I do not remember him at all. My older brother was seven and my sister was nine, so they have some memories, but I have none of my own. And there are no pictures of me with him. The only picture I have of him is with my mother on their wedding day. Pictures were very expensive back then, you see."

"Can I see it?"

"Why sure, follow me." Claire watched in stunned amazement while the two left her standing in the kitchen and wandered off down the hallway deeper into the apartment. Neither one of them had even glanced at her. Last night Claire had asked him and asked him to tell her why he'd done what he'd done to that boy, and she had gotten absolutely nowhere. She'd even threatened to take away his Gameboy, and he'd just handed it to her with a mutinous expression on his face. And here he was sitting in Old Lady Santiago's kitchen, eating cookies, drinking milk, and spilling his guts out to her. *Go figure.*

She finished putting away the groceries and helped herself to a cookie, got a glass, and poured herself a drink of water. She sat down and stared out the back window. The Virgin Mary stared back at her, her hands extended in supplication. *Take the day and get your life together.* How could she get her life together in one day when she hadn't been able to do it in twenty-five years?

When Tyler and Mrs. Santiago showed no signs of returning, Claire wandered down the hallway, hearing the voices get louder as she walked more deeply into the apartment. She found them in the smaller bedroom, Mrs. Santiago seated on the bed and Tyler at her feet, pouring through a box of old photographs. Mrs. Santiago was chuckling. "That is my very stupid brother, doing a trick off the dock at a lake we used to go to in the summer."

"Does he still jump off the dock like that?" Tyler asked.

"No, he died over ten years ago," Mrs. Santiago said. Claire couldn't see her face but she could hear the smile in her voice, "and he was a stupid brother until the day he died."

Tyler laughed and looked up at her. "You loved him a lot, huh."

"Yes, child, I loved him a lot."

"Hope I'm not interrupting," Claire said from the doorway.

"Mom, Mrs. Santiago's brother played for the Brooklyn Dodgers! *Can you believe it?!* She's even got *pictures.*"

Claire was impressed. Tyler looked at her with wide eyes, "Can I stay and look at more of her pictures, Mom? *Please?*"

Mrs. Santiago gave her a brilliant smile. "I would love the company."

"Okay, Tyler, you can stay. Send him home if he gets to be too much for you, Mrs. Santiago."

"He is always welcome company ..." Mrs. Santiago had the look of a child whose been told she can choose anything she wants in a toy store.

Claire wandered onto the back porch and looked out across the parking lots, rooftops and businesses. In the distance were train tracks. When they'd first moved into the apartment, the train whistle used to wake Tyler in the middle of the night and frighten him.

Take the day and get your life together.

I don't believe in chances, luck, superstitions, or coincidences.

Life is all about choices.

She walked into her apartment, rinsed out Tyler's dishes, put them in the drain, and then went into the living room. The pile of pamphlets and list of services sat in a neat pile on the coffee table, along with Daniel Alvarez' business card.

She never took charity. Charity was simply a lure for guaranteed disaster.

Claire sat down and picked up the business card. How strange it was that today of all days, when DYFS had come to her house and accused her of criminal neglect of her son, actually seemed like an okay day. She had laughed. Tyler had shared something personal and important. Mrs. Santiago was smiling and happy.

Life is all about choices.

Her life was out of control. Let's face it, *her life was a disaster.* She was tired and unhappy. *She was done.* Tyler was exhibiting progressively aggressive behavior. *He was suspended for three days from second grade.*

Wouldn't you like the opportunity to get a handle on things before the situation gets so uncontrollable it becomes hopeless?

Making a phone call and asking questions didn't mean she was accepting charity. It meant she was simply making a phone call and asking questions, right? Besides, if DYFS was going to check up on her, then she better have made a good show of doing some of the things Daniel had suggested, right?

Claire picked up the phone, dialed, and listened to the ringing in her ear. "Hello, may I please speak with Janice Strocco?"

But the fruit of the Spirit is love, joy, peace, patience, kindness, goodness, faithfulness ...[7]

Four: Never, Ever Accept Charity

Claire waited on hold for a number of minutes before a business-like female voice came on the line. "Janice Strocco, here."

"Hi, Ms. Strocco. Ummm, my name is Claire. Claire Jenkins. I was calling about the mission house you have for ..." Claire stopped. How did she describe herself? Single, desperate women? Women who can't seem to get their life together? Mothers with children who were potential future criminals?

"Hello? Are you still there, Miss?"

"Ahh, yeah. Your church has some house that they've been fixing up for women that ... need ... some help?"

"Yes, you are referring to Sonrise House. It is a new facility that we will be opening soon. Its express mission is to help single women with children to improve their circumstances in life through professional and personal training and encouragement. We work with all the major government agencies with similar missions."

Claire took a deep breath. "Well, yeah, I was hoping you might

[7] Galatians 5:22, New International Version

consider me and my son, Tyler."

There was a long pause on the other end of the line and Claire suddenly just *knew*. She wasn't going to make the cut. How many times had she been there? How many times had she hoped for a break and been absolutely disappointed at the results? Too many to even count. Janice Strocco cleared her throat. How bad was it that she couldn't even get selected for a miserable charity handout? She was too pitiful even for *that*. "Ms. Jenkins, we are all new at this here at Riverside Church, you see. We so much want to succeed and accomplish what we are setting out to do. The committee that the church has set up to oversee Sonrise House has determined that our initial occupants must pass a rigorous screening process in order to be admitted. And one of the first requirements is that each potential tenant must have an advocate from the committee who champions them. Very much like a sponsor. We determined, with a unanimous vote I might add, that we would not, under *any circumstances*, consider anyone who called us 'cold'. At least for this initial time. I'm sorry. Do you have a place to stay or are you currently homeless? There are numerous agencies available for women having difficulties-"

"You can save your breath, Ms. Strocco," Claire cut in, her voice tight with anger. "I've got a whole list of agencies sitting right here in my lap. Along with a lot of fancy colored brochures. Me and my son, we are *not homeless*. We've got a pretty nice apartment, I might add. I'm not calling looking for any freebies or handouts you might throw my way. I don't accept charity. It's just that Mr. Alvarez thought that we might be better off-"

"Daniel Alvarez?"

"Huh? Yeah, Daniel Alvarez. From DYFS. He was here today because of my son. Mr. Alvarez was real nice and polite to me, too. Only he thought that you might be able to help me out. Even though I've been managing *just fine* on my own. He must not have realized about your committee and your special rules about people like me." Her arm tensed to hang up the phone. Should she slam it down or not?

"Ms. Jenkins, when can you come in and talk with me?"

Huh? "Why do you want me to come in and talk with you? You already told me that I'm not eligible for your house."

"Ms. Jenkins, I sincerely apologize. There's been a misunderstanding. You see, Daniel Alvarez is the chairman of the Sonrise House committee. If he's given you my number and told you to call, he's obviously decided to champion you and your son."

Tyler and Mrs. Santiago were busy playing Gin Rummy at the kitchen table when Claire went over. He was adamant about not going to visit "some lady at a church" and Mrs. Santiago was equally eager to have his company. Why fight it? "I'll be back in time for dinner," Claire said, but they were both giggling and laughing over the card game, having already dismissed her.

The church was pretty much straight down the main street she lived on, at the other side of town. Within twenty minutes she was sitting in her car gazing up at a huge white church that looked like it had just dropped off a Christmas card. Claire had absolutely no memory of ever having attended church. None. It was as foreign to her as ... white picket fences around sweet little homes filled with mothers who baked cookies and fathers who came home every night and said, "How's my princess today?" Church had never ever factored into her life. She had a panicked thought. Would that make a difference in what they thought of her? Should she lie and say something like, "Oh yes, God and church attendance are very important in my life"? Wouldn't they see right through her? She certainly hadn't impressed Daniel with any stunning Godly perceptions. That brought her up short. What *had* impressed Daniel that he had thought enough of her to *champion* her to this committee? She had absolutely no idea.

She walked in the back, to the church offices as she had been directed over the phone. The gentlemen behind the desk looked up as she entered and said politely, "May I help you?" At least he wasn't snotty like Ms. Briggs.

"Janice Strocco asked me to come here and talk to her about the mission house the church is starting."

"Oh, yes," the man smiled at her. "You must be Claire Jenkins." He leaned back in his chair and shouted, "Janice! Ms. Jenkins is here!"

A smiling woman came out of one of the back offices. She was tall and thin with short dark hair streaked with silvery gray. She had an air of causal professionalism about her as she strode forward, smiling. "Claire? Is it okay that I call you Claire?" At Claire's nod, she gestured for her to follow into one of the back offices. She extended her hand and grasped Claire's firmly. "Please call me Janice. Come on into my office."

The room was an absolute mess. Such a mess that Claire hesitated at the door, unable to disguise her shock. Janice seemed amused at her reaction, although not at all surprised. Papers were piled on almost every available surface. Some were in folders, some were loose. There were even a number of piles in various spots on the carpeted floor. On almost every bit of wall space hung children's drawings of every imaginable shape and size. Claire couldn't help but stare, slowly taking it all in.

"I do my best to keep the chairs clear," Janice Strocco chuckled. "Rob, the church secretary, has my permission to throw out anything he finds on either one of the chairs - no ifs, ands, or buts - which helps to keep me under control. It's a good rule, because I suspect that eventually I wouldn't even be able to get in here myself otherwise."

"How do you find anything?" Claire asked in wonder and then, horrified at what she'd just said, she clapped her hand over her mouth and whirled to look at Janice. "I'm so sorry I said that," she said, still with her hand over her mouth.

Janice laughed. "Oh, you're not the first one to make a similar comment. I'll have you know I've got an excellent filing system that works just fine for me and guarantees me job security." Janice leaned over and whispered conspiratorially, "You see, they can never fire me because they'll never be able to figure out where anything is." When Claire looked at Janice, she looked positively triumphant.

Claire smiled. "I guess that's one way to keep from being fired. Somehow I don't think that would work for me at the diner, though." A vision of dishes and glasses and food piled up at all of her tables and even on the booth's bench seats rose up in her mind. Dan would go ballistic!

"So you waitress?"

"Yeah," she sat in the seat that Janice had motioned her to, "I've been waitressing at the All American Diner for almost seven years."

"Do you work there full time?"

"More than full time, actually. I usually drop Tyler off at school to get there by 7:30 and work straight through until I pick him up at school and then I finish up at nine."

"How many days a week?"

"Six"

Janice Strocco sat down and leaned forward across her desk. "*You work thirteen and a half hours six days a week?!*"

Claire nodded. "At least it saves on the grocery bill. I can eat whatever meal I waitress for." She'd tried to be funny, but it sounded pretty pitiful to her.

"And you've been doing this for *seven years?*"

"It's the only way I can manage to make ends meet. And even then it's always terrifying at the end of the month. I've been late twice with the rent, and my landlord told me that three strikes and *I'm out.*"

"Did you always want to be a waitress?"

Claire snorted. "Nah, I used to want to be ..." but she stopped, embarrassed. God, a million years ago she had wanted to be so many things. *So many things ...*

"Claire?"

Claire looked out the window, lost in bad memories. She shivered. "Yeah, I guess I always wanted to be a waitress."

"Tell me about your son. You said his name is Tyler?"

Claire nodded. "Yeah, Tyler. He's seven. He'll turn eight in August. He's a typical boy, loves all sports, won't let me hug or kiss him, and already thinks it's not cool to cry." She looked at Janice. "He's the best thing that ever happened to me, and the only good thing I've got going for me right now. He got in trouble at school yesterday, and they said he has to stay home for three days." Claire looked pleadingly at Janice not wanting for her to have a bad image of her son. "He's really a good kid, honest." Janice smiled at her. "I suppose women with sons on death row say the same thing, huh?" That made Janice laugh. Claire hadn't even been trying to be funny.

Claire sighed. "I screwed up today. Oops, am I allowed to say that here?" Janice just smiled again at her, shrugging her shoulders. "I left him alone at the apartment and someone reported me for 'criminal neglect of a minor.' Mr. Alvarez explained a lot of things to me and although I knew it wasn't a smart thing to do, I didn't realize it was a crime." Claire sighed and closed her eyes for a minute, remembering the fear of loosing Tyler. "He was real nice, that Mr. Alvarez. We talked a long time.

"In the end, he told me about you and this place. When I told him I didn't take charity, he told me it wasn't charity, it was a mission, and I'd have to work hard to stay here." She looked Janice Strocco right in the eyes. "It can't be any harder than what I'm doing already."

Janice looked right back at her and in an absolutely serious voice said, "No, Claire, it can't be any harder than what you're doing right now. Do you know the meaning of 'mission'?"

Claire shook her head. "No, not really. I'm not even sure I believe Mr. Alvarez about it *not* being charity."

"I'll give you my definition of what a mission is. Other people might tell you something a little different." Janice seemed to be gathering her thoughts. "For me, a mission is different from a charity in two major ways: where it starts and where it ends. First, a mission always starts with God. That means that if you dig very deeply to why it all started, you'll find God. Someone, with a heart for God felt God speak to him or her. God might have shown them a need, or an injustice, or made them excited about a certain idea they had. That was the seed that started it all.

"A mission that starts with God and keeps its focus on God is blessed by God. It doesn't always mean that things are smooth, quick, or easy, but there is a steady progression of moving forward. For us here at Riverside Church, we knew that the elderly couple who lived next door to us for years was planning on retiring and moving to Florida. We had spoken with them years ago and had asked them to consider us first when they planned to move. We even told them back then some of the ideas that we had about how we would use the property if we were ever fortunate enough to acquire it.

"Healthy, smart, strong churches are blessed with forward thinking people who make plans and dream what might be. Our Vision Committee began to make plans for raising the money to purchase the house well before we even knew we'd need it."

Janice leaned back in her chair. "So here we are now, proud owners of the property. We prayed for clear direction as to what the Lord wanted us to do with it. We had lots of ideas, but we wanted His guidance. In a month, we will open Sonrise House. Its primary purpose will be to give young women, preferably women with children, an opportunity to improve the quality of their lives.

"And here's where the second greatest difference between a charity and a mission kicks in. Our goal for the women and children at Sonrise House is that we help them personally, professionally, and spiritually. We don't want them to simply be appreciative for the help while they get it, we want them to turn around and decide that they want to help others in the same way they've been helped. We don't want them to find a job that will help them pay their bills, we want them to find a career that will give them lifelong personal satisfaction. Most importantly, we don't want them to think we're just a bunch of nice church folks trying to put in a couple of requisite hours on the volunteer meter. And we want them to realize that God has a unique plan for their lives that only a personal relationship with Him can reveal.

"You see, Claire, a charity gives a handout. A mission gives a new life."

Janice smiled at Claire and rolled her eyes. "Whoa. You got quite a sermon there, didn't you? As you can see, I'm pretty passionate about Sonrise House." She stood. "Would you like to see the house? We love showing it off."

Janice eagerly led the way out of her office, across the parking lot, and towards a modest two story home painted bright white with green shutters. "It's furnished in early American garage sale," Janice said with great pride as they walked in the front door. "We figured that most of the women who would be staying here would have little if anything in the way of furniture to bring, so we wanted it to be stocked and ready." It was a charming house, built in the early fifties, with dark wood accents and big old fashioned windows that let in tons of light. There was a big eat-in kitchen, a dining room, a spacious living room, and the winterized porch had a big wicker couch with cushions covered in a bright flowery pattern. Upstairs were four bedrooms of adequate size, two with full sized beds and two with twin bunk beds. The bathroom was outdated but functional, and spotlessly clean. The house looked scrubbed and shined and polished and ... expectant. Almost as if it were just waiting for the pounding of children's footsteps up the stairs and the smell of fried chicken coming from the kitchen. "About the only problem we foresee is that there is only one bathroom. The church just couldn't afford to put a second one in. The women that stay here will just have to come up with some kind of schedule and be respectful of their roommate's needs."

"What do you mean 'women'?" Claire asked.

Janice looked at Claire. "Well, ideally, we thought that two women and their respective children could share this house. They'll have to decide how they want to handle all the logistics of running the house. The church will take care of the outside yard care."

"I didn't realize that I'd be sharing the house with someone ..."

"Daniel didn't make that clear?" Janice frowned, puzzled by his obvious slip about such an important bit of information. "I'm surprised. Does knowing that make a difference?"

"I, well, I sorta have to live alone."

Janice arched her eyebrows in curiosity but didn't say anything. They were standing out on the front steps of the house, and without asking her, Janice sat down on the stoop. Claire followed.

"I've been on my own since I was pregnant with Tyler," Claire said slowly, feeling that she owed this woman a bit of an explanation, but never willing to reveal much to anyone about herself. "Before that, I, well, I didn't do well living with anyone." She looked down at her hands clasped in her lap. Janice was going to think she was a screw-up *and* a nut case.

"Do you have any family?"

"No," Claire answered far too quickly, revealing even more about herself she realized. Janice didn't say anything. Claire sighed. Heck, she might as well thoroughly educate this nice woman and give her the low down, *the nitty-gritty*. Then Janice would realize just what a huge piece of luck she'd been handed before she made the mistake of allowing Claire to move into the house. "Look, my whole life is one gigantic screw up, Ms. Strocco. From the moment I was born until this very second. As a result, I'm messed up and I'm doing a pretty good job it seems of messing my kid up, too. You and your committee would be very smart to just steer clear of me."

"Daniel didn't think you were such a screw up if he suggested you call me."

Claire shook her head at his obvious failure in judgment. "He only talked with me for about an hour. He has no clue."

Janice seemed completely unfazed. "He's an excellent judge of character."

Claire felt a flash of annoyance. "Why are you being so nice to me?" In Claire's experience *no one* was ever nice to *anyone* without an ulterior motive. Even she didn't expend herself beyond polite necessity unless she was in dire need.

Janice smiled and shrugged. "It's my job."

"I've never been to church and I've never even *touched* a Bible," Claire said. Time to whip out the big guns.

"I've never been to China and I've never even touched a giraffe."

Excuse me? Claire felt the difficult guise of openness and friendliness slipping away in the face of Janice Strocco's continued inability to understand the truth of things. "What does *that* have to do with anything?"

"Exactly," Janice said with conviction.

"Are you saying I don't have to be some big God person to live in your church house here?"

"Yes, that's what I'm saying." Janice reached over and touched her arm and Claire tensed. "You have to be hard working, you have to be willing and wanting to better yourself, you have to be committed to your child and want a better life for him, and you have to be willing to abide by the general rules of the house, but you *don't* have to be the World's Best Christian Woman. At least not immediately." She grinned in a way that

Claire knew she was kidding. "Remember, you would have to sit down and meet with everyone on the committee. I should warn you that while they won't delve into your past, they may ask you some questions you might feel are rather personal."

"Like what?" she said suspiciously.

Janice shrugged. "Committee members were chosen for specific qualities that would make them vital assets to the house, whether it's professional qualifications," she looked at Claire, "like Daniel, or personal passions. I could see them asking you questions like: Do you smoke? Drink? Do drugs? They might want to know how you perceive yourself. Do you consider yourself easy to get along with? Do you have a temper? What job experience do you have? Do you have any personal goals that you would like to pursue?" Janice looked pointedly at Claire. "Can you understand how the way you answer any of those rather personal questions would be important to the success or failure of the house?"

Reluctantly, Claire admitted that she did. All this only further confirmed that this charity or mission or *whatever you called it* was so not for her. "But I'm a real private person, Ms. Strocco. Nobody really knows anything about me. Even Tyler doesn't know too much. And I do have a temper. I'm real quick to tell people what I think of them if they push me the wrong way." Claire looked out at the road and squinted into the sunlight. "I've never been successful at anything. If you want this house to work, I should be the last person you put in it." There, *that should do it.*

"You're forgetting one big factor."

"What?"

"I'm not in charge of this whole thing."

Claire rolled her eyes. "You sure have a lot of confidence in this Daniel Alvarez!"

"Daniel's not in charge of this whole thing, either."

Claire frowned. "I thought you told me he was the, what'd you call it, the chair?" Janice nodded, "of the committee?"

"He is."

"Oh, you must mean the big boss, here. What do you call him, the Main Minister?"

Janice laughed aloud. "'Main Minister', I like that! We usually say 'Senior Pastor'. But no, even the Senior Pastor isn't in charge of the success of Sonrise House." Janice studied her for a minute and then finally spoke in a low, sincere voice. "Claire, it's God who's in charge of whether the house will succeed or fail. *If* you decide you'd like to be considered for Sonrise House, and *if* you meet before the committee and they decide to offer you and your son a place as residents, and *if* Sonrise House is a dismal failure or a rip roaring success, it won't have anything to do with your influence - positive or negative. It's all by God's design.

"Look, I'm a woman after God's own heart. That means I want to please Him, do what He'd like to do, follow His instructions, fulfill His plans for my life. Once a person makes that serious commitment, then her life stops being her own. He or she is no longer responsible for the good or bad that happens to them, for they trust and believe that everything - big or small - is by God's amazing plan." She smiled. "It's very empowering as well as very freeing. I have great responsibilities in my life, but I am never, ever alone. I've got an unlimited source of love, support, and guidance that I can draw on at any hour of any day no matter where I am or what I am doing. It's cool. Really cool."

What made a woman like Janice Strocco believe all of this God mumbo-jumbo stuff, sing songs about love and support, and apparently have a happy la-la-la life? Whatever it was, it sure wasn't Claire! Claire didn't believe in breaks or luck or anything other than what you could fight for or scrape off the floor for yourself. Claire knew that life was about your experiences and the lessons you learned from them. What you saw was what you got and sometimes you got even less than that. Claire was twenty-five years old, and as she turned to look at this nice lady, Janice Strocco, sitting next to her, Claire knew that she was wiser and more experienced than this woman could ever be. This woman could talk all she wanted about a life of fairy tales. Claire knew the truth of things. By sheer force of will she kept her mouth shut and gave Janice a wan smile. Why bother wasting her breath? These people who spouted their own version of goodness and light only heard what they wanted to hear, and only spoke what they wanted you to believe. And truth and fairness were certainly not guaranteed components. Rule Number Eighteen of the Claire Jenkins Rules of Survival Book: *Believe what you see, not what you hear.*

Janice stood. "Can I show you the church? Since you've never been in one."

Claire shrugged. The house was out of the question now. Whether she was willing to swallow all the God stuff that Janice Strocco was throwing her way or not and believe that this *mission* wasn't just another form of charity no longer really mattered. She had killed herself these past years just so that she and Tyler could live on their own away from the complications of living with other people. At any time she could have helped her financial situation by taking in a roommate, but there was no way she could share living space with another person. *Never.* She'd lived with enough strangers to last herself a lifetime. The abject terror of being at the mercy of some other person's emotions and deep dark issues was a nightmare she swore she would never, ever subject herself to again. What's more, she would never allow Tyler to suffer that way either.

They made their way into the back entrance of the church. As Janice opened the door and spoke, there was pride in her voice. "This is called the sanctuary. We worship here on Sunday mornings."

It was a lovely, bright, airy room with light beige walls, blue carpeting and blue cushions on the benches. Claire wandered into the room, suddenly forgetting about Janice. There was a balcony above and the windows that came down on both sides of the big room were so large they reached all the way up through both floors. It was a quiet, peaceful place. Claire felt like she should always whisper here and never, ever run.

"Your parents never took you to church? Not even on holidays?" Janice Strocco's voice seemed loud and out of place to Claire in the stillness of the sanctuary.

"I didn't have parents," Claire answered in a distracted, soft tone, not really wanting to intrude on the silence with conversation. She couldn't resist and walked forward to sit down on a blue cushion in the very front row, center. She looked forward as she rubbed her hand along the soft nap of the velvet. A huge set of pipes filled the front wall. A raised platform was before her. You needed to climb up three blue carpeted steps to ascend to it. Centered on this raised platform were three large chairs, also with blue cushions. On either side of the platform was a spot to stand and rest books and stuff, she guessed. One was larger than the other. "Does the big boss get to use that one?" She pointed to the larger stand.

Janice was watching her silently and glanced to where Claire gestured. "That's called the pulpit. And yes, the minister gives his or her sermon on Sunday mornings from that spot." Janice came over and sat by her. "It's intriguing for me to look at this place I've been in so many times through your eyes. What are your first thoughts and impressions?"

"It's quiet and peaceful. I feel ..." Claire stopped.

"You feel what?" Janice probed, her voice intensely curious.

I feel like home, she wanted to say but that sounded too ridiculous. "I feel ... comfortable here," she finally said.

Janice grinned. "Those are good first impressions. I always thought this was a very welcoming place. When I first came here and saw it for the first time I thought, 'Ahhh, at last. This is it.' I've never regretted my decision, even though people do give me a hard time about my messy office now and then." She chuckled at her own joke. "Maybe we'll see you here one Sunday, Claire."

She shook her head. "I work on Sundays. It's usually my best day for tips." Sundays at the diner, people weren't in their usual rush, even at breakfast and lunch. Families with kids and grandparents came by more often and it was probably the day she most enjoyed working.

They sat in silence for long moments. "How is it you didn't have parents?" Janice finally asked.

Claire shrugged. "I'm a foster kid. I never knew my parents. Never even met them once. By the time they signed all the release papers, I was too old for anyone to want to adopt me. So I just kept bouncing ... One home after another until I was old enough to leave and go out on my own ..."

"You were pregnant with Tyler before you were old enough to go out on your own."

Oh, I was old enough all right. "Yeah, technically speaking I guess." Claire didn't offer any explanations. "Look, I've got to go." Somehow it wasn't so peaceful here anymore.

"I didn't mean to upset you, Claire."

Claire looked at Janice Strocco and tried to be casual and carefree. "You didn't upset me. The bad memories are there whether you bring them up or not." She'd tried for levity, but it had sounded far to bitter.

"Let's go back to my office and come up with a date and time when you can sit down with the committee and be formally interviewed as a potential resident at Sonrise House."

"I, I don't think so, Ms. Strocco. All this sounded good when I talked with Mr. Alvarez, but now, well, *I just can't imagine sharing a home with a stranger,*" she finished in a rush. Claire was dismayed to feel the pressure of tears behind her eyes. She looked down at her hands clasped tightly in her lap. "I just can't."

Janice sighed. "All right, Claire. That's your decision. But, instead of a definite 'no', let's say you are still thinking about things, okay? We weren't going to formally begin interviewing people for another three or four weeks. I know two of the committee members have prospective residents they wish to be considered. Why don't you think about it, and I'll *pray* for you and the choices you are facing."

Claire studied Janice Strocco's face intently. "You're the second person today who's said you were going to pray for me and talked about choices ... I told you. I'm not a God person, Ms. Strocco. All this praying is just a waste of your time."

"Prayer is *never, ever* a waste of time. I'll even go so far as to tell you what I'm going to pray for regarding you. I am going to ask the Lord to show you a clear sign as to what you should do regarding Sonrise House. Clear and unequivocal. And you take the time to really think about what is best for you and Tyler." She paused. "Sometimes, Claire, the best decisions are the hardest ones. It's often much more difficult to make the *right* choices, you know."

They were standing in the hallway, directly outside of the church offices. Claire gazed out the exit door. In the distance she could see a playground. She was relatively sure that she had no idea how difficult 'right' choices were, because to the best of her knowledge she didn't think she'd ever made any. "What does the big boss person here think about your messy office?"

"You mean the Senior Pastor?"

Claire nodded and smiled. "Unless you think God's got some kind of clean office agenda."

"Good grief, I hope not!" Janice laughed. "Here," she said gesturing for Claire to walk forward with her down the hallway, "let me walk you out to your car and I'll show you something."

They went out the door and walked down the handicap ramp. Janice stopped, and when Claire looked at her questioningly, she smiled and looked up. Claire followed her gaze and read: *Riverside Church, Reverend Janice M. Strocco, Senior Pastor.* Claire's mouth dropped open in stunned shock as she turned to look into Janice's eyes, which were twinkling with delight. Janice leaned over and in a conspiratorial whisper said, "I'm quite certain God loves even us messy ones!" As she turned and walked back toward the church, Janice said over her shoulder, "I'm praying for you, Claire Jenkins, and you can't stop me."

The world breaks everyone and afterward many are strong at the broken places.[8]

Five: Never Trust People To Keep Their Word

The next morning found Claire at the diner, rushing between tables still mulling over the events of the morning. Once again, Tyler had fought her tooth and nail about the prospect of spending the entire second day of his suspension with her at the diner. But before she could get out any valid arguments, he'd announced that Mrs. Santiago had invited him to spend the day with her. In fact she was expecting him and had promised to make him pancakes for breakfast. Before she could get out any valid arguments regarding *that*, a persistent knocking had begun at the back door, which Tyler rushed to answer. There stood Mrs. Santiago with a pile of steaming pancakes on a plate. "Tyler can spend the day with me, right Claire? You wouldn't deny an old lady with bad knees and hips the chance to have someone around to help her out now would you?"

"Mrs. Santiago," Claire sputtered, "I can't let you watch Tyler all day. I won't be back until after nine tonight!" She swallowed her embarrassment. *"I can't pay you*, Mrs. Santiago," she finally admitted reluctantly.

---

[8] Farewell to Arms, By Ernest Hemingway, 1929

"Will you do the food shopping for me the next time you go?"

"Sure," said Claire without pause.

"And will you carry it up and put it away like you did yesterday?"

"Sure ..." said Claire.

"Then it's a deal," said Mrs. Santiago nodding and smiling at both of them.

"I get to set the rules," Claire said to both of them, trying to look like she was in command, rather than feeling completely ambushed.

Tyler looked at Mrs. Santiago. "She likes to do that. It makes her feel better." Then he turned to Claire, "What're the rules, Mom?"

If she didn't feel totally overwhelmed with her life in general, having the two of them standing there staring at her expectantly while the smell of hot pancakes floated gently around them would have been almost funny. "Same rules apply today that applied yesterday, Tyler: TV, Gameboy, homework ..." He nodded. "And you both have to come for dinner early, like around 5:00 p.m. before the evening rush, and I'll treat you both."

"Deal," Tyler and Mrs. Santiago said in stereo.

"And Mrs. Santiago," Claire said to her shining face, "you have to promise me that if Tyler gets to be too much for you, you will call me immediately and I'll come get him, okay?"

"Oh, how could Tyler be too much for me? He's such a good, sweet, cooperative boy. We had a wonderful time yesterday. Even if he is a crook when it comes to playing Gin Rummy."

"You should see her cheat, Mom!" Tyler said with real admiration.

"Tyler!"

"Honest, she knows how to deal off the bottom of the deck and everything!"

Mrs. Santiago managed the most innocent of faces and shrugged her shoulders. "Now, is that any way to talk about a sweet old lady, child?"

At the diner, the morning went by in its typical chaos until Dan said, "Claire, table nine's requesting you serve them." Loaded down with hot dishes of steaming breakfast items she nodded to her boss.

It happened sometimes. She had some regular customers whom

she enjoyed serving. They were the ones with kids who looked like the picture-perfect-family. She tended to remember what the kids liked and was happy to bring the little ones back behind the counter when it was finally desert time to let them put their own cherries and sprinkles on top of their ice cream.

But that was usually the dinner rush. The breakfast and lunch rush were usually business people in a hurry who wanted to be served fast and be in and out quicker than was humanly possible. They tended to be impatient and preoccupied. She served the four businesswomen their breakfasts, whipped out her pad and walked over to table nine.

She saw from a distance that the table was all men, which made their request of her very unusual. Six of them. She *never* flirted. With men she was distant and professional. Only with families did she tend to relax and tease and joke. She had a twinge of fear that she quickly suppressed. Never, in all of her time at the All American, had a man behaved inappropriately towards her. That was one of the reasons she never worked past nine. Although the diner was open 24 hours a day, she never had to deal with the inebriated, late night crowd that she knew were served during those hours. Her steps slowed as she took mental note of where Dan was, where Raul and Jamie, this morning's busboys were, and what other waitresses were working this part of the diner. She saw Janelle, and Maddy, the girl who had come in for her yesterday. *You're safe; take a breath, slow and easy …*

"Good morning, welcome to the All American Diner. Can I start you gentlemen off with a cup of coffee or tea?"

She did not look up and make eye contact, but quickly began to write down, in her personal waitress shorthand, the various coffee orders. It was the last voice that made her look up. "Coffee - *not decaf.*" Smiling, friendly eyes, greeted her. "Hey, Claire." It was Paul. The Good Samaritan. She couldn't even remember his last name.

"Hi Paul. Come to check out the fine fare here at the All American?"

"Nah, we know the food's just okay here. We all came to check out *you*." The whole table of men, all six of them, laughed and leered at her.

She felt their eyes on her, looking at her, examining her ... Two of them even winked at her.

She wasn't good at this. There were other waitresses who thrived on the casual, flirty banter that happened often in a situation like this. But she couldn't do it. She didn't have the personal skill. Hell, she didn't really have *any* skills. "I'll get your drinks," she mumbled and scurried away. *Like a terrified mouse,* she thought with disgust.

"Boy, that was a big strike-out, Paul," she heard one of the men say in a teasing tone. She didn't hear anything else.

She stood trembling at the coffee urn, trying to pull herself together. "You okay?" came Dan's voice behind her, making her jump. "You've had a bunch of bad days lately, Claire. What's up?"

Trying to compose herself, she looked at Dan to reassure him that she wasn't going to leave him in the lurch two days in a row. But before she could open her mouth he took one look at her face and said, "Jeeze, Claire! What happened?!" Dan leaned forward to look and see where she'd just come from, and then back at her. "Those guys giving you a hard time? I know you're afraid of men, but you seem to usually manage to do okay with a table of them."

Afraid of men? How did he know? She tried to smile brightly and give a carefree laugh. It came out like a choked squeak. "What are you talking about, Dan? I'm *just fine.* Just trying to juggle all my tables and be bright and cheerful enough to make up for those tips I lost yesterday." She brushed past him, balancing table nine's steaming hot drinks.

Their behavior had obviously been discussed amongst themselves, for by the time she brought their coffees and teas there was an entirely different atmosphere at the table. They politely ordered their various breakfast choices, thanked her, and in general acted like young boys being tested for the table manners merit badges. She relaxed. Slightly. Paul, studying her intently, never allowed her to relax fully. When they finally left, the tip was twice what she should have been given.

Between the morning rush and the lunch rush, she usually had an opportunity to eat a late breakfast or an early lunch. She called Mrs. Santiago, who assured her that Tyler was practically ready to be the poster child for good behavior, and that they were both looking forward to coming for dinner. Sitting on the back stoop in the sunshine eating an egg and cheese bagel and sipping some hot, sweet tea, she struggled to unwind and relax for the few moments she had.

"Can I join you?" It was Maddy. She was an attractive redhead, who had been working at the All American for about four months.

"Yeah, sure," Claire said as she scooted over a tiny bit to make room. "Thanks for covering for me yesterday. Dan would have been a lot more pissed if you hadn't come in so willingly and filled in."

Maddy shrugged. "I can always use the extra cash." She took out a cigarette and lit it and then offered the pack to Claire.

"Nah, I can't afford the habit. I'm trying to figure out how to stop the bad habit my son has of growing. That way I can save on clothes, too."

Maddy chuckled. "How old's your kid?"

"He's seven."

"I've got two, a boy nine and a girl eleven. They keep telling me that teenagers are hell. I'm terrified, because these two have just about put me over the edge already."

They sat in companionable silence for a while, then Maddy said, "Everything work out okay yesterday?"

Claire turned to look at her. She sighed. "Does everyone know?"

"Well, you were pretty hysterical when you left yesterday from what I heard, and Dan mentioned that DYFS was at your apartment ... We were all worried for you." Maddy looked at her. "They say you're real private and that you don't like to share anything about yourself. I'm not prying, honest. But I'm also the type of person who needs to ask when I feel like I should, so here I am. You can tell me to mind my own business and I will." She inhaled deeply on her cigarette and blew the smoke out slowly.

Claire had been working at this diner for almost seven years. She knew all of the waitresses and busboys by name. She had a polite, distant, professional relationship with each of them. But she knew absolutely nothing about any of them because she was not willing *or able* to tell them anything about herself. She shrugged. Wasn't much to tell really. Claire started tearing little bits of her uneaten sandwich off and tossing them in the parking lot to some brave and hungry sparrows. "Yeah, I'm okay. Believe it or not, the DYFS guy was really nice."

"You didn't leave your kid alone again today, did you?"

"No, he's with a neighbor today."

"Oh, good. 'Cause I got a really good sitter if you need one."

"Thanks." She had no desire to go into the fact that she couldn't *afford* a sitter - good or bad.

"Claire?" Maddy waited until they made eye contact. Maddy reached over and touched Claire's arm and Claire made a Herculean effort not to tense. Claire stared down at the hand on her arm and the cigarette that glowed between the hand's fingers. "If you ever have a table of guys like you did this morning that you don't want to serve, and I'm on, I'll be happy to trade with you." She felt like Maddy was walking right into her skull, flipping through all of her private, terrifying secrets and ... understanding.

Maddy didn't let go of her arm. In fact, she put her other arm loosely around her shoulders. Claire felt her chest tighten and was conscious of Maddy's cigarette smoke wafting directly up her nose. "Okay, Claire? No questions asked. Just say, 'Let's trade tables' and I'll know, okay?"

"Why?" Claire had a difficult time choking out the one word.

Maddy removed her hand and her arm and didn't answer right away. She took another long drag of her cigarette, crushed it under her sneaker and then gave it an expert flip in the direction of the dumpster. "Cause *I've been where you've been*, Claire. It was a very long time ago, and I've got a better handle on the terror, that's all."

She knew. Claire exploded, "How can you think you know about me? What makes you such an expert? I just don't like a bunch of guys gawking and smirking at me, dropping funny little comments among themselves that I don't get, even though they're about me. I don't think it's funny and I don't think I should have to put up with it. That's all. Some of you girls like to flirt and laugh and encourage them. That's fine. But it's not me."

Maddy didn't look at her and spoke in a matter of fact voice. "You deal with it with anger and aggression. That's cool. I saw a shrink for a while and she told me that there are all different ways to cope. I deal with it by being a smart mouth. I can fire back one liners so fast that they don't know what hit them, and it so intimidates them that they can't keep up with me. It usually makes them back off to a safe distance."

"I don't know what you're talking about."

"You haven't ever told anyone, have you?"

Enough already, her head screamed. Claire stood, absolutely livid. "Ahh, see. *You don't know me.* I sure as hell told!! I told anyone who would listen to me. And not one damn person believed me. In fact, I'm pretty sure I now believe all the crap they told me to get me to shut up. *It was all my fault.* In fact, everything that's ever happened to me - and most of it's bad - is my fault. I was born a screw up and I'll die a screw up. I'm a walking disaster!" Claire hurled the rest of her bagel toward the dumpster, picked up her Styrofoam cup filled with cold tea, and stalked back into the diner to start the next shift.

Stepping out into the cool night at a little past nine that night she was still seething. Just what did this Maddy want from her? Why, after all these months, did she finally act like she cared and wanted to be friends? Claire searched her mind for something she might have that Maddy wanted. The only thing she could think of was that she had seniority over the shift selections. Maybe Maddy wanted some of her hours. What had she said? *I can always use the extra cash.* Claire had better watch her back and make sure she didn't let Dan down anymore. She was doomed if she couldn't keep up all of her hours ...

"Man, you sure are lost in thought."

She must have jumped five feet in the air.

"Oh, man, Claire, I'm sorry. I didn't mean to startle you," Paul said in a concerned voice.

"What are you doing here?" she managed to gasp out loudly over the pounding of her heart.

"I came by to apologize for this morning," he said.

She moved into the harsh brightness of the neon parking lot lights and searched around for escape routes. She made note of Dan behind the register, visible through the diner's big front window. "Paul, you've got nothing to apologize for."

"Sure I do. I joked with you this morning, and it was obvious to all of us that I upset you really badly. There was no mistaking it, Claire, not only did I upset you, but we plain frightened you. We never meant to do that, honest."

She looked down at her worn sneakers. It looked like they were wearing through near the edge. Darn, she'd need to buy new ones, soon. "You were all very polite and careful after that. I noticed. Thanks for that." She looked up at him. "And thanks for the car and the tank full of gas. That was way above and beyond the call of duty, you know."

"Are you scared of me, or all men in general?"

Claire tried to be funny. "Oh, all men in general. In fact, right after you left, some little old man asked me for more coffee, and I ran screaming out the back door."

"You're not funny." He looked so concerned. "Why are you so scared?"

Like hell she was going to go into detail with this man standing in a parking lot late a night! "It's not you at all, Paul. Honest. Okay?"

"How's Tyler doing? How's the suspension going?"

She was surprised. "How'd you know about that?"

He chuckled. "You were so out of it that day when you got in the truck, I don't think you heard half of what he and I talked about. He told me all about his three day suspension. He even worried he was going to be stuck at the diner with you for the whole time."

"We're doing okay. And he didn't have to spend all the time with me, I was able to make arrangements." *But not before I had the government breaking down my front door,* she thought.

"Could I call you sometime, Claire?"

She looked at him, stunned. "You mean, like, for a *date?*"

He smiled at her. "Yeah, that's usually what two single people do."

"I don't date."

"Never?"

"Nope."

"Can I ask why?"

"Sure, go right ahead."

He seemed a little exasperated. "Why don't you date, Claire?"

"It's none of your damn business."

Paul chuckled. "You're getting feisty again. It seems the nicer I am with you the more feisty you get."

She could hear Maddy's voice, *You deal with it with anger and aggression ... It usually makes them back off to a safe distance.*

Claire got her key out and moved over closer to the door of her car. "Look, you did the Good Samaritan thing. You went way over the top and even delivered the car to my door with a full tank of gas. If you're looking for a payback for your kindness, the best I can offer you is a few bucks from my tips tonight. But *I'm not going to go out on a date with you to even the score.*"

Bingo. She'd made him mad. She could see it in his posture, read it on his face, and hear it in the tone of his voice. As he started to speak in a furious tone, she actually felt herself starting to relax. *Back off to a safe distance, mister ...* "What I did for you, Claire, I did of my own choice, with no ulterior motive whatsoever. I saw someone in need and I was able to provide help with very little skin off my back, and so I accommodated. I didn't even need your lousy thank you, to be honest. You see, what I did, *I did for me.* It feels good to be able to help someone out now and then just because you can."

He sighed and looked uncomfortable *and* angry, now. "*After*, I finished helping you out, I found I couldn't get you and Tyler out of my thoughts. I wondered how you were doing, chuckled over some of the witty perceptions your son had, and quite frankly couldn't stop thinking about those big green eyes of yours. The guys and I came here this morning at my suggestion, but they had no idea that I knew you. I screwed up when I was flip and sassy with you. I just about died when you looked so terrified. So here I am when I should be fast asleep because I've got another double shift starting in less than two hours, making a fool out of myself waiting in a parking lot hoping to talk with a pretty waitress. Who, it seems, would just soon see me drop off the face of the earth as look at me. I get the hint. You can relax. I'm not some crazy stalker or anything. I'm just a jerk who needs to take a hint. Good night." He turned and walked away into the night.

Had the night not been so quiet, he never would have heard her. "I've never been on a date before."

Paul stopped and turned around. "What do you mean you've never been on a date before? *You've got a kid.*"

Claire looked him directly in the eyes to convince him of the truth of what she was about to say. "I have never been on a date before. I have never had a boyfriend. I have never done a lot of things. The person you apparently think I am is nonexistent. I'm one very screwed up lady and you should take the hint and *move on.* Okay?" She inserted her key in the lock and started to open the door.

She heard him walking back to her as he spoke. "I appreciate your being honest with me. At least I know it's not my bad breath or my ugly mug that's frightened you off." He was standing to her right. She could see him out of the corner of her eye looming over her like a big dark mountain. Surprisingly, she was no longer afraid. Claire couldn't help it, she smiled just a bit.

Paul leaned against the car and crossed his arms. "So you don't date," he murmured almost to himself. "That makes getting to know you pretty ... darn ... difficult."

They were both silent for long moments, he, seemingly lost in thought, and she, frozen in the moment of opening her car door. Paul seemed in no hurry to move. She had a momentary break of insanity. At last she said very quietly, "Sometimes, on nice evenings, once Tyler's in bed, I sit on the back porch and watch the stars and the evening lights. It's nice and peaceful." She never looked at him.

"How many seats on your back porch?"

She was nonchalant. "Oh, there's a couple of benches on the roof. It's a public spot really, not my private space."

"Hmmm," Paul said looking down at her, trying to get a read on her she supposed, "so anyone could kind of sit there?"

"Yeah," she said still refusing to make any more eye contact, "anyone."

She was conscious of his car behind her all the way home. Was she out of her mind?! Now he would know where she lived! What had possessed her?! By the time she was home, she was in a real state. Sitting behind the steering wheel of the silent car, she thought she was going to hyperventilate. But she had to go in. She had given Mrs. Santiago her key at dinner, so that Tyler could go into their apartment, shower, and get ready for bed. It had been a long day for Mrs. Santiago, and she couldn't keep her waiting while she had a panic attack in her car. She got out of the car, locked it up, and made her way up the first flight of stairs. Although she strained to hear him behind her, it was as silent as an evening in a small city could be.

Tyler and Mrs. Santiago were relaxing in Claire's living room, watching her ancient television. They were laughing over *America's Funniest Home Videos*. "Hi Mom! Guess what Mrs. Santiago watches every single day? *SpongeBob!* Can you believe it?"

Claire kicked off her sneakers and went over and gave Tyler a kiss on the top of his head. She took her hair out of her ponytail and scratched her scalp until it tingled. "Mrs. Santiago, I'm going to have to buy you groceries for the next three or four times. I can't tell you how much I appreciate your watching Tyler *all day*. It made a world of difference for me at work to know things we're okay with him."

Mrs. Santiago beamed from ear to ear. "It was my pleasure." She looked hesitantly at Claire. "Tyler and I have made plans for tomorrow ..."

Claire padded into the bedroom and took off her waitress uniform. She pulled on a pair of comfortable jeans and her favorite big sweatshirt. "Oh?" she said through the door. "What are you two up to now?"

"We thought we'd go to the library and get some more books out by the author that Tyler's been reading," came Mrs. Santiago's reply.

Claire stuck her head out of the bedroom to stare at Mrs. Santiago. Tyler's gaze was riveted to the television, but Mrs. Santiago was looking directly at her. "He wants to go to the library, Mrs. Santiago?"

"I convinced him it would be fun."

"Where have you taken my son, Mrs. Santiago, and who is this imposter?"

Mrs. Santiago chuckled and looked tremendously pleased. She worked to stand and Claire rushed forward to help her. "Thanks, child. Can I look forward to your son's company tomorrow?"

"Only if he's in bed before I get back from seeing you home, Mrs. Santiago. *No exceptions or excuses.*"

Mrs. Santiago gave her an angelic smile, but out of the corner of her mouth she said, "Did ya hear that, kid?"

"Yup."

She walked to Mrs. Santiago's backdoor. "My eyesight's not what it used to be," Mrs. Santiago said, "but is that someone sitting on our back porch bench?"

"I'll go check, Mrs. Santiago. Thanks again. See you tomorrow."

Tyler was snuggled in bed, smiling at her sleepily. "Was it a good day, honey?"

"Yeah, Mom, it was a *great* day. We ate pancakes, and played cards, and made cookies - there's some on the kitchen counter for you - and we watched TV and she helped me with my school work." He sighed. "You know, Mom, I feel bad that I used to call her 'Old Lady Santiago'. She's pretty cool."

Claire kissed him on the forehead. "I love you, Tyler."

"I love you, too, Mom."

She opened two sodas, poured them in glasses with ice and balanced the plate of cookies on top of one of the glasses. Slipping on flip-flops, she pushed open the back door with her hip and walked out into the evening toward the man sitting on her back porch bench.

Paul was in what was rapidly becoming his perpetual stance. Seated on the bench, arms crossed, head tipped forward, eyes closed, seemingly fast asleep. Claire hesitated as she got closer. Should she wake him? "I'm not asleep," he said apparently reading her mind.

Gingerly, she sat down next to him. "I brought you a soda and some homemade cookies. Don't be impressed. Tyler and Mrs. Santiago made them."

"I can still be impressed if I want to," he said taking a sip of his soda and helping himself to a cookie. "Mmm, good. Thanks."

"I'm not any good at this."

"How would you know? According to you you've never been on a date before and never had a boyfriend. That means you have nothing to compare to. I'm thinking, if I play my cards right, I could impress the heck out of you with very little effort."

Claire suppressed a smile as she looked up at the moon. "It's a fingernail moon." She helped herself to a cookie. "Do you work with all of the guys that came to breakfast this morning?"

"Yeah, most of us have been working for the company for a lot of years. Over that time, we've all partnered with each other at one time or another. We know the area, the routine. If it works out, we get together at the end of a shift and share a bite to eat. We're all at different walks of life, some married, some single, some divorced ... We laugh and tease each other." He shrugged. "It's good." Paul looked at her. "What about you? You friends with a lot of the girls at the diner? You spend enough time there. You must be."

"No. I wouldn't say we're friends. We're polite with each other."

"Who do you have, Claire?"

His question was vague, but she knew what he meant. "Tyler."

"Besides, Tyler." Her silence was his answer.

He sighed and took another long sip of his soda. "I'm the youngest of five. Two brothers and two sisters. All of them will tell you I am spoiled rotten. Please note that's present tense. I'm twenty-seven. Never been married, but got close once." He hesitated. "That's a long story better left for another night if you're interested. I've worked for the power company for almost six years. I have a bachelor's degree in accounting although I never used it. Apparently this is a glaring example of how spoiled I am. I've never been in serious trouble with the police, although I made a couple of stupid choices when I was a kid and have a juvenile record for shoplifting and defacing public property. My driving record is good. I've tried marijuana but was not impressed. No other hard drugs. I used to enjoy a beer now and then, but lately I've been avoiding alcohol all together-"

Claire interrupted him. "Why are you doing this?"

"Two reasons. First, I'm filling in the lull in conversation that's bound to happen and second, I *know* you're not going to tell me anything about yourself, so I figured I'd tell you about me. Then, once I'm gone, you can mull over everything I've told you and decide if I'm as bad as or not quite so bad as you assume I must be.

"I figure it works in my favor to give full disclosure right up front. You can ask me any questions you like and I'll answer them as honestly as I can. Furthermore, I promise not to press you to give me information back."

Why did she feel like crying? *"Why are you doing this, Paul?"*

They stared at each other in the dusky moonlight for awhile. He looked away first, sighed and rubbed his big hand over his whole face and then through his hair. Clean shaven as he was tonight, he didn't look as old as she thought he was when she'd first seen him. His salt and pepper beard made him look a lot older than twenty-seven. The hair on his head stuck out wildly all over his head now. *He needs a haircut,* she thought. "I told you why in the parking lot, earlier." When she just continued to stare at him, he sighed and actually looked uncomfortable. "I said, I couldn't get you out of my thoughts. I couldn't stop thinking about those big green eyes of yours." He picked up another cookie but didn't eat it. "I don't usually have trouble charming women, Claire. It comes pretty easy to me, to be quite honest. My sisters will tell you it comes from being the baby and knowing how to manipulate the situation to get what I want ..."

Paul looked at her with a serious expression. "This is *not* coming out right." He paused. "And I've never wanted to say something right so desperately." He sighed a huge sigh. "I want to impress you but I also want to be honest with you! I can't do that because I'm definitely not perfect! And anything I say to you that isn't positive will only reinforce you're already poor opinion of me ..."

"I never said I had a poor opinion of you."

He turned to her in surprise. "You don't?"

Claire took a deep breath, trying to put into as few words as possible the screwed up state of her head. "Look, Paul, *you're a man*. I have no opinion of you - good or bad. You don't even register on my radar screen, except to be conscious of how much of a safe distance I can keep you at. What matters to me is Tyler and all the things that I need to do to keep our life from falling apart."

"It's a big deal that you let me follow you home, isn't it."

"It was an insane idea," she blurted out.

He gave her an enormous grin. "I think that means that *maybe, just maybe*, you might have a very small opinion about me. And it would have to be a good one, don't you think?"

Claire refused to look at him and answer him. Jeeze, he was quick and smart. That made her uneasy for the first time since he'd frightened her in the parking lot.

Paul looked at his watch. "I better get going. Thanks for the cookies and soda." He stood up, brushed some crumbs off the front of his shirt, and smiled at her. "I'll say goodnight, then."

Claire knew he hadn't gotten the message. "Paul," she said as he headed toward the stairs that led down into the parking lot. *"I'm not what you think I am."* She felt near tears again.

He was already down one step when he stopped and turned to look at her. As she stood at the top of the stairs she was just about eye level with him. "You know Claire, you've never even heard me tell you what I think about you. Why don't you ask me that question? Do you have the nerve to do that?"

It was an absolutely terrify thing to do. She took a deep breath to muster her courage and then asked quietly, "What do you think about me, Paul?"

"You're a dedicated mother and a hard working, reliable woman. Life's been miserable so far, and you have no reason to expect any difference in the future. There's a big, broken heart in there that you think is shattered beyond repair. Your mouth tells me to leave you alone, but those eyes speak to me as well. And they tell me louder and clearer than anything your mouth's said so far that I should keep trying. And you know something? I think *that you just might be worth the effort.*" He reached over with his big hand and touched just the tip of her nose. *"That's what I think about you, Claire Jenkins."* And he turned and disappeared down the stairway into the night.

Many are the plans in a man's heart, but it is the Lord's purpose that prevails.[9]

Six: Men Will Do Anything To Get Their Way

Paul had just wanted to get another look at Claire. He'd given her a ride in his truck and filled her car's gas tank. Yet much as he'd tried, he couldn't seem to keep Claire from his thoughts. What was the big draw? All he knew was that he could think of little else. Was her car cooperating? Were she and the kid okay? How was she managing with the boy at home while she had to work? Maybe, just maybe, if Paul stopped by the diner and saw that she was okay, he could get her off his mind … After their shift was over that Friday morning, Paul had convinced the guys to go to the All American Diner for breakfast. Paul hadn't wanted to show up on his own, fearful that Claire might get the wrong impression. *Which was what?* his grandfather's voice had asked, *safety in numbers?*

"Hey, Saint, isn't this where I picked you up when you put gas in that car?" Josh asked as they walked in from the parking lot early that morning. All of their trucks were parked in the big back lot.

"What car?" asked Vince, looking highly curious.

Paul shrugged, trying to look casual. "I did a good deed the other day and helped someone who'd run out of gas."

"A *woman?*" Vince asked with a knowing smirk.

"Yeah, a *woman,*" Paul said with a tinge of impatience and a wave of concern as they all walked into the diner. Maybe this wasn't such a good idea.

"How many?" said the gum-popping girl behind the register.

"Six, non-smoking," Simon volunteered.

As she gathered up the menus and they followed her to their table, Paul leaned over and said very quietly so the others couldn't hear, "Could Claire wait on us?"

Gum Popper studied him for a minute as the others chose seats and sat down. "Yeah, sure, I'll tell the manager."

"Which one is she, Paul?" Mike asked, scanning the various waitresses and dismissing them one after another.

"Which one's what?" Paul responded, trying his best to sound dumb.

"That one's got potential," Vince pointed out with an arched eyebrow, nodding to the tall redhead standing at a table over in the corner. It wasn't Claire.

And then she was standing at the table. Claire never made eye contact with them, just worked diligently at writing down their requests. Her body language communicated tension. Maybe even fear. Something was really wrong. Vince arched his eyebrow again questioningly at him, and Paul could see Mike getting ready to make a wise comment.

"Coffee – *not* decaf," he said more loudly than necessary. He felt a rush of pleasure, because she immediately seemed to recognize his voice. She looked up and met his amused gaze and Paul felt his face split into a huge grin.

"Hi Paul. Come to check out the fine fare here at the All American?" Claire said.

She'd remembered the sound of his voice. Yes sir, he still had it going on with the ladies, even though he had been out of action for a while. The adrenaline rushed. He remembered the thrill of the chase ... "Nah," he heard himself say in his best sweet-talking voice, "we know the food's just okay here. We all came to check *you* out." Paul heard the guys laughing, and out of the corner of his eye he caught Vince give her a sly wink.

He watched every single one of her lights go out, he saw the shutters get pulled down, he heard the door slam and lock. "I'll get your drinks," she said as she rushed away from their table.

"Boy, that was a big strike-out, Paul," James said.

"Tell me that wasn't the one," mumbled Vince with disgust. He had no patience with women who didn't flirt.

"Something's going on *big time* there," Simon said softly.

"Shut the hell up, all of you," Paul said, furious with himself, the guys and life in general, "just order your food when she comes back, okay?"

The morning's not going so well, his grandfather's voice said disgustedly.

Crap.

Standing in the parking lot after breakfast, Paul had caught Simon's arm as he was climbing into his truck. "What did you mean when you said 'something's going on big time'?"

Simon was a people observer. When the rest of them were talking and yelling, he usually was quietly watching. He always came in handy when they were trying to pick up women because he was more accurate then the rest of them in pegging who would be receptive to their lines or who wouldn't. Simon shrugged. "I'm no expert, Saint, but that lady's been hurt *big time*." He scratched his stubble and gazed at the traffic. "She wasn't just offended by what you said, you *terrified* her. I wouldn't feel too responsible, though. Unless I miss my guess she was pretty scared of all of us before you even opened your mouth."

Paul had caught that, too. Why had he been so flip? He thrust his hands in his pockets, closed his eyes, and sighed.

"What's with her?" Simon asked, his voice filled with curiosity. "You like her that much? Is there more to the story than just coming to her rescue and springing for a tank of gas?"

How could Paul explain it when he didn't get it himself? She was feisty, a single mother, poor ... And now this. He looked at Simon and shrugged. "Hell if I know."

Simon clapped him on the back. "You know, whenever you're

really upset about something, you curse. That's how I know this is really bugging you. It's the only time you slip up." Simon pulled open the door of his cab. "Seems to me like you've got to visit the little green-eyed waitress one more time before you settle this for yourself."

Paul looked at Simon. "You noticed her eyes, too?"

Simon stared at him for a moment. "Yeah, I noticed her eyes."

Paul had gone back to the diner and apologize and ended up following her home. He thought of the conversation they'd had on her 'back porch'. Her 'back porch', which turned out to be nothing more than two benches that had seen better days *a decade ago* sitting on the tar paper flat roof of the store down below. And visiting with her and speaking with her had not done any good getting her off his mind. Paul thought of Claire all the next day through the double shift.

Paul was mostly interested in everything Claire hadn't said. She never spoke of family, friends, fun, or anything that brought joy. Her life was the polar opposite of his. It seemed to revolve around working, surviving, and trying to control her son. It seemed to Paul that she was barely alive. He worked hard, he was single, but he had friends and family and a lot of enjoyment in his life. Claire didn't seem to have any of that. How could that be? Or, more importantly, how could someone go on, day after day, when his or her life was so devoid of ... color?

She had this gray, dull existence. Only Tyler seemed to add color and it was usually bright red flags of trouble. One thing was certain. Each time he saw Claire increased rather than ended his growing preoccupation with her. And that was not good. *Not good at all.*

Vince called him on his cell phone Saturday afternoon as he drove home from his double shift. "Hey, Saint. Got any plans for tomorrow?"

"No, just church in the morning, why?"

"Well, I've got a surprise for you, that's all. Meet me at Buster's around six, okay?"

"Yeah, I guess so." Paul wasn't enthusiastic. Buster's was an old haunt of theirs that they didn't visit as regularly as they used to since Paul had stopped drinking. It was a sports bar that had a fairly good food menu if you liked ribs and steaks and potatoes in various forms. Sitting with

Vince while he packed away beers and leered at the women was no longer high on Paul's list of favorite things to do. Of all the friendships, Vince's and his was the one that had changed the most over the last two years. The other guys seemed content with Paul's changes, but there were times when Vince seemed downright annoyed. Going out one on one had dwindled over the past two years so much that Paul couldn't recall the last time they'd done it.

On Sunday evening, he pulled into the parking lot of Buster's and looked for Vince's car. He spotted it, parked at the far end of the lot away from the other cars that might hit his precious automobile and mar its mint condition. Since his divorce, Vince's only permanent relationship was with his convertible sports car.

The noise of the sports channel as well as the piped in music drowned out Vince's voice, but Paul could see him standing and waving enthusiastically as he entered the bar. As he wove his way through the obstacle course of tables, chairs, and waitresses Paul got a sinking sensation in the pit of his stomach. Seated at the table with Vince were two women smiling their welcome.

"Hey, Saint! This is Tiffany and Marcia. I met them here the other night and they were anxious to meet you. I thought we could enjoy a quick bite here and then go dancing over at the Marquis."

Paul met Vince's grinning face and then smiled politely at the ladies. "Hey, nice to meet you."

Tiffany gave him a broad smile and patted the chair next to hers. "I'm glad you came, Paul. Vince has told me a lot about you."

He settled himself in the chair and gave her a grin. "All good, I hope."

"Actually, after that smile you just gave me, I'm thinking he didn't tell me enough."

Paul sat down and ordered an unsweetened iced tea from the waitress and then turned to Tiffany, "Vince didn't tell me a thing about you, so why don't you enlighten me?" He felt himself slipping into the casual, easy banter that still came so naturally to him. No harm in enjoying himself for a few minutes, was there? He turned slightly sideways, slouched down in his chair, and crossed his long legs in front of him. It wasn't until he felt Tiffany's hair tickle his forearm that he registered he'd put his arm across the back of her chair.

She was in her third year of college, studying to be a teacher. He heard himself say, "I never had any teachers look like you when *I* was in school." Vince caught his eye and winked at him.

Tiffany had long, curly brown hair and big brown eyes. She was just the type of woman that used to appeal to him, tall and leggy with an air of innocence as well as sultry curiosity. Her top was low cut and he caught a glimpse of the edge of the black lace of her bra. *It had been a long time.* As she talked about the rigors of her college schedule he leaned over and inhaled her perfume. *Oh man ...*

She was animated and enthusiastic about teaching, leaning in to talk in his ear over the sounds of the bar. As long as he kept his eyes off her bra lace and away from the legs she kept crossing and uncrossing, he was able to follow most of her conversation. She asked questions about him, and over the noise and the meal they bantered easily. His mind registered that he didn't have to work hard at all with this catch. Just keep reeling her in, slow and steady ...

Across the table, Vince and Marcia were doing as well. Actually better. Vince was into high flirt and tease gear, making her laugh and squeal, and there was significant touching going on.

In the old days, if they reached a certain point with a pair of girls, sometimes the second stage - movie, dancing, walk in the park - *whatever* - never happened because things were moving fast enough that there was no sense wasting valuable time. They had a signal that they used to let each other know that they wanted to move on *solo*. By the time dessert and coffee were finished, Vince had already given Paul the signal.

Vince whispered something in Marcia's ear and she giggled. "Hey," he said across the table to Paul and Tiffany. "Do you mind if we have a change in plans? Marcia's never ridden in a convertible, and I thought I might take her for a ride up in the mountains. The back seat's not too comfortable, otherwise I'd invite you two. You guys all right if we split up?"

Vince and Marcia looked at Tiffany. Apparently, it was naturally assumed that Paul would have no objections. Tiffany gave them a brilliant smile and then turned and leaned over to Paul. "It's okay with me. How about you?" He couldn't help himself, as the front of her top gaped open, he looked. When he lifted his gaze to meet her eyes, she smiled and put her hand high on his thigh. "Vince says you've got a nice home. Care to give me a tour?"

Tiffany rode silently beside him in his truck as he warred with himself. What was he doing? Hello? Hello! *Hello* ... He tried to convince himself he was just taking her home ... For a cup of coffee. So they could talk without the noise and distraction of the bar. So he could give her a tour of the house like she'd asked. *Yeah, right.*

She oohed and aahed as he gave her the tour, especially when she saw the front porch swing: "Oh, I *love* these", and the fireplace: "They're so romantic". When they stepped out on his small back deck she opened her mouth to say something and he grabbed her, picked her up, and kissed her. He pushed her up against the outside wall of the house with her feet off the ground. Tiffany threw her arms around him and kissed him back open-mouthed and they got lost in the game of getting to know each other with their mouths. When they came up for air, she gave him a sideways smile and said, "I think this is my favorite spot in the house." He kissed her again.

Somehow they ended up on the couch in his living room. Paul lost all sense of time and place, of who he was and who he wanted to be. The only thing that mattered was the blood the was raging through his body chanting as it flowed: *It's been so long, it's been too long, it's been so long, it's been too long* ...

He could feel through her top that she had on one of those demibras, the kind that barely covered anything but looked so good. He already knew it was black from what he'd seen at Busters. Paul got wrapped up in the fun of prolonging the inevitable of seeing it and what was underneath ...

He became aware that Tiffany was asking him a question. One that he knew she'd asked at least twice, and it still hadn't registered. "What?" he finally said, struggling to bring his brain up to speed with the rest of his body. "What did you ask me, Beautiful?" He trailed a line of kisses down the edge of her jaw, working slowly and easily towards that bra ... He felt her shiver and grinned to himself with the delight of the victory so close at hand.

"I said," Tiffany gasped, kissing his mouth quickly as he struggled to focus and look at her, "why does Vince call you 'Saint'?"

Seated in the truck in the parking lot at Busters not a half hour later, Paul risked a glance at Tiffany who sat stone faced on the passenger seat staring straight ahead. She'd reapplied her lipstick, but her mascara was slightly smeared under her left eye. He reached over to gently wipe it away. She jumped like he'd slapped her. "Don't touch me."

He let his hand drop and rest on the seat between them and sighed. "It has everything to do with me and nothing to do with you, Tiffany," he said in a low and anguished voice.

"Yeah, yeah, *yeah,*" she said as she looked around the truck cab and began gathering up her purse and her jacket. "Just for the record, I don't do this. I don't meet guys in bars and go home with them on the first date. *I don't.*" Her bottom lip trembled and she worked at fighting back tears. "I *thought* we had some special connection. Vince said that you hadn't dated in a *long* time, and that he knew that you were lonely and wanted to meet someone, and you and I would hit it off, and ..." She choked back a sob and turned to look out into the dark corner of the parking lot.

Paul reached up and grabbed the steering wheel and then rested his forehead on his hands. "Vince is right about some things and wrong about others. It's true, it has been a long time since I've dated, but that was by my choice and not because I'd been hurt or anything. I didn't like the guy I was becoming, and quite frankly, you wouldn't have liked him very much either. But Vince was wrong that I'm lonely or looking for someone. I'm just trying to get my head screwed on straight and get my priorities where they should be. Tonight," he paused not wanting to hurt or upset her anymore than he'd already done, "just proves that I'm really not worthy to be around anyone as nice as you ... yet."

He reached over and smoothed away the mascara smudge that she hadn't let him touch earlier, and he felt the wetness of her tears. "Don't cry. Please don't cry." He drew her into his arms and held her while she sniffled. "Tiffany, promise me something, would you?" He felt a brief nod. "No matter *how nice* the guy is or *how well* you hit it off with him, don't go to bed with him on the first date, okay?" He tilted her chin to look at her. "You're worth too much to sell yourself so lightly. And the fact that I was ready, willing, and anxious to take what you were so generously offering shows that I'm not deserving of anything you have to offer, okay?"

Tiffany pulled out of his arms, took a trembling breath, and sniffed loudly. "But you *didn't* take it in the end. Doesn't that make you the good guy?"

Paul made a sound of impatience and disgust with himself. "You couldn't read my mind, Beautiful. There's no way a body can think the thoughts I was thinking and qualify as a 'good guy'."

Vince saw him on the job Monday with a smile that was all knowing and smug at the same time. "Something tells me that your evening turned out as well as mine," he said clapping Paul on the back.

Paul was at a loss for words and just looked at him. Apparently, that was enough for Vince. His smile slowly faded and a frown replaced it. "Did you screw it up? That was a golden opportunity I handed to you ..."

"I don't need your help in that department, Vince." Paul took off his sunglasses so that his expression and tone could not be confused.

Vince was furious. "Not 24 hours earlier, you were practically drooling over that broken down waitress who showed you not the slightest bit of interest or encouragement. It was obvious to all of us that you needed some help getting back on track." He shrugged. "We go way back. We're almost best friends. I did what any good buddy would do. I fixed you up."

"You're looking at *my* world through *your* eyes. I'm not looking for what you knew Tiffany was offering, Vince. I'm still trying to get my head on straight, and getting involved with old habits isn't going to help me *at all*. Look, I don't know what you thought you saw the other day at the diner ..." Paul looked out into the distance and put his sunglasses back on, "... heck ... I'm not even sure what was going on with me in the diner." He looked back at Vince. "But for ... darn ... sure, I didn't drag all six of you to the diner the other day to check out what I hoped would soon be a sexual conquest."   Paul looked down at his work boots and shook his head. "Jeeze, Vince. I never did that even when I was at my wildest."

"It seemed like you were having a rip roaring time when Marcia and I left," Vince mumbled in defense.

"Yeah, well, old habits die hard."   Paul jammed his hands in his pockets. *"Real hard."*

That afternoon, driving home after his shift he had a long talk with God about his life, his intentions, and his continual failures. "I don't know, Lord. I feel ... like I'm always letting You down. Like I'm fighting with every ounce of my being to accomplish some major purpose You have set out for me in my life, but I have *no clue* what I'm trying to do. How can that be? What do You want from me? *I don't care what You want of me, Lord, just make the path clear.* Paint me some big black arrows and I'll follow them. I promise."

Why don't you go play some basketball? His grandfather's voice said.

No one would love me if they knew all the things I hide ...[10]

Seven: Stay Away From All Men

It was an uneventful week and in Claire's eyes that made it a great success. No calls from the principal or teacher, no breakdowns, and no leering customers. Even Maddy kept a polite distance when they worked the same shifts, and made no more overtures of false friendship.

Tyler was amazingly cooperative each afternoon, working on his homework, doing his reading, and eating his broccoli (which he preferred over green beans). He had even been more interested in being outside on the makeshift basketball court than acquiring 'square eyes' from being glued to his Gameboy too much. Although Mrs. Santiago had offered to watch him each afternoon after he got out of school, and Tyler had begged and pleaded to be allowed to stay there, Claire had remained firm and declined. She never took charity and wasn't going to start now. She did finally cave on her weekend work day, though. It was agreed that Tyler could spend Sundays with Mrs. Santiago, rather then the long day at the diner. In exchange, Claire would regularly do any and all food shopping for Mrs. Santiago (including extra little trips during the week if need be), bring the

---

[10] "Love Alone", By Aaron Tate, Caedmon's Call, Long Line of Leavers, 2000

groceries in, put them away, *and* treat both Tyler and Mrs. Santiago to Sunday dinner at the diner.

Then Saturday rolled around, a day that was supposed to be the best day of the week because it was the only day she had off. True to form, the uneventful week turned into the one of the worst weeks of her life ... *again.*

Things started out nicely. Claire made French toast for breakfast, and she and Tyler padded around in their pajamas until almost eleven, but the beautiful day called. They both set about getting dressed and shouting suggestions to each other about what they wanted to do versus what she had to do.

"We have to food shop. That means for Mrs. Santiago, too."

"Could we go to the park and throw the football around a bit?"

"Yeah, we could go to the park and see the ducks and flower garden. If I do the sports thing, will you do the nature thing?"

"Yeah, okay, Mom." Tyler's enthusiasm was not overwhelming.

"We could food shop on the way back, and maybe we could buy a container of ice cream and some cones."

"You think so?" The longing was so profound in her son's voice that Claire closed her eyes for a moment to quell the sorrow that welled up inside her. *She could do so little because she had so little.*

"Why don't you run next door to Mrs. Santiago and tell her to make up her food list?"

"Okay." He was out the door like a shot. Two minutes later he was back, looking very concerned. "You better come, Mom. Mrs. Santiago is sitting at her kitchen table crying."

Claire found Mrs. Santiago as Tyler had described, sitting in one of her two plastic kitchen chairs, crying as if the world had just ended. "Hey, Mrs. Santiago, what's up? Is there anything that Tyler and I can do for you?"

Mrs. Santiago blew her nose in a paper napkin and then looked up at Claire. "Have you read your mail yet today, Claire?"

"No ..."

"Maybe you should."

Claire saw scattered pieces of mail and catalogs haphazardly strewn around the table, and in Mrs. Santiago's lap was a letter. Claire suddenly got a very bad feeling. "Tyler? Would you run and get the mail?"

In general, Claire hated mail. It never brought good things, only bad. Bills, overdue notices, and junk mail. It was something she avoided if possible, and some days she didn't bother collecting it at all. That had resulted in a nasty note from the postman telling her that if she didn't empty her box each day he would cease delivering the mail to her door and she would have to go down to the post office to claim it. *That* reinforced her dislike of the postal system, however, it did make her collect her mail each day. When would she have the time to go to the post office each day to get her hated mail?

Tyler was gone a few minutes and then arrived breathlessly back in Mrs. Santiago's kitchen. As she sifted through the mail, the letter was obvious. It was the only one that wasn't a bill or junk mail. Her name had been carefully typed by a real typewriter. The return address was for a lawyer. Oh no ...

Dear Ms. Claire Jenkins,

Formal notice is hereby given for you to quit the premises of 61 East Main Street, Apartment 2E within sixty (60) days of the above date. Said premises of 61 East Main, including all tenants both commercial and private, shall consider this a termination of any and all leases currently in place in accordance with Article 7, Section 5, Paragraph 3 of the lease agreement which states, "Owner of said property may at any time, given a notice of sixty days, request in writing the eviction of said tenant from the premises."

Sincerely,

Jacob Dumont, Esq.

When she looked up into Mrs. Santiago's tear-stained face Tyler said, "What's it say, Mom?"

She looked out the back door at the bright spring afternoon. Right on schedule. There was never, ever a break for her. "It says," she said tonelessly, "that in two months I need to find us a place to live or we're going to be homeless."

Mrs. Santiago continued to be so upset that Tyler refused to leave her. He declined the park trip – as if either one of them could have enjoyed themselves anyway - and instead chose to stay and keep Mrs. Santiago company. "I'll get the groceries then and pick up a newspaper to start looking for apartments, okay?" Claire said to both of their unhappy faces. They barely noticed when she left.

The food store that she preferred, because it was big and tended to have slightly better prices, brought her past Riverside Church, where a party was in progress. Kids were running around, crowds of adults were congregating in small groups talking, and balloons were tied to chairs and tables and fences waving in the breeze. She slowed down to read the large banner but didn't stop. It said, *Sonset House - Happy Anniversary! - 50 Years of Love, Laugher, and Service.*

Sonset House? Hadn't Janice Strocco called that mission house, Son*rise* House? This had to be something different, because whatever they were celebrating had been around for fifty years. As Claire picked up speed, she thought she saw Janice Strocco with her head thrown back laughing uproariously.

Claire had a lot of time to think, because food shopping always took her a long time. She had to be careful, down to the penny practically, not to go over her budgeted amount for food. Furthermore, if she could spend *even less*, then that would help her in other areas. For Mrs. Santiago, who also had the added complication of food stamps, it was more difficult. It had never occurred to Claire how difficult it was shopping for another person. What flavor toothpaste? The gel or the paste? Mint or regular? Teeth whitener or for sensitive gums? What kind of milk? Full? 2%? 1%? Skim? She stood in front of the display of apples and was overwhelmed. She'd never realized there were over ten kinds.

Driving back almost two hours later, she noted that things had pretty much ended at the church. Tables and chairs were being folded and put away and the remaining kids now had balloons tied around their wrists to be taken home. Sonset House, she noted, was on the opposite side of the church from Sonrise House. A new, spanking white sign was proudly displayed on its front lawn, surrounded by freshly planted flowers. Slowing down, she read *Sonset House of Riverside Church, Senior Care Housing.* Oh, so that's what Sonset House was. Charity directed at the elderly. Just like Sonrise House was charity for needy women and their children. It had to be charity because no one who could avoid it would ever choose to live with strangers. No matter what Daniel Alvarez and Janice Strocco said, to live in Sonrise House would be charity. Charity was something people gave to you because you were needy. She may be a screw up, but she wasn't needy.

Claire had good reason for not taking charity. It was an undisputed fact that people who gave out charity had hidden agendas. No matter what they said, they wanted either money or control or favors. Charitable people were revered and respected by the community. People who accepted charity were doomed to inevitable disaster: they would always be vulnerable. Unspoken but understood also was the knowledge that those needing charity were lazy, dishonest, and undeserving.

As a child, Claire had grown up on charity and it had almost destroyed her. Hand me down clothes, second hand toys, brutal teasing from the other children, impatience and condescension from the adults ... There had been a constant flow of strangers to whom you were expected to be polite, respectful, and appreciative.

Don't be so sullen, Claire. They are only trying to help.

Claire, say thank you to those children for being so generous to you.

What do you mean you don't like that dress? You'll wear it and be appreciative as well.

You have no idea how bad things could be for you, Claire. You should thank your lucky stars you've got as much as you do.

My mother says your mother didn't want you. My mother says that you have to stay here until they can find someone who wants you instead.

Claire? We have a better home situation we'd like to try with you. Maybe this one will be more successful. I'm sure you'll like this new placement. They have a little girl just your age ...

And *those* were the good aspects of childhood! The bad parts, the *dark* parts were not to be remembered, let alone spoken of. The only time the dark memories couldn't be suppressed was in her nightmares. Thankfully, she was usually too exhausted each night to dream.

Claire was gainfully employed and willing to work hard. She was determined *not* to be needy. Not ever again. There had to be another apartment out there for her and Tyler that she could afford. Maybe it wouldn't have two bedrooms, maybe it wouldn't have a dining room, maybe it would be more run down. But it wouldn't be charity. It wouldn't be living with strangers.

It wouldn't be Sonrise House.

She spent every free minute she had Sunday calling about apartments advertised in the Sunday paper. Tyler spent Memorial Day Monday off with Mrs. Santiago and Claire took an extra half hour at lunchtime to visit three apartments. A pattern quickly developed. If the apartment was in her price range it was invariably so small or so run down or in such a disreputable part of town that she couldn't even consider it. Anything else was out of her price range. At one of the apartments she looked at, the owner had backed her up against a wall and told her in no uncertain terms that he would lower the rent - *by fifty dollars a month* - if she was willing to become his 'friend' once or twice a week. She was so upset when she got back to the diner that she had thrown up in the bathroom.

By the following Saturday, Claire was frantic. There seemed to be nothing anywhere in the area that she could afford. In the depths of desperation, her little internal voice said, *What did you expect, Claire? Nothing ever works out for you, you know that.*

Tyler had been quiet and withdrawn all week and Claire knew he was worried, too. Once again he had been on his best behavior at the diner, spending his time playing basketball outside and doing what little homework he acknowledged that he had. Again, no news from school was good news for Claire.

"Mrs. Santiago thinks she might go live in Florida with her daughter," he volunteered as she came into the living room Saturday morning. He was watching his favorite cartoon, SpongeBob SquarePants.

"Oh?"

"Yeah, she doesn't want to because she doesn't like her daughter's husband, but she doesn't think she has much choice."

At least she's got a place to go, Claire thought and then immediately felt guilty for her attitude. "Florida's a nice place, Tyler. Things aren't so expensive down there, either. Maybe she'll be able to get an apartment where she doesn't have to climb up so many stairs."

"You think so, Mom?"

Claire smiled at him. "Yeah, I think so."

"Paul says he'd keep an eye out for an apartment for us."

Claire froze. "Paul who?"

Tyler at first gave her a puzzled look that said *What do you mean, 'Paul who'* which was rapidly transformed into an expression that said, '*Uh-oh, I goofed.*'

"Tyler, *Paul who?*"

"It's the Paul you're thinking it is, Mom."

She sat down on the couch next to him and switched off the television. "Tyler, when have you spoken to Paul?"

He looked down at his hands. "At the diner."

"When at the diner? He hasn't been in to eat. I haven't seen him ..."

"He comes by on Monday, Wednesday and Friday after his 3 p.m. shift is over and we play basketball. He says he'll only come if I do all my homework first and don't get in trouble at school anymore. Oh yeah, and I have to eat my greens without making a fuss."

"How many times have you seen him?" She was having a hard time fitting her head around all of this.

"He's come by the last two weeks." Tyler's voice turned pleading. "It's been so much fun, Mom! I know you don't want to date him, but please don't make him stop coming by!"

"*What did you say?*"

Tyler looked uncomfortable, but then he seemed to shrug as if to say, *Oh what the heck. The cat's out of the bag already.* "I asked him if he liked you and he said yeah he did, but he said you didn't want to date anybody, and so he thought he would spend time with me instead." Tyler looked real serious. "He's a real nice guy, Mom. Why don't you like him?"

Claire leaned forward and put her face in her hands. "It's complicated, Tyler," came her muffled reply.

"I told him how upset you were about us having to move out of the apartment, and he said he didn't blame you. He said he would scout around and see what he could find, but on Friday he said he hadn't had much luck."

Claire looked at her son. "Tyler, I wish you wouldn't tell strangers our private business. It's not wise."

"I'm not, Mom! I'm just telling *Paul.* He's not a stranger. We rode in his truck and he came to my school and he says he's even eaten at the diner a bunch of times. He even helped me with my homework last Wednesday."

She put her face in her hands again. "Oh, Tyler."

"Did I do something wrong, Mom? Did I? He was just so nice and I knew you knew him and I thought I made good choices this time."

Claire looked up at him and he looked so concerned. *Anguished* came to mind. She pulled him into her arms. "No, you didn't do anything wrong, honey. He is a nice man. One of the nicest I've ever met. You did just fine." And she meant it.

Monday afternoon, Mrs. Santiago agreed to watch Tyler, who was frantic with worry. "You're gonna talk to Paul, aren't you Mom? You're not gonna tell him to stop coming anymore, are you? Please, Mom, *please* don't yell at him."

"I'm not going to yell at him, Tyler."

"Promise me you're not going to tell him he can't come by anymore."

Claire sighed. "I promise."

She was sitting on the steps on break when he came breezing around the corner, whistling. He skidded to a stop when he saw her. He was still dressed in his utility uniform. "Oh," was all he said at first. Then he jammed both of his hands in his pants pockets, leaned against the side of the building by the stairs, and said, "Hi, Claire. I guess I'm in trouble, huh?"

Claire didn't answer him. She just looked at him, really looked at him for the first time. He was tall. *Really tall.* Well over six feet. He had the salt and pepper beard again. He was a hairy guy, with dark hair on his forearms, peeking out of the collar of his work shirt, and curling wildly all over his head. He had a tan, ruddy complexion that distinguished him as someone who worked outdoors. He had his sunglasses on again so she couldn't see the color of his eyes.

"You gonna yell at me or something?"

Quite frankly, she had *no idea* what she was planning on saying to him. None.

He sat down on a lower step, scratched his chin, and looked up at her. "You know, you don't talk much. That's pretty unusual for a woman."

If you only knew what I was thinking, bud, she thought.

Paul shrugged. "I had some free time. Lots of times after work I go to the gym and workout to wind down anyway. I thought, why not go over and shoot hoops with the kid? No harm done. So I did. He seemed happy. Tyler told me he's been doing his homework, not getting in trouble at school, and even eating his broccoli. I figured at least that would help you out a little bit." He just looked at her. "Jeeze, Claire. Say something, *anything*. You're starting to creep me out." He looked at her. "I didn't break any of your rules, did I? Tyler says you've got lots of them ..." Then he gave her a look like Tyler did when he knew he was going to catch it.

Amazed, Claire felt a smile starting. She looked out the back towards the employee parking lot. Finally, she sighed. "Thanks. *A lot.* If I wasn't facing impending homelessness, I would have to admit that these last two weeks have been the easiest I've had with Tyler in ages."

Paul visibly relaxed, similar to an over inflated balloon having some of its air released. "Tyler told me about the letter. I'm sorry, Claire. I've asked around, but there doesn't seem to be much available in the area."

"Much available in my price range you mean." Man, she sounded bitter even to herself.

"What are you going to do?"

"Try to buy a mattress that I can fit into the back seat of my car."

"You know, you're not very funny, Claire."

Claire massaged the bridge of her nose. "I'll manage. I always do in the end. I loose a couple of years off my life to worry and stress, confirm my opinion of my fellow man and my own luck, and then trudge on."

"What's your opinion of your fellow man?"

"That no one does anything for nothing. That God helps those who help themselves. That there's no such thing as catching a break."

"You believe in God?" He seemed to perk up a bit.

She rolled her eyes. "No."

That got him. "Really?"

"Yeah, really, what's so amazing about that?"

Paul shrugged. "I don't know. You tend to run across people who are usually God believing, but not necessarily God fearing, if you know what I mean."

"I have no idea what you mean."

"Can I come sit on your porch tonight, Claire?" Paul said suddenly.

That came out of left field. She intently studied the stone structure of the step at her feet.

"I'll bring you an ice cream cone ..."

"I'm not subject to bribes," Claire said rather primly.

He looked at her intently. "You know, I think that's the first casual, nonsarcastic thing you've ever said to me." He hesitated. "I'll put chocolate sprinkles on it."

She shook her head. "I'm *so* not that easy ..."

He sat forward, as if this whole exchange between the two of them was suddenly terribly important. Perhaps it was. "I'll put it in one of those expensive cookie cones ..."

It was time to start her next shift. She stood up and brushed off the back of her uniform. "You don't even know what kind of ice cream I like ... And I'm not going to tell you. So, you're stuck." She had the ridiculous desire to say, *So there*, and stick her tongue out at him.

"Chocolate chip mint." As she stood there with her mouth open, Paul grinned at her. Chuckling, he said, "I'm not a dope, Claire. You know my agenda. I'm just going slow, that's all. And your son, Tyler is just a wealth of information about you. You should play a game of one on one basketball with him sometime. You'd be amazed at what you'd find out." He stood up, smiled, and then walked around the corner of the diner out of view. She could hear him whistling.

Paul was nowhere to be seen when she left the diner a little after nine that night. Furthermore, he was not anywhere in the parking lot, nor was he sitting on the bench when she got to the top of the first flight of stairs. Was she disappointed? Nah, she was relieved, she told herself. Rule number sixty-three of the Claire Jenkins Rules of Survival Book: *Never trust any man to keep his word, it only leads to disappointment.*

Tyler, she discovered was fast asleep in bed already. Claire was stunned. He had always been such a night owl. When they got back from the diner he didn't usually fall asleep until about 10:30.

"I told him a child his age needed his sleep. Kids grow while they're sleeping you know. I told him he'd be healthier, stronger, bigger, and more handsome with every extra minute of sleep he got." Mrs. Santiago had a twinkle in her eye. "He was asleep by 8:30."

"Jeeze, Mrs. Santiago," Claire said, "the last time he was asleep at 8:30 he was probably two years old. You're amazing!"

"I've raised six children, so I've got some experience. These bones may be old, but the mind and the mouth are still sharp."

Claire had brought Mrs. Santiago a slice of cherry pie from the diner. "Oh, bless you, child. Why has it taken us so long to get to know each other just to be separated? I'll never understand ..." She smiled gratefully as Claire helped her up. "I'm going to go home, make myself a hot cup of tea, eat some delicious cherry pie, and watch some Nick at Night. Ten o'clock is the Andy Griffith Show. I love that show."

At the back door, Mrs. Santiago stopped. "Oh, I forgot. I hope it's okay. I gave Tyler a medal today to wear. It's a Saint Jude medal. People like to say St. Jude is the Patron Saint of Lost Causes, but he is *really* the Patron Saint of *Desperate Situations.* I figured, that for all three of us this apartment predicament means we are desperate. Father Murphy over at St. Bernard's Church was happy to bless one for me, and in the end I thought I'd get one for you, too. Tyler was so taken with mine, that I gave him yours. I hope it's okay ..."

Claire had no idea what Mrs. Santiago was talking about, but she smiled. "Sure, Mrs. Santiago, it's fine that you gave Tyler that medal. It was very generous of you." As Mrs. Santiago made her way slowly to her own back door, Claire couldn't help herself, and glanced out the back door window. Both benches were empty and she was dismayed with herself because she realized she *was* disappointed that Paul hadn't shown.

By 9:45 she was showered and in the worn sweat suit she usually slept in. She went into the kitchen to make herself a cup of tea, and couldn't help herself. She looked out the window one more time and he was there! Good grief! He was there! She rushed back into her bedroom, tore off the sweat suit, threw on underwear, jeans, a long sleeved tee shirt and flip flops, and then went tearing back through the apartment. She tried to calm her breathing and her pounding heart as she walked out to the benches.

"Took your time getting out here, Claire! Darn! The ice cream is really melted."

"I, I didn't think you were coming."

"What do you mean? *I said I was.*" Paul looked at her pointedly. "You didn't tell me I couldn't."

"You weren't here when I got home and you still weren't here when I walked Mrs. Santiago out. I just thought ..."

He thrust the dripping ice cream cone at her and then studied her in the moonlight. "Claire, if I say I'm going to do something, I do it. Maybe you'll not trust my words and you'll have to learn from experience, but aside from hospitalization or car trouble, I'll follow through on everything I tell you I'll do. If you'd just let us exchange our ... dang ... phone numbers I would at least be able to call you if something came up. And you'd have my number to call me if you ... oh, I don't know! ... if you had a question or something," he finished lamely.

"You can have my phone number," she said in a matter of fact voice.

Paul looked at her incredulously. "Claire, I asked you if I could call you sometime and you said you didn't date!" he said with real frustration.

"I know what I said! You didn't ask if you could have my phone number just *in case,* and you didn't offer me yours." She took a lick of the ice cream. "Thanks for this ..."

"You're making me nuts you know."

"I warned you I was screwed up. I can't help it if you don't listen."

They sat for a long time on the benches eating their ice cream in silence. Finally, Paul asked, "Why don't you believe in God?"

"I never had the opportunity."

He looked at her for a moment and she stared back at him. Finally, he chuckled a little bit and shook his head. "Do you know that you never, *ever* say what I think you're going to say?"

For some reason that pleased her and she smiled.

Paul looked out at the train that was rolling noisily into the station. "Wish you hadn't done that."

"Done what?"

"Smile. Those big, green eyes of yours that I can't seem to forget now have some mighty fierce competition."

Claire had nothing to say to that. "Do *you* believe in God?"

"Oh, yeah. I was steeped in it growing up as a kid. Didn't have much choice. Sunday mornings, Sunday nights, Wednesday evenings ... Tried to escape it once I turned into a young adult. Wasted a lot of time rebelling and arguing and denying and challenging." He gave her a soft smile. "Remember, I'm the spoiled baby of the family. There was a lot of eye rolling and 'What did you expect?' from my brothers and sisters. I know I worried my parents something fierce." He looked off into the distance, suddenly profoundly sad. "I still do."

He chuckled softly. "I wised up some once I came to a vague level of maturity, but it took a long time." The sadness was there again. "I hurt a lot of people in the process. But wising up had nothing to do with what my family or church friends said." He thought for a minute, obviously remembering something in particular and then nodded. "Yeah, I'm definitely better off now than then."

Claire was fantastically curious. "If it wasn't your family or friends that made you change your mind, what was it?"

He scratched his chin covered with a shadow of salt and pepper stubble. "Oh, it was God. Sorry I wasn't clear about that. I'm not sure I can put it into words, Claire. During those years when I tried to escape it all, I felt so ... 'lost', I guess is the best word. Alone. Frightened.

Undefended. Yeah, undefended is good! I refused to go to church, declined invitations to parties that had church people in attendance who knew me ... I worked *really hard* to keep myself separate from that part of my past. I threw myself into establishing new friendships, new interests. Filled in all the God spots with other things: sports, work, women." He grinned a wolfish smile that somehow seemed a bit embarrassed. "Not necessarily in that order, mind you.

"Then my grandfather died. My dad's dad. I was very close to him as a kid. He'd kind of taken a special extra interest in me when I was a child, probably because I was the youngest and always crying because I'd been left out of something the big kids were doing. He was always my partner in games, he'd pick me first if we were having a family softball game, he'd let me sit on his lap in his big easy chair and read me the comics. I always used to sit next to him in church. *Always.*

"I couldn't avoid going to church for his funeral. So there I sat, in the last row of the church, looking at my grandfather's coffin, grieving, and," he looked at her with a sheepish expression, "this is probably going to sound so lame to you," he looked out at the night, "I sat there in the back of that packed church listening to the minister speak about my grandfather, hearing the hymns, even smelling the familiar smells, and I felt *like I was home.*

"I didn't feel lost, alone, frightened, or undefended. I felt like I had come home." He took a deep breath and looked at her. "I don't really expect you to get it, so don't worry if you don't. It's okay. I've been attending church ever since. I've still got an ocean full of regrets. There are things in my past – decisions I made – that still ... overwhelm me. My life isn't easier, it's just calmer, more peaceful. Even when everything appears to be in chaos, I still have a place to hang onto. When you look at the world with the attitude that God is in charge of it all, it kind of takes a little of the pressure off."

"Is that what you meant that day when you said you didn't believe in coincidence?"

He seemed thrilled that she'd remembered him saying that. "Hey, cool. You remembered that, huh?" He nodded. "Yeah, I don't believe anything happens by chance. I believe everything, good and bad, can work towards God's purpose if you have the right attitude. Sometimes you need a good wake up call so God can get your attention. My grandfather's death was one of the saddest things I've had to experience so far in my life. But you know what? I'm closer to God than I've ever been in my life. Who knows where I'd be if I hadn't had to go to my grandfather's funeral? The good things I've got going on in my life right now I can trace back to that time of great sorrow. It makes the pain a bit less. I know my grandfather would be happy to have me back at church, back on track.

"Hey, do you know what he left me in his will?" He smiled and looked down at his hands. "No, of course you don't. He left me all the notes and pictures I'd written and drawn him on church bulletins that he'd saved over the years from our times together in church. Funny things like me writing, *If I sit quiet for the rest of church will you buy me an ice cream?* as well as serious stuff like, *I love you the best of everyone Grandpa.*" Paul looked out at the moon. "There's one where I had drawn a picture of me and my grandfather in heaven playing softball." There were a few moments of silence. "Each one of the notes or pictures was carefully dated. Sometimes he wrote little explanatory notes on the history behind the note or picture. They're a real treasure for me. He also left me his Bible. It's pretty worn and you can't really use it much anymore because it's in such bad shape. Sometimes, I take it out and look at it. It's full of notations and special underlined verses. When I look at it, I feel close to him. He left each of us a pretty big chunk of money, but none of my brothers or sisters got anything like those pictures, the Bible, and the saved notes." He laughed. "My sister, Janet, would say that that last comment is an example of how spoiled and selfish I still am."

"You still miss him."

"Oh yeah. Big time. He's been dead a little over two years. There are still days when I think I should call him or stop by." He turned and seemed to be trying to make himself more comfortable on the hard bench. He stretched his arm across the back. "Claire, you know how you told me that you don't date?"

She was immediately suspicious. Her entire body tightened up in a defensive posture. "Yes ..."

"Well, I was wondering if I could ask Tyler out on a date instead." He said this with absolute seriousness, looking directly into her eyes and at that moment she learned something very important about him. She should never, *ever* play poker with him. She decided to play along.

She shook her head. "No, absolutely not. He's too young to date. Jeeze, Paul, he's only seven!" Claire worked to sound firm and unyielding.

"Please? I've got tickets to this Saturday's minor league baseball game. You have to have heard of the new stadium they've just finished building. I promise I'll have him home at a decent hour." He smiled then. A sly smile that gave her a glimpse of the charming ladies man he could be. He started to reach out and touch her arm, but she visibly tensed and he stopped himself.

Claire saw indecision in his eyes, uncertainty as to how to proceed and how far to tease her. She felt an overwhelming sadness settle over her that this kind man - and he *was* a kind man, she was as certain of that as she was of the knowledge that she was a screw-up - felt that he had to be so hesitant and cautious with her. She was so tired of being brittle and tense, always on guard, always in charge. When was the last time she had had some fun? Even these brief few encounters with Paul were clouded with her powerful suspicions and insecurities. An overwhelming desire to cry overtook her and she closed her eyes. "What do you want from me, Paul?" she whispered at last.

He touched her then. His hand was warm and callused as he settled it on her bare forearm and she willed herself to not draw away. Claire sensed instinctively that he knew what a big deal it was that she allowed him this. "Nothing you can't give, Claire. Honest," she heard him say softly. "Nothing complicated. I guess I'd just like to be your friend. Something tells me that just like you've never dated, I don't think you've ever had a real friend. I'd like to be that." Paul sighed. "I'd like to tell you I have no hidden agenda, but I promised you I'd be honest so I can't say that. I like you. I'd like to eventually date you and not just your son." She suppressed a smile as he looked at her pointedly. "Now, don't go asking me why again, Claire. You'll just have to settle for the fact that I do. I've had a different feeling about you from the moment you looked at me through the windshield of that wreck you call a car. I can't explain it to myself, let alone you." He squeezed her arm reassuringly and stood. "I should go. It's getting late and I know your day starts early."

Claire took a deep breath. "I'd allow Tyler to go out on a date with you, but only with a chaperone."

He grinned at her and crossed his arm over his chest trying not to look smug. "Now why didn't I think of that?"

"Do you have a third ticket?"

"I just might."

"I'm not sure, but I think Mrs. Santiago would be willing to go."

Paul leaned forward all trace of humor gone from his face. But wonder of all wonders she realized with a start that she wasn't afraid. At all. "You better be kidding me, Green Eyes," he said.

"Everyone who knows me knows I never kid."

"Yeah, just like you don't date."

"The game's at 1:00. I'll pick Tyler *and his chaperone* up at about 12:15. Don't feed him. Part of the fun is getting sick on all the crap you eat while you're watching the game. And have him wear a hat and sunscreen. You can get pretty crispy sitting there for three hours."

Paul started to walk down the steps, and then half way down turned and came back up. "I forgot. You said I could have your phone number. I'm afraid if I don't take it now, you may change your mind."

She rolled her eyes. "It's in the phone book, Paul. I couldn't afford to pay for it to be unlisted."

"So you're telling me it's okay to look it up and call you? To talk with Tyler and stuff, of course," he added hastily.

"Yeah, it's okay."

"Mine's in the book, too. And it's spelled just like it sounds - *William - son*." He leaned towards her. "But *you* don't have *my* permission to look it up. I'm not that easy." With that, he whistled his way down the steps.

Somewhere inside of me is a someone who longs to be ...[11]

Eight: Establish Safe Boundaries And Never Compromise Them

Claire played the conversation with Paul over and over in her head as she got ready for bed. Of all the things he said to her, what he'd said about church, *I felt like I was home*, was the most powerful. As he'd spoken she'd remembered that exact feeling while sitting on the bench at Riverside Church.

Never in her whole life had she felt the absence of God in her life. The brutal truth was she was simply too busy trying to live. As far back as she could remember there had always been fear. If she was placed in a relatively nice foster home, there was fear that she'd have to leave. And if she was placed, as was more often the case, in a ... difficult ... foster home, there was fear that she'd never get out.

How many times had she sat with a case worker and a foster family listening to them discuss her like she was some annoying piece of furniture that was too big to be stored anywhere? The demanding work of listening, learning, and adapting *fast* was so all consuming in the initial days of a new placement that sometimes she was afraid to sleep for fear she'd get that

---

[11] "Just a Breath", Francesca Battistelli, Just a Breath, 2004

wrong, too.   Then was the inevitable discovery of the reality of her situation. She had learned very quickly that no one wanted to hear her real thoughts, they just wanted to be told what they wanted to hear.

Yes, I like broccoli.

No, my shoes aren't tight.

It's okay. I didn't want to play with it anyway.

No, I'm not hungry.

No, I'm not scared ...

No, I'm not upset ...

No, I'm not going to cry ...

She got caught up in the memories and began to drown in the well of emotions that surfaced as a result. Standing, looking out the window of her locked back door, she could still hear the voices, smell the smells, feel the knot of tension in her stomach ...

"Claire, c'mon and sit down with me and the guys and watch the game!"

"I'm supposed to do the dishes."

"Aww, screw the dishes! Come have some fun! You never have any fun. Here, sit between me and Joe. Joe! Pop her open a beer!"

"I don't drink."

"Hell, there's always a first time! Loosen up, girl! WHOA! Mark! Did you see that pass? What was it? About sixty yards or what? Drink up, Claire."

"I should go, Joel, your mother won't be happy if the kitchen isn't cleaned up. You know it's my job."

"Claire, relax. She won't be home for hours. She went to some artsy-fartsy movie at some theater an hour's drive from here. Said she wouldn't be back until after 11. You've got plenty of time to sit here with us guys, enjoy the game, have a few beers, and then still get your precious dishes done."

"You got a boyfriend, Claire?"

"N-no, Mrs. Burbank says I'm too young to date."

"Nah, that's not what Mom said, Claire. Mom said she didn't want to go through the hassle of dealing with you and strange boys, Claire. You're sixteen. You're old enough to date. Just not strange boys. Don't you agree, guys?"

"Hey, Claire. Sweet sixteen. Have you been kissed? I'll help you if you want to practice."

"Whoa, Claire! You finished that beer already? Whoa! Pass her another one, Joe."

"Here's your beer, Claire. Give me a nice kiss thank you ..."

"My turn!"

"My turn!"

Damn! She'd opened up the thought door. Close it. *Close it.* No, she'd never had time to think about God. She was too busy trying to survive ...

Changed into her sweat suit, curled up in bed, she pushed aside the bad memories and even the anticipation of Saturday's potential fun with Paul. She needed a place to live. She had just four weeks, the end of next month, before she had to move out. Where was she going to go? *Where?*

Tomorrow she'd buy the paper that served the entire state, not just their local area. She'd have to look at apartments that were farther than she wanted to travel. Claire began to realize that she might have to seriously consider moving a distance that would mean she would also be looking for a new job. She didn't want Tyler to have to go to a new school. She fell asleep with the same feelings she used to have as a child when all her things were packed and she knew she was going to a new home the next day. She felt alone, lost, frightened, ... *undefended.* The nightmares started as soon as she was asleep.

Claire knew, because Tyler now felt comfortable talking about him, that Paul had come on Wednesday - *as promised* - to play basketball behind the diner. To say that Tyler was excited about his 'date' on Saturday was like saying Christmas was just another holiday. He talked incessantly about it to her, to anyone at the diner who had the time to listen, and apparently to his friends at school.

"My friend at school, Antwon, says that the Generals," (Claire learned that the Generals was the name of the semipro baseball team they were going to see) "had an almost undefeated record last year, Mom!" he said on the way to the diner Thursday after school. "He also said that if you go early, sometimes you can get the players *autographs!*"

Claire made the appropriate responses as Tyler continued to spout off interesting tidbits about the game, the stadium, and even the available food. "Paul says they have foot long hot-dogs that you can put chili and onions on. He says he can eat *three!*"

"At one sitting?! That's disgusting!"

"I think it's amazing. I'm going to try to eat at least two."

She had a wave of panic. How was she going to pay for that? Wasn't food notoriously expensive at those places? All of a sudden, the prospect of attending the game came into crystal clear focus. The reality was that she couldn't afford one, single thing outside of her budget.

She worried about Saturday throughout the remainder of her shift. Finally, she decided that she had to call Paul. She had to tell him that she'd rethought things and decided it was not a wise idea.

Tyler would never forgive her.

Sitting in her living room at 9:30 p.m. she stared at the telephone as if it was an evil mechanism that could destroy her world. "Get a grip," she said aloud to herself and then picked up the phone and dialed.

"Yo!"

"Hello? Is Paul there?"

"Yeah, sure, who's calling?"

"Claire."

"*Claire? Really?!* Just a minute!" She heard the sounds of a hand covering the receiver and indistinguishable shouting.

"Hello?" It was Paul's voice, but it had a heavy tone of suspicion.

"Hi, Paul, it's Claire."

"It really is you! Mike said it was you, but I didn't believe him."

"Why wouldn't you believe it was me?"

"Well, for one, *it's you.* I just can't believe you're calling me. Second, Mike is a big tease-" She heard 'I am not!' shouted loudly in the background. "Hang on a minute, Claire." She heard Paul say, "I'm going to have a *private* conversation," and then heard whistling and cat calls in the background. After a few moments she heard him say, "Okay, I'm back."

"Am I interrupting something?"

"No, not at all. Thursday evenings I play on a softball team. Usually, since I'm the only one with a house, we all end up coming back here to have pizza or something."

"Oh." Thursday evenings she usually did laundry at the Laundromat right next door.

"What's up? Is everything okay?"

"Actually, I'm calling because we're going to have to cancel Saturday."

"Oh." His disappointment poured out of the phone with that one word. "Why, do you have to work?"

She could lie. It would be the easiest thing. But she'd liked his honesty with her. It made her feel solid, stable. She'd give it back to him. "No, I don't have to work."

"Talk to me, Claire. I'm looking forward to this, Tyler's looking forward to this ... Tyler tells me you're going to chaperone," she heard him chuckle, "Why are you canceling? Tell me the truth."

"I, I can't afford to go."

"What, you planning on buying a ball gown and hiring a limo or something?"

"No, it's just all the snacks and the drinks ... I'm on a really tight budget and I can't even buy a stupid soda, Paul. I've got zero to work with."

"Claire, *I* invited Tyler and you. You don't even have to bring your purse."

"I don't take charity, Paul."

She could almost hear the wheels in his mind turning through the phone. "Okay, how about this? I show you guys a fun time this Saturday - *my choice of how I do it* - and next Saturday, Tyler will have to show me a fun time. Payback. Even-Steven. Fair is fair. No charity, everything's up and above board. You can even keep a financial tally on Saturday if you want." He was quiet for a moment. "Ow, this is *not* the best location for a phone call."

"Where are you?"

"In the broom closet and I've got something sticking in my back ..." she heard shifting and thumping, "Ow! OW!" and then more sounds. "That's better. It was one of those pipes that hooks onto the vacuum cleaner."

"Why are you in the broom closet?"

"I've got a house full of nosy busybodies, that's why Claire. You think women are bad." When she didn't say anything, he said quietly, "Tell me you're still coming to the game, Claire. I've been looking forward to it all week." She could hear tension in his voice.

"I've just realized that if I agree to this, you've somehow managed to get a second date out of ... Tyler."

She could feel him relaxing over the phone. He chuckled. "I told you, I'm no dummy."

Tyler was awake and *finished with his bowl of cereal* by 6:30 a.m. on Saturday. Lying in bed, trying to sleep as she listened to him munch his bowl of toasted oats (they could never afford real Cheerios), Claire groaned and pulled the pillow over her head. But in the end, the early start helped her get the food shopping done before Paul was due to arrive.

She tried to get Tyler to eat a bologna sandwich before they left. "Are you nuts, Mom?! I've got to save room for the hot dogs! Remember?"

"Tyler, don't be asking Paul to buy you a whole bunch of stuff, okay? It wouldn't be polite, and food and drinks at this sort of thing tend to be real expensive."

"Okay, Mom."

Claire felt as though she'd just murdered his pet dog. She pulled him into a tight embrace and kissed the top of his head. Not missing a beat, he ducked his head and wiped it against her arm. For as long as she could remember, whenever she kissed him he automatically wiped it off. They had a running joke that if she could keep him from wiping it off before she counted to ten then it was 'stuck'. She rarely got to ten. "We can still have a good time, Buddy! Just take it easy, okay? Remember that we are Paul's guests and we shouldn't take advantage."

"Yeah, okay, Mom."

She sighed and felt awful. Only she ate a bologna sandwich. Tyler said he wasn't hungry.

Paul was prompt. Tyler was already waiting on the card store roof near the benches by the time he arrived,. "He's here, Mom!! *He's here!!*" He was wearing his treasured Yankee baseball cap that she'd found at a garage sale. "Come on! Hurry up! Here we come, Paul! We'll be right down! Mom! *MOM!!*"

"I'm coming! I'm coming."

Paul drove a beautiful, bright red pick up truck. Not necessarily brand new, it was shiny and clean, inside and out. Tyler sat between them.

Paul was wearing a Yankees cap like Tyler's and Claire wondered if they had planned it. He was wearing shorts and a tee shirt and she was so used to seeing him in his work uniform that she caught herself looking at his big, hairy legs. He caught her and grinned. "Like what you see?"

She chose not to answer, and worked on making sure she and Tyler's seatbelts were hooked properly.

"Where's your hat, Claire? It's a long afternoon in the sun."

"I must have forgotten ..." she said, unwilling to admit that she didn't have one.

Tyler had no such problem. "She doesn't have a hat. I told her I'd share my Yankee cap with her but she said 'no'."

I'm not a child ... "I've got sunscreen on, Paul. I'm not much of a hat person, anyway," she said as he continued to stare at her.

It was a glorious afternoon. The sun shone, but there was a breeze so it was never too hot. They ate and ate and ate. There were taco chips and foot long hot dogs, pizza and ice cream, soda and cotton candy. Tyler never asked for a thing, it just kept appearing in twos or threes. Whatever Paul wanted, he got multiples and shared. Just once she tried to turn down something, saying that she'd already eaten lunch. "Throw it out then," Paul had said to her with a bit of a challenge in his expression.

She was lost in the rules and flow of the game at first, but Tyler had done his research and had extensive wisdom to impart on her. Periodically he'd say, "Is that right, Paul?" and get an answer one way or the other.

At the bottom of the third - she was really catching on to baseball lingo - Paul gave her a pointed look and said, "I'll be right back." Thinking he was going to get more food - and hoping sincerely that he wouldn't bring anything back for her because she was truly stuffed - she returned to watching Neil Patrick Armstrong hit a triple into left field bringing in two

RBIs ('runs batted in' Claire had learned) and tying up the score. She and Tyler were on their feet screaming when suddenly a hat was unceremoniously clapped on the top of her head. Amidst the roar of the fans she turned to see Paul's smiling face. He adjusted the cap and tucked her hair behind her ears. He leaned over and spoke loudly but carefully in her ear, "You look cute." She opened her mouth to decline the gift and found one big finger - smelling strongly of ketchup - placed on her lips. Still leaning over he said, "Put it on my tab."

Tyler drew Paul's attention away as he launched into a vivid description of the play that Paul had just missed. She settled back down into her seat, and as Tyler finished his narrative he caught a glimpse of Claire and did a double take. "Hey, Mom! Good hat!" he said with a huge grin.

They were all seated for only a few moments when they jumped to their feet again shouting encouragement for another great play that put the Generals in the lead. She caught Paul looking at her as she jumped and cheered. She smiled and tentatively touched his arm. "Thanks for the hat," she shouted.

He reached over, adjusted it a bit and examined her critically. "We've got to work on the brim. It needs to be curved properly," he shouted back. Claire had no idea what he was talking about. Paul reached down and took the hand that was still resting on his arm and carefully placed it in the palm of his big hand. As the crowd roared again, Paul turned to shout and cheer with Tyler, but he never let go of her hand. Twice she tried to pull her hand free and his grip tightened. Although he appeared totally absorbed in the game, laughing and talking and responding to Tyler, his actions made it clear that her hand in his was not an afterthought or a simple reflex.

Tyler fell asleep on the short drive home. She turned slightly and put her arm around him as he nestled against her, took off his hat, and stroked his sweat-dampened hair. "He never cuddles like this when he's awake. *Never.*" Paul smiled at her. "Paul, thanks for today. I don't know if you'll believe this, but I don't think Tyler and I have ever had as much fun." She looked out the front window as they whizzed through the traffic. "It's been such a long time since we've been able to just take a day and play. I'll never be able to put it into the proper words."

Paul stopped at a traffic light and looked at Claire intently. They both looked down at Tyler sleeping so soundly between them. He had a smear of ketchup underneath his ear which Claire reached up and gently tried to rub away. Before Paul could say anything, Tyler sighed and smiled in his sleep. Claire's eyes met Paul's. "What is it they say? A picture is worth a thousand words?" he said to her. As the light turned green and Paul stepped on the gas, he glanced at Claire. "I'm pretty sure I get it, Claire."

As Claire walked a very sleepy Tyler to the back stairs of their apartment, Paul called out and she turned. "Just in case you're wondering, Green Eyes," he said with a twinkle in his eye, "this was your *first official date*." He drove away before she could answer.

Monday morning, after the breakfast rush but when things hadn't still officially slowed down enough for Claire to take a much needed break, Daniel Alvarez walked into the diner and took a seat at the counter. She watched him order a coffee and a Danish, her stomach knotted with anxiety.

Was it just a coincidence or had he received another report? Was it a good or bad thing that he was here? Should she approach him on her own or try to ignore him? Finally, circumstances forced the issue. One of her customers asked for a Danish and Daniel was sitting by the fresh baked goods bin. "Hey, Mr. Alvarez."

"Good morning, Claire. Won't you call me Daniel? I think we're about the same age, you know. You make me feel old and decrepit with the 'Mr. Alvarez' stuff." He gave her a kind smile.

"Okay. Do you need anything?"

He shook his head. "Nah, but will you be having a break soon? I'd like to talk with you." He looked at her earnestly. "There is no emergency. It's just one of those follow up visits I told you about. If this is a bad time, you can tell me to come back and that's absolutely fine. I thought, since you work such long hours here, it might be more convenient for us to talk here than trying to set something up at your apartment."

"No, I can talk. I have two more tables and then it usually slows down for a bit before the lunch rush. Can you wait? Are you in a rush?"

"I'll just whip out my computer and some paperwork. You take all the time you need, Claire."

He was a nice guy, even if he had the power to take Tyler away from her if she screwed up again, she thought grimly to herself. At the coffee station, Maddy appeared by her side. "Claire, I know you want me to mind my own business, and last time I didn't you bit my head off, but there's a guy at the counter wearing a DYFS ID badge." She hesitated, seeming to gather up the courage to jump into an icy pond and then plunged right in. "Are you okay?"

Claire studied Maddy's face, and for the first time felt some remorse for how she had behaved the last time that they had talked. Maddy's expression showed sincere concern and a desire to help. Should she believe her? Could she believe her? What was it Paul had asked her? *Who do you have, Claire?* The wave of longing that swept through her, to have someone to look to whom she could trust, was so profound that she wanted to throw back her head and howl. Instead, she closed her eyes and took a deep, cleansing breath.

Claire looked down at the three coffee cups she was filling. "Yeah, I'm okay. He says he just wants to talk when I get a moment. I think it's okay."

"You want me to sit with you and keep you company?"

Claire blinked. "Aren't you afraid I'll bite your head off again?"

Maddy grinned at her. "Are you kidding? I've got a hellova thick skin, girl. You'd have to use a blowtorch to me for me to catch a hint."

It was a casual offer that meant just about the whole world, an offer that showed sincere care and concern. It came from one friend to another. A brave, feisty, outspoken, persistent friend. Claire decided to take her own plunge, although she had no idea if she would survive the jump.

Claire gave a small smile and took a deep breath. "I think I'll take the offer of friendship, but skip the offer of company when I sit down with Daniel Alvarez."

Maddy stared at her for a brief moment and then nodded as though a huge understanding had just been struck. "It's a deal," she said, and walked away juggling four cups of coffee without spilling a drop.

"How's it going, Claire?" Daniel asked when she finally joined him at the counter with her usual cup of tea and a bagel sandwich.

Claire told him about Tyler's improved attitude and the deal she had with Mrs. Santiago regarding baby-sitting and food shopping.

Daniel smiled and nodded as she talked. "Have you called any of the agencies I told you about?"

"Are we speaking on or off the record?"

He smiled. "I guess that will depend on which way the conversation goes."

"Well ... I called that church."

"Nothing else?"

"I told you, Mr. Alvarez ... er, Daniel, I don't like to take charity."

"You know you would be eligible for food stamps and even rental assistance if you applied."

She was silent.

"Janice Strocco told me you declined the Sonrise House opportunity."

She was silent again.

"The committee meets this Thursday, Claire, to discuss potential candidates. Everyone has someone they'd like to bring forward for consideration." He looked at her pointedly. "Everyone but me."

Claire studied her hands, took a bite of her sandwich, and sipped her tea. Still she was silent.

"Janice told me that you weren't happy with the idea of living with someone. But she thought that she really had convinced you that the Sonrise House is *not* a charity endeavor. She told me she told you that she wouldn't take 'no' for an answer from you, and asked you to think about the idea. She also said she told you she'd pray that the Lord would give you a clear sign one way or the other as to how you should decide. Have you been considering this opportunity?"

Claire thought of the letter she'd gotten telling her she had six weeks to vacate the premises. That couldn't be what Janice had meant, could it? Did God send eviction notices? No, of course not. She sighed. "Ms. Strocco was very nice to me. She gave me a tour of the house and the church and we talked for a long time ... But no, I haven't thought about moving into Sonrise House with Tyler."

"You're going to turn down this opportunity simply because you'd have to live with someone?"

"It's difficult for me to explain, but yes, it is as simple as it sounds. You're all expecting me to move in to a house with *a stranger*. Actually, it's bigger than that. It's not just me, it's Tyler, too. We'd have to live with *a stranger* and *her kids*. I've done that my whole life, Mr. Alvarez - Daniel, and it's been a major disaster. I just can't do it anymore."

"You could give it a try. You've made me think about an aspect of Sonrise House that, up until now we hadn't seriously considered. We, with our narrow view, thought that the women and their children would be thrilled at the opportunity, and be delighted about moving in together."

Claire looked at Daniel. "Are you making a joke, ... Daniel?"

To his credit he laughed. Out loud. "It does sound pretty ridiculous, doesn't it? The image of the women disagreeing and the kids fighting like cats and dogs seems highly more probable." He looked down at his empty coffee cup, and when she got up to refill it he smiled his thanks. "Do you have any suggestions for how we could overcome this problem?"

Claire thought. "Well, I don't know exactly what kinds of questions your committee is going to ask the women you're considering, but I think some of the questions should be how they handle conflict, what type of temperaments they think they have, what rules of discipline they have for their kids ... Maybe you should even sit down and talk with the children, too." Claire took another sip of her tea. "And I think the ladies and the kids you finally consider for the house should meet each other with the committee and on their own before the final choice is made by *anyone*." She rolled her eyes. "Let's face it. If the ladies have trouble talking to each other and the kids start fighting the first few moments they're together, that should give you a pretty good idea of if they'll be able to live together in the same house, right?"

Daniel grinned at her. "If we did all those things, would you agree to meet with the committee to be considered for one of the spots?"

Claire chose to ignore his question. "I thought of something, Daniel, after you visited me the other day. Actually, it came up after I spoke with Ms. Strocco." She looked at Daniel. "Hey, should I call her Reverend or Father or Minister or something?"

He smiled at her. "You should call her Janice."

Claire looked at him as though he was making another poor joke.

"What did you think of, Claire?" Daniel asked quietly.

"Well, ... Ms. Strocco explained to me how each of the committee members was allowed to bring forward only one person for the committee to consider. She said, since you'd given me her phone number and told me to call, that you had obviously decided to sponsor me." Claire turned and looked into Daniel's eyes. "*Why me*, Mr. Alvarez?"

Daniel nodded as if approving of her question. "Oh, that's an easy one to answer, but before I do, I want you to promise that you will absolutely believe the reason I give you. No arguments or denials. You'll simply trust my judgment, no questions asked. Can you do that, Claire?"

Never one to make hasty commitments, Claire thought for a moment or two. "Okay," she finally said, "I promise."

"I'm the chairman of the Sonrise House Committee, did Janice tell you that?" Claire nodded. "And this mission, is the single most important mission the church has undertaken, since Sonset House, our house for seniors, was conceived over fifty years ago. It's very, very important to the church that this new mission has as much a success as Sonset House has had. Do you know that Sonset House has been duplicated by over fifteen different churches since its inception?" Claire shook her head. "We've had committees come from as far as Michigan to observe the facility and speak with those in charge so that they could continue to grow and expand upon our initial concept. It's been a powerful testament of God's love and faithfulness toward a program He deems worthy."

Daniel finished his second cup of coffee and shook his head 'no' when she went to get up to refill it. He looked at her intently. "Claire, I want Sonrise House to be celebrating its fiftieth anniversary someday and I want it to have as powerful and as productive a legacy as Sonset House." In his enthusiasm, he reached over and took her hand and squeezed it. She tried not to tense or draw away. "I want it to succeed. The reason I chose to sponsor you, Claire, is that I feel that with you and your son as our first residents, *it will succeed.*"

Claire opened her mouth to argue, then remembered her promise and closed it. Daniel smiled at her. "I know you've had a hard time of it, Claire. But you're an adult now. You have proven to yourself and to many others that you are determined, strong, and independent. However, *it's time to start trusting again.* I'm not telling you to practice blind obedience or to embrace gullibility. I'm telling you to use the wisdom and street smarts you've acquired from a difficult life and *let somebody else in.*"

Claire felt a thousand years older and wiser than this man. "I'm an adult who has never had a life, Daniel. I've never really played or wasted an afternoon doing ... nothing. I've never been on a date or gone on a vacation. I've never had a girlfriend ... or a mother or a father for that matter. People look at me and assume things about me that aren't true. I'm simply surviving, not really living." She stood up, because twice she had caught Dan giving her the eye and she knew she had to get back to work. "I'm not telling you this to get your sympathy. I'm telling you this so you understand the type of person I really am. I don't know why you think I'm the one that will make your Sonrise House a success. I really don't."

Daniel began packing his computer and gathering up his papers. "Claire, I'm going to say this as plainly as I can. I operate my life by prayer and the Lord's guidance. And you're right. I don't know a whole lot about you. *But God does.*" He zipped up his computer case and looked her right in the eye. "And *God's* told me that you're the one I should champion for the Sonrise House. I'm only doing what I'm told."

She watched him walk to the front door of the diner and he turned around. "I've got you scheduled for this Thursday evening at 9:30 p.m. with the committee. We'll wait until 9:45 and then just go home a bit early if you don't show. Think about it, Claire. *Make a good choice.*"

By Wednesday she had visited three more apartments that were in her price range, and every one of them was unacceptable for more reasons than she had time to list. In addition, all of them were too far for her to keep her job at the diner and still manage Tyler as she did now. Going to check on Tyler when she had a few moments after the main dinner rush, all she saw was an empty table with his backpack wedged in the corner of the booth. She told Dan she was taking a break, grabbed three big cookies, and wandered out back.

"Pass it, Ty! Here! I'm open, guy!! *I'm open!*" Paul was drenched in sweat, dodging around Marcus, with his hands high up in the air waiting for a pass. Tyler, tongue stuck in the corner of his mouth - a sure sign of extreme concentration - shot the basketball across to Paul, who tossed it into the basket successfully. Her son and Paul let out screams of triumph. There were high fives all around as Marcus and Luis exchanged good-natured insults back and forth, smiled at Claire, and then wandered back into the diner.

"Mom! Did you see that play? We won by just two points!"

"Congratulations."

"Hey, Claire. How are you today?"

"Hi, Paul." She held up the plate of cookies. "I brought you guys a treat."

"Gee, thanks, Mom. I ate all my peas."

Claire ruffled the hair on the top of his sweaty head. "Good for you, kiddo."

"I'm going to run and get us both drinks, Mom. I do that after our games," Tyler said, and then disappeared into the diner.

She gestured to the basketball in Paul's hands. "I have to thank you for this. I think this is the best part of his day."

Paul grinned at her. "I have a good time, too. Today's even better than usual."

"Why's that?"

He took a huge bite out of a cookie and looked at her funny. "'Cause I don't usually get to see you, too." When she blushed he looked delighted. He popped the rest of the cookie in his mouth. "I'm going to go home now to get cleaned up and eat some dinner." A trickle of sweat rolled down the side of his face, and he ducked his head down to swipe it away on the shoulder of his tee shirt. "I don't think I'll bother with a shower, though. I don't think I need one today." She shook her head at his teasing, but smiled.

It's time to start trusting again.

Claire studied her fingernails. "I might be sitting on my porch tonight. Sure wish I had someone to talk to."

Paul looked at her for so long that she got uncomfortable. "Ask me to stop by Claire," he said quietly, "and I will."

It took an unbelievable amount of courage. "If I bring home some pie from the diner, will you come over and sit on the porch and talk with me?"

At that moment, Tyler came rushing out with two tall glasses of water, and Paul took the time to drain the entire glass in a series of huge gulps. He swiped the back of his hand along his mouth and then fished out an ice cube with his hand and rubbed it across the back of his neck. "Ahhhh," he said with pure delight. "Thanks, Ty." He handed back the empty glass, and then quick as a flash slipped the ice cube down the back of Tyler's shirt. Tyler yelped, but looked delighted. "I'm going, kid. Good game."

Paul hadn't answered her and she didn't know what to say or do, so she stood there like an indecisive ... idiot. Paul picked up his battered baseball hat and clapped it on his head, bounced the basketball a few times, and then, finally, looked at Claire and gave her a sweet smile. "I'll see you later, Claire, whether you've got day old pie to offer me or not, okay?"

She smiled back, relieved. "Okay."

Later that night they sat on the porch eating cherry pie. Claire told Paul about Sonrise House, Daniel Alvarez, and Janice Strocco. She even mentioned Maddy. She asked him his opinion about whether he thought it was charity, and he said who cared if it was? It sounded like an excellent opportunity to him. Furthermore, he pointed out what a tremendous compliment it was that Daniel Alvarez had not only chosen to sponsor her, but sought her out a second time to try to convince her to accept his offer. "Do you realize how many women he must encounter over the course of his job, and yet he chose *you* to go out on a limb for?"

"What do you mean 'out on a limb'?" she asked.

"Claire, he's a *government employee*. He can't go around talking about God and pushing his church agenda with people he's dealing with in the course of his job! He could get fired! *I'm not kidding*. It's just like teachers who can't have their students pray in class or tell the biblical story of Christmas to their students."

"Oh."

"You're going to meet with the committee, aren't you Claire?"

She was silent as he studied her in the moonlight. "You know it's not a charity." She nodded hesitantly. "It sounds like, even though you'd have to live with strangers they're going to make an effort to match you up so that you have at least a chance to get along. You are not alone in this, Claire. There's a whole committee of people behind you." She nodded again. "*What have you got to loose, Claire?*"

Her voice was anguished. "Aren't I a failure if I can't support Tyler and me on my own?" She leaned forward and pushed the heels of her hands into her eyes to keep the tears in.

She felt his big hand on the back of her head and she tensed. He leaned over close enough that she felt the heat of his body next to hers and smelled his subtle after-shave. "No. You're a tired warrior who's made it this far on your own without anyone," he whispered quietly in her ear. He stroked her hair, once, twice, and then withdrew his hand.

After a time he said, "There's something a lot bigger you've got to deal with than this meeting tomorrow night."

Claire sniffed and finally looked up at him. "What's that?"

"You've got a huge tab with me that you're going to have to even out on Saturday. Have you begun to make plans?"

She appreciated his teasing. It helped lighten the mood and got her out of the corner she'd somehow backed herself into. "You'll have to take that up with Tyler. Remember? He was the one that you had the date with. I was just the chaperone."

Paul had the look of a chess opponent who was just two moves away from checkmate. "Do I have your permission to take it up with him?"

She eyed him suspiciously. "Why do I feel I'm getting myself into something I'll regret?"

Paul stood up then, making motions to leave. "Can I make you a promise, Claire?"

She stood and walked with him slowly to the stairs. "All right."

"I promise you'll never regret trusting me. I won't let you down." He reached over and took her hand.

Claire looked down at her hand in his, illuminated by the various evening lights glowing around them. Then she looked up at him and sighed. "All of a sudden I have so many people I want to trust ... I've never had that before, Paul. Ever. There's you and Daniel Alvarez. Even Maddy at the diner. It's scary for me." She looked up at the moon. "And wonderful, too."

"Remember, Claire. I don't believe in coincidences."

Mrs. Santiago agreed to watch Tyler Thursday night so Claire could go to the meeting with the Sonrise House Committee. She agonized over whether she should bring a change of clothes, what they would ask her, how she should answer. Finally she decided to show up in her waitress uniform because her alternate clothes weren't much better. And as for the questions, well, she'd just be what she'd always been: honest and direct. It had never worked for her in the past, why should things change now?

They say that blood is thicker than water. Maybe that's why we battle our own with more energy and gusto than we would ever expend on strangers.[12]

★
★ ★ · ★
★   ·

Nine: Never Reveal What's In Your Heart

What was it about that woman? Paul wondered to himself. She was so down on her luck it wasn't funny, she was practically homeless, she was a single mother with a smart aleck kid that she could barely control, she had no prospects, and no hope in the future. Heck … she didn't even believe in God. *Because she'd never had the opportunity.* Who ever gave such a reason like that? Forty feet up in the truck's cherry picker, he pulled off his heavy duty rubber insulated gloves and tossed them to the floor of the basket. Finished with his work on the high voltage lines, he levered the controls that brought the basket down to ground level. His mind wandered, thinking about this woman who had come into his life. Claire. Claire Jenkins. Jeeze, he didn't even know if she had a middle name.

But he could not get her off his mind. Two days ago he'd held her hand at the ball game. Paul could not remember a time *forever* that he had been more content with himself and the world then those moments that he'd held Claire Jenkin's hand. What exactly was her appeal?

She claimed she didn't date so Paul had knocked himself out to

[12] David Assael, Northern Exposure, Family Feud, 1993

finally get the opportunity to spend a bit of free time with her ... by asking her son out. She was so private that aside from the mountains of mistrust she communicated by look, word, and deed he didn't have a clue about what made her tick. Paul shook his head in amazement remembering the look on her face at the ball game the few brief times she'd really let go and laughed, relaxed, and enjoyed herself. It had been like watching someone trying out skiing for the very first time: hesitant and certain it was going to end up badly. She was a completely isolated island separated from everyone and everything. God, that must be lonely...

Paul sighed. He could hear Simon saying, 'Something's going on big time there.' Did she appeal to him because she seemed so broken and desperate? He had never been the type to bring home wounded birds or adopt stray kittens. He preferred those who surrounded him to be ready, willing and able to keep up with him as he charged through life. That being said, Claire was definitely capable. She'd scraped out the bare existence she and the kid lived with absolutely no help from anyone. Maybe that's what drew her to him: her strength and persistence despite impossible odds? Or was it because she was such a mystery, an enigma? She was as closed about herself as a locked vault. And Paul was certain that there were few good memories locked away. Everyone had skeletons they kept hidden, even from themselves. No one bothered to lock away good memories.

You do, came his grandfather's voice.

"Yeah, but I'm an idiot," Paul said out loud to himself.

"You talking to yourself again, lover-boy?"

Paul looked down to see Mike's grinning face. "And what if I am?" Paul shouted good-naturedly. "At least I know I'm going to have intelligent conversation rather than the ... garbage ... I hear out of your mouth."

Mike pretended to look hurt. "Sexual frustration is making you nasty, Saint. When you gonna hook up with that little waitress of yours so you can relax a little?"

"Mind your own business." Paul grumbled. He always seemed to loose his sense of humor when the guys brought up Claire. "And for clarification, she's not 'mine'."

The guys were fascinated by her. Their obsession had gotten so bad that they were behaving like a bunch of gossipy, nosy old women. And he'd told them so to their faces. They'd gone so absolutely nuts the night Claire had called, he'd had to hide in the ... blasted ... broom closet to get a little bit of privacy! Each one in his own way tried to find out more about her. Joshua and Simon tried to get Paul to invite her and Tyler to one of the softball games they played regularly during the week. James and Maggie invited them over for dinner. Mike and Vince slipped into the more base level of curiosity that at one time had been Paul's most comfortable level as well.

It was his own fault, Paul supposed. For almost two years he'd avoided dating, and the guys had gotten used to him being alone. His love life was like a summer forest in the middle of a drought. Claire was the match. Heaven help him, but the situation showed every sign of getting worse instead of better, mostly because Paul refused to talk about her or bring her around, even though they all knew he was spending time with her. And Paul didn't even know if they were really dating or not!

How could he bring Claire around to meet the guys when he wasn't sure himself about their status? He'd like to call the baseball game a date, but he knew Claire wouldn't. Jeeze ... he didn't even feel comfortable calling her on the ... darn ... phone! He had never felt so inadequate and uncertain around a woman before in his entire life.

Paul sighed deeply. And he'd never felt so right. How could sitting on that stupid bench on a tarpaper roof be so pleasant? And yet it was. Better than pleasant. He felt peaceful and content. The more time he spent with Claire, the more time he wanted to spend with her.

"Wanna go for a b-, drink?" Mike asked after they'd stowed away the gear and the trucks were ready to roll.

It was Wednesday and he knew that Tyler would be waiting for him behind the diner. All the guys needed to find out was that he was spending more time with the kid than with Claire, and they'd probably start tailing him to get more information. Maybe, if things we're just right, he might catch a glimpse of her, or better yet, get a chance to say, 'hey'. "Sorry, bud, I've got stuff to do that I can't avoid. Plus I'm beat."

"Yeah, okay. See you at the game tomorrow."

The kid would be waiting for him, eager like a little puppy. Paul had decided that Tyler did everything fast. He ate fast, did his homework fast, talked fast, played fast. Heck … he even seemed to listen fast which Paul suspected was why he missed so much that was said to him. At first, Paul had to admit that he'd made overtures to the kid because getting even remotely close to his mother had been impossible. But Paul found he enjoyed Tyler's company. There was a lot of himself in the boy, which Paul found amazing given their completely different upbringing. But Paul saw in Tyler the same frantic desire to be just like everyone else that he had had as a child. Tyler wanted to blend in with the crowd and not stand out. Paul had wanted to keep up with everyone else and not be 'just the little brother'.

The problem was Tyler was so far behind in so many areas he couldn't help but be distinctive: he was blatantly poor, he was lacking any male influence in his life, his home life reeked with poverty, and Claire's work schedule made quality time and supervision almost nil. Tyler's desperation to fit in made him all the more obvious in a crowd. His passion to prove himself overrode common sense on too many occasions in Paul's opinion. An open book of information regarding himself and his mother, Paul wouldn't be surprised if he knew more about Claire's son than Claire did. But he couldn't fault her. She was doing the best she could in a bad situation. But that didn't stop Tyler's ride on the train to disaster.

Paul remembered his own desire to keep up, not cry, and not stand out as the baby in the overwhelming group of four older siblings. Sometimes, in the middle of a basketball game, Paul would see a determined expression on Tyler's face, and he felt as though he could read his mind. Consequently, the casual, ulterior-motive based relationship with the kid had turned into something much more important. However, given his tenuous relationship with Claire, Paul wasn't certain that this was necessarily a good thing or a bad thing. For Tyler or for him.

Driving to the All American, Paul viewed his life with something bordering disgust. His life was like one giant unconnected dot – to - dot puzzle. There was his family dot, his church dot, his work dot, his friendship dot, and now recently, the Tyler dot and the Claire dot. Everything was separate; nothing was joined. He wore different hats in

each area which were separate and distinct. It ... stunk. No, it sucked. He
didn't like living piecemeal. He wanted his life smooth, interwoven, and
solid. But joining all the parts together meant he had to allow information
to flow freely between them. Failures, fears, secrets, and sorrows. It was
safer to keep it all compartmentalized. Wasn't it?

Seems like you've got quite a job ahead of you, his grandfather's voice said.
When are you going to get started?

Tyler was waiting for him, grinning from ear to ear, already sweaty
from having 'warmed-up'. Raoul and Jose were standing on the back steps
smoking cigarettes. "You play for a bit, Mr. Paul?" Raoul asked.

No matter how many times he'd asked him to call him "Paul"
Raoul didn't. "Yeah, and I hope you guys ate your spinach or took your
vitamins, because me and Tyler are going to wipe you up off the ground
like wet rags."

The two young men laughed good-naturedly and the brief game
began, taking their entire fifteen-minute break. Once the guys went back to
work, he and Tyler had fun playing one-on-one, and that's when the talking
really started.

"Mom's still not found us a new place, Paul. Have you had any
luck?" Paul knew that Tyler was afraid to discuss this with Claire, not
wanting to upset her any more than she already was.

"Tyler, I've looked just about everywhere, but don't you worry, I'm
praying about it. It will work out." Paul felt a knot in his gut as he said the
comforting words. How did that Bible verse go? Something like if you had
faith as small in size as a mustard seed you could move mountains? What
did it say about his faith if he doubted his own simple words of comfort he
was saying to this boy?

"Yeah, I know you're praying. Mrs. Santiago's gotten both of us
Saint Christopher medals. He's the Patron Saint of ..." Tyler scrunched up
his face in concentration. "I can't remember. It's like the Patron Saint of
Desperation or something like that."

Paul chuckled. "I think it's the Patron Saint of Lost Causes."

"Yeah, maybe that's it. She's lighting all her prayer candles, too,
and when we go to mass on Sundays ..."

"You're going to mass on Sunday's with Mrs. Santiago?"

Tyler stopped dribbling the ball. "Oops. I don't think I was supposed to say that."

Paul studied his expression, willing himself to read the kid's thoughts. "Does your Mom know?"

"Nope. Mrs. Santiago baby-sits me on Sunday, but I don't think we've said anything about visiting the church and lighting candles and singing and stuff."

"Do you think your Mom will mind?"

Tyler thought for a moment. "Nah, I don't think so."

"You really should tell her. She might worry if she called you from the diner one Sunday and didn't get any answer. Don't you think?"

Tyler looked at him and sighed. "Yeah, I guess."

"Don't keep secrets from your Mom. It'll only cause trouble in the end, believe me."

Their basketball game resumed. "You get in trouble one time for keeping secrets?" Tyler asked after they each had turns shooting a few times.

"Oh, man, did I ever. Big time." As the game progressed they swapped stories and jokes. It was a nice, easy time and Paul found that it was a great way to unwind after a busy day in the truck. And if he got to see Claire, well, then it was even better. Turned out *this* Wednesday was even better than any other day so far. He'd gotten to see Claire briefly *and* he'd gotten her to extend an actual invitation to enjoy the evening with her on the porch bench … day old pie or not.

By the time their game was over, Paul and Tyler had made plans for the weekend. Not exactly what they had originally thought they were going to do, but Paul hoped everyone would have fun in the end. He just had to get Claire to go along with everything. How could he manage that? Paul hoped she wouldn't go ballistic when she found out what the two of them had decided.

Surprisingly, his brother, Brian, was waiting on him on his back porch when he rolled in, sweaty and tired from his basketball game with Tyler. Paul groaned inwardly at the unexpected intrusion. "Hey bro." He managed a tight smile as he climbed out of the truck.

"Hey Paul, coming from a workout?" Connie and Rachel were the oldest of the kids in the family. Connie was thirty-five and Rachel was thirty-two. Brian was the oldest brother at thirty. In reality, Paul was closer to him than Elliot, who was only one year younger than Brian. Brian always seemed to have had a bit more compassion for Paul during the growing up years. Elliot, cursed with the middle child syndrome and always battling the 'second to the youngest' label, had been perpetually brutal. Elliot's dogged determination to keep Paul in the 'youngest and least capable' category had cemented a lifetime of animosity between the two. Elliot had never been to Paul's house. Brian had at least been by a few times.

"Yeah, I play basketball with a friend a few days a week. Nothing big, just a chance to work off some steam and sweat a little."

Brian followed Paul into the kitchen and accepted an ice-cold soda from the refrigerator. Paul didn't speak again until he had drained the entire can and tossed it into the recycling. He eyed his brother. "What's up?" Idle chitchat had never been their strong point.

Trying his best to be nonchalant, Brian shrugged and seemed to look intensely curious at the dying spider plant sitting on the windowsill. "Nothing, really," he said as casually as he could manage, "I just thought maybe you'd like to catch a bite to eat or something."

Paul felt a spark of panic unfurl in his stomach. "Something's up. Mom and Dad okay? Janet and the kids okay?"

"Yeah, yeah, they're all fine." Brian watered the plant and began meticulously removing all the brown and lifeless leaves. It was a big job.

Helping himself to another soda, Paul studied his brother. "I'd love to have dinner with you Brian. I've got a couple of steaks I was going to throw on the grill, actually. But you understand my concern that someone has a terminal disease or that you've been notified that the end of the world is near, because you've never come to my house uninvited, let alone suggest we enjoy a casual conversation over a meal." Paul tried not to sound hostile and sarcastic, but was uncertain if he had succeeded.

His brother looked at him with pain-filled eyes. "Is there any law that says we can't start now?"

A stream of sweat worked its way down the left side of Paul's face and he wiped it away with his sleeve. Something was up, big time, and his brother had come to him? What was wrong with this picture? "Look, I smell so bad, I'm offending myself. I'm going to go jump in the shower. Why don't you start the grill?"

Brian nodded and gave a small smile. "Sounds good to me."

In the shower, Paul prayed. The primary area in his life that needed improvement was his relationship with his family, which he had been unwilling and, to some extent, unable to fix. He had always been the baby, spoiled by his parents and resented by his siblings. How many times had he felt excluded, unwanted, and a burden to them? How often had they reminded him of his selfishness and his perpetual ability to disappoint? There was the juvenile record he'd alluded to with Claire, there was the dropping out of high school which had caused him to get his GED through night school, there was the college degree he'd thrown away to work at the power company, there was his blatant rejection of the church and God, there was … How many times had he felt the condemnation from them regarding his failure with Karly and the burden of The Secret he still kept locked away? *Oh God*, Paul prayed, *guide my words and my attitude. Through you I am a new person. Help me to be able to show my family that. Help me to believe it myself.*

Brian had the steaks on a plate ready to be grilled and was munching on taco chips dipped in salsa. In a crowd of people, they would have been singled out as brothers: both with dark, unruly hair, big brown eyes, and substantial height. But Brian had a leaner, less muscular physique, which suited the white-collar engineering career he had chosen. Paul looked the role of the blue-collar worker: ruddy complexion, thick, strong muscles, and work calloused hands. Brian grinned at Paul, "You live all right here," he said with his mouth full a chips. "Hope you don't mind that I helped myself."

"Nah, I'm glad for the company. Want to sit on the porch?"

Between the two of them they carried all the food out onto the picnic table on the porch. Paul threw the steaks on the grill and went back inside to get a bag of garden salad and a store-bought tub of potato salad.

"What kind of dressing do you like?"

"Italian?"

Paul grinned and turned around. Italian and blue cheese dressing were stuck in the back pockets of his jeans. "I thought I remembered you liked Italian."

It was a nice dinner. They talked about work and current events, and avoided speaking of anything related to childhood and church. Paul mentioned the softball games and the little league team he coached. Brian talked about his girls, Mallory who was four and in preschool and Tiffany who was two. Paul chuckled over Brian's stories about trials and tribulations of having two opinionated daughters.

With a package of Oreos between them as dessert, Brian looked at Paul and finally blurted out, "I was wondering if I could stay here with you for a while. I've got my stuff in the car. Janet's kicked me out of the house." And he burst into tears.

Paul sat there with the steak, potato salad, and the Oreo cookies rapidly turning to lead in his gut while Brian poured out his heart and soul. He and Janet had been unhappy for a long time, even since before Tiffany had been born. They'd done the ridiculous thing that many couples try, and decided to have another child to try to heal things that had nothing to do with parenthood and babies. Last night she'd come home from being out late again. When Brian had confronted her she'd admitted she was having an affair and wanted him to leave. Just get out. Go.

Brian looked at his brother, anguished. "I know what you're thinking. You're thinking what a fool I am because I didn't stand up to her, and instead, I just left like she said. But I can't keep fighting in front of the kids! What was I going to do? Make her and the babies move out? I'm the one who works full time and is out of the house all day anyway. She's the one who's home with the kids, doing all of the stuff that needs to be done. I don't need or want the damn house anyway!"

"You don't have to convince me," Paul said quietly. He got up and poured them both a cup of coffee that had just finished brewing. He couldn't remember how his brother liked his coffee so he fixed it just like his, no sugar and a bit of milk. He set the mug down in front of his brother and settled himself back into the plastic lawn chair. He had absolutely no idea what to say, or even where to begin. *Help*, he prayed.

"I never thought I'd be divorced at thirty. Hell, we didn't even make it to the seven year itch." Brian took a sip of his coffee and looked at Paul. "Can I stay?"

"Of course you can stay," Paul said. "You don't even have to ask."

"I can't tell Mom and Dad, it'll kill them. Or Connie and Rachel, they'll nag me to death about what I should have done and what I should do now. And Elliot, he'll just gloat that for once I've failed at something."

"I thought I was the only one who had issues with the family." Paul tried to make it sound like he was joking, but he didn't fool his brother.

"What are you talking about? You don't have issues with the family! You're the only one whose had the guts to do whatever the hell he pleases. Stepped out on your own, chose your own career, even questioned the All Powerful Religious Doctrine we were steeped in." He looked at Paul. "Even with Karly. God, that took guts! You faced us all down, and her family, too, and you made a wise decision." He shook his head. "I wish I had your strength. I've envied you from afar from the time you were little, watching you be feisty and contrary while I killed myself trying to be cooperative and perfect." Brian gave Paul a lopsided grin. "You always seemed to have such a better time at everything you did because of it. It made me nuts." The expression on Paul's face made Brian laugh out loud. "I guess you never realized that, huh?"

"Never."

"Guess you should be glad I came to dinner then, huh?"

The tension in Paul's gut gave way to a soft warm glow. "Guess I'm glad you're moving in, too. Come on, I'll help you unload your stuff."

In the end, Paul made excuses to his brother about where he had to go at about 9:30 rather then tell his brother about Claire. The weight of maintaining all the separate dots of his life dragged him down again. Why couldn't he say, 'Hey, I like this girl, but we're just starting out so I'm going slowly. You'll get to meet her soon though, don't worry.' But he just didn't have … the courage. Still and all, the opportunity to see Claire – and that she had prompted the visit this time – was not something he was willing to pass up. How bizarre was it that he was as unsure of his relationship with his own brother as he was with Claire?

Step out on faith there, young man. Step out on faith, the Granddad voice said. But Paul kept his mouth shut.

Claire had remembered to bring him cherry pie, carrying out the take out containers and cans of soda. They sat on the 'porch' eating in companionable silence. And finally, at long last, she started to talk and tell him a few things. Nothing from the past, nothing really personal about herself, but information nonetheless about the DYFS worker, Daniel Alvarez, Riverside Church (which he was almost certain they played softball against), and even about some of the people she worked with.

Her agony over whether she was a failure for seeking help just about did Paul in. He wanted to reach over, scoop her up, and wipe away her tears as she sat on his lap; a sure way to blow everything. He risked a comforting touch on the back of her head. Her hair was softer and silkier than Paul had imagined, and he felt her tension from his closeness.

A tired warrior, that's what she was, and that's what he had told her. Paul wanted to reassure her, encourage her … date her.

He felt frustrated and angry with himself as he drove home. Jeeze, this was ridiculous! He needed to get up his courage and have it out with her, tell her how things needed to be, put his foot down for once, stop dancing around her like some uncertain school boy. He'd do it Saturday. That is if she was still speaking to him after she found out what he and Tyler had decided to do on their 'date'.

Brian went with Paul to the Thursday night softball game and met the guys. Back at the house, the noise and chaos of a house full of sweaty, victorious men seemed to keep the edge of sorrow at bay for him. The guys were their usual loud, irreverent selves and the laughter and jokes went late into the night. The guys didn't even notice when Paul slipped away at 10:30. He had to know if Claire had gone to see the committee and how it all had gone.

He was moving so slowly with Claire that Paul sometimes felt as though he were going backwards. In the old days … never mind about the old days. Sitting on Claire's 'porch' waiting for her to appear he tried praying rather than thinking … about the old days. And then the cops showed up.

It didn't end up as badly as it could have because he knew one of the officers from one of the softball teams his church regularly played against. But the complaint had been legitimate. He had been hanging around, he didn't live in the building, and although he had his ID and was cooperative, the two officers were hesitant to leave until they'd gotten Claire's reassurance. Seeing her come tearing up the stairs, breathless and terrified, Paul was struck with the enormity of the trust she had bestowed on him with her initial invitation to sit and talk with her on the 'porch'.

Once things were cleared up with the police Claire took another giant leap of faith by inviting him into her apartment. Paul liked 'Old Lady' Santiago immediately, even if she had tried to get him arrested for vagrancy. The idea that Claire had this ferocious old bat in her corner watching out for her made him relax just a bit. Paul tried to answer all of Mrs. Santiago's questions politely and thoroughly. By the time she'd left, he felt that she was satisfied that he was neither a vagrant nor a serial killer. He was certain that the jury was still out on the final verdict, though.

Claire gave him a brief tour of the apartment. He was appalled that she was literally killing herself in order to live in a place so Spartan and grim. Scrupulously clean, it was nevertheless tiny, dark, and very run down. Sparsely furnished, there weren't even any rugs or pictures on the walls. And yet, he heard the pride in her voice as she walked him through the long, dark hallway, showing him the dining room, Tyler's room, the living room, and her bedroom at the far front of the building. Only Claire's bedroom and the kitchen had windows that allowed in any sunlight. Tyler's room had a window, but it opened onto an airshaft between two buildings; the shade was always pulled for privacy. When she turned to face him at the completion of the tour he saw her expectant expression, and he made some appropriate noises about the place. His heart just about broke.

Paul was amazed at how small her circle of acquaintances was. Just the night before, she'd spoken for the first time of other people in her life. None seemed to be friends. No family of any kind was referred to. Even he, for all his bluster and talk about distancing himself from friends, family, and church people, was amazed at the extent of her isolation. At any given time, in less than an hour, he could make just a few phone calls and have the world at his feet ready to help him. But not Claire; she was well and truly a woman on her own. Suddenly her tiny, drab apartment was visible to him through her eyes: it was a sanctuary for her remoteness, a monument to her tenacity.

Paul was conscious of the enormity of what she was giving him. She was sharing and trusting and cautiously venturing out into unexplored territory. He caught himself praying the same prayer over and over: *Give me the right words, Lord, Give me the right words.* He did not want to … mess … this up.

Paul did everything in his power to escape Brian on Friday night, but was unsuccessful. Loading up the back of his trunk with his softball equipment, Brian was more than content to go along for the ride again.

"You don't want to watch another boring group of amateur sports freaks running around trying to recapture their youth do you?"

"Yeah, I do," Brian said with a puzzled expression. "I had a great time last night, and I even laughed a couple of times. You're offering me the same opportunity tonight. Why would I turn it down?"

Paul shrugged. "I don't know," he mumbled. "The team's different tonight. You might not have as good a time as last night." *This is my church dot, Brian. It doesn't connect with my family dot.*

Brian studied him. "Clue me in if you don't want me to tag along …"

Paul shook his head. "No, no, you're welcome." When Brian continued to stand there and stare at him quizzically, Paul said, "Honest."

Now's as good a time as any to begin connecting the dots of your life, his grandfather's voice said quietly in Paul's head.

As Brian continued to study him, Paul took a deep breath and said, "It's a church softball team, Brian." At Brian's stunned expression, it was clear that nothing could have surprised his brother more. He stood there, speechless. "It's the second season I've played with them. I've got Josh and Simon playing, too, but they don't attend church or anything."

"But you do? Attend church, I mean," Brian finally said.

"Yeah, I've been attending church pretty much since Granddad's funeral." Paul picked up his equipment and started walking out to the truck with Brian following close behind.

"Why the big secret?"

Paul leaned against the side of his truck and looked his brother in the eye. "What would everyone have said if I'd shown up two years ago after Granddad's death and said, 'Hey everyone, I've decided to recommit my life to Christ and start fresh'?"

Brian maintained eye contact. "Mom would have cried, Dad would have been relieved, Connie would have begun making a list of suggestions for areas where you needed to improve, Rachel would have added more to the list plus given numerous examples of your previous failures, and Elliot and I ..." He hesitated and could no longer meet Paul's gaze. He stared off into the neighbor's back yard. Finally, he sighed. "Elliot and I would have laughed and said, 'Yeah, sure.'"

Paul nodded, agreeing with him. "You just answered your own question."

As they drove toward the game, Brian finally asked, "What made you recommit your life?"

Staring ahead at the traffic, Paul said, "I didn't like the person I had become. The pleasures I found were shallow and the rewards I achieved were fleeting." He glanced at Brian. "Sounds corny, huh?"

"So you're living happily ever after now?" Brian said with bitterness.

"Why the sarcasm?"

Brian sighed and scrubbed his face with both of his hands. "My life sucks right now, Paul. My wife wants to be with another man. I'm in imminent danger of losing everything that I have ever valued as precious and dear. I'm so far down in this pit of self-pity that I'm having trouble seeing ground level." He was quiet for a moment and when Paul glanced at his brother he seemed to be struggling to maintain his composure. "Why is God letting this happen to me, Paul?" he whispered almost to himself. "Have I done something terrible to deserve this?"

What do you say to a person when he says that? Paul had no

insight into God's plan and design. He had no psychological or theological degree with which he could impart stunning wisdom that would make his brother sit up in awe. Brian had no idea the extent of Paul's own unresolved issues. No idea at all. *Help*, he prayed. Paul took a deep breath. "I've been on both sides, Brian. I've tried a life that rejected God and all He stands for. I've done things that I'm so ashamed of that I can't think of them without becoming physically ill. For the past two years I've tried to walk a life that is focused on God. I screw up all the time, but I continue to refocus each time I drift. The main reason why I haven't told you or Mom or Dad is that deep down I'm afraid I'll fail, not so much by choice but because of lack of faith." He shook his head. "How stupid is that? I'm more worried about my family witnessing my failure than God."

They were in the church parking lot now. A warm pleasant breeze wafted through the open truck windows. Paul looked at his brother and continued, "I think we have a different view of what God is like. I've come to believe that He is, above all else, a God of love. He has to be, because I am so often such an unlovable person and yet … I know I never have to doubt His feelings for me. When you told me about you and Janet and what was going on between you I was filled with such sorrow for the two of you and for Mallory and Tiffany. A real grief. I think that's how God feels, Bri. I don't think He's saying, 'So there, Brian! That's for that time you failed me and that's for all of the opportunities you let slip by that could have brought Me pleasure.' I think He's up there agonizing right along with you.

"The only thing I know for sure is that you're not on your own through this, though you may think you are right now. God doesn't leave you stranded. He didn't leave me stranded, even when I rejected Him. He let me make my mistakes, but He didn't desert me. Furthermore, I think that God not only is with you, He's already anticipated this rough time in your life and made preparations to help you get through this."

"What are you talking about?" Brian asked.

At least he's not going to cry again, Paul thought. "I'm saying that God has already put in place things in your life to help you get through this. Think. Can you see what they are?" Brian remained silent, but Paul was certain that he had his brother thinking so he began to list, "You've got your job, close friends, your health. You've got your family, including you're newly discovered good-buddy relationship with your brother. You've got your girls who mean more to you than anything, and will be the force that will keep you putting one foot in front of the other no matter how hard it gets. You've got your church family, too. But most importantly, even if you didn't have any of these things, you've got a relationship with God. Now, more than any other, is a time to draw closer to Him, rather than pull away. Why would you do that? What would that accomplish for you aside from making things worse?

"You have a right to be angry and bitter, but direct it correctly. Be angry at Janet, be angry at the man she's gotten herself involved with, be angry at yourself for when you've allowed opportunities to slide by that you should have taken. But don't be angry with God. Make use of the resources available to you so that this situation doesn't destroy you, but makes you better and stronger."

The silence in the truck was profound when Paul finally stopped speaking. *Well done, kid,* his grandfather said, but Paul wasn't so sure. Studying his brother's profile, Paul had no clue if he'd accomplished anything positive at all.

Finally, after long moments of silence, Brian turned and looked at Paul. "You think they'd let me play third base?"

Paul hesitated for only an instant. "You'll have to talk to the coach - I'll introduce you to Pastor Buurman. I'll give you one more piece of advice tonight, though."

"What's that?"

"Whatever you do, don't tell him you're a Red Sox fan. He'll put you so far out in left field we'll never hear from you again."

Call it a clan, call it a network, call it a tribe, call it a family.
Whatever you call it, whoever you are, you need one. [13]

Ten: There's No Such Thing As Love

Claire had been lost in thought when she pulled into her
parking space at almost 11 p.m. that Thursday evening
after meeting with the church committee about Sonrise
House. The meeting had been just about everything she had expected.
There had been five committee members waiting to talk with her, including
Janice Strocco and Daniel Alvarez. They had all been polite and friendly,
trying their best to put her at ease, which was impossible.

As Claire had answered their questions and tried her best to keep
her attitude under control, the reality of the situation *that she was seeking help
from strangers* kept rearing its ugly head. And it was a bigger, stronger, uglier
presence than anything else in that room. Although not one member of the
committee appeared anything but sincere, her stomach was knotted and her
palms remained damp. She was breaking Rule Number Nine of the Claire
Jenkins Survival Book: *Never accept charity. It will absolutely destroy you.*

Afterwards, each committee member had shaken Claire's hand and
spoken privately with her before leaving. Janice Strocco had told her that
they were all going to pray for a week before they made their final decision.

---

[13] Jane Howard, "Families"

Claire wasn't sure which decision would upset her more: if they chose her or if they didn't.

Walking across the parking lot at her apartment in a daze of thoughtful apprehension, it took her exhausted mind a few moments to register that there were two police cars parked haphazardly in the lot. *Oh no* … It never crossed her mind that the police cars had nothing to do with her. Never.

Gasping for breath at the top of the stairs, she came face to face with two police officers … and Paul.

"Hey, Claire." He was standing by the porch bench with his hands at his side and his Yankee baseball cap pushed back from his face. He looked intimidating nonetheless, shadowed by the intermittent evening lights and towering over both police officers by a good three or four inches. "Would you mind verifying to these two officers that you know me and that it's okay that I'm sitting here on the roof waiting for you? Seems one of your neighbors called and reported me for loitering."

Claire glanced back toward the six apartments and although she wasn't exactly certain, she could have sworn that she saw the curtain over her kitchen sink move just a bit.

"Do you live here, miss?" one of the officers asked.

Claire nodded, still slightly breathless from running up the stairs. "Yeah, I live in apartment 2E."

"Do you know this gentleman?"

Paul gave her a slow smile, perhaps, she thought, enjoying being called a 'gentleman' by a police officer. She looked at the officer whose name badge said 'Keyes'. "Yeah, Officer Keyes. This is my …" She hesitated, stuck on the question, What was he? Paul's grin widened and he arched his eyebrow at her. He was curious to hear what he was to her, too. Claire took a deep breath, "*friend*, Paul Williamson. It's okay that he's here waiting for me."

"Could I see some ID?" Officer Keyes asked her. As the policeman checked her license she puzzled over the reality of things. This mountain of a man, who towered over the two armed police officers, caused her absolutely no concern or anxiety. Had she wandered up the stairs and found him sitting on her back porch – at 11:00 p.m. – she would simply have been happy to see him. The realization overwhelmed her.

"Ms. Jenkins? Are you all right?" Lost in thought, Claire had totally forgotten her company. Officer Keyes was holding out her driver's license. When she reached to take it he said, "You have a nice night now, you hear?" He and his partner ambled down the stairs and into the night.

"I didn't mean to cause all this fuss, Claire. Sorry." Paul had taken off his baseball cap and stuffed it in the back pocket of his jeans.

"What are you doing here at 11:00 at night?"

"I wanted to know how your interview went."

"So you *drove over*?"

He had shrugged, "I still don't think you'd be too happy if I started calling you to have idle chit-chat."

"So you *visit* to have idle chit-chat?"

Paul had grinned at her. "Are you getting feisty?"

Claire struggled to contain a smile. She looked out into the parking lot and watched the two police cars slowly make their way down the alley and out to the street. "You want to know something crazy?" she heard herself saying. "I was more nervous around those two police officers than you."

Paul gave her another grin. "Sounds like good progress to me."

As she turned to look up the second flight of stairs to her apartment, she definitely saw the kitchen curtain move. Making a decision, she turned and looked at Paul, standing like a huge, dark sentinel behind her. "If I invite you in to introduce you to Mrs. Santiago, will you promise not to make a big deal out of it?"

He glanced up at the window of her kitchen. "That who called the cops on me?"

She shrugged. "I'm guessing ..." Claire stood her ground, now wrapped in indecision. What was she doing? *Establish suitable safe boundaries and never compromise them for any reason.* What was that? Rule Number Eleven or Twelve?

Paul walked toward her. "It makes sense that you introduce me to Mrs. Santiago. I don't want her having me hauled away sometime when you're not around to save my sorry … butt." He had smiled a reassuring smile. "Relax, Claire. Trust your instincts. It's *okay.*"

Mrs. Santiago *had* called the police, and before she left Claire's apartment gave Paul a brief but thorough interrogation. "She used to work for the CIA or something?" he asked after she left.

Claire laughed because once again his thoughts had mirrored hers. Later, sitting outside on the back porch sipping sodas she told him of the Sonrise House interview and surprised herself by sharing her indecision about whether she wanted to be chosen or not for the house.

Paul was quiet for a while and then had finally said to her, "I know you're not into God at all Claire. I remember you saying that you don't even believe in Him. But I also remember your reasoning behind that; you'd never had the opportunity. Why don't you give God a chance? Why don't you try praying about all of this? Why don't you decide to give this whole situation to the Lord and let Him work it out?" Paul held up his hand when she started to interrupt. "Before you give me your list of arguments, just answer one question: *What do you have to loose?*"

She had no answer to that question so she kept her mouth shut in the end.

Saturday morning, the phone's harsh ringing woke Claire from a deep sleep. As she struggled to reach for the offending intrusion, she glanced at the alarm clock by her bedside. *6:48 a.m.*

"Hello?" her voice was slurred.

"Hey, Claire. It's Paul. I'm at the food store with a pen and paper. Do you have your shopping list ready?"

She struggled to get her mind wrapped around consciousness. "What …? What are you doing at the food store?"

"People usually come here to buy food, Claire."

How dare he sound sarcastic *with her!* Her anger sharpened her wits and she sat up in bed. "At 6:50 a.m. on Saturday morning?!" she shouted into the receiver.

Her anger got his attention. "Jeeze, Claire, did I wake you? Tyler said you were an early riser." Claire could distinctly hear the sound of SpongeBob coming from the living room. "Paul, *Tyler* is an early riser.

During the workweek, *I'm* an early riser because otherwise we'd be starving and living out of our car. *On Saturday*, I sleep unbelievably late. Sometimes until *8:00*." Anger and sarcasm were evident in her reply.

There was silence on the other end of the phone. Claire pictured Paul standing in the fresh food aisle in between the avocadoes and the pineapples. The mental picture made her giggle. Just a little bit.

"Are you laughing or crying?"

"I'm crying."

"No you're not."

She sighed. "What would possess you to call me and offer to do my food shopping at this hour? Besides," she said as an afterthought, pushing her tangled hair out of her eyes, "on Saturdays I have to do Mrs. Santiago's shopping, too."

"I've got that list already. Tyler got it on Thursday night."

Claire sat up straight. *"He did?"*

"Claire, didn't Tyler talk to you about today?"

"No ..."

"Well, you and Tyler are spending the day with me at a local park. We've got to get going by 10 to be there by 11."

"TYLER!"

Tyler appeared in her bedroom door, fully dressed including his Yankee cap, eating a toaster pastry. "Yeah, Mom?

It was hard to look stern and intimidating sitting in bed wearing a faded Mickey Mouse tee shirt, but Claire did her best. "Do you have something to tell me about today, Tyler?" she asked.

Tyler shook his head. "Uh-uh."

Claire said into the phone to Paul, "He says he doesn't have anything to tell me."

She heard Paul sigh. "Let me talk to him."

Tyler took the phone and sat on the edge of her bed. "Hi Paul ... No, I didn't say anything ... You said you'd take care of it ... Oh. OH ..." Tyler listened to Paul talk and then shrugged his shoulders. "I don't know ..." Tyler looked down at his knee and picked absently at a scab. "I suppose so ... Yeah, okay ... You want to talk to Mom again?" Tyler handed her the phone and went running from the bedroom.

"So what's the deal? Obviously, I'm awake now."

"Tyler and I have a wonderful second date planned. We just slipped up in the communication part of things."

"Here, Mom," Tyler thrust the shopping list at her. "Read this to Paul."

Into the phone, Claire said, "You're not doing my food shopping, Paul."

"Sorry, we're on a tight schedule today and you don't have a choice. I'll give you the receipt and you can pay me back. Anyway, I've got to buy some stuff for the party, er, I mean picnic anyway."

"What are you up to?"

He sighed. "Look, I've been standing in the doorway of the food store so long people are starting to give me money thinking I'm panhandling. You *said* Tyler and I could plan things. I promise you'll have a nice day."

What else could she do?

It was another beautiful Saturday, with the temperature warm but not uncomfortably hot. The phone in the apartment rang once at about 8:45, and Tyler was out the back door like a shot responding to some obviously secret communication. Before she knew it, Claire was putting away groceries for her and then for Mrs. Santiago.

"Hurry up, Mom! Paul's gonna be late!" At Tyler's instructions she'd gone back inside to get her Generals baseball cap. She was dressed in a faded tee shirt and the best pair of denim cut off shorts she owned. She was glad it was warm enough for her flip-flops, because her diner sneakers were well on the way out. As usual, her hair was pulled up into a ponytail, secured with a rubber band. The sun blazed down on them as they walked over to Paul's truck, and she wished that she owned a pair of sunglasses.

"Did you pick up all the food?" Tyler asked looking out the small back window to the truck bed.

"Yeah, we've got enough to feed a large army."

As she went to climb into the truck after Tyler, Claire noticed a large blue tarp spread out covering the entire bed of the truck. She felt a big knot of uncertainty. "Is the whole back of your truck filled with food?" Paul avoided looking her in the eye as he fumbled with his seatbelt and helped Tyler fasten his.

"Oh yeah, Mom," Tyler said breathlessly, "there's fried chicken and cold cuts and a bunch of different salads and sweet pickles, not dill because I told Paul you and I both like sweet, and soda and ..."

Claire stood up outside the open passenger door, crossed her arms, and said, "Out with it."

"Whad'ya mean, Mom?"

"Not you, Tyler. The big, nervous, suspicious one behind the steering wheel."

Paul looked at her pleadingly. "Claire, I'm running late. I'm *always late* as far as they're concerned. I'm gonna catch ... heck ... before I even get a chance to do something to really ... annoy ... them. Could you get in the truck and I'll answer anything you ask on the way?"

She looked from Paul's intense expression to Tyler's. Tyler leaned forward conspiratorially and said, "He always catches ... heck ... with his older brothers and sisters no matter if he does things right or wrong. But if we're late for this party, Mom, he'll never hear the end of it."

She looked back up at Paul. *"Party?"*

At his pleading look, she climbed in and shut the door. The truck roared off. She decided as they drove that she was going to have to keep her son and Paul separated if she ever wanted to get the upper hand. Every angle, every complication, every argument she may have brought up was carefully and completely addressed and solved.

"You see, Mom," Tyler explained, "Paul's got to help out at this birthday party for his Mom, and he was in charge of picking up all the food since he's got the truck, only they didn't think he'd be reliable enough so no one's really happy that he's doing it."

Paul jumped in, "My Mom is turning 70 and they're having a big party. It was supposed to be a surprise, but she found out talking to one of her friends." He glanced at her and rolled his eyes. "Thank *goodness* I haven't talked to her in over a week, or I guarantee you I would have been blamed for spoiling the surprise."

Tyler looked at her with all the wisdom and knowledge of a seven year old, "Paul's sisters drive him nuts, *big time.*"

"I don't understand why *we* are included in this family celebration," Claire said at last.

"Oh that's easy, Mom," Tyler began, "you see, Paul and I were making plans for our next adventure, and Paul said it was my turn to plan. You know, like he did the ball game and everything. So I told him how we had to be careful with money, since we've got none, and that maybe a day in the park would be good, and we got talking and planning and then all of a sudden Paul shouts, 'Oh … *darn it* …'" Tyler leans over and whispers, "only he didn't say 'darn', if you know what I mean, Mom," to which Paul uttered an audible groan, "and he starts telling me all about this party he was supposed to help with and everything, and it was me who suggested that we come along and help Paul out. After all, Mom," Tyler finished, "you know all about serving and helping with parties and food and everything."

"I *did not* invite you to make use of your waitress skills, Claire," Paul said to her, and for the first time he no longer looked up tight but slightly angry instead.

"Why'd you invite me then?" she asked as Paul whipped the truck out onto the fast lane of the highway to pass some vehicles going only the speed limit.

"Oh, he invited you so that he could see your green eyes," Tyler answered helpfully. Paul groaned again, and Claire smiled … just a little.

The park was one that had a baseball diamond, a paddleboat pond, paved pathways for roller-blading and biking, an enormous playground, and even a small amphitheatre. The site of the party was obvious the moment they drove into the park. Someone was working on tying helium balloons of all colors randomly onto chairs and picnic tables, trees and even children. Some of the balloons bore funny sayings like 'Over the Hill' and 'You're HOW old?!' Paul didn't park the truck in the lot, but drove right onto the grass heading toward what looked to be the center of the action. As one, the group of people turned and headed toward the truck.

"You made it." It was a statement made with profound relief by a woman, perhaps in her mid thirties, who had hair the exact shade of Paul's.

"I told you you could count on me, Connie," Paul said with a hint of exasperation. "Connie, this is my friend, Claire and her son, Tyler. Tyler's a real man of action and he's ready, willing, and able to do any job you want him to."

Connie looked at Claire, studying her intently for a brief moment, and then smiled widely. "Welcome! I can always use another capable set of hands! I'm so glad that Paul brought you both," she put her arm around Tyler, "and that I've got such an excellent helper to assist me." Claire, always cautious when meeting new people, liked her immediately.

Over the next hour and a half everyone pitched in hauling, setting up, and making decisions. There were heavy doses of teasing as well as plenty of laughter. Claire, never comfortable in group situations and solitary for so many years tried to hang back and be as invisible as possible. But it was not to be with Tyler yelling, "Mom! Come here!" every five minutes it seemed, and Paul yelling, "Claire, help!" every two. Pretty soon, others caught on that she was comfortable dealing with hostessing and serving, feeding and organizing large masses of people, and before she knew it, Paul's brother, Brian, was heard saying, "Ask Claire. She knows what she's talking about, and she's not half as bossy as Connie."

There were tables loaded with breads and salads, the smell of Sterno wafted on the breeze, and huge buckets of cold drinks were strategically placed. The picnic tables had been covered with colorful red and white checked table clothes and big buckets filled with citronella candles waited to be lit once evening came.

"What time is your mom due to arrive?" Claire asked Connie.

"Noon. All this was supposed to be a surprise, did Paul tell you?" Claire nodded. "That mother of ours. I don't think we've ever managed to surprise her, ever. She knew everything when we were kids, anticipated everything when we were teens, and now that we're adults, seems to have sources in every area of our lives!" Connie smiled and shook her head. "She's seventy years old and sometimes I have trouble keeping up with her."

The two of them helped themselves to bottled water and sat down on lawn chairs under the shade of a huge oak tree. "How long have you been dating Paul?" Connie asked after they both had chances to take long gulps from their water.

"Oh, I'm not dating him. We're, as he said, 'just friends'."

Connie studied her for a moment and then shrugged. "Whatever you say. I'll tell you this, though. Paul rarely comes to this type of get - together anymore, and when he does he always seems pretty up tight and miserable." She looked across the field and nodded her head. "Just look at him. He almost seems like the 'old Paul'."

Claire followed Connie's gaze to see Paul standing with his big hand resting on the top of Tyler's head, laughing uproariously at something his brother Brian was saying. Brian was holding one little girl in his arms and another tightly by the hand. To Claire, Paul seemed exactly as she had come to know him: happy, smiling, carefree … She turned to Connie. "Why's he always uptight and miserable?"

Connie's expression turned sad and she looked down at her hands now clasped tightly in her lap. "He knows we miss him – the *old* him. He knows we worry about him. These kinds of get - togethers always have lots of our church friends and family, and there's always prayer and talk of God along with the fun and the laughter. The fact that he doesn't like to have anything to do with that now makes times like this awkward for him and for us."

Claire looked at Connie and then at Paul, who was walking toward them and then back to Connie. "Look," Connie said quickly, seeming to regret what she had said, "don't say anything to Paul about what I've just said. We're so happy he's here. I'm thrilled he felt comfortable enough to bring you and Tyler." She looked over at her brother and Tyler as they approached and lowered her voice, "I miss him so much, and I just seem to always get it wrong when I talk with him. *Always*."

"Hey, you two. Get back to work. Who said you could loaf around and enjoy yourselves?" Paul shouted at them when he got within range.

Tyler came running up to Claire, breathless. "Mom, Paul said that we could go over to the big playground and try it out before his Mom shows up. Do you want to come along?"

Claire looked at Connie, "Do you need anymore help?"

Connie grinned. "Are you kidding? Thanks to you we're ahead of schedule!"

Claire stood and looked at Paul and her son. "Guess you two have got company."

"Are you okay?" Paul asked her as they walked slowly towards the park equipment and Tyler ran on ahead. "My family can be pretty overpowering, especially my sisters."

"I'm fine. Actually, I'm having a better time than I ever imagined. You introduced me to your brother, Brian, but I didn't meet his family. Were those his two little girls with him?"

"Yeah, Mallory's four and in preschool and Tiffany's two."

Claire frowned. "Have I met his wife? I'm trying to keep all of these people straight."

"Nah, you haven't met Janet. Nobody on the planet knows it but they're having trouble. Such big trouble that he's living with me at my house right now."

"Oh, no …"

"Yeah, he's a wreck, but he's hiding it pretty good today, huh?" Paul looked at Claire. "I think the story he's circulating is that Janet's sick with some stomach flu and couldn't make it." Paul shook his head. "With the way things are with this family, everyone will probably assume she's pregnant and they'll start planning a baby shower."

Claire walked beside him for a bit. "Your sister Connie seems wonderful."

Paul looked at her like he suspected her to have heat stroke. "Connie? Wonderful? She's the bossiest, most narrow minded woman I've ever met." He hesitated. "Besides Rachel. That's my other sister. You'll meet her soon. She's supposed to be coming with my Mother and Father." He looked at her pointedly and rolled his eyes. "My parents fall into a completely different category," he said ominously.

"Connie thinks we're dating."

Paul shrugged. "Well, let them think that rather than the truth that

I'm actually dating a seven year old boy." He grinned and winked at her.

"We're not dating, Paul"

He sighed. "Whatever you say, Claire," he said and reached over and took her hand in his.

"Paul."

"What?"

She tried to pull her hand away but he held on tightly. "Let go."

They were at the playground now, and Tyler was scrambling up one particularly complicated series of ropes and tunnels and ladders aiming for the top of the massive center structure. "Look, Claire, believe it or not this *situation* between us is as confusing to me as it is to you. All I can say is that when I'm with you I feel peaceful and good and *right*. I don't feel like such a screw up. I've learned over these past two years that God makes me feel *exactly like this* when I'm on the right track." He rolled his eyes. "It doesn't happen as often as I'd like, so believe me, when it does happen *I take note.*"

He dragged her over to a bench by their still clasped hands. They both smiled and waved at Tyler as he shouted and waved from the top of the tower. Claire looked at Paul, stunned. "You're not a screw up! You've got a good job, lots of friends, a wonderful family, a roof over your head, you're healthy and active, you have a wonderful sense of humor, and you're working hard to lead an exemplary life. It seems to me you are the picture of success! Why would you say such a thing?"

He was silent, squinting out towards the playground. Claire got the distinct feeling he was not seeing what was in front of him.

Claire tried a different tact. "Why does your sister think that you don't want to be around 'prayer and talk about God' as she put it? You're the most Godly man I know. Next to Daniel Alvarez," she amended.

"She didn't waste any time, did she?" he said bitterly.

Claire was surprised at his tone. She had never intended to get involved with family matters, let alone ones that were volatile. She was completely unskilled at dealing with something like this. Heck, she couldn't handle her own personal issues, let alone someone else's. What should she do? What should she say? *Be honest*, she heard as clearly as a bell in her head. *Speak with your heart.* Was that a new rule? Maybe so ...

"Paul, I don't know what I'm dealing with here. It seems a lot more complicated than I can understand in a little over an hour of being here. But I will tell you what I saw when I talked with your sister, Connie. I saw someone who loves you, who's worried about you, who has no idea what the right course is, and who's fantastically glad that you're here today. That's what I saw. That's what I heard. I saw no condemnation and no anger. The only person I see whose hostile since we've gotten here is you."

Paul studied her face, perhaps searching for hidden truths. He got a determined look on his face. *"We're dating, Claire,"* he said fiercely.

She threw up her one free hand in exasperation. "Hello? We're not talking about me and you, we're talking about you and the hostility you have toward your family."

"I think that it's all connected, Claire. You're right. You don't know what you are dealing with here. But I'd really appreciate your taking the time to listen and learn and tell me what you see. *No one* has ever, *ever* said what you've just said to me. Maybe I need to see my family through your eyes instead of my own."

"Why does your sister think that you don't want to be around prayer and God talk, Paul? *Why?"* she asked quietly.

"Because I'm a coward. Because I'm stubborn. Because I'm a ... darn ... fool," he said just as quietly.

He looked so miserable, and Claire felt herself soften. "Okay."

He looked at her, with surprised eyes. *"Okay?"*

"Uh-huh."

She felt Paul studying her profile intently as she watched Tyler laugh at something another child said to him. Without turning to look at him, she peered at Paul out of the corner of her eyes, and he suddenly got a very calculated, knowing expression. "If we're dating, I get to call you and talk to you when I want. I get to hold your hand when I want. Even if there are people around to see." He'd been holding her hand the entire time they had been on the bench, and he tightened his grip ever so slightly.

Claire faced him. "And if I tell you that I don't want to date you anymore, that I can't handle it or I don't want it, then you'll go away, no questions asked, no arguments and no tricks like asking Tyler out on a date again," Claire countered back.

Paul shook his head. "No, Claire. If you decide you don't want to date me anymore, *we'll talk*. We'll do our best to be honest and then we'll go from there, okay? I hope we talk a lot. I like talking with you. This is a fifty-fifty deal." He scratched his head. "Wait a minute, does Tyler have a cut in this?"

"No."

He chuckled. "I knew you'd say that." As Claire continued to stare intently at him, he reached up and cupped her cheek with his free hand. She froze. The warmth of his big hand covering the side of her face was a sensation she had never, ever felt. He ran his thumb over her cheekbone and Claire inhaled manly soap and aftershave. No one but Tyler had ever touched her with warmth and affection. "Close your eyes, Claire," he said low, "I want to whisper something to you."

She hesitated for just a moment and then did as he'd asked. This whole trusting thing was so novel, but so nice, too. She felt him lean forward and waited, listening. His warm breath feathered the side of her cheek and she heard him say, "I'm going to kiss you." Before she could react, his warm mouth settled on her cheek and for a wonderful, brief moment she was held immobile by his big hand on one side of her face and his lips on the other. "There," she heard him say with satisfaction, "we've sealed this with a kiss, Green Eyes."

Paul kept Claire by his side for the entire party, only separating from her when Connie claimed him or Claire for help and advice. He was attentive and relaxed, introducing her to numerous family and friends, all of whom seemed to know him and be genuinely pleased to see him.

Meeting Paul's parents was not as eventful as it could have been given the lively atmosphere of the party. Claire had an opportunity to note where Paul had gotten his size and looks from – his father - and his energy and outgoing nature from – his mother. When they were finally introduced, Paul's mother was gracious and friendly. "How do you like this?" she said in mock frustration, "I've been telling everyone *for years* that I'm only sixty – two and then they have to go and tell the world that I'm really seventy!

What kind of birthday present is *that?*"

Claire had laughed and said, "Better to look sixty-two and be seventy than the other way around."

Paul's mom winked at her and turned to her son. "I like her, Paul, she's quick and she's smart," she said with a loving smile. Mrs. Williamson put her hands on her hips, "How are you holding out with all of these Bible - bangers, young man? Is it killing you?"

Paul sighed. "Jeeze, Mom, I'm here, okay? Can't you just be glad about that?"

Hannah Williamson stepped forward and gave her son a fierce hug. The top of her head came barely up to Paul's chin. "I *am* glad you're here, you dope. That's all I've been praying about since I found out about the party."

She pulled back and eyed him mischievously. "Too bad we haven't talked more recently; I would have had more time to adjust to this attack of honesty," she said looking at a black birthday balloon that said 'You're seventy and I'm not!' Hannah grinned at Claire and explained, "Paul could *never, ever* keep secrets from me. He's got this invisible sign on his forehead," she reached up and brushed his mop of hair off his brow, "and whenever he was hiding something I'd tell him it flashed 'You're an idiot, Mom'. That's how I always knew he was up to something." She laughed and lowered her voice conspiratorially to Claire. "When he was little and I'd tell him his 'Idiot Light' was flashing he used to take his hand and try to cover it. It was a sure sign that he was definitely up to no good."

Paul looked absolutely disgusted with himself. "It took me *years* to figure out that covering my forehead before I talked with her was a dead giveaway that I was trying to con her." He leaned over and kissed his mother's cheek. "She's a very evil woman. Watch yourself ..."

Hannah laughed uproariously and made no effort to defend herself. "With five kids, Claire, you do what you have to do." She excused herself, hinting directly that Paul should show up sometime soon to a Sunday dinner with Claire and Tyler, and went off to a cluster of people who were wearing tee shirts that said 'Hannah Williamson: Miss American 1902'.

"She's great, Paul," Claire said wondering what type of woman she would have become had she grown up in a family like this. When Paul didn't say anything, she looked up at him and was shocked at his anguished expression. "What's wrong?"

"She's a master at making me feel guilty," he said glumly, taking a deep breath and scrubbing his face with both of his hands. "Want to go get something to eat? That fried chicken looks great."

"What did I miss?! How did she make you feel guilty?"

"Oh, the cracks about Bible - bangers and making reference to Sunday dinners. They're all subtle digs at me and my failure in the good son department."

"Ohhhh," Claire said in a knowing but sarcastic tone, "I see. You're bent out of shape because your mother was worried you wouldn't feel at ease here and that she invited you to Sunday dinner." She shook her head in mock disgust, "You're right. She's evil incarnate."

"There's a lot of history here, Claire, that you don't know about," Paul said defensively.

"I know that. But what I also know is that I've spent my whole life, dreaming of having a family just like this. I know nothing's perfect, but unless you can tell me that there are criminal activities hidden beneath this Bible-bangin' surface, I'll tell you about one of the Claire Jenkin's Rules of Survival. Number Thirteen says, 'If you dream about it, it's never gonna happen.'" She stopped and looked at him, holding a plate piled high with food. "I didn't even know something like this existed *to* dream about it. Do you even know what you've got here?"

Paul looked at her intently. "Believe it or not," he said to her, "yes, I do."

In the final hours of the party as the lightning bugs made their appearance and the citronella candles cast aromatic light, every adult – all one hundred plus guests – settled down on folding chairs and picnic benches. Tyler, though completely exhausted, joined the children in a rousing game of flashlight tag in a nearby field. Paul's father John Williamson, stood in the flickering light with a piece of paper and a flashlight.

"Oh, no," Hannah Williamson said, and almost everyone burst out laughing. When the laughter died down, she said in a pleading voice, "Haven't I been put through enough already?" But the expression she gave her husband as she looked up at him was filled with love.

"I have something I'd like to read," John said to the group, although he had eyes only for Hannah. "One time, many, many years ago, Hannah told me that the woman she most idolized was this woman I'm going to read to you about."

He looked down at the paper in his hand and began to read, "Who can find a virtuous and capable wife? She is worth more than precious rubies. Her husband can trust her, and she will greatly enrich his life. She will not hinder him but help him all her life ...[14]" Paul's father's voice was deep and rich and filled with emotion. Claire heard Mrs. Williamson say, "Oh, John," as he began to read, and then she sat quietly with everyone while he read on. Connie, midway through, reached over to rest her hand on her mother's shoulder. When Hannah turned to smile at her daughter, Claire could see tears glistening on her cheeks.

When Paul's father finished reading, someone in the group shouted, "Amen!"

John grinned into the darkness and then looked at his wife. "This woman from Proverbs may have been your idol, Hannah," John said to her, "but you have always been mine. Happy Birthday! I love you, Wife."

For Claire it was the defining moment in her life. She wanted to stand up and shout. She scanned all the faces near her shadowed by the evening twilight, features flickering in lantern light, and none seemed to recognize the momentous discovery being revealed before their eyes. It was real. She'd never seen it before, never experienced it personally, and had ceased dreaming that it really existed. At last she had witnessed it with her own eyes. She had found it. *There really was such a thing as true love.*

She would never be the same again.

---

[14] Proverbs 31:10-11, New Living Translation

Courage is fear that has said its prayers.[15]

Eleven: No One Wants To Hear Your Problems

Claire was silent on the drive home. Paul despaired, fearful that she was so angry with him that she'd never speak to him again, let alone acknowledge that they were dating. Where to begin? He'd start with the complications of his family …

"Don't take my mother seriously, okay Claire?" he spoke softly so he wouldn't disturb Tyler who was once again fast asleep between them in the truck "She pressures everyone to come by and eat dinner with them on Sundays."

When they had said their good-byes, Hannah had looked Claire in the eye and said, "Don't let *him*," she glared lovingly at her son, "keep you from coming to visit us, Claire. We'd love to have you and Tyler come by for Sunday dinner one of these days."

"Claire works on Sundays, Mom," Paul had said.

"So? Pick another day. We didn't have much time to talk today and I'd like that. Plus, John is always looking for an excuse to show off his culinary skills." Hannah leaned forward conspiratorially to Claire, "I hate to cook, but don't mind clean up duty at all." She winked at Claire. "I mean

---

15 Dorothy Bernard

it; get that son of mine to bring you by or come without him."

Sitting across from him in the truck, Claire blinked at Paul. "So I'm not to take the invitation seriously? She really doesn't want me to come to her house to eat dinner?"

"No, I," Paul sputtered, "I just don't want you to be any more upset than you already are ..." he finished lamely.

"What makes you think I'm upset?"

"You're so quiet."

"I usually shout when I'm upset. Ask Tyler." Paul thought he caught a small smile as she looked out the windshield.

She wasn't upset? "Then why are you so quiet?" he asked quietly.

"I'm just thinking, that's all."

"Am I allowed to ask about what?"

"Sure, go ahead."

"I'm having a little déjà vu here," Paul said cautiously. "I remember vividly stepping into this trap and practically getting my head bit off once before."

She smiled again. What was with her? "Sorry about that," she said softly. "I was thinking about your family. They're nice. *Really nice.* I never had a family like that."

Paul stayed absolutely silent, willing her to open up and tell him something personal and private about herself. Something, anything, that would fill in this shadowy, black and white outline he had of her. He craved color and definition, darkness as well as light. She reached down and stroked Tyler's hair. "It's always been just me and Tyler since he was born." She sighed and looked out the passenger window, absently fiddling with the frayed hem of her shorts. "And before that, it was always just me on my own." Claire looked at Paul then. "It's not a nice story, Paul. *None of it.*"

She was warning him. Letting him know that you had to be strong to *hear* the story, let alone live it. He had a moment's panic. Was he strong enough? The last thing he wanted to do was to disappoint her, let her down.

"I've been honest with you since the start, Claire. I'm not very good with words, but you don't have to have any special skill to listen. If you want to tell me something, I'll be honored to listen for as long as you want to talk." They pulled into the parking lot of her apartment building. When Claire went to gently shake Tyler awake, Paul laid his hand on hers. She looked up at him. "Let me carry him in. Don't wake him." She gave him the quiet smile again and nodded her head.

Claire tucked Tyler into bed, clothes and all. She pulled his sneakers and socks off and wiped his hands and face with a warm, damp cloth. Both she and Paul chuckled when the cloth came away almost black. "I think it's hopeless," he finally whispered.

"I agree." She tucked the sheet around him, kissed him, and they backed quietly out of the room. "He'll probably sleep until ... 7:00 *at least* tomorrow," and then chuckled at her own attempt at mother humor.

Paul followed her out to the kitchen, leaned against the doorjamb, and watched her open the refrigerator, take out sodas, fill the glasses with ice, and pour. When she turned to head out to the 'porch' he went ahead of her to open the door. They were greeted by the sharp sent of ozone and torrential rain. "I hadn't even noticed any clouds," Claire said.

Paul took one of the sodas from her, clasped her hand, and walked her slowly back down the dark hallway into the living room. Claire switched on a small lamp, softening the room with the warm glow of a fifty-watt bulb. She looked out of place in her own home. "I'll go, Claire, if you want me to." Paul finally said.

She gave him another small smile. "You don't have to go. I'm not uptight about you; I'm uptight about the things in my head. Whether you're here or not, they never go away." She gave him a wry look. "That's part of my problem." Claire plopped down on the couch and gestured for Paul to sit. "Besides Daniel Alvarez, you're the only man who's ever been in the apartment since I moved in."

"I'm honored."

Claire looked at him pointedly. *"You should be."* She took a sip of her soda and played with the water ring it had left on the top of the table's surface. "You need to know what you're getting yourself into Paul. You keep pushing this dating thing with me. I struggle with what you see in me and ... well ..." she swallowed, fiddling with the glass in front of her, "I find myself thinking about you and looking forward to talking to you and ..." she put her head in her hands, "I'm starting to get afraid," she finished lamely.

"Afraid?" Paul had anticipated some of the things she might say to him, but not this. "You're afraid of me? I thought we were past that one."

She shook her head and he knew he wasn't getting it. Jeeze, they'd only just started and he was already lost. *Think*. He couldn't stop himself, acting before he could reason it all through. He reached over to her, put his arms around her waist, and pulled her against his side in a protective backward embrace, and she instantly became a frozen block of ice in his arms. "Easy, Claire," he whispered against her cheek, immediately recognizing his mistake. "*Easy*. This is nothing more than the way I was brought up. When you know someone's hurting or frightened or in need of something that you're not sure how to give you *hug*. You give them what strength and support you have with a physical touch." He slowly disentangled his arms from her waist, putting one along the back of the couch and one in his lap. He no longer held her; in fact sitting rigidly next to him as she was, they weren't even touching. Paul realized she was trembling.

"I, I don't do well with touch-touching," she said to him, her teeth almost chattering.

"How are you at leaning?" he asked again against her ear.

She gave him a puzzled look, and then seemed to realize what he was talking about. Slowly, as though she were lowering herself into a scalding tub of water, she gradually moved until her entire back was leaning against him. He didn't move a muscle.

Moments went by and then she said quietly, "You always smell good, you know."

He chuckled. "We'll try this after a full day's work and one of my basketball games with Tyler. You'll change your tune quickly."

His humor relaxed her more and she finally rested her head against his arm on the back of the couch. "I don't ever remember doing anything like this ..."

"Jeeze, Claire," he said in exasperation, "where have you been all your life?"

"Lost," she said in a voice that sounded like a frightened child.

She reached up and took the hand that was resting on the back of the couch, drawing it down so that it was held by both of hers. In doing so, she was once again in a partial embrace. "I've been working hard these past few years trying to carve out a place for myself and for Tyler. I have," she hesitated, "Rules of Survival that help me stay together. Stay sane. You're messing with my rules, Paul, making me question things that I know for fact, causing me to shift and change things that I've put in place to *keep me alive*. I'm afraid because ... you're adding complications to the mix that I can't deal with."

He was mystified. "Like what?"

She shrugged against him. "Like hope, trust ... love. I was doing okay without them, really I was, Paul. And now, all of a sudden I'm faced with having them be a part of my life and, well, it's terrifying."

Paul couldn't help it, his arm tightened around her. He leaned forward to whisper again to her, "I *think* I'm complimented. But somehow I feel like I should say 'sorry', too. How weird is that?"

Claire didn't stiffen at his movements, but didn't respond either. She seemed lost in thought. "I was a foster kid from the moment I was born," she began in a distant, flat voice. "I left the hospital a ward of the state and stayed a ward of the state until I turned eighteen. My parents were 'unfit to care for me', although no one ever elaborated any more than that. Those unfit parents didn't think enough of me to sign the necessary papers that would have released me for adoption. My earliest memory is crying over a stuffed bunny that could not be found when I was being picked up to be taken to another 'permanent' foster home." She sighed. "I must have been about three, three and a half.

"I heard a homeless person described as 'transient' one time and took the time and trouble to look it up. It meant 'remaining in a place for only a brief time'. I could not understand what the difference was between a homeless person and me. There was absolutely no distinction as far as I could tell." She was silent again for a moment. "I was about eleven.

"By the time I was in my teens I was an angry, sullen, bitter kid. I was wise to grown-ups and their lies, knew how to play the game to survive." Claire was quiet for a minute. "Or so I thought."

She sat forward and took a sip of her soda, and then another one. She looked at Paul and smiled briefly at his intense look. He said nothing and made no move to draw her back beside him, but his body was cold where she had been. Did she feel that, too?

Apparently she did, for Claire settled back down beside him, her back to his right side. When she sighed again, he wrapped his right arm around her waist and pulled her back even more tightly against him. This time she seemed to have no objection.

"It was in my teens that the Rules of Survival began to form. They were rules I made up based on experience. Every single one of them I learned the hard way and I never ever doubted their truthfulness." At his continued silence, she turned and looked at him. "Aren't you going to ask me what the Rules are?"

"You'll tell me if you want me to know, Claire. You're teaching me to be a patient man." He gave her a sweet smile and she felt his hand caress her waist briefly and then be still, perhaps realizing he might have gone too far again.

Claire began to speak in the monotone voice of someone who had repeated something a million times, "Never accept charity because it will absolutely destroy you. Establish suitable safe boundaries and never compromise them for any reason. If you dream about it, it's never gonna happen. Believe what you see, not what you hear. Never trust anyone to keep his or her word because it only leads to disappointment. Men always have hidden agendas. Men will do anything to get what they want. Stay away from all men ..." She turned and looked at him. "I've got a million of 'em. *A million.*" And then she started to cry.

He gathered her against him, and his other hand cupped the back of her head to hold her carefully under his chin against his chest. At some point he began to rock her back and forth as she continued to cry. Paul had no words; he just sat there silently as she soaked his shirt with her tears.

"I lost count of how many foster homes I went to," she finally continued, making no effort to pull away from his embrace. "I learned to be very cooperative if it was a good one and a demon from hell if it was a bad one. I had a goal: get my high school diploma, get into a county college, get a nursing degree, and get out on my own as soon as I could. I began to look at my situation as an opportunity to grab everything I could get my hands on, literally and figuratively. I'm not proud of it, but I stole if it suited me and I thought it would speed me along to my goal.

"My last foster home was nice at first. They didn't make me do too many chores and when I look back on it they were strict with me just like real parents should be. They had a son ... he was a year younger than me ..." Claire clutched at Paul's shirt and swallowed with difficulty. He held her a little bit tighter. "His friends came over one night and they brought beer. His mother was away at a movie."

She sat forward and Paul let her go, watching, knowing what was coming. It was like seeing a car fatal wreck happen from a distance and being unable to prevent it. Claire laughed bitterly. "They invited me to sit and watch the game with them. They offered me some beer and I drank it. Somehow ... somehow ..." Silence filled the dark living room, a huge, awkward, horrible silence. She hunched her shoulders and bent low over her knees as though she was trying to withdraw into herself. He watched a tear trickle down her cheek and drip onto the bare floor.

Paul reached over, scooped her up, and settled her on his lap. He circled her with his arms and tucked her head under his chin. She was so far within herself she didn't even seem to notice his touch this time. "You don't have to say it, Claire," he said quietly. "I get the picture." He kissed the top of her head and settled back against the couch, rocking her in silence.

Time drifted. Paul took advantage of the moment, getting his fill of holding her close, inhaling the clean scent of her, stroking the silkiness of her hair. Heck ... he was comfortable; he'd sit all night with her if he could.

"You don't have the whole picture," she said quietly perhaps an hour later, "unless you know that one of those six boys is Tyler's father, although I don't know which. You don't have the whole picture unless you know that they cleaned me up and tucked me into bed when they were done with me. You don't have the whole picture unless you know that when I tried to tell someone - *anyone* - what had happened, but no one believed me. I *had* joined the guys to watch the game of my own choice, I *had* drunk alcohol, I couldn't remember ever telling them 'no'. Who'd believe *me*? I was only a troubled foster kid who'd been thrown out of too many foster homes to count ..." She stopped and a small moan escaped from the back of her throat.

"Ah, Claire, *Claire,*" Paul felt a sorrow well up from deep inside of him. A sorrow that mourned the truth of all her Rules, a sorrow that cried over the irrevocable loss of her innocence. He rocked her, he rocked himself. He remembered her talking to him in the dark of the parking lot weeks ago. *I have never been on a date before. I have never had a boyfriend. I have never done a lot of things. The person you apparently think I am is nonexistent. I'm one very screwed up lady and you should take the hint and move on. Okay?*

Long moments passed again. The information was so heinous that it could only be given in small doses and then time was needed to overcome the awful taste. Against the top of her head, Paul finally spoke what was in his heart, "I don't think I've ever admired anyone so much in all my life, Claire. With nothing to start with, with attacks on every side, you've turned into a strong, independent woman who works harder than anyone I know, who has an ironclad determination to succeed, who loves her son with every fiber of her being, and who is far more beautiful inside than out. And let me tell you, *that's saying something.*" Still sitting on his lap she sat up to look at him with an incredulous look on her tear streaked face. Paul reached up and cupped her cheek and his thumb brushed away a tear. In a voice gruff with emotion he said, "I noticed you first because of those green eyes of yours; I'm fighting to stay because of your heart, Claire."

Her mouth trembled and more tears streaked down her face. He wanted to kiss her so badly that for a moment it was an all-consuming thought. Paul fought it down; time enough for that later. He suddenly wanted their first *real* kiss to be wreathed in happiness and joy rather than surrounded with darkness and evil ghosts. He used his big, calloused hand to wipe away the tears from her cheeks and dried off his hand on the front of his shirt more than once. "I think the dam has finally broken, Green Eyes," he said to her at last. He gently guided her back down to nestle against his shoulder underneath his chin and he rocked her again as she cried some more and sniffled.

Sitting on her battered couch in her dingy, bare apartment, Paul finally felt as though he'd arrived home. It had been a long, arduous trip, but he'd made it.

At some point, she fell asleep in his arms, softly 'whuffing' a sleepy breathing rhythm against his neck. He had no idea what time it was, but it was late. Making a decision, he stood and carried her to her bedroom, taking in the neatly made bed and the threadbare cover visible from the glowing streetlights from the street. Paul laid her down and took off her shoes, just as she'd done for Tyler so many hours earlier. She never stirred. He tucked the covers around her and then stood, watching her sleep.

These past weeks since he'd first met her he'd been struggling with what it was about her that kept drawing him back. Why did she continue to haunt his daily thoughts and nightly dreams? What was it about her that made him look forward to the next opportunity to be with her? Finally, tonight, he'd figured it out.

She was the most courageous person he knew, and she was going to teach him how to be courageous, too.

Thank you, he prayed, *thank you very, very much.*

The phone woke Claire Sunday morning. "Hello?" she said in a voice filled with sleep.

"Claire? It's Paul. I worried that your alarm wasn't set and that you'd oversleep and be late for work ..."

Claire's brain struggled to function. What day was it? What month was it? What year was it? "What time is it?" she finally managed to ask.

"A little before seven. I couldn't remember what time you had to get to work on Sunday. Tell me I did right calling you." His voice had a desperate edge to it.

She sat up, yawned, and stretched. "You did right calling me. I should have been up fifteen minutes ago. I think even Tyler's asleep." She strained to hear the television but heard only silence.

"Okay," she heard a sigh of relief at the other end of the phone, "so now I can stop having a crisis. I've been up since six, wondering if I should call or not." She smiled to herself, enjoying the fact that there was someone somewhere thinking about her. "I thought of another reason why I'd like you to get a place at that Sonrise House, Claire."

"Oh yeah? Why's that?"

"Because you could have Sundays off. Then, the next time my mother guilts me into showing up at her house to eat, I can drag you along for protection and distraction."

"You think I'd do that, huh?"

"I'd drag you by the hair. You'd have no choice."

She got ready for work with a smile on her face.

Sunday was her favorite day to work. The tips were often the best, she saw more families than any other day, and after four o'clock things often slowed down to a pace that didn't make her sweat. Tyler and Mrs. Santiago came to dinner as usual and she even took a few minutes to sit and chat with them over their desserts. Wiping down their table after they'd left, Claire felt a twinge of guilt. She'd been so wrapped up in her own disastrous life circumstances she'd completely forgotten that Mrs. Santiago was in a similar situation. Although her daughter in Florida had said Mrs. Santiago could move in with her, it sounded as if neither was too happy about the situation. Straightening up, Claire scanned her section to check her two remaining occupied tables and met the sincere faces of Janice Strocco and Daniel Alvarez. Her heart skipped three beats.

"Hi Claire," they both said, with identical friendly smiles.

"Hi Mr. Alvarez, Hi Ms. Stroc - ," she stopped and blushed.

"Janice," Janice Strocco said. "And this is my sidekick, Tonto, but you can call him Daniel."

Claire sighed. "I know, you've both told me. I'll keep trying." She flipped open her order book. "What can I get you?"

"You wanna come live at our house?" Janice said with a huge grin. She reminded Claire of Tyler waiting for Paul to show up on the day they went to the baseball game; so eager and so excited she could hardly stand herself.

They wouldn't joke about something like this, would they? Claire looked at Daniel, who had a kind, satisfied smile on his face. "It was unanimous, Claire. Exactly what we had prayed for. No dissension in the committee at all. Everyone was impressed with your sincerity and honesty."

Claire's knees felt wobbly and she sat down next to Janice in the booth. "Really?" she finally managed to croak out. Could it be true? Could she have finally been cut a break after all these years?

Janice reached over and gripped Claire's hand. "Really, Claire." She leaned over to make direct eye contact. "The committee met after church today and decided. You will accept, won't you Claire? Daniel and I were so thrilled that you were chosen, and then we got this sinking feeling that you would change your mind." She nodded toward Daniel. "We couldn't wait, and decided to come here and tell you ourselves. We hope we don't have to convince you to say yes."

Claire looked down at Janice's hand still clutching hers and then up at Janice. "No, you don't have to convince me to say yes. If you hadn't made this offer, then Tyler and I would be sleeping in our car in another couple of weeks. I don't really have any other choice."

"Do you remember what I was going to pray for, Claire?" Janice asked quietly. "Remember I said I was going to pray that God would give you clear direction about your decision?"

Claire nodded.

"God says 'no' and 'yes'. God allows circumstances to steer us in the direction He wants us to go." Janice looked like all of this made absolute sense to her.

Claire couldn't help if she sounded a bit sarcastic. "Are you saying God caused me to be evicted from my apartment?"

Daniel piped up. "Would you have seriously considered Sonrise House otherwise?"

"No, but ..."

"Look," Janice said. "Why does your eviction have to be perceived as 'bad luck' for you? Why can't it be God's way of making sure you don't pass up this opportunity of a lifetime? Who says that He didn't realize just how adverse you were to this entire concept, and He knew that it was going to take something major to get you to accept? Who says that God doesn't have wonderful plans for you and for Sonrise House, and that He's ready to finally put it all in motion?

"And isn't it a whole lot nicer to think of it my way?" Janice said with a grin.

Claire looked at their faces; Daniel's calm, peaceful one and Janice's open, enthusiastic one. Why would she ever consider fighting this good fortune? Whether it was God or luck, who cared in the end? Wasn't it time she was cut a break? "When can I start moving in?"

Daniel reached over and put his hand palm down on the table. When he took his hand away a shiny brass key attached to a key ring sat in the middle of the table. The key ring was a big Lucite rectangle that had a picture of a sunburst with the words 'Press on to know the Lord, He is as certain as the dawn. Hosea 6:3' written on top. "We've got to sign a few papers to make it all official, but we know you've got to be out of your apartment very soon. Plus, with the hours you work, we know how tough it's going to be to get everything packed and moved, and to resettle.

"There are a lot of people in the church who are not on the committee who want to help. When you're ready, we have numerous people with pick-ups and such who are willing to help get you moved in and settled. Just say the word, okay?"

Claire looked down at the key and then back up at Daniel and Janice's excited faces. These two people were putting a lot of trust in her. Claire knew how important the success of Sonrise House was to them, and she was suddenly overwhelmed with the responsibility of it all. She had a thought. "Who else will be moving in with Tyler and me?"

Janice and Daniel looked at each other. "Go ahead," Janice said, "it was your decision."

Daniel's face was intense and serious when he turned to look at Claire. "I remembered your reservations about living with strangers, Claire, and I remembered your valid points about different people – adult and child – trying to live together and do it happily. We talked in the committee and I voiced your concerns. Surprisingly, there were a number of people on the committee who shared your opinion. We decided we'd take things slowly at first. We'd like you to move in first, get settled, help us get through the transition involved in setting things up with the county and state agencies as well as the church family. Then, once you and Tyler are settled and we've worked out the initial 'kinks', say six months or so, then we'll interview some other candidates and make a decision." He smiled at Claire. "We even discussed having you sit in on the committee and interview any prospective roommates as well. But that's getting ahead of ourselves."

"You also need to know," said Janice, "and this is a tremendous compliment, Claire, that you were the only one to get a unanimous vote of approval from the committee. For all other candidates, the committee was divided. We felt that this was God's way of confirming our decision about you and Tyler being the only family for the first few months."

The key sat in the center of the scuffed Formica table. It was more than just a key to her new home; it was a key that opened doors to a whole host of possibilities. When the committee had interviewed her, they had asked Claire questions about her goals – professional and personal. She had struggled to be honest with them, dredging up long ago hopes and dreams. At the time, Claire had wanted those committee members to understand that she wasn't just some down and out waitress looking for a free handout; she wanted them to realize that she was vital and intelligent even if she was also overwhelmed and slightly desperate. She could hear herself stuttering out the answers to their questions.

I, I used to want to be a nurse, the kind that helps those tiny preemie babies, you know? I used to go to the library whenever I could when I was a kid and get books on nursing and biology … For a while I knew the names of all the bones in the body from the tip of your toe to the top of your head. Studying stuff like that helped fill in the time when I was … you know, on my own and stuff.

Free time? I don't have much free time, but if I had it, well, I guess I'd spend more time with Tyler. I think most of his problems – and they're not big problems, mind you – are because I just don't have the time to sit and talk with him. Sometimes he gets talking to me and telling me stuff about friends and school and I'm so tired that I fall asleep on him right in the middle of our conversation. I wish I had more time to just laugh with him. I'd like to spend a day with him not worrying about the stuff I have to do and just enjoy the stuff we want to do. We went to a baseball game the other day and he acted like he'd been flown to the moon, he was so excited. I, I'd like to do more stuff like that, you know? Nothing big or expensive like Disney World or anything. Just going to the park, or the movies, or ... McDonalds for dinner.

God? I told somebody just the other day that I didn't believe in God because I'd never had the opportunity. But maybe that's not quite right. I think I believe in God, but I think He's got better things to do than worry about someone as small and unimportant as me. Don't get me wrong, I think I've done pretty good on my own and all, but there are a lot of people out there who are in more desperate situations than me and are probably more deserving of ... Godly help, I guess. I guess I think that God figures I'm tough enough to handle my life on my own, and He's focusing His energies where He's more needed.

I've got a temper, I won't deny that. When someone pushes me into a corner or tries to get in my space, I don't take very kindly to that. I wasn't always like that. I used to be kind of meek and quiet and shy, but well, life changes you, you know? If you sit around all silent and sloppy then people will just plow right over you, take what they don't deserve, and leave what you don't want. I've got rules in my head that have helped me survive and make it this far. I'm living on the edge, I guess, but I'm not stupid and I'm not oblivious. I'll figure something out for Tyler and I if this doesn't work out with you guys and you decide one of the other women needs this house more than I do. Don't you worry about that. One way or another, Tyler and I will end up just fine.

Up until this very minute, though, Claire realized that she had begun to loose faith in her ability to provide for herself and her son. The rubber band of tension that twisted tighter with each day she got closer to the eviction had reached a point where it was going to snap rather than stretch anymore. Absolutely, this shiny brass key was more than just a new home for her. It was her new future.

"Remember, Claire," Janice said as she and Daniel began to leave, "we didn't arrange all of this. God did." She chuckled to herself as though she was remembering a private joke. "In His own unique and puzzling fashion, God has put all this in motion in just the way He wants it all to be."

Claire stood up and let Janice slide out of the booth. Janice handed her the key. "You've got my number, right?" When Claire nodded, Janice impulsively hugged her. "I'll see you soon, okay?"

Daniel smiled and touched her arm. "Who would have thought that getting reported to DYFS would be such a great thing, huh?" Janice and Daniel headed for the door.

"Hey! I almost forgot," Claire said, stopping the two of them just as they were walking out the door. "That Sonset House that the church owns. How do you get to move in there? I know someone who needs a place …"

When Daniel and Janice had finally left, Claire heard "You okay?" Turning, she saw Maddy's concerned expression.

Claire broke into a smile. "Look what I've got, Maddy. It's a key to my very own house." Maddy looked puzzled for just a moment and then let out a loud whoop as she pulled Claire into a fierce embrace. As their shift progressed and they passed each other carrying trays of steaming food, Maddy shouted decorating ideas to Claire. It took Claire a while to realize that part of the joy of her good news was wrapped up in the fact that she had a friend to share it with.

Claire finished her shift in a daze, preoccupied with all that had to be done. Later that night after, having said her thank - yous to Mrs. Santiago, showering, and crawling into bed, as tired as she was Claire couldn't fall asleep. Looking at the phone, she made a hasty decision and called Paul.

"Did I wake you, Paul? It's Claire."

"Nah, I'm kind of a night owl if you haven't figured that out yet. That's why I show up on your porch all the time and get arrested for loitering."

"Did you have a nice day?" Claire was at a loss about making casual conversation. Her skills in the area extended no farther then the few brief words said before she asked, "And what can I get you from today's menu?"

He sighed. "Well, I went and had dinner at my mother's, so that should tell you everything."

"I think I'm supposed to believe that you had a miserable day, but from what I saw of your Mom and Dad I think it must have been a wonderful afternoon."

"Let's just say it was a long afternoon."

"What did your Mom cook?"

Paul burst out laughing. "Oh, my Mom doesn't cook! Dad does all the cooking, especially now that he's retired. She does all the inviting and cleaning up, though."

"You're kidding!"

"Nope, I'm not. It's been that way for as long as I can remember. She cooked during the week when we were little and Dad still worked, but it was only to keep us all alive. She hates to cook. Dad was in the mood for Indian today, so he cooked some turkey curry and made his own vegetable somosas. I'm going to reek of Indian spices for a week."

"You're serious." Claire had enough trouble conjuring up a 'typical' Sunday family dinner, let alone one with all these added twists.

Paul chuckled. "Oh yeah, I'm serious."

"Were your brother and sisters there?"

"That was the best part, just Brian was with me. I went because he insisted I go. Otherwise I would have tried to escape the whole experience like I always do."

Claire couldn't help but ask, "What am I missing? Your family seemed so wonderful on Saturday. Why do I only hear negative things from you about them?"

He was silent for a moment before he answered. "I've kind of always been the black sheep of the family, Claire. The spoiled black sheep. I've worked really, really hard to achieve that status, too. There's not a lot of love lost between me and my brothers and sisters, although things have really improved lately with, Brian."

"Are you still the black sheep? I just don't get it. The Paul I know is kind and patient and good. You've gone out of your way too many times to count for both me and Tyler. You even go to church! If that makes you the black sheep of the family then your brothers and sisters must be saints!"

"I've kind of been reinventing myself these last few years," he said with some hesitancy. "You've met the 'new me', while the rest of the family is still reeling from the old me."

"That's not what I saw Saturday," she said with certainty.

"What did you see Saturday?"

"I saw a sister who wanted to talk with you so badly she had herself all worked up into knots about doing it correctly. I saw a mom who loved you like crazy and missed you maybe even more than that. I saw a whole pile of people grinning from ear to ear because 'Paul came to the party'. Tell me," she said with a teasing tone, "when my back was turned were they spitting and throwing rocks at you?"

"I screwed up pretty badly for a while, Claire. It'll be a long time before they all forgive and forget."

"I think it's something completely different."

Paul sighed. "Are you going to tell me or do I have to guess?"

"Oh, I'll tell you all right, but I'm not sure you'll be happy to hear it. I think rather than it being a long time before your family and friends forgive and forget I think it's you who needs to forgive and forget. They don't seem to have a problem with you, you seem to have a problem with you." He was silent on the other end of the phone. "All this God and church business has to have something about forgiving and forgetting, doesn't it?" she finally asked him quietly.

"You just might be more trouble than you're worth, Claire Jenkins," he said after moments of silence. "What, do you have a psychology degree hidden underneath that waitress uniform?"

"I did try to warn you. Repeatedly."

"Yeah, you did."

"How about we make a deal, you and me?" she finally said.

"What kind of deal?" He sounded completely wary, like suddenly he'd just discovered a trap door he was on top of.

"I'll try to remember and believe all the nice things you said about me last night if you do the same about what I say about you. Okay?"

"You drive a tough bargain. I know what I tell you about yourself is true." This time it was her turn to be silent. "Okay, it's a deal. I'm going to hold you to this though. No more talk about your bad luck and being a screw up."

"Right back at you Mr. Williamson. Hey, you didn't ask me about my day," she said, smiling as she curled up in her bed. And when he finally did ask, she told him all about her new key.

The foolish man seeks happiness in the distance, the wise grows it under his feet.[16]

Twelve: Nothing Is Ever As Good As It Looks

The week flew by with too many things to get finished in too little time. Monday and Tuesday Claire had gone to visit Sonrise House on her lunch hour, walking from room to room, looking out the windows, sitting in the chairs. The reality of her good luck overwhelmed her. The realization that she was no longer living a hair's breadth away from financial disaster and homelessness was a tremendous relief. She lost count of the number of times she'd become melancholy and tense only to realize that she was stressing about things that were no longer a concern. She had been doing it for so long she was more used to worrying than not.

Wednesday, Daniel Alvarez came to the diner to discuss details. Her first month would be completely rent free, purposely releasing her from her brutal work schedule so that she could begin to reorder her life. He wanted her to get herself over to the county college first chance she had to look into taking some nursing courses in the fall. Daniel went through her finances, asking her specific questions about her salary and financial obligations. While Claire was completely free of debt (no one would

---

[16] James Oppenheim

consider giving her a line of credit!) her income was staggeringly low even with all the hours she put in. "I think you should reduce your work load to no more than fifteen hours a week, Claire," Daniel said in all seriousness.

"Are you nuts, Daniel?" she'd asked him. "How do you expect Tyler and I to eat and me to put clothes on our backs and gas in the car?"

"Well, first you have to understand what the rent on the house will be." He wrote a number down. "By my calculation, this is exactly one week's salary working about fifteen hours a week, right?" When she nodded, he said, "Good budgets allow for only a quarter of the income to go toward the rent or a mortgage. So that's what you'll be required to pay us for Sonrise House."

Claire rolled her eyes and shook her head in disgust. "You're a really nice guy, Daniel, but you're a lousy business man."

He gave her one of his rare grins, leaned over and whispered, "This isn't a business, Claire, this is God's work." He then outlined where she was supposed to go to apply to other organizations for assistance regarding food, medical needs, and financial aid for college. "You'll be stuck standing in some pretty long, tedious lines registering for all of this, but that's another reason why we wanted your first month to be rent free. Work at the diner, but take enough time off so you can get all these things done and out of the way."

Claire finally decided to take Thursday, Friday and Sunday off to finish packing and begin moving things over to the house. After school on Thursday she took Tyler to see the house. They sat in the car for a long time just looking at everything through the windshield. "We're really going to live here, Mom?"

"Yeah, we really are, buddy. Just us two for the first few months, and then eventually another lady and her kids will move in. So it's not totally ours."

Tyler shrugged. "I don't think I'll mind having another kid living here with me. I hope it's a boy or at least a girl that likes to play baseball."

Claire needed to keep him grounded. "She could be a girl who loves Barbie dolls and fingernail polish who you'll never get along with."

"Do I have to share a room with her?"

"No."

"Do I have to play with her?"

"No, but you'll have to be polite."

"Is she allowed to play with my things?"

"No, as long as you keep them in your room, that will be your own private spot. Of course, if you leave them lying all around the house, well, that's a different story."

"Your gonna bug me about keeping things neat even more here than at the apartment, aren't you?"

She smiled and touched his cheek. "No, it will probably be about the same."

"Can we plant some flowers in the garden?"

"I don't see why not."

"Do I get to pick out which room is mine?"

"I guess, within reason. Let's check it out, okay?" Claire had already decided that she would take one of the larger bedrooms and wanted Tyler to take one of the smaller ones. She hoped they wouldn't have a fight about this. But they didn't. Tyler picked the room she'd thought would be just right for him, next to hers with the two big windows shaded by a huge oak tree. There was a nice closet with a built in set of drawers that Tyler decided was perfect for all of his "private stuff". Whatever that was.

"Can we paint my room if we want to?"

"I think so. I'll have to make sure."

"Can I put up posters?"

"Sure."

Tyler looked at her. "I'm going to miss the apartment, Mom, but this place is nice. How long can we stay here?"

She squatted down in front of him. "We can stay here for two years, maybe a little bit more. I'm not going to work as much, Tyler, and I'm going to have a chance to go to school to become a nurse! Then, when I work I'll make better money and we won't have to struggle so much with everything. I should have more time to do stuff with you. Maybe we can go to the park or the movies or something."

He looked down at his toes. "I'm going to miss Mrs. Santiago,

Mom. She doesn't want to go live with that stupid daughter of hers." He looked up at her. "Hey! Could she come live here with us?"

Claire took Tyler's hand in hers. "One of the things I had to promise was that no one would live with us in this house unless they were approved by the church committee. That means Mrs. Santiago. But I told Pastor Strocco and Mr. Alvarez about her, and they were going to see what they could do."

"Mrs. Santiago's been lighting a lot of candles, you know, Mom," Tyler said. He fingered the St. Christopher's medal he wore beneath his tee shirt. "At church on Sunday she prays the whole time she's there for a new place for all of us to live. I'd hate for only us to find a happy place to stay …"

What could she say? "Well, maybe we have to add our prayers to Mrs. Santiago's."

Tyler looked thrilled. "Really, Mom? I told Mrs. Santiago that I didn't think that you ever prayed. I didn't think you even believed in it."

She shrugged. "Do you think it will make Mrs. Santiago feel better if she knows that we are saying prayers for her?"

"Oh yeah, she really gets into that stuff, Mom."

"Okay, then we will."

"Right now?"

"Ah, er, okay … sure. You want to say a prayer?"

"I'm not too good at it, Mom."

"I think you might have more experience at it than me," Claire felt compelled to point out. They'd had a long talk about him visiting church with Mrs. Santiago and praying and lighting candles and everything.

He shrugged. "Okay." He closed his eyes, bowed his head, and folded his hands. Then he peeked out at Claire. "You gotta do this, Mom, that's how it works."

"Oh, okay," she said trying not to smile.

"Hey, God, it's me, Tyler Jenkins. This is my mom, Claire Jenkins. She doesn't talk to you very much but we're both worried about Mrs. Santiago and so we're both sending up prayers today." Tyler leaned over towards Claire and said out of the corner of his mouth in a whisper, "How does this sound so far, Mom?"

"Perfect," she said in the same conspiratorial whisper. This was the kind of stuff she missed working all the hours she did. It was glorious.

"God, me and my Mom are worried that Mrs. Santiago won't find a place to stay that will make her happy. Will you help her find a place just like you did for us? Me and Mom would really appreciate it." He leaned over again to Claire. "Want to add anything, Mom?" he said out of the corner of his mouth.

"Oh! Er, well, thanks God for giving us this house to stay in for a while. It's a really nice house and Tyler and I really appreciate it. A lot."

"Oh, good, Mom!" Tyler said in an excited whisper. "Mrs. Santiago says you're supposed to always say things you're thankful for before you go asking for a whole bunch of stuff. I forgot that." He assumed his praying stance again. "In Jesus' name, amen!" Tyler opened his eyes, unfolded his hands, and smiled at Claire. "That's it, Mom. We did it. Now we just wait and see."

Claire couldn't resist. "How soon until we get an answer?" she said still trying not to smile.

"Oh, Mom," Tyler said to her in a tone that implied she had so much to learn but he was willing to be extremely patient with her. "Maybe you don't realize. God works in mysterious ways. You don't always get to see the answer or understand the answer, but you always get an answer. Mrs. Santiago told me that, too. Come on! Let's go look at the back yard!" She watched in stunned amazement as her son rushed out the back door.

Paul was waiting in her parking lot Friday morning when she got back from taking Tyler to school. "I'm taking you to breakfast," he said in a rather commanding tone, "and then I'll come help you pack to make up for the time you'll loose eating." He crossed his arms and tried to look fierce and commanding.

"Who's paying for breakfast?"

"Me," he said, "or we could arm wrestle and the winner could pay."

He took her to a place that was smaller and more intimate than a diner, but not much fancier. There were tables outside on the sidewalk, and they both got steamy hot croissants fresh from the oven. As she wiped a dribble of butter off her chin, Paul smiled and said, "The guys are showing up with their trucks tomorrow to help you move." He looked a little bit uncomfortable. "I hope they'll behave, but it's just possible that they will drive us both absolutely nuts. They can be rather ... irreverent ... when they get going. I'm worried that they'll make you uptight." He took a sip of his coffee. "If you tell me you'd rather they didn't help, Brian and I will just show."

"None of you have to come help. There is a whole bunch of church people who were eager to help."

"You won't do that," he said with absolute certainty.

"How are you so sure?"

"They're strangers and you don't like to ask for help. That's why I'm *telling* you Brian and I are going to help. I'm *asking* you if you want the wild bunch along for the ride."

"Are you different when you are with them?"

That made him thoughtful. "I try not to be." He made a face. "You saw me with them that time at the diner for breakfast."

"How could I forget?" He gave her such a pained look that she smiled at him.

"When you smile I -," he stopped himself.

"What?"

Briefly he made eye contact with her then he scratched his chin and motioned for the waitress to bring the check. He didn't look at her and he didn't answer her, just glanced briefly at the check, threw bills on the table, took her hand and walked with her out to the parking lot. Claire stared at Paul while he held the truck door open for her, still silent but now looking at her intently.

"Are you going to tell me what's on your mind?"

"You sure you wanna know?"

"Yeah, I'm sure," she gave him a cocky look that communicated she could handle it.

"When you smile," he leaned forward, purposely invading her space, "all I want to do is kiss you. You're smiling a lot more nowadays and it's becoming a bit of an all consuming fixation with me." He reached up and cupped her cheek with his hand, and after a brief hesitation touched her mouth with his thumb. He sighed. "It's bordering on an obsession. Then I start thinking that you've probably never been properly kissed, and so I want the setting and the circumstances to be just perfect. *Then* I get all wrapped up with the when and the how and the why and the where ..."

Claire reached up and touched his face the same way he was touching hers. Long, long moments passed and he felt her thumb trace the outline of his mouth. He froze, afraid to move, afraid that she would startle and withdraw her hand. "I suppose you've kissed hundreds of women," she murmured, looking directly at his mouth.

"Millions," he breathed.

"So you've got lots of experience; enough for both of us. So the fact that I have no experience shouldn't be too much of a problem for you, huh?"

"No, not too much of a problem. Of course, we might have to practice a bit. To work out the kinks and so that eventually we get it just right. That's important you know, the practicing."

"Hmmm," she said, "so I've heard," as she stared directly at his mouth seemingly memorizing every pore. She licked her lips.

Paul exerted a little bit of pressure to draw her closer. So what if it was a shopping mall parking lot? So what if he hadn't shaved since yesterday morning? So what if he hadn't brought her roses and they weren't all dressed up from a fantastic night on the town? He'd kiss her now, right this ... darn ... minute.

Claire withdrew her hand from his face, suddenly all business. "We'd better get going, I've still got a lot of packing to do." She made motions to climb into the truck.

He forced down the strangled, agonizing moan that threatened to come from some profoundly frustrated place deep inside of him. Then she turned and grinned at him. "Now what are you thinking?"

"That you're killing me, Claire. You're really killing me."

She turned back to him, laughing and touched his face again, this time with both hands. Paul closed his eyes and took a deep, calming breath.

She smelled clean like Dial soap and some fresh kind of clothes detergent. "I, I have felt lighter, freer, happier than I've felt in ... probably my whole life, Paul. I keep thinking about that night you spent talking to me, listening to me." She brushed his forehead and he felt her touch his hair. "Actually, what was most important was that you believed and didn't condemn me." She traced the bridge of his nose and the outline of his mouth again. "Now, I've got the house and at last things seem to be falling into place for me. I hear you saying 'I don't believe in coincidences,' and I think and think about this kind, loving man who's gone out of his way to show me that there really is some goodness in this life. A man who's been patient and tender and understanding and loving. At the birthday party for your mother," Claire said quietly, "something important happened to me. I saw true love between your parents, Paul. In my entire life I've never seen that before." She shook her head. "I didn't think such a thing existed. You are a product of that loving kindness. That's what makes you so unique and special."

What beautiful things she was saying to him, giving him. Still with his eyes closed he let her words seep deeply inside, making him feel like the person he so wanted to be in God's eyes. Was that really how she saw him? She made him feel ten feet tall. She believed in him. Claire's hands dropped to his shoulders and he opened his eyes just in time to see her lean forward and give him the lightest of butterfly kisses on his lips: fleeting, soft, sweet ...

He went with the moment, gathering her in his arms and looking at her, meeting her unwavering gaze. Was her pulse racing like his? Holding her against him, he reached up and smoothed back a strand of hair, tucking it behind her ear. "Need me to smile again?" Claire said, and she gave him a dazzling grin. So they had their first real kiss, right there in the parking lot, with no moonlight and no roses.

And it was just perfect.

Paul attacked packing Claire's apartment like he did everything: head on, gun's blazing, taking no prisoners. Glasses were wrapped, clothes were folded, toiletries were boxed, and by the time Tyler was picked up from school they were just about finished.

"What are you doing?" Paul asked Claire in a puzzled voice.

"Cleaning the toilet. Tell me you've never seen this done before and I'm never going to your house."

He chuckled. "I clean my toilets, and I resent the implication that I don't. What I don't get is why you're cleaning *this* toilet *now* when you're moving out *tomorrow*."

Claire sat back on her heals and blew a wisp of hair out of her eyes. "I'm going to clean this apartment from top to bottom before I leave. No one's going to say that Claire Jenkins is a slob."

"Claire, they're going to *refurbish* the entire building. Change the place into expensive condos! They're probably going to rip that toilet right out of the wall and throw it out."

She gave him a little sniff and went back to her scrubbing. "Then it will be the cleanest toilet they tear out."

He shook his head. "I was thinking that we could bring a load of your stuff over to the house after we pick Tyler up from school. I carried down a bunch of boxes from the kitchen to the back of my truck. Would you and the kid like to go to my softball game tonight? This is the church team that I'm on. It would give you a chance to at least meet Simon and Josh. It might make things go smoother tomorrow."

Claire turned around to study him. "You're really nervous about my meeting your friends. Are you worried about what *I'll* think of *them* or what *they'll* think of *me*?"

He slid his massive frame down the hallway wall and sat looking in on her in the bathroom. "Neither. I'm worried about how *all of you* will view *me* when you're together. My life's kind of weird, Claire. Everything is separate and distinct. Like an undone dot - to - dot puzzle. Nothing connects. You should have seen what a basket case I was bringing Brian – *family* – to the softball games - *friends* and *church*." He shook his head. "I was a wreck."

"How'd it turn out?"

"Fine."

"What were you afraid of?"

He shrugged, trying to look casual. "Discovery. Disclosure."

Claire had a flash of his mother describing how he could never lie to her when he was a kid. What did she say he had on his forehead? Oh yeah, an idiot light.

"What are you, some mafia hit man or drug runner or something? What's so awful in your past that you're working so hard to keep everything separate?"

Paul looked at his watch. "What time do you usually pick up Tyler? We don't want to be late."

Claire got a knowing smirk on her face. "Who - ho! Seems like the big guy's got a few secrets of his own stashed away. If we connect all the dots of your life, Paul, does it draw a clear picture?"

Christmas, she had no idea ...

"Seems like your tidy little life of compartmentalized places is starting to run together. Let me think." She whipped off her rubber gloves, stood and started washing her hands in the sink. "There's the dots you've already mentioned: family, friends, church. There's a work dot. Then there's me and Tyler. Are we one or two dots?" She dried her hands and looked at him expectantly as she slipped past him into the living room to put on her flip-flops.

He struggled to stand. "Two. Well, you were two, but now that you know about me and Tyler and the basketball games and we're dating you're kind of one dot. But ..." This was too weird, trying to explain to her about how she was an unconnected dot in the map of his life. *Way too weird.* He looked at his watch. "Claire, don't we have to go?"

She stood with her hands on her hips in the middle of her boxed up living room. "You asked me a question a while back that kept haunting me even when you weren't around to do it personally. It was, 'Who do you have, Claire?' That question went right to the heart of all that was glaringly wrong in my life." She walked up to him and looked him in the eye. Or as best as she could, given the fact that she was more than a foot shorter than he. He was almost a little afraid of her at this moment. "Here's your question, big guy. *Who do you trust, Paul?*" She looked at her watch. "Damn, we're going to be late ...!"

Claire had been told that the possessions she wanted to keep that didn't fit in the house could be stored in the basement. After picking Tyler up from school, the three of them worked for a few hours (fortified with a box of Dunkin' Donuts) unpacking and arranging the kitchen at Sonrise House. "As poor and destitute as we are, we've got an awful lot of stuff!" Claire finally laughed. Paul was suspiciously quiet as they worked, and when Tyler went to use the bathroom Claire said quietly to him, "Are you regretting the invitation for us to come to your softball game tonight?"

He'd been tightening something under the kitchen sink and bumped his head when he came up to look at her. "Sh-, Ow!" Sitting on the kitchen floor rubbing his head, he looked up at her with a sheepish expression. "Simon told me once that the more I swear the more upset I am. Yeah, I want you to come tonight."

"You're awfully quiet. I'm not very good at being tactful and gentle when I'm trying to make a point. I'm sorry if I upset you back at the apartment."

"Look at me, Claire. Do I look like 'tactful and gentle' would work with me?"

She grinned and shook her head.

"Okay, then. Just keep operating in whatever way that comes naturally to you. That's one of the things I like so much about you. You're original."

Claire helped herself to another donut and passed him one. "Oh yeah? What are the other things you like about me?"

He worked to unfold himself from under the sink and pull himself up to standing. "Do you realize that you're flirting with me? I'm thinking that you're so inexperienced with life that perhaps you're not aware of it. So I'm just helping you out here by pointing out that leaning against that counter with chocolate frosting on the corner of your mouth and the know – it - all smirk on your face, not to mention the blatant attempt to get me to list all of your personal charms, is definitely in the category of flirting …" He advanced on her as he spoke and she kept right on grinning. "God, it's nice to see you happy, Claire." He wiped away the chocolate smear and then licked his finger. "Really nice."

"Don't be down on yourself, Paul. Remember our agreement

about believing each other's perceptions. There's nothing you could say that would change my opinion of you." The lead suit descended on him, pressing him down. He stared at her, feeling himself drown in his ocean of regret. She reached up and dusted powdered sugar off his shirt. "Now it's *my turn* to say, 'Take your time, Paul. You don't have to tell me anything you're not ready to tell me. You're teaching me to be a patient woman.'"

He sighed and rested his chin on the top of her head while he gave her a hug. "You're killing me, Claire. You're really killing me."

Was this how real people lived? Claire sat in the bleachers of the softball game with Brian, watching people laughing and joking, talking and playing. Tyler had been recruited as bat and water boy and was thrilled to be running around with 'the big guys', even sitting on the bench with them. Periodically he turned and waved to her, grinning from ear to ear.

"All packed?"

Claire smiled at Brian. "Yeah, thanks to Paul. He showed up today and everything shifted into high gear."

"Paul has a way about him, huh?" He smiled as Tyler waved at them for the four hundredth time.

"Will you see Tiffany and Mallory this weekend?" At his pained expression she immediately regretted her words. "Oh, Brian, I'm sorry."

"My life's pretty screwed up right now."

"I'm a pretty good expert at screwed up lives, so if you ever want to talk, I'll be happy to listen. Just don't expect any profound insights or helpful suggestions. If I have any, I'm grabbing them for myself, first."

His bark of laughter made even Paul turn around with a questioning look. "Touché. Maybe we should avoid each other. I'd hate for us to get too close and combust or something." They shared smiling glances. "Thanks, I needed that."

"I'm not exactly sure what I did," she said in a puzzled voice.

"You reminded me that I'm not the only one on this planet with troubles. I'd pretty much convinced myself of that over these last few weeks."

"Oh. Yeah, well, sorry. I've had the monopoly on that reality my whole life."

"I hear the house is nice."

Claire looked at him. "Yeah, and so's your brother."

He grinned. "I'm discovering that for myself."

In deference to Tyler's, Paul, Claire, Josh, and Simon went to the local ice cream parlor after the game instead of to the local restaurant. They sat outside under the stars on a grassy hill next to the store's parking lot eating their various selections. "How's the car running?" Josh asked Claire between bites of his cone.

"Terrific. It runs fantastic. Want to buy it?"

That made Josh laugh. "No way. You forget, I had a real close look at it when I helped Paul put gas in it that night."

"I purposely tone down all of its impressive features so that the theft insurance stays low."

"Yeah, I bet." He turned to Paul. "She's going to keep you on your toes, Saint."

Paul winked at her. "She tried to warn me."

"What time do you want us all tomorrow, Claire?" Simon asked in complete seriousness.

"I don't want you to give up your day off, Simon. It's okay."

"What are you talking about, Claire?" Josh spoke up. "Paul said you're cooking a huge dinner for all of us. There's one thing you should know about single guys. They'll do anything for a good meal." He gave her a teasing grin.

Paul looked at her with concern, reeking with insecurity and worry. "I told them I'd spring for dinner, Claire. I never said you'd cook for them."

"What? You're embarrassed about my cooking?" Claire tried to look and sound hurt.

Simon jumped in, apparently just as uptight about Claire and the guys as Paul was. *This might be fun,* she thought listening to him stutter, "No! No, Claire. I think Paul just knows you're probably going to be exhausted after a full day of moving and doesn't want you to have to cook for us."

"So you think I'm some weak, girly-girl type, Simon?" Now she tried to sound defensive.

Simon exchanged a worried glance with Paul. At the same time Claire looked at Josh and grinned. He'd caught on quickly. "What they're both trying to say, Claire, is that Paul usually only dates brainless bimbos, and if you fall in that category we don't want to overtax you," Josh said with a huge grin. Simon looked horrified and Paul put his face in his hands and groaned.

"Oh, *that's all*," Claire said and took another bite of her cone. "Why didn't you say so?"

Paul lifted his face from his hands, looking first at her, then at Josh's grinning face, and finally at Simon. "See what I mean? She's killing me …"

Saturday was exhausting but fun. The guys arrived early (but not as early as Tyler, who had already been waiting on the roof for them for more than a half hour) and organized chaos ensued. Claire insisted on doing Mrs. Santiago's food shopping, despite her arguments to the contrary. "You've got enough on your mind, child, go on ahead and supervise those men in your apartment."

"No, I'll do your food shopping for you, Mrs. Santiago. And furthermore, next week, Tyler and I will be by to help you finish packing. We'll even save our boxes for you, okay? We've still got almost two weeks until you have to be out. We've got to keep our fingers crossed, Mrs. Santiago."

Mrs. Santiago patted Claire's cheek and gave her a tired, sad smile. "My daughter's trying to get off work and come up sometime next week to help get everything settled here. She's told me that I don't need to bring any of my furniture or anything. Seems she can't fit it and doesn't want to pay to have it brought down anyway." She sighed. "I've been in this apartment for fourteen years, Claire. *Fourteen years.* I know it's not much, but it's my home." She shrugged her stooped shoulders. "It's my independence."

Claire didn't know what to say. There really was nothing to say.

"Tyler told me that you and he prayed for me the other day."

Claire was embarrassed. "Yeah, well, I know it is important to you and it was important to Tyler."

"You're a good mother, Claire. You love that boy and it shows. He knows it, too. And he loves you right back."

Mrs. Santiago's praise meant a lot. Looking at this stooped, nosy, bossy old lady, Claire felt a fierce surge of protectiveness towards her. "You've helped me out a lot these past weeks, Mrs. Santiago, and Tyler has grown to really love and care for you. You're like the grandmother he'll never have." Claire reached out and clutched Mrs. Santiago's bony hand. "We're still in this together. I'm just getting into the lifeboat first, okay?"

The old lady's tired blue eyes looked at Claire. "Okay, child. You keep that boat steady because you know these old bones of mine aren't as spry as they used to be."

Claire met the entire crew of Paul's friends in the end. She already knew brother Brian with his sad eyes, Josh with his teasing grin, and Simon with his intently serious demeanor. She met James and his wife Maggie, who brought a bowl of homemade macaroni salad that was so large one of the guys had to carry it. "I thought it would go with anything we eat for dinner," she explained with a friendly smile. "I'm real good at making beds and organizing things, so James said I could come along." Claire was glad for her female presence and told her so.

Of all the guys only, Mike and Vince made her uneasy. By the end of the day, were she forced to admit it, she really didn't like Vince at all. Both men had assessed her in a way she found uncomfortable, but Vince's looks held an air of familiarity that was unwanted and unwarranted. Vince went out of his way to be around Claire, alternately offering flirty little comments or sly innuendos. While she was comfortable laughing and teasing with Josh or Brian or even Simon, she kept her distance from Vince, and offered him no encouragement.

Dinner was a loud, boisterous affair with Maggie's macaroni salad, bottles and bottles of soda (Paul had said no alcohol because they were all driving back and forth between the house and apartment), and *ten* pizzas. "Paul, that's *one whole pizza* for each one of us! Including Tyler!" Claire had said as the deliveryman strode back to his truck pocketing the tip he'd just received from Paul.

Paul looked puzzled at her statement. "Yeah?"

"*Ten pizzas?*"

As they both turned to look at the crowd surrounding the food, Josh picked up an entire pizza and an entire bottle of soda and wandered over to sit beneath a big oak tree. Paul grinned at her. "And your point is?"

"I guess I should be thankful that you didn't expect me to cook for this bunch," Claire said as she watched Josh good-naturedly shoo Mike away from his claimed pie and drink directly from the soda bottle.

"You okay?" Paul asked her quietly as he looked at her intently.

She looked back. "Yeah, I'm okay. *You* okay? How are all those dots of yours?"

He smiled at her and then looked out at the chaos. "Getting connected. But so far my life hasn't fallen apart."

Sitting quietly waiting for Paul to join her and eat, Claire heard a deep voice ask, "This seat taken?" Claire looked up from her cooling pizza to see Vince's challenging expression.

"I don't believe so, but you should probably ask the host."

"Nah," Vince said as he lowered himself down next to her, juggling pizza, soda and macaroni salad skillfully, "the hostess is *a lot* cuter." He winked at her and Claire flashed back to that morning in the diner. He'd winked at her that time, too. Vince nodded to the house. "Nice place. Some people have all the luck," he said with a tinge of envy.

Claire bristled. Was she the one with 'all the luck'? "What do you mean by that?" she couldn't help ask. She took a bite of her pizza and tried to look casual, but she had begun to steam.

"No offense, Claire. You're just one lucky chick, that's all. How many other people do you know who get a furnished house practically rent-free? Plus, what else did Paul say you were getting? Food stamps? Financial aid? Sounds like a sweet deal to me. Payback must be a bitch though." He took a long gulp of his soda. "Ahhhh. Plus a free dinner and a good looking labor force. You seem to have Paul hooked pretty good, too. Yessiree, things are really looking up for you compared to when we first met you in the diner."

The tone, the innuendoes, *the whole experience* was too familiar for words. The pizza congealed in her stomach and she watched a horse fly work on her potato salad. "I think I better start cleaning up," she mumbled, unwilling to make waves with any of Paul's friends.

"Hey, don't run away! Least you could do is keep me company while I eat my dinner since I've spent my Saturday helping you move."

"I'm not much of a conversationalist, Vince," she said, but didn't leave like she wanted to.

"No? You must have some other sterling qualities then that are attracting the old Saint back to familiar pastures. He's been avoiding skirts for almost two years, and now I watch him with you and he's just about turning himself inside out to make you smile."

Claire looked Vince straight in the eye. Okay, she was done. "Are you trying to make some point? I'd rather you just spit it out than listen to you do this subtle little dance. I don't have the desire, patience, or skill to play word games with you."

He gave her a sly smile. "So the green eyed waitress has got spark after all, huh? I thought so." Vince looked over at Paul who was deep in conversation with Maggie and James. "Me and Saint go way back. You know what I mean, Claire? Before he was called Saint and was embracing all of that mumbo jumbo God crap. I'm just being honest with you. I miss the old Paul. I'd like him back. I was just curious as to which side you're on. Are you all dewy eyed with church, thanking Jesus, Mary, and Joseph for your good luck, or are you just grabbing everything you can get your sweet little hands on? I was just curious about what the Saint was hooking up with."

Claire stood and collected her things, biting the inside of her mouth to keep it shut. She saw absolutely no benefit in responding. Rule Number 22 of Claire Jenkins Rules of Survival: *Never try to defend yourself. No one will ever believe you.*

It turned out to be the only black mark in an otherwise great day.

Your character is essentially the sum of your habits.[17]

Thirteen: Never Defend Yourself. No One Will Believe You

"**M**om?" The voice was distant, a child's whisper. "Moooom."

"Tyler?" Claire opened her eyes to see her son freshly scrubbed from the shower, with his hair combed, and wearing a clean, buttoned shirt. The strong smell of Dial soap and store brand baby shampoo wafted over her. She looked at the clock. 9:00 a.m. "What's up, kiddo? How was your first night in your new room?"

Tyler grinned. "It was great, Mom. It's so quiet here. No horns or train sounds." He wrinkled his forehead. "I never told you, Mom, but sometimes the train still used to scare me in the middle of the night."

Claire sat up and plumped the pillows behind her. "You can always come get me, you know."

He sat on the edge of the bed and picked at the bedspread. "I'm too old for that."

She smoothed his collar. "You look nice. What are you all dressed up and ready for?"

[17] Rick Warren, *The Purpose Driven Life*, Zondervan Publishers, Grand Rapids, Michigan, 2002

Tyler got the look that made Claire's stomach tighten and her head think, 'Oh no …' "Well, Mom, I was thinking that since they gave us the house and Mrs. Santiago is still all worried about stuff and everything that maybe we should … you know, since you're not working today or anything … go to church."

Huh? "Today? This morning?"

Tyler nodded his head enthusiastically.

"Gee kiddo, I'm so beat from yesterday. It's the one Sunday that I don't have to get up and work. I thought we'd just have a lazy day here hanging out and getting familiar with the house and the neighborhood." The last thing in the world that she wanted to do was go to church. The last thing.

"Oh, okay." He hesitated and then plunged on. "It's just, you see, well, Mrs. Santiago has only got two more Sundays before she's got to get out of her apartment and go live with that daughter she doesn't like so that mean's we've only got two more shots to go to church and light candles and send up official prayers and stuff."

"Official prayers?"

He nodded. "Yeah, I think, doesn't this make sense to you, that prayers said in church with all those candles and smells and stuff have got to be more official than prayers you do anywhere else? I think Sunday Church Prayers have got to be the strongest."

Claire sat there with her mouth hanging open. He's really thought all of this through? Good grief.

"Mom, if you don't want to go, could I just go? It's just across the back yard and the church parking lot. You could watch me from the kitchen window while I walk over. Please? Please?"

She threw back the covers and stood up, and her son started dancing around the room with excitement. "I suppose you know what time service is," she said as she rummaged through her closet looking for something decent.

"Are you kidding, Mom? You can read the big sign right from here! Look. It says, '9:00 a.m. and 10:15 a.m. Worship Services'." He looked at her and grinned. "Man, we've go no excuse for not going to church now, Mom!"

Walking in to the back of the church at 10:00 a.m. Claire did not feel as "at home" as she had felt the other day sitting in the front pew with Janice Strocco. She felt nervous and glaringly obvious. She insisted on sitting in the very back row, in the corner beneath the balcony section. She felt like she should be wearing dark sunglasses and a wide brimmed hat.

Tyler was all worked up. "There's no holy water or candles or big statutes! There aren't even places to kneel down and pray." He looked at her in absolute seriousness and whispered tensely, "I'm not sure this is a real church, Mom. It could be a fake."

That made Claire relax. Just a little. She put her arm around him and whispered. "This is a real church, honey. They come in all shapes and sizes, I think. Just like people. Let's go for the whole ride and then we'll discuss it at the end, okay?"

"Do you think our prayers will work when there's no candles and holy water and stuff?"

"I'm positive." He studied her for a minute and then seemed to agree with her, for he relaxed and leaned against her in the pew.

A woman with a badge that said "Usher" came and gave Claire a program, and Tyler something that said "Kid's Korner" at the top. It had puzzles in it, and while she read through the program he started working on the various activities. People came in and smiled and greeted each other. Some laughed and embraced. Children ran around, and gradually the room began to fill. Then the organ began to play and a hush settled over the place giving the entire room a serious but soothing atmosphere.

Claire caught on to following the program she had been given. It told when to stand and when to sit, what to say and what was next. She didn't sing and she didn't close her eyes when everyone prayed, but otherwise she was pretty sure she did everything according to the rules. The bulletin said "Children's Sermon", and Janice Strocco in fancy flowing black minister robes came out onto the pulpit and said, "Come on down, kids! Time for the Children's Sermon!" She seated herself on one of the three blue carpeted steps up front. A distant thundering came from the balcony, and children of all ages, shapes, and sizes seemed to come out of the woodwork. They joined Janice up front, sprawling on the carpet in front of her or wrestling for the prime spots on the stairs next to her.

"Are you going?" she whispered to Tyler.

"Can I?"

Claire shrugged. "Sure. Why not?" He was gone in a flash.

"I'm going to tell you about two people today," Janice began, "but you're going to have to use your imagination because I don't have any pictures of them." She held up her right hand. "Imagine that one of the people I'm going to tell you about is seated here." She held up her left hand. "And imagine that the other one is seated here." She leaned over conspiratorially. "Now, I'm going to ask you just one question at the end of all of this that I want you to answer, so listen carefully, okay? And I'll make it really easy because I'll tell you the question now: which one of these two people do you think God loves more?" She looked at the forty odd bunch of children at her feet. "Got it? Which one of these two people do you think God loves more?" Claire could see the kids nodding their heads.

Janice held up her right hand. "This woman, from the time she was a young girl decided that she loved God and wanted to follow Him and do things that would make Him happy. But a lot of sad things happened to her over the course of her life. She had a younger sister who was born with a sickness that was so bad that that sister finally died. She had another sister that got very sick with another sickness called cancer and almost died because of that. Her mother got something called a brain tumor and had to have a very serious operation to keep her alive. This woman, more than anything wanted to be a wife and a mother, but she made many, many bad choices about who she fell in love with. She got very discouraged and sometimes she was quite angry with God that He wouldn't help find the perfect man for her to marry. In the end, she didn't get married until she was over thirty years old."

"Wow, that's old," said one little girl sitting next to Janice, and everyone in the church burst out laughing.

Janice smiled. "You bet it's old! And then, remember all she wanted to be was a mother?" Many of the children nodded, fully engrossed in the story. "Two times her body got ready to have a baby but things didn't work out and the babies died." Janice looked at the children sitting around her in rapt attention. "This lady had a lot of unhappiness in her life, didn't she?" Claire saw even a few adults nodding their head.

Janice held up her left hand. "Now I'm going to tell you about this woman. She also made a decision early in her life that she wanted to live a life that would make God happy. She grew up in a family that loved God, and even though times were tough she felt loved and treasured. Do you know that early on God told her what He wanted her to be when she grew up? She had a whole bunch of friends that worried and worried about what they were going to be, but this little girl knew when she was only six years old what God wanted her to be. She didn't have a lot of money growing up, but God provided for her and she worked hard in school and managed to get a scholarship to college. Do you know that before she even finished with all of her college work she got offered a job to do what she had always wanted to do? How cool is that?

"She became very successful in her career. She met a man and fell in love with him later in life, and they eventually had three beautiful children: two boys and a girl. She has many friends and family surrounding her even today."

Janice looked at everyone, including the congregation sitting out in the pews. "Okay. Who remembers what question I was going to ask you?"

"Which person did God love more?" a large, redheaded boy volunteered.

"That's right, Ian," Janice smiled at him. "Which one of these two people do you think God loved more? Let's do it by a show of hands, okay? Raise your hand if you think this woman was loved by God more." She held up her right hand, the sad woman, Claire thought. Few people raised their hands. "Hmmm," Janice said, "seems like you guys don't think she was too popular with God, huh?"

Janice held up her left hand, the happy woman. "How many think that God loved this woman more?" Almost every child raised their hand except for the two year old who was busy toddling around behind Janice sucking his thumb. "So you think this lady was more loved by God, huh?"

Heads nodded.

"Well, what if I told you," Janice said in a conspiratorial whisper, "that both of these women are really just one woman, not two?" She joined her two hands together in a clasped fist. "What if I told you that all of those happy and sad things happened to just one woman? What would you think about that?"

Silence. Claire could hear the cogs whirring in people's heads as they digested what Janice had said. Janice slapped both of her hands loudly on her knees. "This is what you need to remember about God," she said. "God loves you during the good times and during the bad times. He loves all of us equally. No one gets an easier ride because they are better or wiser or prettier or more cooperative. And no one, no one has a life of all good times or a life of all bad times. It just doesn't work that way. When hard times come, God rides right along with us, sorrowing just as we do. When joyful times come, God sings and dances and laughs and smiles with us as well. You need to remember that keeping your eyes focused on God gets you through life, good or bad."

Janice closed in prayer and dismissed all the kids to Church School. Claire saw Daniel Alvarez come up, put his arm around Tyler, and whisper something in his ear. Tyler nodded, smiled and pointed back towards Claire. Daniel made eye contact with her, nodded a brief greeting, and then walked out of the front of the sanctuary with his arm around Tyler.

Who was that woman Janice spoke about? Was she real? Claire really wanted to know. Or was it just some made up story to help illustrate Janice's point?

Claire thought about herself. She was the sad woman. No doubt about that! But what had Janice said? No one has a life of all good times or a life of all bad times. It just doesn't work that way. Claire would have to sit down and talk with Janice. Her life was a glaring example of the fallacy of Janice's point. There were no good times in Claire's life.

None at all.

Well, until recently, she amended to herself. Things were certainly going pretty well now with Sonrise House and Daniel Alvarez and Janice Strocco and Paul and his family and his friends. What about Claire going to college? Living in a house? She had to admit that that was amazingly good as well. Nothing else, except …

Of course there had always been Tyler. As long as he wasn't doing something criminal, or almost criminal, she was so darn proud of him she could hardly stand it. He was loving and kind and sensitive and sweet. She thought of him praying for Mrs. Santiago and standing at her bedside this morning all clean and ready to go to church. How could anybody love a person as much as she loved that boy?

And Mrs. Santiago. How could Claire discount her? How would she have made it through these last few weeks without her help watching Tyler? She had, in a few short weeks, given Tyler love and laughter and … even faith.

Claire sighed. If she was counting good things, then she really must add her job to the list. She was fortunate to have the job at the diner that offered her flexibility, meals, and allowed her to bring Tyler when necessary. Even though she was always struggling financially, things really could be worse in that category and she knew it.

Janice was standing at the big podium – the pulpit – talking. Claire thought of the fact that she and Tyler seemed to never get sick, so she rarely had to deal with doctor bills. Aside from his suspension, Tyler had never missed a day of school. Not once. Other waitresses at work were always sniffling and coughing and coming down with the flu. Claire never got sick. Her health was another good thing she couldn't discount.

But there was nothing from her past at all that was good, she thought to herself. Nothing at all. Well, except that one foster family that let her come back and stay with them for a bit right before and after Tyler was born. And when they moved they helped her find her apartment. And told her about the All American Diner, because one of the daughters of that family had been a friend with one of Dan's daughters. So that was one good thing from her past she guessed …

Oh yeah, there was that one foster family that was so passionate about school (Claire had thought they were nuts), but they were the ones that got her interested in school and made her start to dream that maybe one day she could become a nurse … They'd taken her to the library and gotten her a library card and a bicycle, and she used to spend hours and hours studying and dreaming about becoming a world famous nurse …

On the bulletin, she began to write words. Good words. Nursing. College. Sonrise. Janice. Mrs. Santiago. Daniel. Paul. All American Diner. Tyler. Health. The Symborskis. The Jankowskis.

She looked down at the words she had scribbled all over the bulletin. They were her dots. She could connect them in order and they would be the path of stepping-stones that had gotten her through all the muck and mire and horror of her life. Good things really had been there amidst the bad! Waddaya know. And unlike Paul's, hers were all connected - with chain links! For if just one had not been there to keep her moving, to keep her putting one foot in front of the other, guiding her to safety, she would not have made it.

But she had.

She was here.

They had been there.

Maybe she was really going to make it after all.

Monday morning like a bolt of lightning from the sky, Janice Strocco knocked on the front door. She was holding a plant and grinning from ear to ear. "Welcome to the neighborhood." She leaned over conspiratorially and said, "Watch out for those neighbors, though," her head nodded toward the church, "I hear they give wild and crazy parties every Sunday."

Claire invited Janice in and they ended up seated on the front porch sipping steaming cups of coffee. "Thanks for all this," Claire began, but Janice held her hand up.

"I didn't come over here to bask in your appreciation, please. Understand this Claire: you earned this opportunity, you'll be working long and hard, and this church has great hopes and dreams for you and this new venture we're starting together. You can thank me when you're moving out under your own steam, having accomplished all you are setting out to do. And we'll thank you right back for making this idea a success. Deal?"

Claire gave her a small smile. "Deal." She took a deep breath. "Can I ask you a question?"

"Sure! Shoot! Pastors love questions so they can spout out reams of intelligence and wisdom," Janice said while rolling her eyes.

"Was the woman you talked about yesterday in the children's sermon real or made up?"

Janice hesitated and then said, "She was real."

"Do you know her?"

"Why? You want to talk to her?"

"Yeah. No. Well, kind of." Claire groaned. "I don't know ..."

Janice chuckled and patted her on the shoulder. "You can talk with the woman, Claire. It's not a big deal."

"It's just ... well, it's just that her life had so many hard parts. And then you said that no one's life is all happy or all sad and I thought, 'Ha, you should take a look at my life, Janice Strocco! I'll prove you wrong.' But then I got really thinking about my life and I was just amazed that I could trace a pattern of at least one good thing all the way through it. And the good thing was always just enough to get me through all the bad."

Janice looked at Claire intently. "Claire, it's true that no one's life is all good or all bad. Even the people you look at who seem to have it all invariably, if you could scratch beneath the surface, have had all kinds of pain and sorrow. Even church people. We always like to put our best face on when we march off to church, and we like to talk the talk and walk the walk. Then we get out into the real world and we fall flat on our faces. That's why so many people think Christians are nothing but annoying hypocrites."

Janice was thoughtful for a moment. "I think a truly good Christian witness – that's showing what God has done in your life – is not putting on a false front trying to dazzle and impress. It's about laying it all out on the table. Letting people see how broken or bad or unwise you were and what a huge powerful force of change God has been in your life." Janice reached over and touched Claire's forearm. "That's why I told my life's story to the kids on Sunday, Claire. Many people who know me knew I was talking about myself. It's no big secret. I just told it that way so I'd keep the kids hooked."

Claire looked into Janice's smiling face. "And some of the

unsuspecting adults.”

Janice threw her head back and laughed. “I’m always careful to make sure that my children’s sermons are interesting enough to keep the adults tuned in, too. What did you think about my adult sermon? I carried the idea of renewed life and changed personalities even further with the story of the Woman of Samaria.”

Claire looked absolutely mortified. “I’m sorry! I didn’t hear your sermon! I was too busy thinking about your children’s sermon.”

“Hey, don’t be sorry! God speaks to us in all different ways during our time at church. That’s why a worship service has so many parts, because everyone is so different. Some people are moved by the music, some by the sermons, and some by the prayers. Some are just moved by the love and welcoming atmosphere of the people attending. It’s all part of the package.”

Claire looked lost in thought. “Go ahead,” Janice said, “nothing compliments a ministers more than having parishioners not only remember their sermons, but wanting to discuss them.”

Claire spoke slowly, “You said that you knew early on what you wanted to be … ‘God called you early’, that’s what you said.” Janice nodded. “So early on you knew you were going to be a minister.” Claire stated it as a fact and Janice nodded again. “How could you, a minister, or an almost-minister, get discouraged or angry at God over the way stuff went in your life?”

Janice gave her a wide-eyed look. “What? You think because I knew I wanted to be a minister that everything would just smoothly fall into place for me over the course of my life, or that I should have just been calm and patient and well behaved as the years slipped by for me? You think because I’m a minister I’m perfect? You think I don’t curse under my breath when someone cuts me off on the road when I’m having a bad day? You think I didn’t yell at my kids and make mistakes when I raised them? You think that my husband falls down on his knees each night and thanks God for the gift of me?” Janice grinned a small, far away grin. “If only …” she said and then chuckled. “Claire, there are no levels of Christianity. One person is not better or worse because of her calling or her personal status. But there are steps. First, you either are or you aren't. There is no in - between. God says He's going to spit the lukewarm ones, the ones that can't make a real decision, right out of His mouth.

"To become a Christian is relatively easy, but it's a monumental commitment. You have to believe that you're a sinner and that there is absolutely nothing on your own you can do to change that. Next you have to believe that Jesus, God's Son, came to earth and died on the cross to take the punishment for all the sins we are responsible for – and rose from the dead. Lastly, you have to ask for forgiveness of your sins and ask Jesus to come into your heart to live and dwell and guide you all the rest of your days." Janice shrugged. "That's it."

"I was never baptized."

"So? Baptism shows the world a personal decision you have already made. Baptism doesn't save you, it's the choice that saves you." Janice smiled at her. "You make the choice and I'll baptize you. That's simple."

"But I'm not a baby!"

"So? You think that you missed the boat and now it's just tough luck the rest of your life? Don't you think that God will take you any time He can get you?"

"I suppose …"

"Look, Claire. Jesus said that we were to come to him with the heart of a child. That means that you don't need lots of flowery words or high - fallutin' college degrees. He wants us to have the same level of trust that makes a child believe that Santa can fit down a chimney, that Easter Bunnies deliver candy, and Tooth Fairies leave money under our pillows. He wants all consuming trust that doesn't question, but has glorious, uninhibited belief. Once you make that step, then the next step is to grow and learn and pray.

"Praying is by far the most important. It's talking to God and it works. Listening is next. You can't pray and ask for things and then be unhappy with the answers. It doesn't work that way. God works in His own time, His own style, for His own purpose." She laughed. "And praying to win the lottery or for your team to win the Stanley Cup doesn't fit into the prayers we're supposed to do.

"You should pray about things you're thankful for and pray about things you're concerned about. Any requests you make should be at the Lord's wisdom and discretion, not based in your own selfishness or lack of knowledge. No one knows what's best other than God. Prayer changes things. That's an absolute fact."

Janice grinned at her. "So, I'm the happy and sad woman. All those things happened to me, and I'm sure I'll have plenty more good and bad moments in my life. The greatest test of life is: What am I going to do about it? Am I going to become bitter? Angry? Spiteful? Vengeful? Or am I going to rise up above it, let it strengthen me in areas where I was weak, let it empower me in areas where I was once uncertain, let it educate me in areas where I was once ill informed. It's an attitude. It's a choice. And it's a way of life. It's empowering. It's joyful."

Janice looked at her. "Can I say one more thing? I don't want you to be thinking, 'When will this woman ever leave?!'"

Claire laughed. "No, you can say one more thing. You've really got me thinking."

"I think God has great plans for you." Claire rolled her eyes. "No, Claire, hear me out on this. I think that God has had His eye on you from the start. You are an amazingly strong, capable woman. A woman who, seemingly without the help of anyone to love or coddle or teach her, has become someone who is good and committed and loving and seeking of good things." At Claire's skeptical look, Janice said sincerely, "You know that your life could have turned out in so many other different, horrible ways, right?" Claire nodded slowly. "You could be on drugs, into prostitution, embracing a life of crime, neglecting your child ... right?" Claire nodded again. "But you haven't done any of those things, have you? Even when it seemed nigh onto impossible you have worked like a dog to maintain a life of goodness for you and for Tyler. Haven't you?" This time Claire didn't answer. She stared down at her tightly clasped hands. "Haven't you?" Janice whispered quietly.

"Yes."

"And now God is stepping in and putting the rest of the puzzle pieces into place. You suddenly have so many good and wonderful things happening in your life, right?" Claire's eyes were full of tears when she looked at Janice. She didn't answer Janice's question, just continued to stare at her intently. "So now, God is putting the finishing touches on one of His glorious masterpieces, getting ready to launch a powerful, strong, loving, committed young woman out into His world to make her mark. To make a difference. Look out world, here comes Claire Jenkins."

Claire wiped her streaming eyes, took a deep breath, and looked again at Janice. "I want that to be so. All that you said about me. I want that for me, and I want that for Tyler, too. I want it so bad I can almost taste it."

"It's a simple choice, Claire. Nothing complicated. No tricks. No gimmicks. Just a step in the right direction."

"So what do we do first?"

"Pray," said Janice as she put her arm around Claire, "always pray first."

★

★ ★ ˙ ˙ ★

★ ˙

Fourteen: No One Wants To Hear The Truth

There he goes, Paul thought glancing at his bedside clock, just like clockwork. The glowing digital numbers read 2:05 a.m. He could hear his brother's muffled sobs in the spare bedroom. Four nights in a row this had been going on, ever since Brian had gone to see Janet and she'd served him with preliminary divorce papers. But the fact that Paul had been unable to get a decent night's sleep for the past week had nothing to do with his brother. He was haunted with his own personal demons that seemed to grow bigger and louder with each passing day. Whom do you trust? Claire had asked him. She had no way of knowing how deeply she had hit pay dirt, but the true question was, Whom do you trust enough to tell your Secret to?

For three years he tried every tact to submerge it, escape it, erase it, forget it, but it grew larger and more horrible with each passing month. He hadn't been able to drink it away, bluster it away, and the most awful truth of all, he hadn't been able to pray it away. The Secret followed him wherever he went, even to bed, and was much more disruptive than his brother's muffled cries.

---

[18] Frank Lloyd Wright

"What can I do, God?" he mumbled out loud into the darkness of his bedroom. Last night his brother had been awake grieving until at least four a.m. when Paul had finally fell into a fitful sleep. "I can't seem to solve my own problems, let alone someone else's." What a pair these two Williamson brothers were.

Maybe he's thirsty, his grandfather's voice suggested.

Paul levered himself up out of bed, hitched his boxer shorts up a bit and absently scratched his bare chest. Padding barefoot into the kitchen, he got down two glasses, filled them with ice, and added iced tea. Padding back down the hallway, he walked into the spare room without knocking. In the darkness he could hear his brother's quick intake of breath and hasty sniffle. He plunked the drink on the bedside table and settled into the easy chair in the corner of the room. "Thought you might be thirsty."

"Oh. Yeah. Thanks." Brian sat up, shifted the pillows, and then helped himself to the iced tea.

"Nice night," Paul said in an easy conversational tone, like it wasn't two o'clock in the morning and they weren't both drinking iced tea in their underwear.

"Yeah."

"Think it might rain tomorrow."

"Is that so?"

"That's what the weather channel's saying."

"They've been known to be wrong."

"What are you going to do about Janet?"

His brother picked up the hem of his worn tee shirt and wiped his face with it. "There's nothing to do, Paul. She says she wants a divorce."

"Can I ask you a question?"

"Yeah, sure, go ahead."

"It might upset you."

"You're not sitting in here with me at two in the morning because I've been singing happy songs and making daisy chains, Paul."

"*Could* you take her back after she's been with another man, and forgive and forget?" Paul hesitated. "I don't think I could do that."

Brian sighed. "I love her, damn it. I kind of took it all for granted, though. I got wrapped up in being the big provider, feeling impressed with myself with all I was accomplishing. At the same time I felt truckloads of pressure about needing to keep advancing at work, have the right kind of car and house and clothes. I pressured Janet to make changes right along with me." Paul's eyes had adjusted to the darkness, and he could see Brian's anguished profile as he looked out the window. "I bought her a membership to a health club so she could get back in shape after Tiffany, and insisted she hire a decorator to fix up the house." His voice was filled with loathing. "I had one of the office managers call Janet and offer to take her clothes shopping in the hopes that she'd class up her image. Do you know," he took a deep shaky breath, "how many times she wanted to invite people over from work for dinner or a party, and I said no because I was embarrassed about her cooking and the middle class way we lived?

"I've had plenty of time to play this all over in my head, Paul. I'm not exactly sure, but I think that I effectively communicated to her that there was not one, single area in our lives where she performed up to my standards." He looked at Paul in the darkness. "Hell, I'd like to divorce myself, truth be told. Think if you were Janet you could forgive and forget *me?*"

"So, you're just going to sign the papers and move on?"

"What else can I do?" Brian's voice was a choked sob.

Paul yawned and stretched. "Well, as far as I can see you've communicated for the last few years that you aren't proud of her, and you don't think she's a worthy partner. Now that she says she wants a divorce you're letting her walk away without a fight. Seems like you've been consistent all along, and will be right to the moment you finish things up in court in front of the judge."

Brian shook his head at the ridiculousness of it all. "What? I'm supposed to go stomping over there, tell her I love her, and that over my dead body am I going to let her get away?"

"Have you tried that yet?"

"No ..."

"You seem to be getting pretty desperate to me. What have you got to loose?"

Even though the room was lit only by the soft glow of Brian's alarm clock and the full moon outside, the two brothers stared at each other intently for a few long moments. "Okay, I'll do it," Brian said with determined finality. He stood up, slipped his sneakers onto his bare feet, picked up his wallet and car keys, and headed out the bedroom door in his boxer shorts and an old Giants tee shirt.

"Hey!" Paul shouted.

"What?"

"Well, aren't you going to wait until morning? Or at least until you take the time to get dressed?"

Brian thought about it for a moment and then shook his head. "Nope."

Paul laughed quietly to himself and sipped on his iced tea while he listened to Brian's car start up, pull out of the driveway and roar off down the street. At last he stood up and wandered over to the window. It was one of the beautiful summer nights that had an edge of coolness to it, and his toes curled on the bare wood floor as a cool breeze drifted through the open window and collected around his feet. The moonlight was so bright that the trees actually cast shadows on the lawn. He sighed with a moment's brief contentment and took a deep breath. Simple pleasures. "Give them both wisdom, wise words, and soft hearts, Lord," he said quietly into the night.

Brian wasn't back by morning, and Paul wondered on the way to work if that was a good or bad sign. He sure hoped his brother wasn't driving around crying in his underwear. Or worse yet, sitting in a jail cell.

Worry about yourself why don't you, his grandfather said loudly and clearly.

Too true. It was time for him to face all the things he was running from. Paul needed to talk to someone. He went down the list of people he knew and respected trying to feel the right choice. All he managed to do was dismiss everyone, one by one. He knew instinctively that he wanted someone who had a spiritual base. That let out all of his friends, including Claire. Whomever he talked to had to be someone who had some years under his or her belt and could draw on a life of experiences – successes or failures. That eliminated his brothers and sisters (thank God). It made sense that whomever he sought out would have had some history with Paul and understood a little of what made him tick and why. His new minister knew him, but only from these last two years of church attendance and the fact that he still couldn't contain his temper in a competitive situation.

And Paul wanted to talk to a man. Paul didn't want to listen to any smarmy talk about getting better in touch with his feelings and all the crap that women would be quick to tell him. "Damn it, Granddad, why do you have to be dead?" he finally said aloud in the truck as he made his way to the morning's first site.

There is another, his Grandfather said mysteriously back. Why did Paul suddenly feel like he was in a Star War's episode?

Leaving the job, sweaty, sunburned, and stinking, he decided to forgo the gym and just head home. He was tired and hungry and he needed a cool shower. There was still no evidence of his brother as he flipped through the mail and drained a can of soda. The concern in his gut about Brian being stranded somewhere in his underwear again rose to the surface.

And then with a sudden crystal clear burst of clarity, Paul knew exactly whom he was going to talk to. It was Tuesday. Like a blinding flash from a camera that leaves you momentarily unable to do anything but blink, he knew. Leaving the mail unopened on the counter, he walked back to the truck and headed to his parents. To talk to his father.

Tuesdays in the Williamson house had been Dad's Night for as long as anyone could remember. Through babies and diapers, baseball games and ballet classes, through rain and snow and even hail, on Tuesday night Hannah Williamson had a night off and she disappeared. Of course everyone knew where she went. She went over to Gail Maggio's house and drank herbal tea and ate junk food and played Canasta until well after midnight, but come … heck … or high water Tuesday night Hannah was off. John became King of the Castle for an evening, cooking and mediating, helping with homework, and driving the kids to wherever they needed to go. The word 'Mom' was not spoken or thought of. Sometimes it was a night of hilarious fun and laughter, and sometimes it was a night of chaos and confusion, all depending upon the schedules and moods of those involved.

Paul would go talk to his father. Or, at least visit. He wasn't sure he had the courage to really do anything much but show up.

Classical music poured out the open living room windows along with the heavy spices of curry and turmeric. Seemed like his father was still on his Indian kick. To the best of his knowledge, Paul had not been present in his parent's house on a Dad's Tuesday in about five years, and yet his father smiled and greeted him like he'd been expecting him all along. Within minutes Paul was dicing onions and staring incredulously as his father sipped a glass of white wine.

"What?" his father shouted over the music. Paul remembered when they were teenagers and how they used to try to hide their dad's cassette tapes in the hopes of avoiding the 'long hair' music, as they called it. Paul pointed to the glass of wine. He couldn't believe what he was seeing. John grinned and shouted to him, "I love dry white wine! It's my Tuesday night treat! I get to listen to my tunes, make a mess in the kitchen, and drink a glass of fine wine." He adjusted the flame under the skillet, "and if I'm fortunate, I end up with some pleasantly surprising company."

"Does it happen often? The company, I mean," Paul shouted back.

"You'd be surprised," was all he'd say, cryptically.

They worked preparing the meal in companionable silence with Paul serving as general gofer and clean up patrol. No one was ever elevated to anything higher when John was in the kitchen.

Seated in the formal dining room with the sterling cutlery, Wedgwood china, linen napkins, and Waterford crystal goblets, Paul should have been surprised, but he wasn't. His dad had put on a new CD, and the music was turned down now to a bearable decibel so they no longer had to shout. "You would be eating here like this all by yourself if I hadn't shown up, wouldn't you Dad?"

"Sure. You guys know I do. Every Tuesday night come rain or shine."

"Mom playing Canasta?"

"Nah. I think she went to the movies."

"So who's been by to visit lately?"

"Oh, all of you show up sooner or later. Some more often then others. When Connie's two were little she used to show up here almost every Tuesday and I'd cook her dinner. Mark was home with the babies while she took a night off."

"Really?"

"Yeah, you were already away at college. Rachel shows up quite regularly, but only when soccer season is over. Elliot's more regular than all of you, but that's because he's cheap and always looking for a free meal."

Paul burst out laughing. "You're calling Elliot cheap?"

John shrugged. "Yeah. He is. Don't you think?"

Paul didn't want to get into it. "Yeah, I guess. Among other things."

His father sighed. "I'd hoped you two would have gotten closer as you got older. It's not going to happen, is it?"

"Stranger things have happened …"

"Brian's been by."

"Yeah …" Paul was unwilling to reveal private things his brother had shared.

"It was good of you to let him move in with you while he's going through all this confusion with Janet."

Paul had a flash of his brother driving around in his car last night in his boxers. "Have you seen him today?"

"No. Have you?"

Paul shook his head. "Nah, we talked last night though. He's missing Janet. A lot."

Dad took a sip of his wine. "Sometimes you don't truly miss something until it's gone."

"So it seems like I'm the only one who doesn't regularly show up on Dad's Tuesday Night, huh?"

"Oh, I have plenty of nights on my own. But I never know who's going to show up, so I always plan accordingly. Sometimes I get you kids, sometimes I get my friends, and sometimes I get your friends …"

"What do you mean 'sometimes I get your friends …'?"

His dad took a bite of the lamb. "I put too much spice in this dish. Too much of a good thing …" He looked at Paul. "I've had lots of interesting guests over the years. There seems to be some underground communication system for people who remember that Tuesday Night is Dad's Night at the Williamson house." He shrugged. "Like I said, I never know who's going to show up." He glanced at Paul. "I don't want to make you uncomfortable talking about God, but it's kind of like my own personal ministry. It's gotten to the point where I pray long and hard Monday night in preparation for Tuesday, just so I'm ready for whatever's going to step through that door. It started out as Mom's Night Off, but Hannah knows she's gotta get her tail out of this house on Tuesday whether she wants to or not now. It's more my night and whoever shows up than her night now."

Paul and his dad ate for a while as they listened to the soothing sounds of the music in the background. "This is Pachelbel's Canon, isn't it?" At his father's nod, Paul said, "I always liked this one."

His dad gave him a sly smile. "I know."

"It's okay for you to talk about God, Dad. I've been attending church for the past two years, since Granddad died."

His father looked at him intently for a moment and then said, "Is that so?"

"Yeah, I go every Sunday. I'm on the church softball team. I coach the church's little league baseball team, too."

"And why's this been such a big secret?"

"Because I'm an idiot."

"Besides that," his father said with a slight smile.

Paul smiled, too. "For a while it was just easier to keep my life in separate little compartments. It was easier to control."

"And now?"

Paul shrugged. "Lately, keeping everything separate has been harder work than it's worth."

"Why this sudden turnaround at Dad's death?" John said quietly.

"You know how you said you don't always miss something until it's gone? Well, after Granddad died, I realized that I was missing a lot more than just him."

"Which brings me back to my original question. Why was this wonderful decision kept in the shadows?" When Paul remained silent John continued. "You know, each one of our children is so amazingly different and unique." He chuckled to himself, lost in memory. "You think, once you become an all - knowing parent of two, healthy, rather well adjusted children, that you know just about all there is to know about parenthood. You get a little cock sure of yourself and start to spout out advice to others. When you see other people struggling with their unruly kids, you have condescending thoughts like, 'My, if they only did things the way we did them', or even worse, 'What a terrible example those parents are setting for their children'.

"And God lets you get full of yourself and lets life just continue on. You have a third child and a fourth child, and by the time the fifth child rolls around, you and your wife, if you're still speaking to each other, know the reality of the situation which is," he smiled at Paul, "that you've got absolutely no clue how to get yourself out of this mess you've gotten yourself into." He took another sip of his wine, seemingly finished reminiscing.

"Yeah, so what do you do, Dad?"

His father chuckled. "Oh, you do what you should have been doing all along. You start to pray. Really hard. For help, guidance, patience, wisdom … and you buckle your seatbelt for a wild ride." His father looked at him pointedly. "That's what good parents do, Paul. They love their children unconditionally, they bathe them in constant prayer, they allow them to make the inevitable mistakes, and they're always available for hugs and advice." Paul's father stared at him for long moments, and Paul could see love, tenderness, pride, and … anguish.

Suddenly, Paul knew. "Karly came here on a Dad's Tuesday, didn't she Dad?"

John was silent for a moment and then nodded slowly, "Yes, son. Yes, she did."

"So I'm guessing that this gigantic Secret that I've been running from hasn't been such a secret after all."

"It's been your secret, Paul. No one's invaded the sanctity of it. Only your mother and I have known about it, and we just added it to our list of prayers for you, that's all."

Paul pushed back his chair, stood, and went to look out the back window. He thrust his hands in his pockets and said furiously through gritted teeth, "You've got a grandson out there, Dad, that you'll never get to know. How can you sit there calm and collected, talking about praying when you have lost something so huge that you can never regain?!"

John sighed and didn't immediately respond. "Your mother and I have shed many tears over this together, Paul. But that's what marriage and parenthood is all about: tremendous joys and cavernous sorrows, and you hold each other tightly through the bad parts so that you don't get destroyed. You're missing the boat here, though. Your mother and I have had five beautiful children to love and cherish and laugh and cry over." Paul felt his father's presence directly behind him. "We were a little too worried about *our own son* and what he was going through to focus on ourselves too much. We know what you're missing and can only imagine what you're going through. We've been busy loving and praying for you. We've been busy waiting for you to forgive yourself and start living again."

It was suddenly crystal clear to Paul. All the family get - togethers, all the times he'd felt condescension and disappointment and disgust directed towards him. Paul realized with a powerful rush that those emotions had come only from inside *him*. Not from his family or friends. There was nothing here but love. In an anguished voice he said to his father, "I can't forgive myself. It's too big. What I did to Karly. What I did to that child. It's too big. I'm going to carry this with me for the rest of my life."

John put a hand on Paul's shoulder. "Some of what you say I can't argue with, Paul. You will carry this with you for the rest of your life, there's no doubt about it. But, this does not need to be the point of destruction for you. Your mother and I have prayed for you and Karly and … the boy. You can chose never to forgive yourself, but that's a choice. God can forgive you. That's all that really counts, isn't it? Sometimes our greatest hurts and sorrows turn out to be our greatest ministry, our greatest witness to the world. Right now, your greatest hurt and sorrow is keeping you hidden. It's paralyzing you, slowly strangling you to death. That's what your mother and I see, and that's what we pray so hard about. We want your Secret, as you call it, to be a point of triumph for you. It can be, you know."

Paul turned to look at his father, heedless of the tears still wet on his face. "How, Dad? How could I do that?"

John pulled his son into a tight embrace. "I can't answer that, son. That's your job. But I'd guess your first step would be to visit Karly."

Visit Karly. Maybe Paul should just take the hedge shears and begin lopping off his toes one by one. That would be a hell of a lot easier.

Wednesday as Paul played basketball with Tyler, Claire came out and sat on the steps. "Mr. Williamson, I was wondering if you'd like to come home and have dinner with us." Paul stood there; sweat pouring off him, frowning in puzzlement.

Tyler gave him a huge grin. "Mom only works up to five now, Paul. She drops me off at school early and picks me up at three like she used to but now we go home at five and eat dinner together. And starting next week, when I'm finished with school, she's going to be finished at three when I'm done with summer camp. That is, unless her nursing classes change things."

"No more late nights, Claire?"

She smiled at him. "No more late nights."

"And she's got Saturdays, Sundays, and Mondays off now, too!" Tyler said.

"Really ..." Paul looked at both of their smiling faces.

Claire was a good cook, it turned out. Paul watched her dicing chicken breasts and sautéing them in onions and garlic and fresh mushrooms, while he and Tyler played a cutthroat game of Monopoly sprawled out on the living room floor. At her request, the boys set the table and poured the drinks.

As they were seated and getting ready to eat Tyler said, "Mrs. Santiago says you should always say grace before a meal," as Claire halted with her fork midway between her plate and her open mouth.

Claire carefully put her fork down. "Oh, okay, big guy. You want to handle it?"

Tyler looked just as awkward as Claire.

"How about this?" Paul suggested. "We'll go around the table and each say something out loud we're thankful for. No big deal. No fancy words. We'll just pick one thing out of our day that we'd like to express our appreciation for." He looked at both of their skeptical faces. "I'll start. I'm thankful for this dinner invitation and the great company."

Claire caught on and volunteered, "I'm thankful that I'm not standing up at a counter stuffing in fast mouthfuls while I'm between tables."

Tyler's concentration was evident. Finally he blurted out, "I'm thankful for ... broken down cars!"

"What?!" Claire said.

Tyler shrugged. "If you hadn't broken down on the side of the road, Mom, we never would have met Paul," he explained matter – of - factly. It made perfect sense to him.

Paul grinned and shrugged his shoulders, taking a big mouthful of food. "This is delicious, Claire."

Once Tyler was in bed, they sat on the wicker couch on the screened in front porch. "You're quiet tonight, Paul, is everything okay? How's Brian?"

"I haven't seen him since he left my house in his underwear Tuesday night." Claire looked at Paul as though he was crazy, and he laughed out loud. "It's true! Don't look at me like that! He hasn't called me from jail, and it doesn't seem like he's come back to the house at all, so I'm hoping that's a good sign."

They sat in companionable silence for a bit and finally, with a big sigh, she leaned over and put her head on his shoulder. It was absolutely natural for him to respond by putting his arm around her. It was better than nice; it was just right. "I found someone I could trust, Claire," he finally said. "I talked to my Dad."

"Wise choice," she answered promptly.

"How would you know? You hardly know him."

"First impressions are powerful. His packed a wallop."

Paul sighed. She had a point. "Yeah, I guess so." He rubbed his cheek against the top of her head. "I'm gonna trust you now, okay?"

She snuggled in closer and said quietly, "I'd be honored."

"You know how I told you I got close to getting married once?" When she nodded her head he began his story. He tried hard not to leave out any details, and the story took a long time. He brought her right up to the point where he told his family and had to deal with their disappointment and condescension. All of a sudden, he didn't want to reveal anymore about himself to her. This seemed bad enough. The Secret came and sat down right between them on the wicker couch and smiled at him.

After a time Claire finally spoke. "So that was the last time you heard from Karly? You've never spoken since that day?"

Well, technically ... "I've not seen or spoken to her since that day."

"Oh."

Paul sighed. "But I did hear from her."

Claire sat up and looked at him. "You did? Have you heard from her recently then?"

His palms were sweaty and his heartbeat was thumping irregularly in his chest. Wasn't what he did with Karly in some ways what those six boys had done to Claire? Left her alone, pregnant, and defenseless? What if Claire saw him in the same way as Karly did? What if she didn't want to hear from him or see him again either once she knew the Whole Truth about The Secret?

"Paul?"

Who do you trust, Paul? Was that Claire or his grandfather speaking? He couldn't tell. Paul leaned forward and put his face in his hands.

"Paul?" He felt her put her arm around him and tenderly touch the top of his head.

"I didn't hear from her recently Claire. I heard from her about eight months after we broke things off. I got legal papers. Asking me to sign away parental rights to the baby boy she had given birth to." Paul looked at Claire then, because he wanted to see the hatred and loathing right there on her face. Just get it over and done with so he wouldn't be able to play any games with himself in the future. "I signed the papers, Claire. Just like that, I said, 'Sure, you can give my kid away. I don't want him either.'"

Claire sighed a deep, sorrowful sigh, but didn't draw away from him. "And you didn't care one bit, did you? You still don't. You were just glad to put it all behind you and move on," she said tenderly, reaching over to stroke his face. "It didn't mean a thing to you. You didn't think twice about it."

"You're supposed to be disgusted with me Claire," he said with barely controlled fury. "You're supposed to think what a miserable example of a man I am."

She wrapped her arms around him and kissed him on the cheek. "Oh, I am. I just can't stand the sight of you, you awful, terrible man. I expected you to be perfect, just like I am. All shiny and squeaky clean." And Claire hugged him tighter and Paul felt her try to rock him but he was really too big for her to move much.

He pulled away from her, gripped her face, and looked intently at her. In an anguished voice he tried one more time to get her to see and understand the horrible picture that was being revealed to her. "I've got a son out there and my parents have a grandson out there and my sisters and brothers have a nephew out there that we'll never know, never see." Didn't she get it?

Claire had tears in her eyes when she said, "But you'll still love him won't you, Paul? All of your family will still love him. You'll still love him with all your heart because that's what your family is all about, isn't it? Your family is all about love." Tears trickled down her cheeks and collected in the palms of his hands while he still held her face. "You'll keep him in your heart and your prayers your whole life, won't you? Won't you?"

And then Paul let her rock him while he cried.

After a time they wandered into the kitchen and Claire poured them both cups of coffee. Finally, Paul broke the silence. "Dad says I need to go talk with Karly."

Claire sighed. "That's going to be the hardest thing you'll ever do, Paul."

"Do you agree?" Paul hesitated. "I mean, do you think it would do either of us any good?"

"I, I don't know, Paul. I really don't."

"Would you be … any better … off … if someone from your past sought you out and tried to … talk … with you about things?"

Claire didn't answer him right away. "It would depend. On who. On why. On what. But, in a lot of instances, I could see … closure … happening." She gave Paul a tremulous smile. "Please understand I'm not telling you it would be a happy ending. Closure can mean harsh words but they may make the speaker feel a lot better for getting things off … her … chest. She might rip you to shreds in more ways than one. You risk feeling even worse after seeing her."

"I don't even know where she is. I'd have to start with her parents."

Claire looked at him. "Have you prayed about this?"

Paul looked at her like she'd grown another head. "What did you just ask me?"

Claire looked surprisingly confident for a few moments and then blushed. "Janice Strocco called me today, Paul. She wanted Mrs. Santiago's phone number. It seems that there's a place opening up in Sonset House. She wants to talk with Mrs. Santiago to see if there is a possible match between her and the current residents." She bit her lower lip seeming to decide what more to say and then plunged on. "Paul, Tyler and I *prayed* about this. When I listened to Janice talk to me about this wonderful opportunity that had suddenly become available, all I could think about was me and Tyler and our puny little prayer the other day. I suddenly felt so powerful. I keep hearing you and Daniel say that you don't believe in coincidences. All this 'good luck' is starting to be too much for me." She hiccupped a little laugh and then shrugged. "I'm just saying that something as huge as what you're considering needs to be done in the best possible manner. Prayer can't hurt, can it?" Suddenly she needed his reassurance and confirmation.

"No, prayer can never hurt, Claire. Ask my mother and father. I'm beginning to think that my entire life – all the good parts – are a testament to their faith and prayers." Paul drew her into an embrace standing there in the kitchen. "Tyler told me all about waking you up and you going off to church with him on Sunday. That's so cool, Claire. You two are so good for each other."

He felt her hands touch his back tenderly, "And you're good for both of us."

"My dots are connecting, Claire. With each connection I feel stronger and more capable. Maybe," he said quietly as they stood embracing in the kitchen, "one of these days I'll be as strong and courageous as you."

I'm not gonna lie about feeling fine and knowing everything's okay
I just gotta believe that His hope inside will lead me to a better place[19]

★
★ ★ ⋅ ★
★ ★

Fifteen: Keep Your Secrets To Yourself

Karly's parents didn't tell him he couldn't come visit them the next day. (No sense putting it off, Paul already wasn't sleeping from the stress anyway.) However in barely civil tones they did communicate that they could see no benefit in talking with him. He politely pressed them and was at last given a day and time on Sunday, July 3rd. The drive took two and a half hours, and then he stalled another half hour by stopping at a local restaurant to use the bathroom and chug a cup of steaming black coffee. He also drove around their block three times before he finally parked and got out of the car.

Standing on the front walk he wasn't surprised that he actually felt worse than he had the last time he'd been there, almost exactly six years ago. The front door opened and a young man, probably nineteen or so, stood framed in the doorway. He scrutinized Paul for a moment, and then as Paul walked forward he said, "Man, you've got balls."

It was Michael, Karly's irreverent little brother who had grown into a strapping, smart-mouthed man. Paul looked him in the eyes and said in the same tone, "But not for long, probably." Michael snickered and held

19 I Will Not Lie Down, Margaret Becker, Simple House Album, The Sparrow Corporation, 1991

the door open.

"I'm supposed to tell you that they're on the back patio and then disappear. I'd pay cash to hang around and listen." There was malice in Michael's tone.

Paul remembered playing touch football with the ten-year-old version, and the boy's thinly disguised idol worship of him. He remembered that Karly (and only Karly) called him "Snake" in honor of the time he'd left a real live snake in her underwear drawer or something like that. Jeeze, it had never occurred to him that there was a subset of people that hated him besides Karly and her parents. "Guess you could always go hide in the rose bushes and eavesdrop."

"Don't worry. I'll manage." Michael walked away without a backward glance.

Mr. and Mrs. Martin sat on their back patio gazing out onto the yard made brilliant and alive by the smell of warm earth and cut grass cooked in summer sunshine. Both were obviously tense but made a good show as they sipped iced tea from tall frosty glasses. A third chair and a third empty glass sat by a table that held a full pitcher of something cold and wet. Mr. Martin stood as Paul came outside, but did not extend his hand. "Paul," he said by way of a greeting.

"Mr. and Mrs. Martin, thanks for seeing me. I know how difficult this is. I've been driving around the block for the past half hour trying to get up the courage to come in."

Mrs. Martin looked at Paul but didn't say anything. Mr. Martin motioned to the empty chair. "Have a seat, Paul. Would you like some iced tea?"

"Sure. Thanks." He settled his long frame into the cushioned lawn chair and had a blinding wave of panic. What in God's name was he doing here?!

Exactly, said his grandfather. *And don't forget it.*

Paul took a sip of his drink, cleared his throat and took a deep breath. He'd been so worked up about the visit it had never occurred to him to rehearse or plan what he was going to say. *Guide my words*, he prayed desperately. "I, I've done a lot of growing up in these past few years, Mr.

and Mrs. Martin." He smiled wryly, "It's been a long, difficult journey." They stared back at him blank faced. They had no reason whatsoever to give him an inch and Paul hadn't really expected them to. "At the time Karly and I were together I was struggling with a lot of things besides growing up. I was questioning my faith and who I was, and who I wanted to be – not just professionally, but personally. Karly, well, Karly always *knew* what she wanted out of life. She had a goal and a purpose and strength of character. As I slipped further and further away from what was *good* and *right,* her focus and drive made my issues that much more obvious. As much as she tried to keep me on the straight and narrow, I worked just as hard to drag her down, away from that. I don't know why it was so important to me, but it was."

Paul looked down at his hands. "I'm sorry about that more than anything. I shouldn't have made her doubt herself and her faith. I shouldn't have challenged her to compromise her principles to show her love. I knew she loved me, I really did."

"But you didn't love her back, did you?" Mrs. Martin spoke at last.

Paul faced the accusation directly, looking Karly's mom right in the eye. "No, ma'am. I didn't love her as much as she loved me. But I hope it counts that I loved her as much as I was capable of at the time. It's hard to love someone else when you don't think much of yourself." They stared at each other for a few moments. Mrs. Martin looked away first.

"Why are you here, Paul?" Mr. Martin finally asked in the awkward silence.

Paul looked at Karly's father. He'd always been polite, even on that last horrible morning six years ago. Had he held up? Had he been there for Karly when everything went down about the baby? Paul couldn't ask, he didn't dare. "I'm a twenty-seven year old man now, sir. I'm certain that over the course of my life I will continue to make mistakes, but I'm ever hopeful that the glaring ones are behind me. I've recommitted my life to Christ and have been making every effort to at least get to the point in my spiritual walk where Karly was back in college. In answer to your question, I'm here because I'd like the opportunity to speak with Karly. I can't tell you why because I don't know why. I just know that is seems to be what the Lord wants me to do. I don't want to upset her, rekindle any relationship, or reclaim lost opportunities. I guess I'd just like the opportunity to tell her I'm sincerely sorry and give her an opportunity to accept or reject my apology."

"She's moved on with her life. She doesn't need your apology or to hear your story. I think you'd be best off to go back to wherever you've been these past six years," Mrs. Martin said in a hiss.

"Madeline …"

"No, Tom, why can't I have my say? I'm tired of being polite and accommodating," she said in a bitter tone. "Always the exemplary Christian." She turned to Paul. "You destroyed our little girl, young man. Just destroyed her. If you'd taken a bomb and set it off here in the living room that day you would have done less damage. We're still grieving for what we lost," her voice caught and she put her balled fist up to her mouth almost as if to shove the sobs back inside herself again.

"Madeline, don't …"

Mrs. Martin glared at her husband and then turned back to Paul. What had Claire said to him? *Closure can mean harsh words, but sometimes they make the speaker feel a lot better for getting things off … her … chest. She might rip you to shreds in more ways than one. You risk feeling even worse after seeing her than you do now.* Paul looked at Mrs. Martin getting her closure wrapped in his pound of flesh. "This family has never recovered from your selfishness or your cowardice. Your presence here is unwanted and if you think that we're going to blithely hand over Karly's address and phone number so you can amble on down to see her and tear her up to shreds again, *you're out of your mind.* Just because *you're* ready to talk and *you'd* like an opportunity to settle things from your deep dark past doesn't mean *we're* inclined to accommodate." She stood, visibly fighting back tears. "I've had my say. You can see yourself out."

Paul stood and then looked at Mr. Martin. "I appreciate you're taking the time to see me. I'm sorry … for stirring all of this up again."

Mr. Martin stood, took a deep breath, and thrust his hands in his pockets. "Oh, you haven't stirred anything up, Paul. It's been swirling around here for years. It never settled. The last thing this family agreed on and was happy about was the vacation we took fifteen years ago to Disney World." He looked regretfully at Paul. "I'm sorry. I had mixed opinions regarding whether to give you contact information for Karly should you request it. There's too much dissension in this house already. I'm not going to go against Madeline's wishes."

"I understand," Paul said. He made his way out of the house, down the front path, and over to his truck. He'd parked it in the shade down the street, not wanting the Martins to see him having a crisis about going in. Michael was leaning against his truck.

"They still intact?" he said with a glance at Paul's shorts, a smirk on his face.

Paul sighed. "I didn't realize I owed you an apology, too, but I suppose I do, Michael. I'm sorry. With you, I'm not exactly sure the extent of what I've got to apologize for, but I'm hoping you'll believe me when I say I mean this to be one of those all encompassing apologies. Okay?" He reached in his pocket and pulled out the keys to the truck.

"So who won the battle?"

"I'm not sure anyone's the winner or loser."

"Oh stop being so damned polite. I wanted to know which one of my parents won. They've been arguing since you called three days ago. Dad wanted to let you know where Karly was if you asked, and Mom said no. Who won?"

Paul stared at Michael. "Your mother."

"Thought so. He always lets her win."

"I really should get going, Michael. Can I drop you off somewhere?"

"The last time Dad won an argument was when he sided with Karly about giving the baby up for adoption. Mom didn't want her to."

"Somehow I feel like you shouldn't be telling me these things, Michael."

"I can give you Karly's address."

Paul walked over to the truck and leaned back against it, crossed his arms, and looked at Michael. "And why would you do that, Michael, knowing how your mother feels about things, knowing how divided your parents are over this?"

"Because I agree with Dad. Because I'm on Karly's side. Because I think she might like the chance to tell you to Go To Hell right to your face. That's why."

Paul had to know. "Is she okay, Michael? Can you tell me that? Can you give me just that little bit of information?"

Michael seemed to think about the question for a bit. Perhaps debating which way he answered would cause Paul more misery and pain? "She's doing missionary work, teaching with the Navajo Indians down in New Mexico at a place called Huerfano Station. I can tell you she's okay, but that's about all I know. She stays away from the battling, bickering Martins as much as possible. I haven't seen her since she moved down there." He held out a piece of paper. "Here's her address. There's no real reliable phone service there. She calls us when she can."

All of a sudden the desire to contact her and endure more *closure* was more than Paul could handle. He pushed himself away from the truck, ignoring the piece of paper that Michael held out, and headed toward the driver's door, key in hand. "I think I'll pass, Michael. I'm going to trust your parent's decision."

Michael continued to hold out the piece of paper. "She has contact with the kid, you know. Pictures and emails and stuff. His name is Benjamin."

Paul felt like he'd been hit by a freight train. He looked at Michael, desperate to determine if he was serious or playing some twisted game. *"She has contact with our son?"*

Michael nodded. "Yeah, it was one of those 'open adoption' things. Where Karly got to pick where the baby went. She chose the couple. I think that's why Mom doesn't want you to contact Karly. She knows if you do, it won't be a one-time deal, and she doesn't want Karly to get hurt again." Michael narrowed his eyes at Paul. "It took Karly a lot of years to get herself together. She did the whole close to suicide thing and everything. You really screwed her up. Now that she's better, that's what makes me think she'd like a chance to really tell you what she thinks of you."

"I see."

Michael walked past the driver's door and slipped the piece of paper in through the window Paul had left open to keep the heat from building up. "Another discussion I'd pay real money to hear, between you and Karly. Man, that should be rich." He shuffled across the street toward home, his pants riding so low Paul swore he caught a glimpse of his boxers.

"Thanks, Michael," Paul called out but he didn't receive any response.

Paul's parents were having their traditional 4th of July barbeque celebration the next day. Claire had been excited about going and insisted on bringing along a dish of potato salad. They'd had a long talk by phone when Paul arrived home from the Martins. He struggled with accurately communicating all of the volatile emotions that he'd experienced with the Martins, with Michael, and by himself on the way home. *She has contact with the kid, you know.* He heard Michael's casually uttered statement over and over in his head and each and every time he felt like he had been sucker punched in the stomach. On more than one occasion he caught himself massaging his gut, looking somewhat like an oversized, modern day Napoleon.

Claire had listened silently, asking pertinent questions to clarify certain points that he'd missed in the telling. When she heard about Benjamin she was quiet for a few moments and then said quietly. "There's your purpose."

"What do you mean?" Paul pinched the bridge between his eyes trying to dull the pounding headache that was growing there.

"You've said all along how you felt *compelled* to contact Karly, but for the life of you, you couldn't figure out why or to what end. I think you've found your purpose. Your goal."

"The kid?"

He heard Claire sigh into the phone like she did when she was trying to organize her thoughts and words before she said something important. "Where's the greatest guilt, Paul? Is it with Karly and the way you left the relationship or is it with the loss of the child?"

Paul sat slumped on the hanging swing on his back porch with the cordless phone gripped in his right hand. "I don't know …"

"You've said to me that you know, as hard as it was, that it was best that you and Karly never married. You admitted you should have handled it differently, but you would have wanted the same result, right?"

"Yeah …"

"And yet you're still racked with guilt. Lots regarding Karly, I know, but I think the biggest portion is regarding that faceless, up until now nameless son that you have somewhere out there." Claire hesitated and then said quietly, "If you had one wish, what would it be, Paul?"

He rocked the swing backward, and resting his elbows on his knees, cradled his pounding head in his left hand. He felt his throat tighten and his eyes burn with emotion. "I'd want my son to be … safe, happy, loved, protected, treasured. I'd like to know that," his voice caught, "he's okay."

"So, here's your chance." And then she'd asked him when he was going to fly to New Mexico.

"Are you nuts, Claire? I can't just fly down there and show up at Karly's front door and say, 'Hi! Remember me?'"

"Why not?"

"Because …" He couldn't come up with a reason that didn't smack of cowardice and the easy way out.

Claire sighed and Paul had a sudden wave of comfort and peace that he had someone like her to talk to about all this. Where would he be right now if she wasn't a part of his life, he thought with a sudden flash of panic? Claire's calm, soothing voice filled his ear. "Look, there's no rush, right? No big clock that's ticking. Take your time. *Pray* about it." Paul could feel her smiling at the other end of the phone. "Maybe you need to talk with your dad again. It sure turned out well the last time, didn't it?"

She was right. Lately, she was always right, it seemed. "I don't know," he grumbled. "Look, I'm tired. I've got a monster headache. I'm gonna get to sleep, okay?"

"You're a good man, Paul. If all of this weren't causing you a bit of thought or concern, *that* would be a *big* problem."

"Claire?"

"Yeah?"

"I'm glad you're a part of my life. I'm glad I have you to talk to about this stuff. I'm glad your car is a piece of … junk … and that it broke down."

She chuckled quietly. "You know what I'm glad about?"

He stretched out along the swing's length, draping one long leg over the back and bracing the other one on the ground to cause a gentle rocking motion. He smiled to himself, and just the change in his facial expression lessened the pounding of his head. "No, what are you glad about?'

"I'm glad that you are *exactly* the man that you are, Paul. Because anyone else would never have had the patience or the tenderness to work through this wall I've had around myself for all these years."

There was long silence on both ends of the phone, a wonderful, contented silence. *I love her*, Paul thought to himself. *I really do love her.* "I'll pick you up about eleven tomorrow, okay?" he finally said. "You got your fantastic potato salad already made?"

"Yup and yup."

"Sleep tight, Claire."

"You too, Paul. You too."

Paul could tell that the whole crew was there by the pile of cars parked out front and by the shouts of laughter and boisterous conversation when he, Tyler, and Claire arrived just after noon. Standing in the shadowy interior of the house looking out onto the big wrap-around deck, he could see his father was where Paul knew he would be, in front of his massive grill cooking for the crowd. John wore a baseball cap that said 'Too Hot', with chili peppers embroidered on the front of it, and an apron that said 'Kiss The Cook' in bright red letters. Croquet, horseshoes, and badminton were being played on the lawn, and piles of assorted appetizers were scattered around on the deck tables.

"Remind me again who they all are," Claire whispered next to him, slipping her hand in his.

"Dad," he pointed to the grill, "and Mom," he pointed to his mother, who was wearing a tee shirt that said 'Well Behaved Women Rarely

Make History'. "My sister Connie's wearing the blue top and that's her husband Mark that she just handed a shrimp to. Their kids Evan and Janine are playing badminton on the lawn. There's my sister, Rachel, she's giving my brother Elliot a hard time. Rachel's husband is Andy, he's trying to," Paul snorted, "hit my other brother, Brian, with the croquet mallet. I don't see their son Ryan. He's only six, and he's a soccer nut. They've had him on a soccer team for two seasons already. Oh! There he is. See over there by the wooded area? He's kicking the soccer ball showing off for ..." Paul hesitated.

"What?" Claire asked turning to follow the direction of his gaze.

"Well I'll be," Paul said with a slow smile. "Seems like showing up in his underwear did a world of good for Brian and Janet. That's Mallory, Brian's oldest that Ryan's showing off his soccer skills to, and I see Janet walking across the yard there holding Tiffany's hand. She's *smiling*," Paul said in wonder. "Jeeze, Claire. I haven't seen her smiling in about a year and a half."

Sure enough, the woman in question strolled across the lawn, stopped to watch the crochet battle going on, and smiled when Brian blew her a kiss. "That sure looks promising," Claire said under her breath.

"Sure does," Paul agreed, and he sighed. "I'm glad for him. He was one pitiful mess."

"Maybe they just needed time apart to miss each other."

Paul took Claire's hand. "Maybe. You ready to face the masses again? Hey. Where's Tyler?"

Claire laughed and pointed. Suddenly Tyler was joining the croquet game and Elliot and Brian where chasing him across the lawn.

It was the most relaxed Paul could ever remember being with his family. Ever. He sat and laughed and took their teasing and threw it right back at them. Paul made cracks about Brian driving around in his underwear causing Janet to blush furiously. Mark made comments about Paul needing to go in and peel the potatoes. To everyone's delight Paul went in, found the bag and peeler, and dropped them all at his brother-in-law's feet and announced that he was officially passing the job to him. *For life.*

The entire family played a ferocious game of croquet that involved good - natured insults and extensive cheating. One disagreement took the air of a tackle football game. When Paul tackled his sister, Rachel, in response to her blatant attempt to cheat and therefore beat him she laughed up into his face, "Just where have you been all these years, little brother? I've missed you."

The comment meant the world to Paul. "Lost, Rach, really lost. But I'm back."

Putting her hand up to his cheek she smiled and said, "It's about time."

Dinner was spectacular as usual. No one was disappointed and everyone was uncomfortably full. Barbequed mushrooms, peppers, filet mignon, shrimp, and miniature, homemade pizzas for the kids. *All done on the grill.*

"I think I'm going to explode I'm so stuffed," moaned Elliot in mock agony.

"Look at it this way," Connie said to him with an absolutely straight face, "at least you won't have to put out any money for the next few meals, and you can pinch a few more pennies."

With a burp, Elliot grinned at his sister. "Exactly my thinking, sister dear."

Paul watched the interplay between his family, and for the first time saw that the teasing and the ribbing that he'd taken such offense to was an integral part of the familial interaction. When had he begun to feel that it was always and only directed at him? No one was particularly singled out, and yet everyone was fair game. Even Claire and Tyler got their own share of teasing – Claire for her poor taste in men and Tyler for his amazing ability to eat *eight* hotdogs. (At least that's what was actually observed.)

"What? Do you have a hollow leg or something, kid?" Brian asked picking up Tyler's skinny leg so high that he ended up dangling upside down laughing and flailing. "You got those hot dogs in your pockets or something?" Brian gave him a shake.

"You're cleaning up whatever shows up," Janet said with a smile.

"Hey, don't blow on me kid, okay?" Brian said, but put him down rather gingerly in the chair next to Claire.

While the kids ran around the backyard playing flashlight tag and catching fire flies, Paul took advantage of the lull in the conversation, over coffee and tea, brownies and apple pie (not cooked on the grill!). "If I say to all of you as a group "I'm sorry", do you think that would be enough to start with a clean slate?"

"That and about two hundred bucks," Elliot said with a grin.

"Paul, you don't have to apologize for anything. We've loved you and prayed for you and did our best to support you and encourage you …" his mother began.

Paul interrupted her before she could really get going with a huge, mushy, speech. "Well, you're wrong about that, Mom. I *do* have a lot to apologize for. Unfortunately, at this point in my life I can't spell everything out to all of you, but eventually I will. I'm asking for your forgiveness for being an … idiot … in years past, I'm asking for your continued love and support, and, most importantly, I'm asking for your prayers. I've got some big decisions facing me over the next few weeks, and I'd appreciate your prayers as my back up."

"You're asking us to *pray* for you?" his sister Connie said in a stunned voice.

Paul met her surprised expression over the flickering candlelight. "Yeah, Con, I'm asking for your prayers."

"Now it's all starting to make sense," Rachel said with an intense look. "Now I get why you seem so … different, so *peaceful.*" She grinned at Claire. "I thought you were some miracle worker or something."

Claire gave her a shy smile and shook her head, "No, it wasn't me."

Paul reached over and took her hand. "Yes, some of it *is* you, Claire." He gave his family a grin. "*Finally*, at long last, I seem to be getting all my … stuff … together in the right order. I'm asking that you keep me in your prayers while I finish up some of the last, few, *really difficult* things, okay?"

"You got it, bro," Brian said. "But you need to know that you actually had it even before you asked."

Paul carried a sleeping Tyler up into his bedroom and then stepped back while Claire took off his sneakers and socks and covered him with a sheet. She glanced up at Paul. "We seem to do this a lot with him, don't we?"

"He goes full tilt and then hits the wall and collapses. We better not let him get a driver's license."

"You want a cup of coffee or something?" Claire asked as they made their way downstairs.

"You're not too beat?"

"No, it was a wonderful day, and actually I'm pretty wound up still." They wandered into the kitchen and prepared the coffee. She chatted about school and about Mrs. Santiago, who was settling into Sunset House with only a few minor compromises. "I had to carefully suggest that she could not assume the role of Master and Commander within the first few days of moving in or she was going to end up sitting on the roadside hitching a ride."

"How'd that go over?"

Claire smiled at him over her shoulder. "She actually laughed and said she'd been living alone for so many years she had forgotten about the nuances of compromise." Claire shook her head. "I hope it works out over there."

"I love you, Claire."

She froze, her back to him, as she was putting milk in both of their coffees.

"You gonna say anything?" he finally said to her rigid back.

Still with her back to him, she managed to shake her head in a jerky 'no'.

"You don't have to tell me you love me back. I didn't expect that, you know. It's just, well, I've never wanted to say that to a woman before *just because*, you know? I've said it to a few women in the past, but, I'm ashamed to say, I usually either had some sort of hidden agenda or I just plain felt pressured to say it." He took a deep breath. "I almost always have taken the coward's way out, Claire. But, well, with you, this feeling I have for you it just kind of fills me up inside and I, well, just kind of started to feel this need just to tell you how I feel. So," he shrugged his shoulders although she still had her back to him and couldn't see, "I decided to say it." He walked the few steps across the kitchen and around the small table to stand behind her. "I guess I could have waited until we were in a more romantic setting, but I just couldn't hold it in anymore." He dropped his voice low and standing behind her he whispered into her ear, "You make me happy, Claire. You make me peaceful. You make me want to please you and protect you ... I like the woman you are, Claire. You're no nonsense, but you can be silly, too. You're serious and thoughtful, but you have a great sense of humor. You're responsible and dependable, but you can tease and play. When I'm away from you, Claire, I look forward to being with you again, and when I'm with you I never want to leave."

There was no sound but the nighttime sounds of cicadas and crickets. Still with her back to him, Claire remained frozen and silent.

"You ever going to speak to me again?" Paul finally asked her, wrapping his arms around her, drawing her back against his chest, and kissing the top of her head. It was in his arms that he felt her tremble, and realized she was crying silently. "Hey! Hey, what's this?" He leaned over her shoulder and gently cupped her chin making her look up and around at him. "I know I'm no prize catch, but I didn't think you'd be sobbing your eyes out over my declaration of love," he teased.

"Oh, Paul ..." Claire turned in his arms and he crushed her to his chest.

"Easy, love, easy. Come sit with me on the porch." He grabbed her hand and dragged her out to the porch swing, sat down, and then pulled her onto his lap. She buried her face in his neck. "Last night," he said to her, "when we were talking on the phone, I thought about how I loved you. I was sitting on my porch and I thought, 'I really love her'. It was a ... darn ... good feeling."

They rocked for a long time on the swing as Paul enjoyed the closeness of the woman in his arms. Finally, Claire sniffed and said quietly, "Tyler loves me. It's that wonderful, unconditional kind of love that a child gives his mother. You know, 'You're pretty, Mom', 'You're the best cook in the whole world, Mom', 'I want to live with you forever, Mom.'

"After the ... rape, I was homeless for a time, wandering. I'd decided that I wouldn't go back to the agency or to another foster home. I'd rather be dead." She sighed. "I meant it, too.

"I lived on the streets for about a month and a half, but winter was coming and I was cold and, I guess, pretty scared. I'd left with just the stuff I could put in my backpack and the money I could find in my foster parents' house. It wasn't much at all. I was afraid to go to the shelters because I was obviously underage, and I knew I'd get snapped up back into the system. You would have thought that when I realized I was pregnant I would have been devastated, but knowing I was going to have a baby who would *love me* was what made me try to pull my life together.

"I hitchhiked to a family that I had fostered with for about six months when I was thirteen or so. I had fond memories of them. I'd been moved out of that home because another family had expressed an interest in adopting me." She was quiet, lost in thought for a few moments. "But that never worked out. I knocked on this family's door and pretty much stood on their front steps and cried my eyes out. They let me stay with them for Tyler's pregnancy, and it was through them that I ended up getting the job at the diner."

"Why didn't you stay with them after Tyler was born, Claire?"

Claire shrugged. "The dad got transferred. A job opportunity in Europe. They helped me find my apartment, and gave me the security and the first month rent, too. I still get letters from them every now and then."

Claire sat up on Paul's lap and wiped her face on her shirt sleeve. With feather light fingers she touched his face: his brow, his nose, his cheeks, his lips. "Until now, Tyler's the only person in my life who ever told me that he loved me, Paul. He loves me with a child's love, deep and unconditional, and I treasure it. I didn't believe that anyone would ever love me besides Tyler. I, I didn't even really believe that love existed outside of the realm of a mother/child kind of relationship! All that stuff in movies and books was just *fluff*. Made up stuff in other people's minds who had too much time on their hands to do something more practical."

Gently, she leaned over and kissed him on the mouth. "And here you are telling me you *love me*. That I make you happy and that you want to be with me. You tell me that I have good suggestions and ideas. You say I am responsible and dependable and you want to please me and protect me." She shook her head, looked him right in the eye and said, "*You cannot be real.*"

"I'm real all right," he breathed into her mouth and kissed her hard. "I am very real. *I love you, Claire Jenkins.* What do you have to say about that, huh?"

She drew a shaky breath and snuggled back down against his chest, tucking her head under his chin. This was so nice. This being told she was loved and being looked at with eyes that shone with happiness and ... desire. Claire trembled with the wonder of it ... and the terror of it. *Intimacy.* Being intimate with a man – emotionally and physically - was something she had promised herself *would never happen.* It was the bedrock of her rules of survival. It was what kept her from going off the deep end, and enabled her to climb out of bed and face each new, difficult day. Even looking into Paul's handsome face, a face that showed nothing but care and concern, she'd felt the terror begin to grow and churn in her gut. Against his neck she said, "I'm full of unresolved problems, Paul. I've got issues that have issues. I've limped along, keeping my head just barely above water. I'll drag you under." She felt the tears press at the back of her eyes and she squeezed them shut taking a deep shuddering breath to gain some courage and control. "I drag everyone under."

Paul shifted them on the swing so that she was lying in his arms but looking up at him. One arm cradled her and with his free hand he touched the side of her face. He stared intently at her and his big, callous thumb gently rubbed her mouth and the smooth plane of her cheek. "*So soft,*" he murmured almost to himself, "so pretty, so kind, so good ..." Unable to resist, he leaned down and gave her a long, slow, sure kiss. The churning in her stomach was there but had stopped growing. It just sat there like some undigested, unpleasant meal. Paul looked at her. "Remember what you said to me on the phone the other night? About there being no clock ticking? No rush?" She nodded. "I've still got stuff to settle from my past. You've got stuff to settle from yours. What's the race? Where's the big hurry? We work on it slowly but surely *together,* Claire. Seems to me that both of us are a ... heck ... of a lot better together than apart. Do you agree with me about that?"

If she could have stopped the tears she would have, but instead they trickled out the far corners of her eyes. She nodded.

Paul spent long moments just looking at her, trying to read her mind like it was the most important piece of information he was ever going to acquire. "I ..." he began and halted. "I ..." he began again, never looking anywhere but right into her eyes, "don't want to be anywhere but ... here with you. Okay? We'll sort out what we can sort out between the two of us, and if that isn't enough, if there are still things that are bigger than the two of us put together then ... well, maybe ..." his massive shoulders lifted into a shrug, "we'll go talk to a professional about these issues, okay? *Together. The two of us.*

"I look at it this way, Claire," he said rather fiercely to her, "God's gone to a lot of trouble to hook us up, and the least we can do is pay attention and try our best." His eyes challenged her to disagree with him. He suddenly looked like a pit bull staring down a threatening opponent.

Claire closed her eyes at the intensity of his gaze and sighed. *I love him with all my heart and my newly discovered soul,* she thought. *If all of my trials brought me right here to this place and this moment with this man then perhaps it was all worth it. I've got Tyler and Paul.* She opened her eyes to smile at him. He'd become like a marble statue as he held her and poured out his heart: hard and tense and rigid. Claire reached up and touched his face and brought her hand down to wrap around the side of his neck. "I love you, too, Paul Williamson. I have never, ever said that to another person beside Tyler, and I am *so glad* that I've discovered it and can give it to *you."* Wrapping her arms around him she said, "When you met me I was an empty glass. Slowly and surely with patience and love you have filled me with only good things: faith, love, hope, goodness ... Thank you..."

Paul placed a big finger across her lips to stop her. "It's a fair trade, Claire. Even Steven. A partnership. I'm getting as much as I'm giving. So let's just trade 'I love yous' and leave it at that, okay?"

"Sounds good to me ..."

My happiness is found in less
Of me and more of You[20]

Sixteen: Nothing In Life Is Free

Ten days later, Paul sat crammed in the economy section of an airplane bound for Albuquerque, wishing he could have just *five minutes* with the miniature sized designers who thought what he had in front of him was considered *ample leg room*. Even the young mother next to him, struggling to keep her squirming toddler content and belted into the seat between them, looked cramped. She had a bag full of goodies that she dipped into whenever it seemed like the kid was going to explode and had successfully diffused imminent disaster a number of times.

The woman said in a patient tone, "Luke, if you throw that on the floor we're going to loose it. When you're finished with that, hand it to Mommy and she'll put it in her bag." She smiled hesitantly at Paul. "I'm sorry. You probably were hoping for a nice, peaceful flight, and instead you're stuck next to … Godzilla in diapers."

Paul laughed and gestured to his legs folded up like a pretzel, "Forget it. It provides a good distraction from the pain and torture of this 'ample leg room'."

---

[20] The Answer, by Shane Barnard, Shane & Shane, Upstairs, 2002

Reaching down, she pulled her bag closer to her in the window seat. "Feel free to take some of Luke's leg room, he doesn't need it just yet."

Paul shifted a bit. "Thanks." Reaching up he popped the air phone that was embedded in the seatback in front of Luke and handed it to the boy. "Here, make a call, Luke."

The boy looked thrilled to be holding such forbidden fruit and immediately began pushing the buttons. "Do you think that's okay?" the woman asked.

Paul rolled his eyes and grinned. "Sure. These things are indestructible."

"Do you have children?"

No. Well, yes. Well, sort of. "No." It was the safer, easier answer.

"We're on our way back home. We went to visit Grammie and GP for a week, didn't we Luke?" She reached up to touch the child's silky brown hair.

"Beep-Beep," Luke said as he nodded, dragging his attention away from the air phone and looking up at Paul. "Minnie."

The woman grinned. "That's how he says GP – for Grandpa, and Grammie. Isn't that cute?"

Paul smiled and nodded politely, then closed his eyes and rested his head against the seat back. He attempted to rein in his chaotic thoughts. What was he doing? What did he hope to accomplish? What was he going to say? How would Karly react to him showing up unannounced and completely unwelcome? He wished he knew the answers.

At home he had felt such a compulsion to *get on a plane and get down to Karly* that it had invaded both his waking and sleeping thoughts. Sharing his frustration with Claire had finally led her to say to him on the phone, "What are you waiting for, Paul? It seems to me as if the feeling to go is getting *stronger and stronger*. I'd get down there and get it over with. You're always telling me you don't believe in coincidences. Seems to me that this is a fairly clear big black arrow. *Get yourself to Albuquerque.*"

Huerfano Mission School, Huerfano, New Mexico, two hours by car north of Albuquerque, thirty-five minutes from the nearest town,

Farmington, New Mexico, and forty-five minutes from the Four Corners area. Four Corners was famous because four states, New Mexico, Arizona, Colorado, and Utah all met at one point. He'd looked it up on the map, and read about it on the Internet. At first Paul had thought that the school was an orphanage. He knew a little Spanish and "huerfano" meant "orphan". But through his research he discovered that "Huerfano" had gotten its name from the large, lone mountain that rose up out of the flat open vista like a lost, abandoned child. An orphan. No orphanage, Huerfano Mission School "catered to the spiritual as well as the educational needs of native children in and around the Huerfano area in grades kindergarten through eighth." He scanned the website for pictures or descriptions about the teachers, but the web site was carefully generic in its information. The directions had been there though, and as he drove north up Highway 44 in his rental car Paul agonized over what was his next step.

He had talked with his parents before he left, so he knew they were praying for him. Claire had given him a sweet smile and a wink and told him that she and Tyler would be praying for him as well. *Guide me. Help me. Give me words. I'm here because of Your Guidance. Don't let me make a mess of this.*

In the end, he saw no sense in going immediately to his hotel room. Heaven knew he wasn't going to sleep a wink that night with the anxiety of facing Karly. Why not just get it over with? He found the school, and some old guy at the gas pumps in town with one eye, a long gray braid, and very few teeth told him that the "pretty teacher" lived out back behind the school in a little white trailer. He parked his rental car in the school parking lot and followed a dirt road behind the school. Just when he was beginning to doubt the old guy's information, a little white trailer came into view, sparkling white and absolutely surrounded by flowers of every shape and color. This was Karly's trailer. *He felt it in his bones.* When no one answered his knock, he settled himself down on the front steps, pulled his baseball cap down to shade himself from the sun's glare, and got ready to wait as long as it took.

He heard her coming before he saw her; she was humming a tune quietly to herself. As she came around the bend, Paul's heart started to pound, and he felt a flush of nerves that caused him to sweat. Big time.

Oh man. What was he doing here? Why had he come? What did he think he was going to accomplish? Had he lost his … stupid … mind? He knew Karly had seen him when her steps slowed and her humming stopped. He stood to greet her, gathering his thoughts and his nerves.

He didn't speak until she finally stopped dead in her tracks staring at him. *Pale and horrified* described her. "Hey Kar." His voice felt old and rusty and his brain felt absolutely paralyzed. "You look as beautiful as I remember you." *Oh great, you idiot. The first thing you mention to her is her appearance? Knowing all you know about her and her opinion of herself and her looks? Just get in the car and go back home. Now.* Paul cleared his throat and willed his brain to kick into some semblance of capability. "I know this is a shock, me being here and all. I would have called, but you probably know better than anyone that phone service isn't the most reliable out here."

She said absolutely nothing. Just stood there, staring at him as though he was her biggest of nightmares come to life.

And he supposed he was.

Desperately trying to lighten the mood, Paul smiled at her, felt himself shrug and say, "I was just in the neighborhood and thought I'd stop by and say hello."

Nothing. Not a smile. Not a frown. He didn't even think that she'd blinked. Karly just stood there like a frozen, appalled statue. Paul felt a wave of pity for her. Good God, how many weeks, *months*, had he pondered and agonized over this very meeting, and here she was being blindsided by him? What had he expected? For her to flash him one of her gorgeous smiles and invite him in for … flipping … tea? "Look, I can leave if this isn't a good time and come back later if you'd rather. I've had weeks to get up the courage to come here. I could at least give you the courtesy of a few hours."

And then she spoke in that same, smoky, melodious voice he remembered so well. Only he didn't quite remember it dripping with venom. "A few hours won't do it, Paul. I think I need about ten more years." She walked right up to him and he could see the blue of her eyes and the flush of her cheeks. She was *ballistic* with fury. Holy … cow.

Through gritted teeth she said, "Excuse me. I need to go into my home."

Paul held his ground and couldn't help himself. "We need to talk."

If looks could kill he would have been in worse shape then the piece of road kill he'd seen on Highway 44 a few miles back. "No, *you* need to talk," she spat at him. "I feel no compelling need whatsoever." Karly stepped around him, climbed the stairs, ripped open the door, and then slammed it with enough force to make her point.

Strike one, you're out.

Walking down the hill toward his car, Paul began to doubt his intentions, his abilities, ... and his sanity.

Paul chose to give Karly most of Saturday to get used to the idea of speaking with him in terms that were – hopefully - close to civil. He'd found a room in one of those small, roadside motels where you parked your car in front of your door. It wasn't the Hilton, but it was clean and quiet. He spent the day driving around sightseeing, traveling down to a place called Chaco Canyon. He wandered around the Anasazi ruins in awe of the history and the sheer age of the *ancient* place. The brochure referred to 900 A.D., and Paul was unable to wrap his brain around the scope of it all. He caught himself walking quietly and respectfully the way you would in a church, or better yet, a cemetery. Here had been an advanced civilization from long ago, and he had the privilege to walk where they had walked.

But by Sunday morning he was no closer to his goal of having a polite conversation with Karly than he'd been at home in his own living room. He knew some local history and interesting facts about the Navajos. Last night Paul had practically come to blows with some local guy in Karly's driveway when he'd made a second unsuccessful attempt at seeing and hopefully speaking with her. Had she posted guards to keep him away? Currently, Paul was the recipient of dagger-filled looks from Karly when she'd walked into church and discovered him sitting in one of the back pews. Here it was, going on the third day, and they hadn't exchanged one single word beside the venom filled ones outside her trailer. And things showed no signs of improving, Paul thought to himself as he watched Karly's 'driveway guard' send him more than a couple of challenging glances throughout the service.

What the … heck … was he going to do? He couldn't stay here indefinitely waiting for Karly to decide – if ever – to cut him a break. Paul had taken a week of his vacation to fly down here. It was becoming more and more apparent that a week was not going to be enough time.

Sitting in church Paul felt frustrated and lost, unwelcome and foolish. Why exactly had he come here? He sighed. *God only knew.*

Help, he prayed. *I don't know how to handle this situation. I don't know what my next move should be.* His stomach gave a loud, embarrassing rumble. He was tired of fast food. Maybe he'd go to a nice restaurant and at least have a decent meal. Yeah, that sounded good.

Reverend Jamison seemed nice. He exuded that comfortable 'I've-been-doing-this-forever' style of ministry that showed he was content with his life. He put others at ease with his warmth and charm. Medical updates were given and prayers were offered regarding Edith Jamison, Reverend Jamison's wife. Paul listened to them discuss her "hip replacement surgery" and her current battle with a "second round" of colon cancer. The concern was palpable throughout the congregation. This was a woman who obviously, when in good health, had been one of the movers and shakers of the church community.

After the service Reverend Jamison shook Paul's hand and made the standard inquiries as to who, what, when, where, how, and why Paul was visiting. Nothing nosy, just the standard 'make conversation with the visitor'. When Reverend Jamison extended the invitation to dinner Paul declined, feeling awkward and less than enthusiastic about making polite conversation with strangers over a meal – even if it was home cooked. Especially in a home in which someone was significantly ill. But when Reverend Jamison persisted, and then made note that Karly was a regular guest for Sunday meals, Paul jumped at the opportunity.

The Jamisons lived in a small ranch-style home within walking distance of the church. It was a cozy, welcoming place that Paul would have enjoyed and felt right at home in had it not been for the reason for his visit and the one guest who was definitely not happy to see him. More than once, Paul was thankful that looks could not kill. Nor could sharply spoken words. And just when Paul was questioning the wisdom of accepting

Reverend Jamison's dinner invitation, Karly's 'driveway guard' showed up to join them as well. Paul sincerely prayed that things would *not* get any worse. *Please, God, this is about all I can handle.* The guard's name was Earl, Earl Nezbegay, and watching the way he looked at Karly told Paul that he was interested in a … heck … of a lot more than just keeping her private property safe from would be trespassers. Strangely, Karly was only mildly more receptive to Earl's presence and attempts at conversation than she was to Paul's. Interesting, very interesting.

The conversation flowed around the standard topics of where Paul was from, his family, his work, and his life. He answered honestly, and when the question about his faith came up, Paul pretty much laid his cards right there on the table for both Karly and the rest of the group. "It's been a long time in coming, but I've finally realized that the only life to lead is one rooted in Jesus Christ. About two years ago I rededicated my life to the Lord, and I've worked diligently to remain on that path. I slip up all the time, but it only makes me more determined. Lately, I've worked hard at trying to come to terms with *most* of the foolish choices I've made over the course of my life. I know I can't change anything or go back and rearrange my life, but I would like to make amends for some of my mistakes. I've made peace with my family, I've … met a truly wonderful young woman the Lord has seen fit to bless me with and … I feel that maybe, *just maybe,* I might someday become a fruitful, productive, solid man after God's own heart. I still have a few major hurdles I need to get over before I can begin to look completely forward, instead of regularly backward, but each day is better. That's what we should pray and aim for, right? That each day be better than the one before?" *There,* he thought, *if that doesn't send a clear message to Karly to let her know what his agenda was, then nothing would.*

Although he wasn't sure what he'd hoped for, it certainly didn't involve Karly and Earl leaving abruptly only minutes later, driving off in a cloud of gravel and dust. One minute Karly was going in to check on the dinner in the oven, and the next thing anyone knew Earl and Karly were making patches in the driveway.

Edith Jamison, ill but still extremely feisty, gave her husband an arched eyebrow. "What's that all about?" she fired at Reverend Jamison.

"How should I know, Edith?" He turned to smile politely at Paul, trying to smooth over any awkwardness. "Can I offer you more iced tea?"

"No, thanks Reverend Jamison, I'm fine."

Edith gave Paul a piercing stare and then said, "What are you to Karly?" While Paul worked to gather his thoughts and formulate a politically correct response, Edith said, "Just tell me this: are you Benjamin's birthfather?"

Reverend Jamison, failing to hide his stunned expression, sighed and slouched down into the well-worn couch. "Give it up, boy. Just spill it. There's no use fighting Edith's inquisitions. I'll say I'm sorry now, as it seems to appear that I set you up for this, but please understand I'm only an unwilling and totally clueless minion."

"Oh, Samuel, stop it now," Edith said with a small chuckle. "Why beat around the bush? It's obvious that there's something between the two. Paul's done a relatively good job trying to be calm and polite, but have you *ever* seen Karly behave in such a manner? I may be terminally ill, but I'm not stupid. I can only imagine one reason for Karly being so upset and on edge." She pinned Paul with her direct stare. "So? Am I correct in my assumption?"

Paul looked first at Mrs. Jamison, then to Reverend Jamison who rolled his eyes, and then back to Mrs. Jamison. "Yes, ma'am, I'm Benjamin's birthfather. I'd hoped to have the opportunity to speak with Karly and just clear the air between us but that doesn't seem like it's going to happen, does it? I can't even get the opportunity to speak with her ..."

"Didn't welcome you with open arms, huh?" Edith chuckled.

"No, ma'am, not at all."

"Did you really expect that?" Sam asked in complete seriousness.

Paul looked at both of them, scrubbed his face with both hands, and sighed. Reclining back in the easy chair, he stared up at the ceiling. "Would you believe me if I said I don't know what I expected? All I know is that I felt a strong, compelling urge to come down here and speak with Karly." He sat up and looked at both of the serious, elderly people looking at him. "I started all of this before I even knew that Karly had contact with ... Benjamin." He shook his head and looked down at his tightly clasped hands. "It never occurred to me that such a thing was possible. I just wanted ... I just needed ..." Paul stopped and took a deep breath. There was a large lump building in his throat, making speaking, breathing and swallowing increasingly difficult.

"What did you want and need, son?" Edith asked him quietly.

"I just wanted to say I was sorry for everything I put her through. I just needed to know that I had done everything humanly possible to rectify the terrible wrong I did to her." He looked up and made eye contact with Edith Jamison. "My girlfriend, Claire, calls it 'closure'. She said that that was what I was looking for, but warned me that after I met with Karly I might feel worse than before I'd started all this. I've prayed long and hard about it, and it is *very clear* to me that the Lord wanted me to come here." He snorted. "But now that I'm here, I haven't a clue what I'm supposed to do."

"God works in His own time and at His own pace," Reverend Jamison said finally. "How many days do you have until you have to get back?"

"I have a flight booked for Wednesday afternoon, but I've taken the whole week off. If I haven't seen Karly by Wednesday, I'll stay on until the weekend. But if I'm still unsuccessful by Saturday, I have to go home no matter what. I'm working the midnight to seven a.m. shift Monday morning."

"Then we'll just pray that things all fall into place by this weekend," Edith Jamison said matter – of - factly.

Paul looked at the elderly woman, who seemed frail and tired physically, but whose eyes sparkled and snapped with determination and conviction. "I'd appreciate that, Mrs. Jamison. I've got my prayer warriors working overtime for me back home, but I could use some serious support down here as well.

"You've got it," she said. "Sam," she said turning to her husband, "I'm starving. Let's forget about Karly and Earl and eat supper."

"Yes, ma'am," her husband said with a smile.

Karly and Earl arrived just as they were sitting down at the table. Karly had obviously been crying, her pale skin blotchy and her eyes puffy and swollen. But they both sat down at the table and made polite, albeit sporadic conversation over the course of the meal. Karly made no effort to speak or respond in any way to Paul, and yet the tremendous anger she'd exhibited every time he'd seen her seemed to be gone. The anger was replaced with a different emotion that Paul couldn't seem to identify. It wasn't until dessert, over his apple pie, that he finally realized what it was.

It was resignation.

Monday afternoon, Paul waited for Karly outside the school in full view. No more sneaking around. No more surprise attacks. He'd approach her in a polite, adult fashion and hope like ... anything ... that she'd respond in kind. She stepped out of the school building looking tired, lost in thought, and oblivious to everything around her. *Great. She'll be startled again by his unexpected appearance.* "You look lost in thought," he said to her across the length of the playground tarmac as it sizzled in the August heat.

She stared at him for a heartbeat and Paul felt himself tensing as he prayed, *Please, please, please talk to me* ... "I'm trying to decide which Bible story to tell tomorrow. Today's was a big hit, and I've been asked to do a repeat performance."

"Oh? What was today's production?"

She grinned at him, a smile that filled his head with sweet memories of times long gone before betrayals and heartbreaks and life altering mistakes. "I told my all time favorite story about Deborah, the only female judge of Israel. It's a great story: blood, guts, war, and women's empowerment."

"Hmmm, I'll have to read up on that one. I'm not familiar with it."

"Judges four and five. It's a good one. I think I'll do Joseph tomorrow so the boys will get equal opportunity with good biblical examples."

"Are you allowed to choose what you do in the classroom? How much freedom do they give you?"

The conversation flowed easily while both of them carefully kept things in the safe, unemotional areas of work and her daily routines. Within minutes though it seemed they were standing outside Karly's trailer feeling awkward and tense. She sighed and a resigned expression flitted across her face. "Would you like to come in and have a drink? It's not much, but it's my home."

Paul nodded. "I've traveled a couple of thousand miles just for an offer like that."

She busied herself in the kitchen getting out glasses and plates. He wandered around and took in this place she called home. It was tiny ... darn ... tiny. He had to keep his back perpetually bent or he would probably scrape the ceiling with his head. He took off his baseball cap and sunglasses and set them on the small table on which she obviously ate her meals. There were lots of Navajo artifacts around the place with other eclectic decorations here and there. It was nice, cozy, *home*. It was a place that you could come home to, kick your shoes off, and curl up with a good book or a cup of tea. There were snapshots of family and friends. He recognized her brother Michael. There was a cute shot of her sitting on the playground at the school surrounded by about ten or eleven Navajo children of various ages.

And then he saw it. A picture of a small boy sitting in a green miniature easy chair holding a stuffed bunny and grinning at the camera. Paul hadn't expected to see a picture of the boy out there for anyone to see. He couldn't help himself and bent over to study it closer. Brown hair. Blue eyes. Freckles across the nose and cheeks. Sesame Street Band-Aid on the left index finger. Right shoe untied. Red tee shirt with what appeared to be sailboats on the front. Yellow shorts. One sock pulled up, the other one slouching down. Looking even closer it appeared that he had a slight milk mustache. Paul touched the picture reverently and his chest felt as if it were going to explode. The sensation passed up through his throat and traveled and landed directly behind his eyes. His vision blurred as the tears pooled and then slowly fell down his cheeks. It was a picture.

Of his son.

"You can have the picture, Paul. I can have reprints made."

He whirled around, heedless of the tears on his face. *She'd give him the picture?* "Really? You mean that?"

Karly nodded. Paul picked up the photo and made his way over to sit down on the couch. He couldn't stop looking at the photo. Any awkwardness was averted through the comic relief provided by Karly's cat, Goliath. Paul watched, amused as the cat put Karly through her paces: letting him in, greeting him as if he was royalty, providing him with a pile of snack treats. By the time the cat had finally settled – grudgingly - on the back of Karly's chair, Paul had had the opportunity to pull himself together … somewhat.

She let him have his say. He poured out his heart and soul to her, while she sat silently and still with her cat kneading her head. At first he stuttered and stammered, sounding like an idiot he supposed, but he plowed through the initial fits and starts and finally found his groove. He worked hard to explain about his profession of faith. He wanted her to understand that *none of this* goodness or responsibility she saw was related to anything but his change of heart, mind, and soul. He talked about needing to be accountable for the mistakes he had made and the responsibilities that he'd failed miserably in. He acknowledged that a simple apology was completely inadequate and admitted that he really didn't have a clue as to what he was supposed to do now that she'd given him the opportunity to speak to her. He tried to explain a little about Claire and her good advice. Finally, he took complete responsibility for his lack of maturity and courage. He even admitted that had he known about the baby he wasn't sure he'd have behaved any differently. Paul knew that Karly knew he was a looser and a creep. He just wanted to make sure that she knew *he knew* that he was a looser and a creep.

She seemed to become upset only once when he admitted that for a brief time he had entertained the idea of fighting her to keep the baby when he'd first received notification of the child's existence. She'd gotten pale, tense, and furious, but before she had a chance to speak Paul asked if she'd just let him finish. "I looked at my life and the person I was and the future I was headed for and I knew that I had absolutely *nothing* positive to offer anyone, especially a baby." It was at that moment that she stopped looking angry and had gotten teary. "And I remembered the person you were and I knew that no matter how much you may have hated me, you would *never* hurt any child, let alone your own. So I had to face the fact that you were always more together and mature and focused and *good* than I ever was and that this choice of adoption must have been what you felt was the best and wisest thing for the child. And suddenly I wanted to do something wise and good and noble *for once*. So I signed the papers and sent them back. I tried to do the right thing."

When Paul looked at her tear-streaked face his eyes filled with tears too, and made wet tracks down his cheeks. Suddenly he desperately wanted to hear her affirm what he'd done. *"Did I?"*

A simple yes would have done, but instead she stood up, walked over to a bookcase and pulled out two photo albums. "Here," she said handing them to him. "You need to look at these. Take the time to read *everything*. I'm giving you permission. It will take you a while. There's iced tea in the fridge and cold cuts and bread there, too." Karly looked at her watch. "I'll be back in about ... two hours." She was gone before he could make complete sense of what she'd handed him.

The first photo album was really a story of a couple in love. So in love with each other that their love spilled over abundantly and made them want to share it with someone else.

If I were to use just one word to describe my wife, Viv, I would have to say committed. She puts her heart and soul into all she commits to: our marriage, her teaching call, her church, her friends, her family, and me. To be included in Viv's inner circle of those she loves and cares about is to know unconditional love and support. She claims you as her own. I have many things to be thankful for in my life, but she is at the top of my list ...

My husband, Darin, is one of those guys who is unaffected by the world's definition of 'macho' or 'manly'. He is so confident and sure of himself and his soul that he embraces the unique individual he is with an enthusiasm that takes your breath away. He is positive and affirming of all he meets, willing to listen and encourage while at the same time offering sound advice and unique suggestions. He loves to cook (thank goodness, because I sure don't) and has the uncanny ability to be able to fix just about anything. I fell in love with his giving spirit, I stay in love with him because he encourages and loves and cherishes me like no one else in the world could ...

This is our home. It's a home not because it has four walls and windows and a flower garden out front. It's a home because of the love and commitment that we share with each other on a daily basis in all walks of our life: spiritual, personal, and professional. Anyone can have a house, but it takes real work to have a home. God is at the center of all we do. We can feel His presence, and we pray that many can feel it as well ...

Our life is full and rich. We have been blessed with things we didn't even know enough to ask for! We would like to share our life with a child, and so have put this book together. We have filled it with our essence and sewn it together with our prayers. Our prayer for you is that the Lord is working powerfully and strongly in your life and that His presence is a comfort and a blessing to you. Our nightly prayer is that the Lord will guide our heads and our hearts as we begin this new journey of adoption.

We pray the identical prayer for you.

Paul read pages and pages of email printouts. Hesitant, initial notes were then followed up with conversational get – to – know –you letters that progressed to loving, encouraging correspondence. Paul read with wonder and amazement what Karly had written about him and his family:

... Benjamin's birth father was 6'5" in stocking feet! He had lovely brown eyes and sandy blonde hair. I always admired his casual, easygoing attitude concerning life – I was always so uptight and full of must do plans! And he was poetry – in - motion with just about any sport. I remember going skiing with him and standing at the bottom of a run waiting for him. He came zipping and gliding, flipping and flying down that mountain making it look like the easiest thing in the world. It may be hard to believe that a 6'5", 250-pound man could be beautiful, but I was in awe of his grace and rhythm that day. Were Benjamin to have even half of his birth father's coordination, he will be quite an athlete ...

... Paul's family is the stuff that dreams are made of. Picture Ward and June Cleaver with three boys and two girls. Some of my best memories of Paul involve times with his family. There was an unconditional love and acceptance that permeated that family that I still miss. It may sound strange, but I always felt more at home with Paul's family then I ever did with my own. Regarding Paul's hair, it wasn't particularly curly, but he usually kept it quite short, so who really knows? But Paul's sister, Connie, had glorious long, thick wavy hair, so that must be where Benjamin gets his curls.

... I can't stop thinking about my visit with you. Thank you again and again and again for letting me come and stay with all of you. Benjamin is all you have said about him and so very much more. I see flashes of my brother Michael's mischievousness

and glimpses of my own personal stubbornness and determination. The morning that I was getting ready to leave and go to the airport, I caught him in my room, in my suitcase, in my make-up bag. I said to him, "Just what do you think you're doing, young man?" and he turned and gave me this confident look that communicated 'I know I'm not supposed to be doing this but I also know that you can never get truly angry with me'. Paul used to give me that look all the time, and it completely stunned me. He is truly a part of all of us. What an amazing miracle he is!

Sitting reading what Karly had written about him, at a time in which Paul *knew* she had to be still hurting and grieving over what he had done to her, he was amazed to discover that Karly never, *ever* spoke unkindly about him. Each inquiry about him was answered politely and as honestly as she could manage. He read descriptions of himself, his talents, and his family, all of which painted a fair and positive image of him. *How could she have managed that?*

The second album was all photos, each picture carefully dated with notations of the child's age. For a long moment as he gazed at just the first page he wondered if he could get through the entire book.

As he viewed each picture, reading each carefully noted comment, the well of emotion inside him grew and grew. There was one picture that drew Paul's attention of Benjamin and Viv and Darin sitting on the front steps of their house grinning at the camera. It was a recent photo, because Benjamin looked to be about four. Everyone in the picture was relaxed and casual. Studying it, Paul saw that Viv and Darin were holding hands and that Darin had his other arm wrapped around Benjamin, his hand splayed across his belly, and that Benjamin was casually holding onto his index finger. Benjamin had reached his little arm up and wrapped it around Viv's neck so that she was slightly bent over close to his cheek. It was not a picture that a photographer would orchestrate. "Put your hand there, hold his finger there, put your arm around …" It was a completely casual shot of a family that loved each other and drew strength from being near each other.

His son had that kind of love.

Thank you, God. Thank you for taking care of things when I was too dumb and self absorbed to even think about them. Thank you for providing my son with what he needs to make him into a good man. Thank you for answering prayers before I even had the wherewithal to say them.

The tears came then. A great flood of emotion that encompassed years of repressed sorrow and grief and guilt. They were cleansing, washing away fears and smoothing over torn surfaces in his soul. Paul prayed for himself, for Karly, for Benjamin. He was thankful for God's constant guidance, for Karly giving him time to talk, Viv and Darin, the Jamisons, his family, and Claire. On the periphery of his prayers he thought of Earl and Karly, his parents and their sorrow of never knowing a grandchild, him and Claire ... *Thank you. Guide me. Mold me. Make Me. Help me listen and obey ...*

Monday night the phone rang at about 12:30 p.m. Claire's time. "Hello?" Her head was swimming with all of the general college information she was supposed to be understanding. Booklets, pamphlets, schedules, choices!! If it was *this* hard with the basic stuff, how was she *ever* going to handle the serious business coming up?

"Claire?" Paul's voice sounded tired. Drained.

"Paul!" She did a quick mental conversion. "Are you okay? It's 10:30 your time." They had talked twice and she knew of his frustration in trying to speak with Karly.

There was a pause and then a long sigh. Claire's heart hitched. She could only imagine how tough this was for him. "We finally talked, Claire."

Claire struggled to read between the emotions she heard in his voice. "I've been praying." All day. An all consuming feeling in the pit of her stomach that she couldn't escape and had just kind of surrendered to. "All day. For both you *and* Karly."

"I've got pictures."

Claire didn't have to ask of whom. *"Tell me."*

"He's got my hair color, and it curls like mine did when I was little before I kept it short. Same color as Brian's youngest, Tiffany. Freckles. Not a lot but enough to show up in the photos I've seen. He has Karly's smile. There's a shot of her and him taken recently, and they're both grinning at the camera ..." It was like a flood, a damn bursting, and he talked nonstop for almost an hour telling her about photo albums and emails and things he had just learned and things he was still desperate to know. "I wonder what his voice sounds like?" he finally wondered out loud.

"Is Karly okay?"

"Yeah. Yeah, we're both okay. It turns out it was good closure for both of us. I had no idea what I needed to say to her besides the inadequate 'I'm sorry', but in the end the Lord helped me say the right stuff. I told her that I understood why she'd given the baby up, Claire, and that made her cry. Good crying, I mean, but … apparently it was a big deal-"

"That you got it," Claire interrupted.

He was silent for a moment. "How'd you know?"

Claire sighed. "Tell me why she gave her baby up for adoption, Paul."

He was silent again. "I may not have loved her enough to marry her and spend my life with her, but I knew what a good person she was. Pure good. Kind good. Loving good. That kind of good. The kind that wouldn't let hurt or anger or embarrassment or social pressures influence a decision that would harm a child. Harm *her* child. I told her that I knew that the choice she made to give up … Benjamin … had to have been the best choice she could make. And that that was why I signed the papers and didn't fight it."

"You told her that?"

"Yeah. I did."

"I love you, Paul Williamson."

She felt his smile over the phone line. "You do, do you?"

"Yeah. I do."

"I'm missing you. Big time."

"That's nice to hear."

"You're supposed to say you're missing me, too."

"Honestly? I'm so stressed over this school registration I'm barely functioning."

"You'll do fine, Claire. Just relax. It takes a while to get back in the groove of studying for someone like me who doesn't have a disciplined bone in his body. But for you, it will be a piece of cake. You'll organize your schedule and set aside specific times with the most optimal atmosphere for learning, and you'll make up little study aides and strategies, and you'll even have Tyler drilling you on stuff." He chuckled. "Go ahead. Tell me you've already thought about most of that."

He heard her sniff over the phone. "I will not. You're already too full of yourself thinking you know what's best for everyone. Me, Tyler, your brother Brian, Karly ..."

"I don't know about that, but I know what's best for me."

"Yeah? What?"

"*You.*"

"Are you still coming home Wednesday?"

"I don't like being separated from you, Claire. I don't like it when we're separated only by a town or two. When it involves thousands of miles and plane flights I down right hate it."

"I'm still planning on picking you up at the airport."

"I'm talking seriously and your talking travel arrangements."

"If I don't talk travel arrangements then I'll get all soupy and start crying."

"I'll take you any way I can get you, Claire."

"Are you *sure* you're real?"

A garment of praise for my heaviness
Beauty for ashes
Take this heart of stone and make it yours[21]

Seventeen: There Is No Such Thing As A Happy Ending

'*A*nd *we know that God causes everything to work together for the good of those who love God and are called according to his purpose for them.*'[22]

Claire sat on her porch swing surrounded by the darkness and the crickets, staring down at the words illuminated by the dull porch light printed right there in black and white. The house was quiet. She should be asleep but she needed to read just one more thing… With the massive changes in her life – personally and professionally – she'd discovered new and amazing things about herself: she was an early riser, she absolutely adored reading and learning and stretching her mind, and – here was the most stunning part – she craved human touch. Simple hand holding touch, possessive arm around the shoulders touch, sitting close enough to feel the warmth of another individual next to you touch. *All of it.*

She sighed, trying to examine the changes. The analytical part of

[21] Beauty For Ashes, By Shane Barnard and Kendall Combes, Shane & Shane, Upstairs, 2004, Inpop Records
[22] Romans 8:25, New Living Translation

her, the one that had rationalized her life away, categorizing and compartmentalizing while it ruthlessly carved out the rules of survival, needed desperately to understand the why of this. Being an early riser part wasn't so surprising. Having eliminated the substantial worry, stress, tension, and fear from her life she had fallen into the peaceful, comfortable pattern of deep, renewing sleep that was followed by excited, anticipatory wakefulness. No big puzzle there.

The reading and learning wasn't too surprising either. She'd had vague memories of that passion over the course of her life; she'd always enjoyed school, and the quiet and peacefulness of a library had been as close to worship as she could remember. The fact that life had gotten in the way and literally snuffed out that spark – with a forty-foot tidal wave – wasn't particularly surprising either. *That was real life.* Hey, you just learned to cope. And she had.

But the human touch, now that was as foreign and new as discovering a newborn baby in a basket on your front steps. Where had that come from? Never, ever, in her entire life had anyone ever spontaneously and without a hidden agenda or necessary obligation touched her. She had a flashback of never minding scraped knees because it always got you a cuddle; even if you didn't shed a tear. There was a time in her early teens when she remembered being fixated on couples: couples who kissed or held hands or put their arms around one another. What was that like? Why would you want to do that? Then everything went down with that one night, and in a flash she knew exactly what being touched was like. Never again. Never again. *Never again …*

Her car had broken down in June. It was almost September. A little over three months, and her life had done a one hundred and eighty degree turn. Claire smiled to herself.

And we know that God causes …

Trouble was, up until a month ago, *maybe everyone else knew,* but she sure didn't. This whole God business had seeped into the cracks and crevices of her life even when she had been certain there was no more room for anything more. Like a bucket full of rocks. Filled right to the top with no room for one more pebble or the bucket would tip over and spill.

That was her life three months ago. A bucket full of rocks, filled to overflowing. And yet God had fit in just perfectly. The cynical part of her wanted to roll its eyes at all of the nice words and well - meaning overtures by all of the goody – two - shoes Bible - bangers. But there was absolutely *no way* that the fatalistic part of her could ignore the changes in her life – *good changes*. Her Rules of Survival were shot to … heck … as Paul probably would have said.

    And we know that God causes everything to work together for the good of those who love God and are called according to His purpose for them.

    Claire could not escape the image that Janice Strocco had put in her head of herself: *So now, God is putting the finishing touches on one of His glorious masterpieces, getting ready to launch a powerful, strong, loving, committed young woman out into His world to make her mark on things. To make a difference. Look out world, here comes Claire Jenkins.* Who in their right mind wouldn't want that for themselves?

    Claire may be poor and uneducated and unsure of a lot of things, but she was *definitely* in her right mind. She wanted all of what Janice had said, and here was the truly amazing part, *she wanted even more.* She wanted love and happiness, security and hope, a future that was so much brighter than a past that you couldn't be bothered even to look back at and remember. And suddenly none of this seemed out of her reach.

    Daniel Alvarez had given her a Bible last Sunday when she came to church with Tyler. Attending the worship service, she had been just as hesitant and uncertain as the previous time, but now with an excited curiosity that drew her nonetheless. She'd politely demurred and tried not to take the Bible he set down on the pew next to her. "It's another investment in the future, Claire. I give this to you, and one day maybe you'll do the same for someone else." When she'd looked up into his sincere brown eyes, she was surprised to see a hint of tears. *"Someone did this for me, Claire.* That's why I am what I am today. I'm just passing it on." And he walked away.

    It was a lovely, rich looking book with a blue leather cover and golden edged pages. Inside it had her name and the date and the words 'Philippians 4:6-8' written in careful, neat script. She had no idea what it meant. Tyler did though. Turning to the front of the Bible he found the Table of Contents, and his grubby finger skimmed down all of the foreign words until it stopped on the word 'Philippians'. Page 967. Claire watched in fascination as he thumbed his way through the golden edged pages, found Philippians, flipped through even further and then planted his finger on a spot. She watched his lips move as he read silently. Looking up at his mother he grinned, "Cool, Mom. Read it." He passed the book to her.

'Don't worry about anything; instead, pray about everything. Tell God what you need, and thank Him for all he has done. If you do this, you will experience God's peace, which is far more wonderful than the human mind can understand. His peace will guard your hearts and minds as you live in Christ Jesus.

And now, dear brothers and sisters, let me say one more thing as I close this letter. Fix your thoughts on what is true and honorable and right. Think about things that are pure and lovely and admirable. Think about things that are excellent and worthy of praise.' [23]

Her newly discovered love of learning had literally exploded. There was stuff written like this? This whole book was filled with this wonderful stuff? Claire looked up with stunned amazement and wonder, skimming the crowded room for a view of Daniel. He was talking with an elderly woman, and she watched him, smiling and solicitous. Sincere, too. There was no doubt about it. Finally, when the conversation ended and he made his way back toward his seat, he glanced over at her. Their eyes met, and she couldn't help herself, she gave him a dazzling, thousand watt smile. He grinned back at her and nodded. *Someone did this for me, Claire.* He knew.

Forget about hearing the sermon. What had Janice said? That the reason the worship service had so many parts was because people needed all kinds of ways to be spoken to? Flipping through the Bible, correction *her* Bible, Claire found a slip of notebook paper carefully folded in the back. *My favorite verses,* Daniel had written in his careful script. *You'll eventually find your own, but here's a start anyway. Some of these I have memorized. That way I carry them with me all the time.* It was followed by a long list of words and numbers, some of which she couldn't even pronounce. The Table of Contents became her best friend that day as she quietly flipped and turned and read

---

[23] Philippians 4:6-8, New Living Translation

and absorbed.

For God is not a God of disorder but of peace... [24].

'And I am sure that God, who began the good work within you, will continue His work until it is finally finished on that day when Christ Jesus comes back again. [25]

For we are God's masterpiece. He has created us anew in Christ Jesus, so that we can do the good things He planned for us long ago. [26]

That night, long after she should have gone to sleep, she had read:

The Spirit of the Sovereign LORD is upon me, because the LORD has appointed me to bring good news to the poor. He has sent me to comfort the brokenhearted and to announce that captives will be released and prisoners will be freed. He has sent me to tell those who mourn that the time of the LORD's favor has come, and with it, the day of God's anger against their enemies. To all who mourn in Israel, He will give beauty for ashes, joy instead of mourning, praise instead of despair. For the LORD has planted them like strong and graceful oaks for His own glory. [27]

Beauty for ashes.

Joy instead of mourning.

Praise instead of despair.

There it was in a nutshell.

She wanted to stand up and shout, "I WANT THAT!" Who could she call? Who could she talk to? What should she do? She looked frantically at the alarm clock. 12:15 a.m. There was no one she was going to call at that hour. What had Janice said? *"To become a Christian is relatively easy, but monumental in commitment ... sinner ... believe ... Jesus, God's Son, ... ask ... with the heart of a child."*

Claire took a steadying breath. She could do this. She wanted to do this. She *needed* to do this. "Dear God," she began hesitantly, "First, I want to thank you for all the good things that have been coming my way lately ... and, I guess, all the good things you've allowed over the course of my life ..."

Yeah, it was easy.

Paul thought there was something different about Claire the

---

[24] I Corinthians 14:33a, New Living Translation
[25] Philippians 1:6, New Living Translation
[26] Ephesians 2:19, New Living Translation
[27] Isaiah 61:1-3

moment he spotted her waiting in the concourse at the airport. But what was it? The dazzling grin was new, but he'd seen that a few times recently. The hesitancy and uncertainty was still there but it was no longer the deer – in – the - headlights kind, more like the 'I have no clue what I'm doing but I'm game'. Again, new but not completely novel. As he walked toward her, matching her smile with a big, stupid one of his own, she stood there watching him while the busy airport swirled around her. He stopped about a foot away from her and studied her, liking every … darn … thing he saw.

"Hey," he said finally, filling in the silence of their own personal bubble of privacy.

"Hey yourself," she said back to him and, impossibly, her smile got bigger and brighter and traveled up into her eyes. It was then that he understood what was different. She was fairly vibrating with excitement, no *joy*, standing in front of him like an enthusiastic puppy trying but failing to control itself. He wanted to grab her and crush her to him, but all of the careful control stops he had faithfully practiced to avoid upsetting her kept him still.

Suddenly, Claire launched herself, jumping the distance that separated them, and looped her arms around his neck. He reflexively dropped his duffel bag and caught her around her waist, holding her tightly against him. He grinned crookedly. "Missed me, huh? Maybe I should go away more often?" He leaned in to kiss her and then caught himself, still unsure and unwilling to upset her. She was changing the rules he'd only recently learned.

She kissed him there in the airport, tangling her right hand into his hair and wrapping her left leg around his thigh. It was a kiss out of a soppy romance movie, and it just about dropped him to his knees. When she finally pulled back to look at him she said quietly, "No, I don't want you to go away again. I want you to stay here with me."

"Believe me, I'm not going anywhere," Paul promised her, and he gave her another mind melting kiss.

Sunday, Claire, Paul, and Tyler went to dinner at Paul's parents'. There was a perpetual standing invitation, but his father had specifically called him to extend a request, and Claire had clearly expressed interest in going. So there they were, in the condition that every guest for Sunday dinner found themselves: stuffed and content, sipping coffee and tea, and trying to figure out how they could possibly manage even one small bite of the sumptuous desserts – chocolate cheese cake and blueberry pie.

Paul took a sip of his coffee and looked around the big wooden picnic table in the center of the deck. Everyone had managed to make it: Connie and Mark, Rachel and Andy, Brian and Janet, Elliot, and what sounded like five hundred kids running under a sprinkler in the yard, shrieking and laughing. Not one child seemed to mind that it was almost dark and nowhere near as warm as it had been just a few weeks ago. "Uh, I have a bit to say and I was hoping you'd give me a few moments to try to muddle my way through."

"If you're in debt, I'm not lending you any money," Elliot said.

"Thanks, Elliot, I knew I could count on you," Paul said and everyone laughed. He looked at the group surrounding him, illuminated by the flickering citronella candles. "I'm not in debt and I'm not in trouble. I just feel the need to clear the air and ask a favor of you all."

As he cleared his throat, Claire reached out and took his hand. "Bear with me, okay? This is kind of tough." Paul closed his eyes, took a deep breath, and let it out slowly. When he opened his eyes to speak, everyone was sitting silently and expectantly.

"I've made a lot of poor choices over the last, oh let's just say ten years. Like a snowball going down hill, the bad choices started out in high school and kept rolling on getting bigger and bigger. It's not anyone's fault but my own. I take full responsibility. But that doesn't lessen some of the pain, hurt, and sorrow I caused along the way.

"One of the biggest hurts was the way I handled my relationship with Karly. She was a kind, good, loving woman who I pretty much completely destroyed."

"Paul," his sister Connie interrupted, "all of us here have dealt with heartbreak in one form or another. I think you're being too hard on yourself. *Let it pass.* It's not worth beating yourself up over something that happened so many years ago. I'm sure Karly has moved on," she smiled a sweet smile at Claire, "just like you have."

Paul nodded at his sister. "Thanks for the kind words, Connie, but I think you're wrong. I'm pretty confident that none of you have had to deal with the consequence of a child conceived out of wedlock and the decision to give that child up for adoption." Even the crickets and the cicadas seemed to become silent in those few moments as everyone processed what Paul had just said. He saw his father reach over and take his mother's hand out of the corner of his eye.

He plowed on. "When I broke up with Karly, what neither of us knew was that she was pregnant. I left her with the enormous consequence of being an unwed mother. She handled the situation with the same careful consideration she handled everything in her life, and decided to give the baby up for adoption.

"I'll tell you honestly that at first I was furious with her. I thought – ridiculously – that I would fight her and raise the baby myself. However, that was when I was living with Vince …"

"Oh man," Brian rolled his eyes and shook his head.

"… and," Paul continued, "I was in no way equipped to care for an infant. I finally decided that Karly had *always* had a better head on her shoulders when it came to serious things, common sense things, spiritual things …" Paul smiled, *"every*thing, and so I decided to trust and respect her decision. I signed the papers and gave her no trouble with the decision."

"*Wow*," Rachel breathed, and her lip trembled and a tear escaped down her cheek. *"Wow."*

Paul smiled at his sister. "Yeah. Wow." He sighed. "You guys know the other stuff. I went off the deep end for quite a few years, but what I've kept to myself is that since Grandpa's funeral I've been steadily making my way back to the straight and narrow. I've, well I've recommitted my life to God, and I've been trying really hard to repair any damage I could."

Paul looked over at Claire and she gave him a wink. "God seems to be pleased with my efforts, because lately lots of *good* things have been happening in my life. Some things," he grinned at Claire, "were just laying right on the side of the road waiting to be picked up." Claire blushed and looked down at her lap.

"I wanted to come clean with all of you. I want you to know where my head and my heart and my soul are at, and *have been*. I'm not asking you to forgive me or forget, but I am asking you to understand that I'm *trying*. Okay?"

At everyone's serious nods, Paul continued, "I recently worked up the courage to fly down to where Karly currently lives. She and I have … well, talked and had some closure about all of this. I'd like to ask you to specifically pray for me because I *think*, that I *may* have the courage to go one step further." He reached into his shirt pocket, pulled out a white envelope, and took out three color photographs placing them reverently on the table. "And try to contact *Benjamin's* adoptive parents and see if, perhaps, I could establish some kind of relationship with them."

His sister Connie picked up a picture first, studying it in the flickering candlelight. "Oh, Paul," she said, her voice choked with tears, "he's gorgeous, *just gorgeous*. He, he looks like you, you know …"

It took Paul a minute to respond because his throat was constricted with emotion. "Yeah," he finally said in a husky voice, "yeah, I know."

"Mom! MOOOOOM!! Paul's going to be here any minute, *hurry up!!*"

"I wish I had a dollar for every time you've said that to me, Tyler," Claire called down to her impatient son from the top of the stairs. "You know darn well Paul's going to come in, say hello, grab a soda, sit down and chat with you for a bit, hear your latest school adventure, play a video game or two, and then finally, once I have my coat, my gloves, and my boots on, and am beginning to sweat, *I'm* going to say, 'Hey you two, can we leave *please?*'

Tyler looked up at his mother, and Claire noted that his coat and boots, hat and gloves *were* already on, "But Mom, we're going to his house to exchange Christmas presents. He's not going to want to wait any longer than *me*." Tyler had a point. Even Claire had to admit that she was excited. They had decided to exchange gifts on Christmas Eve in the relative calm and quiet, versus tomorrow's chaos at Paul's parents. Paul had managed to weave a bit of mystery into today's get - together. He'd insisted that they come to his house in the late afternoon to spend time together, and then go to Christmas Eve service at her church after dinner. Furthermore, he'd been insistent that Claire not drive over to his place as she usually did, but that he would pick them up. Claire knew he was up to something, but couldn't quite figure out what.

"Do you have Paul's present?"

"Yeah, it's in the bag by the door where you told me to put it." Tyler paused. "I think he's gonna *really* like my present, Mom. Don't you think?"

Claire grinned at him and turned to go back into her bedroom to finish getting ready. "How could he not?" she called down to him. No grown man in his right mind would turn down the latest video game edition of Super Smash Party Animals, right? And, of course, given the tremendous enthusiasm Tyler had over the game, *well* ... it was just about the perfect present! She smiled and shook her head, and studied herself in the mirror. Was this smiling woman with her eyes twinkling with excitement really her? She'd splurged and gotten herself a new dress, deep green velvet with fitted sleeves and a full sweeping skirt that stopped just below her knees. New shoes, too. *High heels*, no less. She'd really gone all out. When was the last time she'd had the desire, let alone the means, to do something like this for herself? She twirled around and stopped abruptly, feeling the rich fabric swirl around her legs. "Thank you, Lord," she whispered, "for my life."

It had been almost four months since Paul had gotten home from Huerfano. Tyler was blazing through the third grade; he'd never be the best student but Claire had not had to make even one visit *or had even received a phone call* from the school. She'd take that over straight A's anytime. Tyler and Claire usually sat at the kitchen table in the evenings doing their homework. It had turned into a special time that both of them enjoyed.

Claire was totally immersed in her studies, fulfilling Paul's prediction of being organized, on top of things, and completely in the groove. Thanks to Claire Paul, Tyler, Maddy, and even Dan now knew more about biology, sociology, advanced algebra, and beginning physics than they had ever dreamed. Paul, in particular, had turned into a wonderful study partner, especially in the math area, although biology seemed to be disgustingly easy for him, too. He had a unique gift of being able to break down a complicated subject into tiny bites, making it easier to understand. He admitted that he surprised himself at times. Gradually, Paul had insinuated himself into almost all aspects of Claire and Tyler's lives. With the reduction in hours at the diner, she found herself with free time. If they weren't going to school or studying, then invariably she and Tyler were with Paul doing *something.*

Claire and Tyler continued to attend church next door. Besides the regular worship service, they'd gone one step further, and with the start of Sunday morning church school in September had decided to attend small study classes geared to their ages and interests. Tyler had made some new friends and she had begun the slow process of learning what being a Christian was all about. Claire liked the opportunity to ask questions and hear the thoughts and ideas of others. And Paul now came to her church. She couldn't pinpoint exactly when, but one Sunday he'd just slid into the pew next to her and Tyler, and that had been that. They shared a hymnbook, wrote silly notes to each other on the bulletins, and regularly had intense discussions about the sermon afterwards. Sunday afternoons they usually ended up doing things that any busy adult had to do on a rare free day: laundry, cleaning, food shopping … But it was done together and with lots of laughs and teasing. Sunday evenings usually were spent at Paul's parent's house, much to *everyone's* delight – even Paul's. He was different around his family now: relaxed and open.

That her life could be so very different from what it had been only six months ago was, for Claire, a testament to the fact that miracles still happened. Her life was stable, her future was promising, her outlook was positive. *Thank you …*

"He's here!!! He's here!!! Moooooooom!" There was a pounding of booted feet, the sound of the safety chain banging against the opening door, and the crash of the front door slamming shut.

Paul's laughter could be heard from downstairs as the front door reopened. "… all the excitement about? You'd think you were in a hurry to get going or something. I thought we'd have a soda, play a few video games, maybe see if your mom needs me to fix anything ..."

"*Paul!* We're *both* all ready to go! *Come on!*"

"Hold your horses there, kid," Claire said as she made her way down the stairs carefully, not wanting to fall flat on her face because of the unfamiliar high heeled shoes. "I was going to ask Paul to look at the dryer. It was acting up this morning." She struggled to keep a straight face.

"*Mom.* Don't do this to me."

Claire and Paul both burst out laughing. "He's a little bit excited," she pointed out to Paul with a big grin.

Paul stared at her intently. "You look fabulous."

"It's a new dress – and new shoes. She got it at the mall," Tyler volunteered. "It cost -"

"Tyler!" Claire interrupted, "You don't usually go telling people things like that."

Tyler looked completely baffled. "What's the use of spending seventy - five dollars on *one dress* if everyone doesn't know how much it cost? That doesn't make much sense to me."

Paul chuckled. "Well, people might think you're bragging."

"Oh."

"I'd say," Paul said with a twinkle in his eye as he looked a Claire, "it was worth every penny, though."

The three of them were out the door driving to Paul's house in record time. Claire and Tyler had been over to Paul's house numerous times in the last few months. Tyler thought it was the greatest place in the world: every kind of sports equipment known to man, including a pool table in the basement, *plus* a faithful supply of all types of soda and junk food. Recently, much to Tyler's tremendous disappointment, Paul had been trying to tone down the junk food, making himself profoundly unpopular with Tyler as well as his numerous other guests.

"Can we open presents as soon as we get to your house?" Tyler asked seated between Claire and Paul in the front seat of the truck. "I can't wait for you to see what I got you."

Paul glanced at Claire and she grinned and shrugged her shoulders.

"That's okay with me," he said, "I just hope it's not a turtleneck. I hate turtlenecks."

"It's not! It's a -"

"Watch out, Tyler! He's trying to get information out of you. Don't let him trick you," Claire cautioned.

Paul winked at Tyler and Tyler squinted his eyes at Paul. You could almost hear the cogs whirring. For the remainder of the drive the conversation flowed between the two of them as they tried to trick each other into revealing what each had bought the other for Christmas.

Claire thought about her gift for Paul. There were a million things she could have gotten, but her finances were limited and she didn't want to get him just anything. She'd tried to get him to promise not to go overboard with presents, and he'd just told her to mind her own business. She'd been so excited when she'd finally thought of what she would give him. *It was the perfect gift.* Paul had shown her the church bulletins his grandfather had left him along with his grandfather's Bible. The bulletins were precious mementos of Paul's childhood and his relationship with his grandfather. The Bible was just as precious, but crumbling and fragile with age. It must have been in pretty rough shape when Paul's grandfather had carried it. Claire had taken the Bible without Paul's knowledge and had it refurbished and rebound. Even the edges of the pages had been restored to their original silver shine. In the end, it had been more expensive than she'd anticipated, but Claire thought that it was well worth the cost. Afterwards, though, she had agonized over whether she had overstepped her bounds. Should she have asked? Maybe she should have run it by Paul's parents? *Oh well, too late now.*

Paul had a dinner waiting when they reached his house. A *real* dinner with turkey and mashed potatoes, green beans and biscuits. There was even an apple pie. Claire was speechless. "Don't get used to it," he said in a rather gruff tone. "What work! I've been up since 6 a.m., making that … dang … stuffing and chopping and peeling vegetables. Why does my father enjoy this so much? *He's nuts.*"

She laughed out loud. "That makes the meal all that more special, knowing what a labor of love it was." Paul rolled his eyes and continued to grumble under his breath.

The guys exchanged gifts. From Paul, Tyler received lessons in karate as well as a beginner's book on the sport. "The lessons are on Wednesday afternoons," Paul explained. "I figured that since it's been too cold for our outside basketball game, we'd switch over to this. I've signed up for a class, too." Tyler was ecstatic. Paul's video game was a big hit, too. "Another reason why this meal is such a big pain in the … butt. If I wasn't in charge, I could be playing this right now," Paul said in all seriousness.

"Mind if I try it out, Paul?"

"Nah, Tyler, you go right ahead."

"Do you want to exchange gifts now?" Claire said with a smile, watching Tyler rip open the plastic on the game.

Paul looked uptight as he glanced towards the kitchen. "Could we wait until later? I don't want to rush, and I've got to check that … stupid … turkey."

"I'd rather do it later, too." Her stomach was in knots over his gift. Why hadn't she just bought him a turtleneck or something?

The three of them enjoyed every bit of the meal and then worked together to clean up. Christmas carols played on the stereo and they laughed and giggled and then ate pie sitting on the couch watching Tyler smash video bad guys.

Even though they got there early, the church was absolutely packed. Claire and Paul managed to squeeze into the pew in the very back of the church, while Tyler went up front to be part of the singing presentation. Claire felt that there was something special about the church tonight, the dim lighting, the candles, the scent of the pine bows decorating the window sills, the feel of the velvet seats against her skin, the warmth of Paul's arm around her shoulders. It had a magical, otherworldly quality about it. Sitting in church, singing the wonderful hymns, and listening to the choir and the scriptures, Claire felt for the first time what all the talk about "Christmas Spirit" really meant. It might sound corny, but it was true.

"Then pealed the bells more loud and deep:

God is not dead, nor doth He sleep;
The wrong shall fail, the right prevail
With peace on earth, good will to men."[28]

This is my first Christmas that really means what it's supposed to mean, Claire wrote on her bulletin.

This is the first Christmas where I've sat next to the person I love in church, Paul wrote back.

Claire sighed and rested her head on Paul's shoulder. Tyler's church school class was part of a large group of children getting ready to sing 'Silent Night' with the church choir. She watched him focus intently on the choir director.

He looks cute in his bowtie, she wrote.

You look almost too beautiful in that dress, he wrote back.

I didn't know you hated turtlenecks. What am I supposed to do with your present?

Still got the receipt?

No.

Will you marry me, Claire?

The children began to sweetly sing the opening strains of the hymn. *Silent Night, Holy Night, all is calm, all is bright …*[29] In an echo, the adult choir sang softly followed by trumpets and flutes, the organ and the piano.

Claire looked up from the bulletin into Paul's serious eyes. Who would have thought that she could ever have said that *anyone* would have been worth the wait, worth the life that she had led to reach this point? And yet there he was staring at her intently.

Glories stream from heaven afar, heavenly hosts sing Alleluia!

Paul wrote on the bulletin, *No receipt. Gotta say yes.*

They say that your life flashes before you when you die. But, just as her rules of survival were untrue, so was that statement. Claire's life since Paul flashed before her: standing with his hands on his hips looking at her through the windshield of her broken down car, looking at her

---

[28] Henry Wadsworth Longfellow (1807-1882) "Christmas Bells"
[29] Josef Mohr, 1816-1818, Silent Night

incredulously and saying, *What do you mean you've never dated? You've got a kid!,* at her old apartment standing with his hands in his pockets between the two police officers arching his eyebrow at her, looking fiercely at her at the picnic saying, *We're dating, Claire,* the look of tender compassion on his face when she explained to him about her life, the expression on Tyler's face whenever Paul appeared on the scene, Paul telling her he loved her in her kitchen that night not so very long ago ... With a start, Claire realized that your life doesn't flash in front of your eyes when you're dying, it's when you're just about to start living.

Radiant beams from Thy holy face, with the dawn of redeeming grace ...

Dear God, Claire loved this man. There was no place else she wanted to be other than right here by his side, no matter where he went or what he was doing. With him she felt ... whole. Felt that anything big or bad that could or would happen to her she could handle. With him she felt ... joyful. She actually trusted the reality of her life that had shattered her rules of survival into smithereens. A part of her still could not believe that *this man* was willing to take on everything that committing to her and loving her entailed.

You're getting a lot more problems than you deserve, you know, she wrote.

He took the pen and paper out of her hand and made a show of crossing something out and writing only one word. He handed the piece of paper back, and she read how he had changed it.

You're getting a lot more love *than you deserve, you know.*

She nuzzled her face into the crook of his neck, breathing in his warm clean scent, and his arm wrapped around her, holding her so tightly she could barely move.

"Give me the answer I want, Green Eyes," he whispered in her ear. "You're killing me here."

"Yes, yes, yes, yes, *yes,*" Claire whispered into his neck. "Yes."

"That's a better present than any turtleneck, I tell you."

Epilogue

My Family Heritage

By Benjamin McKnight

Everybody has a family, but mine is different from everyone else I have met. I have a Mom, her name is Vivian, but everyone calls her Viv. And I have a Dad, his name is Darin. My Mom says to say that she calls him 'Honey', but lots of times I hear her call him 'That Man!' while she is rolling her eyes. My Mom is a really good teacher (4th grade) and my Dad is a financial consultant (Mom says he plays with other people's money). Our favorite things to do are to go camping (at places like the Four Seasons Hotel where they have flush toilets and put chocolates on your pillow at night), swim in our pool in the summer (Dad and I are building a deck), and travel to places like England and California and Florida and New Mexico to see new places and learn new things. Oh, and I am also a sports nut: skiing, hockey, baseball, football, soccer, and kickball. Mom says that anything that involves sweating has always appealed to me. (In the spring I do baseball and in the fall I do soccer.) I'm not really, really good at any one of these sports, I just love to play.

When you first look at us, it looks like we are a small family of just three but that's where you are wrong and that's where things get really different. You see I have another mom, another dad, and *almost* SEVEN half brothers and sisters. (I have to say almost because the twins aren't born yet.) Now you might think that you know how this could all be but I'll bet you a hundred dollars you'd be wrong.

I am adopted.

I have always known that I was adopted. Mom and Dad told me that to really love someone you have to be able to do things for them that maybe are pretty hard. My birth mom, I call her Karly, knew that she couldn't care for me the way she wanted me to be cared for. So she worked real hard to find a couple who could give me all the things she couldn't. While she was doing that, my Mom and Dad were looking to find the perfect child to fit into their life. Everybody prayed about it. A lot. And God brought Karly, Mom, and Dad together. I write to and talk to and see Karly all the time, although you need to fly in an airplane to do the seeing part. She's married to a real, live, honest to goodness Navajo Indian! And he's a preacher. They have two kids already, a girl named Lydia (she's seven, almost six years younger than me) and a boy named Jacob (he's five). Right now as I write this, Karly is pregnant with twins – a boy and a girl. I don't know what their names will be because Karly and Earl (that's her husband) can't agree. (I hope they decide soon!)

That's how I ended up with two moms. And a kind of stepfather. And *almost* two brothers and two sisters. And don't forget the part about the Navajo Indian. That's the *really* cool part I think.

But that's not all.

My birth father's name is Paul. I didn't get to meet him until I was almost six and a half. It's a long story, but Paul said it was because God needed to work on him a lot more than the average person. Paul is real cool. He is a GIANT. Mom says that one day she wouldn't be surprised if I'm that big, too. Dad says if that happens I will come in handy as his own personal bodyguard. Then he laughs. (Dad isn't too tall. Don't tell him I told you that though, because Mom says he's overly sensitive about that.)

Paul contacted my parents and talked with them for over a whole year before I got to meet him. Mom said she and Dad had to establish a relationship with him before I got involved. I don't know what the big deal about that was because like I told you, he's really cool. By the time I met Paul he was married to Claire. Claire has one son named Tyler and now she and Paul have two kids, both girls. Tyler is almost sixteen (he's really funny and really cool) and Ruth is five and Sarah is three. Both Ruth and Sarah are really cute but really bossy. Paul is funny because he says that between Claire and Ruth and Sarah he and Tyler, are doomed to be under the control of bossy, opinionated women for the rest of their lives. But he usually looks pretty happy about that so I wouldn't feel sorry for him or anything.

So that's my family: two moms, two dads, one step dad, one step mom, and almost seven half brothers and sisters. I'm not even telling you about all of the aunts and uncles and cousins! It's fun being a part of such a big, "unique" (that's what my Mom calls it) family. Mom says that from my Dad I get my sense of humor and my generally positive outlook on life. She says I get my organization and my ability to relate to children from her. From Paul I get my size and my love of sports. From Karly, well, Mom says that from Karly I get my loving personality. That sounds pretty mushy, but I guess it's true. I think love is the most important part of a family and we sure have a lot of it.

I wish everyone could have as good a family as I've got.

The End

(At least for now!)

About The Author

Susan McGeown is a wife, mother, daughter, sister, friend, aunt, uncle (don't ask), teacher, author ... but, most importantly, a "woman after God's own heart." Living in Bridgewater, New Jersey, with her husband of over fifteen years and their three children, writing stories is just about the best way she can imagine spending her free time. Each of Sue's stories champions those emotions nearest and dearest to her: faith, joy, hope and love.

Philippians 1:20-21

For I fully expect and hope that I will never be ashamed, but that I will continue to be bold for Christ, as I have been in the past. And I trust that my life will bring honor to Christ, whether I live or die. For to me, living means living for Christ, and dying is even better.

www.ingramcontent.com/pod-product-compliance
Lightning Source LLC
Chambersburg PA
CBHW031102260626
47172CB00001B/184